**_"When are you going to realize that I'm always right?"_**

"That's still to be proven." Tara went to stand, and Reeve quickly was at her side. He didn't ask permission, but then, had he ever? He did what came naturally. He scooped her up in his arms and carried her to the bed.

"You needn't carry me," she said. "I can walk."

"Your ankle needs rest." He hadn't meant to whisper. But then, maybe now was the time for whispers and murmurs and stolen kisses and exploring touches.

*Rein it in,* he silently warned himself.

He sat her on the edge of the bed and knelt to take her boots off.

"I can do that," she protested.

"It's no trouble."

He moved his hand to take hold of her leg and his fingertips brushed along the crevice at the back of her knee. The itch to explore further overwhelmed him.

He planned to leave, let her sleep. And then he looked at her and saw his heated desire mirrored in her eyes.

He sunk down in front of her. "I need to kiss you."

He didn't wait for a response; her deep lavender eyes had told him what he needed to know.

She was as eager for his kiss as he was for hers . . .

**By Donna Fletcher**

Loved By a Warrior
Bound to a Warrior
The Highlander's Forbidden Bride
The Angel and the Highlander
Under the Highlander's Spell
Return of the Rogue
The Highlander's Bride
Taken By Storm
The Bewitching Twin
The Daring Twin
Dark Warrior
Legendary Warrior

# DONNA FLETCHER

# LOVED BY A WARRIOR

AVON

*An Imprint of* HarperCollins*Publishers*

AVON BOOKS
*An Imprint of* HarperCollins*Publishers*
10 East 53rd Street
New York, New York 10022-5299


ISBN 978-1-61129-775-1



Printed in the U.S.A.

# Loved by a Warrior

# Chapter 1

Reeve stood hidden amongst the snow-laden pine trees. He didn't move a muscle and slowed his breathing. He didn't want to be detected as he watched the scene unfold before him with interest.

A lone woman stood circled by four men, thieves for sure, though not one of them approached her. She held no weapon, and though she was sturdy in weight and height, the men outnumbered her. They would surely have no problem capturing her.

He noticed she didn't appear upset with her dire situation. The men actually eyed her with more fear than she did them. Her features were common enough, not that one could refer to her as a beauty, but by no means was she unsightly. Perhaps it was her large eyes that dominated her round face that made one take notice and question her features. Even where he stood, a few feet away, he could see that the color of her eyes was uncommon. He had been with his share of women and had seen many lovely-colored eyes and some not so lovely, but never had he seen her eye color. It was deep lavender, though actually more purple, a royal color for sure. Add to that her raven-colored hair, which fell in ringlets around her face and down near to her waist, and one would wonder her heritage. Born of royalty or born of magic?

The men surrounding her apparently were thinking the same, for they did not approach her. She stood stock-still, her muted red, fur-lined cape hanging open revealing a velvet gown gathered high beneath her full breasts, which looked as if any moment they would spill forth.

Odd though, she was devoid of jewelry, unless, of course, the thieves had already confiscated it. Why then, though, did they continue to surround her?

The enclosed wagon she obviously had ridden in had been torn to shreds, pillows and blankets and chests lay strewn about the ground, along with the guards who apparently had tried unsuccessfully to protect her.

"She must have the wealth on her person," one thin man said sharply.

"Then go fetch it," said another heavier man in need of a good washing.

"You go fetch it," the thin fellow shouted back at him.

"Is there not a one of you brave enough to confront me?" the woman asked, defiance shining in her strange-colored eyes.

Reeve had to admire her courage, or was it foolishness, goading them the way she did.

"She is no bride to any of us, so the hex won't work," another said, and took a step back.

"Then you go wrench her *bride price* from her," declared the heavy fellow.

Reeve furrowed his brow. Could it be so? He had believed a *death bride* was a mere myth.

"I'm not touching her," spat the thin fellow.

The woman grew more defiant. "You are cowards, every one of you."

The heavy man huffed and shook his head. "She knows she has the power to snuff the life out of us if we touch her."

"But I thought it was only husbands she killed?" asked another

"You willing to take a chance?" queried another.

They all shook their heads vehemently.

"We have no choice," the heavy man said. "She must die."

Reeve grinned. He had no intentions of letting the woman die even if she was a *death bride*. Besides, you would need to wed her for the curse to work, and if that was the case, then he would free her to go wed whatever desperate man had been unwise enough to agree to such a foolish arrangement.

One brave soul stepped forward though it was not the thin or heavy one; they remained where they were while urging the courageous, or idiotic, man forward.

"Get her and be done with it," one shouted.

The sole man approached the woman cautiously, sword in hand, and Reeve almost laughed aloud when he saw how the man's hand trembled violently.

What surprised him, though, was the way the woman defiantly tilted her head and squared her shoulders as if she defied him to approach her, and with not a weapon in hand to defend herself. She was either boldly courageous or bloody stupid.

There was no thought of leaving her to her own foolish devices even though Reeve wished to be on his way home. He had partially succeeded in carrying out his mission and wanted to return to his family to see how his brothers had fared with theirs and to continue on course to make certain that the true king of Scotland took the throne.

The reminder that his mission took priority over everything else made him realize that he would need to see this done and be on his way. Time was precious, and he did not wish to waste a moment of it.

With a few cautious steps, he left his hiding spot and stopped just behind the four men.

"I think you should leave the lady alone," Reeve said calmly though firmly.

The men jumped, swinging their raised swords as they turned in unison. They remained where they were, no doubt assuming one man presented no danger.

One spoke. "She's a killer of men."

Reeve looked from one to another. "None of you appear dead. Of course, I could be wrong, since you all *stink* like rotting corpses."

The woman smiled though she made no comment.

"There are four of us and one of you," the thin man pointed out.

Reeve rubbed his chin and frowned. "A shame it isn't more evenly balanced. But if you wish, I'll wait while you get more help."

"Are you stupid?" the heavy one asked with a snort, stepped forward, and threw his arms out wide. "I am three maybe four times your weight. I could crush you with one blow."

Reeve was used to men underestimating his strength. He was tall and lean with muscle, whereas most Scotsmen were thick and of average height. Their misconception gave Reeve an advantage since most thought him no threat though it never took long for the poor blokes to realize their mistake.

Reeve's hand struck out so fast that the heavy man was on the ground flat on his back with Reeve's booted foot at his throat before he realized what had happened. Reeve kept his foot firm at the man's throat even though he flopped around like a fish out of water, as Reeve spoke to the other three.

"Leave now, and I won't hurt a one of you," he told them. "Think otherwise, and your already offending stench will join that of the rotting dead."

"We'll split the wealth with you," one offered, and the others nodded agreeably.

"I'll give it all to you if you'll help me."

The three men turned to glare at the woman, while Reeve slipped his boot off the man's throat, leaving him gagging for air as he stepped over him and walked to the woman's side.

Reeve was no fool. People didn't part with wealth that easily. He didn't for one moment believe that if he disposed of these men, that would be the extent of it. He knew it. He could feel in his gut that she wanted more from him.

And he was curious.

"We got to her first," the bolder of the men shouted. "She's our prisoner, and the booty belongs to us."

Reeve drew his sword and pointed it at the man. "The booty belongs to whoever is the strongest to take it. Are you strong enough to take it from me?"

The men huddled together, the one on the ground having finally gotten to his feet and joined them. They mumbled amongst themselves until they finally separated.

The bolder one spoke again. "How about you give us a bit of the booty, and we leave you alone."

Reeve grinned and brandished his sword. "How

about I run my sword through every one of you and leave you to rot." With a quick step and a jab, he nicked the one fellow's ear with the tip of his sword.

The other men stumbled back, knowing it took a skilled swordsman to perform such a feat. Most would have just lopped off the whole ear.

"Be gone with you, or I'll cut you open and leave the animals to feast on your innards," Reeve warned, and jutted forward, scaring the men so badly that they turned running into each other and tripping over their own feet as they scrambled to run away.

"Won't they follow us?"

Reeve turned to the woman, her eyes steady on where the thieves had disappeared into the woods. He realized that while her voice had turned soft, her violet eyes held a hint of apprehension. "Not if they know what's good for them."

"But they could follow and attack—"

"Let me worry about that," he advised, sheathing his sword. "That is, if you still wish me to help you."

"I hope that you can help me."

It sounded as if she pleaded, yet with courage, and Reeve admired her bravery since she truly wasn't in any position to haggle. He could easily take what wealth she carried and be rid of her.

And so he had to ask, "Why trust me?"

"You didn't join forces with the thieves."

"Perhaps I wanted the wealth for myself," he suggested.

"Then I would be dead by now."

He stepped closer to her. "What if I wanted something else from you?"

Her soft voice turned as hard as solid stone. "Kiss me or touch me, and you'll die."

"What if I don't believe the tale of a *death bride?*"

"If you know that I am one," she said, "then you truly would be a fool to take the chance."

Her eyes turned a deeper shade of purple and filled with such heavy sorrow that Reeve couldn't help himself. He reached out and was about to touch her when she stumbled back, in a rush to avoid him.

He drew his hand away. "You are not my bride, so therefore I have nothing to fear."

"There is more to the tale than you know."

Her blunt tone warned she would say no more, but that wasn't what stopped him from satisfying his curiosity. It was the utter despair so visible in the slump of her shoulders, the slight drop of her head, but mostly the way she hugged herself, her arms tight around her middle.

How long had it been since someone had embraced her?

He knew she wouldn't let him near her, so he offered comfort the only way he could. "How can I help you?"

"I don't wish to bring death to any more men."

Reeve wondered just how many times she had been a widow.

"I wish to find a safe place where I may live in peace and harm none. In return for helping me find this haven, I will give you my substantial bride price."

He certainly had no intentions of leaving her on her own. He also couldn't help but think how her offer would benefit his mission. His three brothers, not by blood, though as close as if they were, would surely agree. They had been working hard in gathering forces to help bring the true king to the throne when the time was right. This offer could help bring that to fruition.

"Agreed," he said firmly.

"I'll have your word on it as a Highlander warrior."

He saw no reason not to give his word since he intended to see her safe. "You have my word."

"Let me gather a few of my things, and we can be on our way," she said.

"First, call me curious, but I would like to know your name and the name of your intended," he said.

"Does it matter?" she asked, a bit startled.

"Well, I could call you lass, bonnie, darling," he shrugged. "Take your pick."

"Tara," she said quickly. "My name is Tara. As for my intended, I prefer not to share his name. I wish only to slip away into oblivion and let everyone assume what they may."

"More than likely they will assume you dead, your bride price stolen."

"That would be best . . . for all."

Reeve could not imagine slipping away from his family, leaving them to believe him dead. Besides, if there was no body to be found, his parents and his brothers Duncan, Trey, and Bryce would search until they found him and then bury him on MacAlpin soil where he belonged. Was there no one who loved her enough to make certain of her fate? Or would her family be relieved that they were finally rid of her?

He watched her gather a few of her belongings and some clothing, rolling them up in a dark green wool blanket and tying it with gold cord that she stripped from one of the garments she was leaving behind.

He was surprised that no servant maid had been sent along with her. That she worked without complaint and not asked for help made him wonder if she was accustomed to tending to herself.

Reeve had to smile. She was certainly sturdy enough to handle chores, not petite like his brother Duncan's wife, Mercy. Mercy could stand behind her husband and not be seen; that was how tiny she was, or perhaps that was how big Duncan was.

Tara was no wee woman. He was a good two inches over six feet, and her head reached past his chin. She wasn't slim and certainly not weighty, though there was solidness to her. Her red dress displayed her plentiful bosoms nicely though it failed to distinguish her other curves. So, naturally, he couldn't help but wonder what lay beneath all that red velvet. Narrow waist, full hips? He loved full hips, loved the feel of thick flesh in his hand when a woman rode him.

*Why?*

The question echoed in his head. Why was he thinking about this now? He almost laughed since the answer was simple. He was a man, and men enjoyed drinking in the beauty of women. Yet Tara wasn't a beauty, attractive, but he'd seen far more beautiful woman. Duncan's wife being one of them. Why, then, did he find her enjoyable to gaze upon?

"I'm ready," she said.

Reeve reached out to take her bundle from her, but she ignored his offer and slipped the cord over her head so the rolled blanket could rest against her back. She certainly was an independent lass. Another trait he admired.

"The bride price?" Reeve asked, not having seen her retrieve any coins or jewels.

"I have it. And you'll receive it when I am safely ensconced in my new home."

# Chapter 2

"And your name?" Tara asked, intending to remain focused on the immediate situation as they kept a steady gait. If she allowed her mind to wander off in memories, as it so often did, she'd be in tears soon enough. And if there was a time that she truly required her wits about her, it certainly was now.

"Reeve," he answered.

"Of the clan?" she asked wanting further clarification of the man she had entrusted with her life.

"What does it matter?"

Tara knew he was merely mimicking her own response to his similar query. And he was right. She should have thought of ascertaining that information before asking for his help.

"You're right. It makes no difference," she said. What did make a difference was that she believed him an honorable man. And that was the only thing that kept her feeling safe, though the dirk she had slipped into her fur-lined boot also helped her feel safe. So did the fact that she knew how to use it.

The few inches of snow crunched beneath their footfalls, and the air was crisp, but, then, it was the deep of winter. And they were in the Highlands, the precious, beautiful Highlands that she loved so dearly. She had not wanted to leave her home. She had not wanted this arranged marriage, but her father had insisted. She would have much preferred to have remained living the solitary life she had planned on since her last husband had died three years ago, when she was barely twenty.

However, her father had a different idea, and so she had been sent from her home to wed a man she had never met and had never wanted to wed. It seemed, however, that fate had interfered and had sent someone to rescue her, and she couldn't be more relieved.

She cast a quick peek Reeve's way. Strong, bold lines made up his fine features. And no doubt many a woman thought him handsome, and rightfully so. He had dark, piercing eyes that just about matched his long, dark hair. Thick braids entwined with the wool stripes the color of his plaid, red and black, hung at the sides of his angular face. His lean body wore his black shirt and plaid well, and he had wrapped an additional plaid around himself for warmth, draping one end over his shoulder.

He was lean in body though not by any means lacking in strength. That had been obvious from the way he had so easily handled the thieves. Add to that an unwavering confidence, and that made him a man who stood out amongst men and one much sought after by women, though not her.

She couldn't allow herself to think of him in any terms other than her rescuer. She had been lucky that he had happened her way and had unknowingly provided her with an escape and a good one at that. Surely, her father would believe her dead, her bride price stolen, and he, as well as she, would be free at last. And sadly, she wondered if he would be relieved.

Enough dwelling; she needed to remain focused on the present situation, and so she asked, "You know where you will take me?"

Reeve nodded. "That I do."

"Is it far?"

"Four or five days' journey at most."

"Far removed from people?" she asked.

Reeve stopped abruptly, and she halted, cautiously avoiding him.

"It is a clan—" He held up his hand when she opened her mouth to protest. "I will finish."

She bit at her bottom lip to stop from speaking and folded her arms across her chest.

"This clan will take you in. There are a few empty cottages on the outskirts of the village. You can have your pick. You can make friends or not, the choice is yours. But at least you will have some modicum of protection."

Tara almost objected, worried that the men might seek her out. Word would spread soon enough though, about whom she was, and then no man would dare even talk with her. And Reeve was right. She did need some degree of protection. While she was self-sufficient to a point, it would be unwise to think she could survive entirely on her own.

"These are good people. You will do well there," he said, and turned to continue their journey.

She trudged behind him, his strong footfalls clearing a good path for her through several inches of snow that had fallen since yesterday. She tugged her cloak more closely around her, the cold air biting the flesh. And she glanced with worry at the sky. Sure enough, a heavy cloud covering had moved in swiftly, and she had no doubt it promised additional snow.

"We need to find shelter," Reeve said.

"More snow," she said.

He nodded. "Finding shelter is essential. There's an abandoned croft a few miles to the west."

"Will it take us out of our way?"

"Not much," he said, and switched direction.

Tara followed, pulling up the hood of her cloak and keeping pace with Reeve. Traveling behind him, she couldn't help but admire his tireless strides or the ease in which he vaulted over fallen and decaying trees. The good-sized boulders proved no hindrance to him as well. She, however, skirted around them before he could offer her help.

The sky grew darker, and it took from midmorning, when he had come upon her, until midafternoon for them to reach the croft. Snow started just as they spotted the empty cottage in the distance.

"Are you hungry?" he asked.

"Yes," she answered, feeling quite ravenous, having not eaten since early morning.

"I'll hunt after getting a fire going."

Before they reached the cottage, the wind increased along with the falling snow, and Tara feared a substantial snowstorm. If so, they could be trapped alone for days.

The wind stung the flesh, and Tara kept her hood pulled down to protect her face though it hampered her vision and slowed her pace.

"Keep up," Reeve yelled against the swirling wind and snow.

She raised her head to see that she had lagged behind him, and so she hurried her pace to catch up. With the snow heavy on the ground and it blurring her vision, it was no wonder that her foot got snagged by a snow-covered log, and she went tumbling head-first.

Before she hit the ground, Reeve's arm grabbed her around the middle, yanked her up on her feet, and planted her firmly against him.

"Hold on," he shouted above the din of the storm.

"No!" She tried squirming out of his tight embrace.

"Stop!" he yelled near her ear, and pressed her hard against him.

She was stunned by the strength of his grip and his fearlessness. He had not given thought to his actions; he had simply reacted. He had saved her from falling face-first into the snow, and now he kept her tucked against him, safe from the harsh wind and the possibility of being separated in this wicked storm.

Surprisingly, she found herself complying with his command and burrowing her head against his chest. Once done, he wrapped his other arm around her, and they trudged through the swirling wind and snow to the cottage.

It had been forever since she had been held so tightly. It felt almost as if he never wanted to let her go, or perhaps she merely wished to believe it. It didn't matter that a snowstorm swirled around them; her only thought at that moment was how utterly wonderful it felt to be held again.

She fought the tears and the memories of being loved and all it entailed. She hadn't realized how very much she missed not only the intimate touches, but the simple ones, like now and how he held her so protectively against him, his warmth seeping into her and his strength wrapped around her. And kisses, Lord, it had been too long since she had been kissed. To feel a man's lips again, to know his touch and to be able to touch him . . . no, she couldn't think about it. It just wasn't possible, at least not for her.

He hurried her inside and struggled to shut the wooden door against the storm while keeping her tucked in the crook of his arm.

A brief shiver took hold of her, more from her thoughts than the cold.

He yanked her hood back as he asked, "Are you all right?"

She tried to step away from him, but he refused to let her go. "I'm fine. You should release me now."

"Why? You fit rather nicely," he said with a teasing smile.

And she did; she had noticed the perfect fit herself. Her body's contours seemed to meld precisely with his. It was what had churned her memories; for there had been another time she had felt the same. It was as if two missing halves had been reunited, but instead of the thought bringing joy as it once had, now it brought only sadness.

"Please, let me go," she pleaded softly.

"I am not your intended; therefore, it is safe for me to touch you."

"You must trust me on this," she said with sorrow. "It is not safe for you, and I truly wish no harm to come to you."

He slowly let his arm fall away from her, and as he did, she stepped away from him. She didn't dare look at him. She wasn't sure why. Perhaps she feared she'd see pity, or disgust; or perhaps she more feared what she would *feel* since for the briefest of moments, his innocent touch had stirred dormant feelings within her.

"You'll not be able to hunt in this storm," she said, wanting to think on anything but that brief spark that had faintly ignited her desire.

"It would be unwise," he said. "But we will need firewood."

Tara glanced around the room and saw that two broken chairs and shards of broken crocks were the only items in the one-room cottage.

Reeve didn't waste any time. He grabbed both chairs and smashed them against each other, splintering them further. He broke some other pieces over his knee, and then he piled them all in the fireplace and had a fire going in no time.

"We'll need more wood. I think I saw a woodpile near the door."

He was out the door and back in no time, and he repeated his actions until there was a good-sized stock of wood inside.

"Hopefully, the storm will stop before morning, and we can be on our way," Reeve said, pulling the plaid he had wrapped around his chest off and hanging it from the end of the mantel.

"Or it could last for days," Tara suggested.

Reeve shrugged, as if it didn't matter to him. "Then we'll certainly have enough time to become better acquainted."

Tara had no intentions of becoming better acquainted. The less she knew about this man, the better for him and for her.

She slipped the bundle off her back and took off her cloak, spreading it on the hard-packed dirt floor in front of the fireplace. Her hand disappeared into her wrapped bundle, and when she finally found what she was searching for, she smiled.

She opened the cloth-wrapped parcel and tore the hunk of dark bread in two, offering one to Reeve. "It's what's left of the bread I baked for the journey."

He took the bread from her and sat down beside her before taking a bite.

He sat cross-legged like she did, and their knees looked as if they touched, but they didn't. She cautioned herself to move away, not to remain close.

*Keep away. Keep away.* The chant repeated like an echo in her mind.

Unfortunately, she didn't listen to her own advice. She remained as she was, allowing herself a modicum of closeness to this man.

"This is delicious," Reeve said after finishing the piece. "You baked it?"

"I did," she admitted, realizing he would find it odd.

"You're obviously of noble class, and I've never known a woman of your status to cook, let alone know how. That is usually left to servants, is it not?"

She turned his question on him. "You know *many* women of my status?"

He laughed. "I will satisfy your curiosity, and then you will satisfy mine."

He was even more handsome when he smiled, and his lighthearted, teasing nature made him all the more appealing. And both were dangerous thoughts.

She nodded and silently cautioned herself that she didn't need to know anything about this man, but she was too curious to listen to her own warnings.

He leaned closer to her, their shoulders near

touching. "I'm such a devilishly handsome creature that born noble or peasant, women can't resist me."

Tara had to laugh since his dark eyes danced with merriment, and his grin was too mocking to take seriously. "That is no answer."

"But it's the truth," he said with a wink.

She almost reached out to touch his face, but clasped her hands together instead. She wanted to make certain he was real, that she wasn't dreaming that she was truly sitting beside a man in front of a hearth talking. It simply felt too surreal to be true.

"Now your turn," he said.

"That was no answer," she argued lightheartedly. "You claim you are irresistible to women and have known many, even noblewomen. Does that mean you are of nobility yourself?"

She detected a brief change in his eyes, as if a shield had been raised, and she wondered if he hid something from her as she did from him.

"I am of no noble birth, though my numerous travels have allowed me to meet people of all classes."

Before she could probe for more, he was quick to claim once again that it was her turn.

She was reluctant to explain to him why she could bake bread. The less he knew about her, the better, though perhaps if he learned the truth, he would then be more willing to keep his distance from her. Then, if she should happen to fall again, he would not be so quick to catch her.

"I spent time in the kitchen with the cook who was a jovial and caring woman, and one my father favored, being her food was quite tasty." She paused, not truly wanting to share the story, but knowing it was for the best. "Then, one day, her husband suddenly died. He was standing there one minute talking with her and on the ground next, dead as dead can be, and the following day he was buried."

She continued not knowing if Reeve was too shocked to comment or that her revelation had left him speechless.

"Tongues started wagging, and, before I knew it, his death was blamed on me. The women believed that somehow I had infected the cook with my death bride curse, and from then on not one woman would speak with me or come near me." She paused again, and when Reeve continued to remain silent, she went on. "Soon after, my food began to taste bad. Instead of complaining to my father, I took matters into my own hands and, with the knowledge I had acquired from the cook, I began to cook for myself in a tiny cottage that I had claimed."

Tara hadn't expected Reeve to respond, so she was surprised when he asked, "What about your father? What did he do?"

"He didn't object to my actions."

"Why not?"

He sounded affronted, and Tara was quick to explain. "There was no reason. I settled the problem for him."

"*No,*" he said. "He should have defended you."

"It would have done little good," she said, pleased that he once again thought to protect her, even from her own father. "Not soon after I kept my distance from the cook, she met a man and married him. So you see the whole thing proved true."

"Nonsense. Regardless, whether you had kept your distance or not, she would have met the man.

"You're not superstitious, are you?"

"Superstition is just plain fear that breeds more fear," he said. "Your father is duty-bound to protect you, and that duty comes before curses, hexes, or the like."

His brief tirade startled her. "You truly are an honorable man."

"A man has nothing if he has no honor."

"You will make a fine husband and father one day, or are you already?" she asked, thinking how lucky the woman who was, or would be, his wife.

Reeve shook his head. "I have no time for such distraction. When I am free of present responsibilities, then I will find a good woman to love, wed her, and sire a gaggle of children, who I will raise with honor just as I have been."

"You have many siblings?" she asked, recalling she had wanted the same, a good man to love and wed and to raise many children. That was the hardest part of this whole ordeal, realizing that she would never have children.

"I have three brothers, and though they are not by blood, they are my brothers nonetheless. We were all raised by Trey's parents. He and I are of the same age, six-and-twenty years, while Duncan and Bryce are one year older. We are family. There is nothing I would not do for them or them for me. And what siblings have you?"

"I have none," she said, though she did have three half brothers. They were simply not worth mentioning. They cared little for her and mocked her as much as others did, so she did not think of them as family. They certainly never defended her; they more tormented her when she was young.

"And what of your mother?"

"She passed on before I took my first step. I barely remember her."

"I recall little of my own mother," Reeve admitted, a bit of sadness in his voice.

The more she spoke to this man, the more she felt a kinship to him, which was why it would have been wise for them to remain strangers, knowing nothing of each other. For the little she had learned had her wishing she could be friends with him. Unfortunately, she couldn't take the chance. She would not be the cause of another man dying.

She hoped this storm would not hinder their journey. She needed to find a cottage where she could live out the rest of her days alone.

Reeve added more logs to the steadily burning fire and stepped outside, returning several minutes later, shaking off a good coating of snow.

"The snow has worsened," he said, returning his extra plaid to hang on the end of the mantel.

The news upset Tara though she kept her worries to herself. She feared sharing such confined quarters with him, especially for a prolonged period of time. Reeve did not understand the dire consequences of such action. And she wasn't sure she could explain it so that it made sense, for it certainly had never made sense to her.

The only thing she was certain of was that the curse was real, and if she wasn't careful, Reeve would die.

# Chapter 3

Reeve watched Tara sleep, her fur-lined cloak wrapped around her curled-up body. She reminded him of the cats around the keep, the way they would curl tightly into a ball while they slept. But unlike the cats who curled next to each other for warmth, Tara lay alone.

He could not imagine never being touched. Whether it was a brotherly hug, his mother's comforting touch, or even her occasional teasing smack, he knew he was loved. And he could not imagine never being able to hold a woman in his arms, kiss her, or be kissed. And he certainly could not fathom never coupling with a woman ever again.

He looked forward to the day that he would fall in love, like his brother Duncan had. They were inseparable, and that was how he would be with the woman he loved. He would crawl in bed with her every night, and whether they made love or not, he would hold her in his arms and protect her always.

Reeve wondered over the origin of the curse that had dubbed Tara the death bride. Was it a series of unfortunate circumstances? Or gossiping tongues that turned unfortunate events into a woman being cursed?

He intended to find out more about her. Why? He couldn't precisely say. He didn't feel sorry for her. She had courage enough to seek freedom for herself with the help of a stranger. And she had the strength to keep her distance from him for fear of causing him harm even if it had meant getting lost in a snowstorm.

She had fought his embrace as soon as he had her in his arms. And when she had calmed, and he had been able to tuck her more snugly against him, he found she fit, as if she had been made for him.

It had been an odd feeling. One he had never experienced before. That a flare of desire had risen up in him he couldn't deny, but it had been more than that though he couldn't exactly explain it. It had been much too strange a sensation, one that overwhelmed, grabbed at him, rattled him, and excited him.

Could he be treading a dangerous path? He presently had no time to pursue a woman, which was why he satisfied himself with willing women now and again. And he certainly had known noblewomen quite intimately. They had pursued him more vigorously than the peasant women he had known. But it had all been nothing more than a satisfying of needs. There had been no love involved, nor had it ever been implied.

Reeve yawned and stretched himself away from where he sat near the hearth. He continued stretching as he stood; his arms near touching the thatched ceiling. He hadn't realized he had groaned along with his mighty stretch until he looked down and saw Tara's eyes open wide with fear.

He fell to his knees beside her. "It's all right. I was just having a stretch, that's all."

She shrunk away from him, pulling her cloak

more tightly around her, and with a bit of a tremble to her voice, she said, "I thought you a demon rising from the depths of hell."

Reeve smiled. "Now that is what I want my enemies to believe of me, but you are not my enemy. You are a friend, and a demon always protects his friends."

He was pleased when she giggled.

"You are no demon. You are a good man."

"Shhh," he said with a finger to his lips and a quick glance around the room. "That's a secret best kept between you and me."

"I will keep your secret," she whispered.

His smile faded, and he so badly wanted to reach out and touch her, just a gentle friendly touch to let her know someone cared. But he knew she would not receive it well, so he tried to do the same with words.

"And I will keep any secret you, my friend, wish to share," he said.

When a glint of a tear appeared in the corner of her eye, he wanted to take hold of her and cradle her in his arms. But again he knew it was not a wise thing to do.

"Thank you," she said in a bare whisper.

She closed her eyes after that, and he wrapped his extra plaid around himself and settled a few feet behind her on the floor to sleep. As tired as he was, sleep eluded him for too long, his mind rushing with chaotic thoughts.

He had decided at the onset that he would take Tara home with him. She needed a place where people would treat her kindly, and he believed his village would accept her, curse and all. But after hearing her story about the cook, he wondered if her presence would cause problems. Wagging tongues could do a rash of harm, and if anyone knew . . .

*Why did anyone have to know?*

The question rang loudly through his thoughts. No one need know her history. He need only tell them that he had rescued her from robbers, and she in turn asked for his help. He could concoct a good tale that would have the village wanting to protect her. And perhaps with the curse ignored and fear expelled, Tara would be able to have friends and perhaps find love.

Of course, he would have to be a good man. One who would protect her and treat her well, and Reeve would make certain of it. He wouldn't let just any man trail after Tara. After all, he was the one who found her and helped her. It was his duty now to see her safe.

With that satisfying thought in mind, Reeve finally fell asleep.

Reeve wiggled his nose, trying to get whatever caused the pesky tickle off. Though he had to admit there was a nice scent to it, sweet with a touch of pine. He slowly opened his eyes and as he did he saw another pair of eyes opening as well.

Both pairs of eyes shot wide open, and Reeve realized that he and Tara had rolled toward each other sometime in the night, and he had wrapped himself around her. She, in turn, had snuggled into his arms, and there they rested, nose to nose.

When she had finally realized the same, she scrambled to get away from him, but her cloak and his plaid had become entwined, and there was no getting out of it.

"We can't be this close," she pleaded.

"I have not died yet," he said with a teasing laugh.

"It is not funny. You are in danger being this close to me."

"Why? If you help me to understand where the danger comes from, perhaps I can help you."

"You can't help," she said adamantly. "Why can't you just believe me and let it be?"

"Because it makes no sense," he said, realizing that when she had struggled to free herself, she had inadvertently forced her body closer against his, and she fit snugly against his suddenly growing mound. "You're right; this isn't a good time for this discussion."

He hoped she didn't feel him springing to life against her, and so he hurried to untangle them. She helped. Their hands and arms wound around each other as they tried desperately to disengage themselves.

When it was done, they rushed to separate, each taking a deep breath of relief when finally apart.

"I'll see if the snow stopped," Reeve said, needing a shot of brisk, cold air right now.

He took an even deeper breath once outside. He was relieved to see that the snow must have stopped early in the night, only a few inches having covered the ground. They could continue their journey home.

He entered the cottage, glad that the cold air had tamed his desire and pleased that they could be on their way.

"Can we leave?" she asked with concern, before he had a chance to speak.

He nodded and smiled. "Only a few inches, though there are drifts. We can leave now, or I can hunt, and we can eat then—"

"I'm not hungry," she said, interrupting him. "Perhaps later, unless, of course, you're hungry?"

"I can wait," he said, preferring to get started as well.

Reeve saw to putting out the fire while Tara gathered her things and once more hung her bundle on her back. They were on the road again in no time.

There wasn't much chance for chatter, focus was essential. There was no telling what was hiding beneath the fallen snow. More than once, Tara almost fell from her boots catching on a hidden rock or fallen branch.

Reeve had been quick to grab her arm and steady her. She didn't object, but then there was no need for him to wrap her in his arms as he had done in the snowstorm. And he thought what a shame. He actually wouldn't mind holding her again.

*Where had that thought come from?*

Sure, she had felt good in his arms. *Damn good.*

He shook his head. He didn't need to be thinking about this.

"Something wrong?" she asked from behind him.

"Nothing," he said, not turning around.

"You shook your head."

"Clearing it," he said truthfully.

Silence followed, and Reeve thought the matter settled until. . .

"Are you having second thoughts about helping me?'

He stopped abruptly and turned around, causing her to come to a similar abrupt stop though nearly on top of him.

"That wasn't a thought in my head," he answered honestly.

"Then what troubled you?"

"Too many thoughts."

"I suffer from the same affliction myself," she said.

"Then you know it takes a good shake to rid yourself of them."

"A chore I do quite regularly."

"Good, then we understand each other better than most," he said, finding more things in common with her and also realizing that her lips were ripe for kissing. Slightly plump and moist, having worried at both with her teeth as they had spoken.

Damn, but he wanted to kiss her, and when she scurried back away from him, he realized that his desire to do just that must have shown in his eyes.

"We'd best keep walking," she said.

He nodded, turned, and did just that. He silently berated himself for his foolish thought. Whatever had he been thinking? She certainly wouldn't be receptive to a kiss, and what if this myth was true?

Now he truly intended to berate himself. He never believed in foolish nonsense. It was usually ignorant people saying ignorant things that caused problems. He had used his brawn to settle such matters. And it had never failed, people always surrendered to strength.

"Reeve!"

He turned at her scream and lunged for her, grabbing hold of her hand just as she went over the side of an incline, her momentum pulling him along with her. They slid down the steep slope on their stomachs, facing each other, picking up speed as they went. Reeve gripped her hand tightly, letting her know there was no chance of her slipping away from him. She clung just as tightly to him, and for a sheer moment, it felt as if their hands melded together as one.

With a thud, a whack, and a bump, they came to rest at the bottom of the hill. Reeve landed on top of her, their limbs all tangled.

"Are you all right?" he asked before trying to move.

She turned her face, and having no choice, she rested her cheek against his. "I believe so."

Her skin was silky soft and lightly flushed, and he liked the feel of it pressed to his. "We need to slowly untangle ourselves and make certain there are no severe injuries."

She gave a brief nod and winced.

"Something pains you?" he asked, concerned.

"My arm is twisted beneath me, and it's beginning to hurt."

Reeve slowly untangled his one arm from beneath her and eased his legs from around hers before gently moving himself off her to stand and give a stretch. Ascertaining that he had no injuries, he was quick to drop down on his haunches to help her.

She sighed. "With you off me, I feel much better."

Reeve grabbed at his chest and grinned. "You are the only woman who finds *relief* in me not being on top of her."

Tara laughed and struggled to sit up. Reeve was quick to help her, his hand slipping behind to rest at her back. Oddly enough, she didn't protest, though Reeve let his hand fall away as soon as he sat her up.

"That is because I am different from all the women you have known," she said with a wide smile.

When she smiled, her lavender eyes darkened to a sultry purple, and with her cheeks flushed, she was far prettier than Reeve had first believed. And yes, she was right. She was different. He wasn't quite sure how, but she was different.

"Your arm?" he asked, seeing how she cradled it.

"Just sore, nothing more," she assured him moving it up and down so that he could judge for himself.

He instinctively reached out to help her stand when her eyes opened wide, warning him not to touch. So they were back to that again, and he shook his head. "This will not do." And with that, his hands went to her waist, and he brought her to her feet in one gentle swing.

His hands remained firm at her waist as he spoke. "There is no way I can keep my hands off you."

"What?" she asked, startled.

"Not in an intimate sense," he corrected, and damned if images of him touching her intimately didn't pop into his head. He shook the vivid scenes away before they could do more damage, and explained, "I cannot stop myself from reaching out and helping you when you need it. It's simple instinct. And evidently you wish my help since you called my name when in trouble. So there will be no telling me that I cannot touch you or warning me with that evil eye look. I will be touching you, so get used to it."

Tara glared at him wide-eyed and wide-mouthed.

Reeve glared right back, folding his arms across his chest.

"You're placing yourself in danger," she said.

Reeve looked himself up and down. "I look just fine. You, on the other hand," he said, pointing his finger at her, "have had a couple of close calls, which I"—he thumped his chest—"saved you from. And so far, I am still standing, as you can plainly see. I am not deader than dead. I am alive and well."

"You are," she said as though it were a miracle.

"Perhaps the curse is gone," he suggested.

"I doubt that."

"Then why am I still alive?"

Tara shook her head. "I don't know, but I fear taking chances with your life."

"It isn't you taking the chance. It is me. I chose to help you; therefore, whatever happens is my own fault."

"But I have warned you—"

"True, you have, and still I choose to help you," he said. "So the consequences are of my own making."

She worried at her lower lip, and Reeve watched it plump further to life. Damn, but he was in need of a woman. That was the problem; he had been too long without one. Who was he kidding? It had been only three days since he had coupled with a very willing widow who had provided him with water when he had stopped at her croft, then suggested he share supper with her until finally she had invited him into her bed. They had had a good time, and when he left, after a delicious morning romp in her bed, they had both been smiling.

Why had he suddenly begun to think of intimacy with Tara? The answer came as fast as the question. When he had held her against him and she had fit so perfectly. With such a precise fit, he couldn't help but wonder if they were perfectly sized in other ways.

"A simple helping hand, that's all," she clarified.

"What else would there be?" he asked innocently.

"I'm not an ignorant woman, Reeve. I felt you grow hard against me this morning. I saw the look of desire in your eyes when we spoke, and I see how you focus on my lips. Wondering how a kiss would taste?"

He saw no reason to deny the truth. "The thought did cross my mind."

"Thank you for being honest. It is good to know that I was not wrong about you being a moral man. With that said, I am sure I have nothing to worry about. You will touch me only when I am in need of help."

"Agreed," he said. "Just remember, I will be there to help you with *all* your needs."

# Chapter 4

Tara concentrated on keeping a steady pace behind Reeve even though her ankle pained her. She probably gave it a good twist in the fall, and walking on it wasn't helping. If she alerted Reeve to her injury, he would surely stop and refuse to continue until her ankle healed. And there was no telling how long that would take.

She also knew it was not wise to linger with this man. She had been well aware that thoughts of coupling with her had danced in his head. She had seen the desire in his eyes more than once and had felt it when she woke wrapped in his arms.

It had surprised her, but what surprised her more was that she had stirrings of desire herself. A tiny spark had tickled her dormant passion, and she had briefly felt the urge to couple. Not that she had ever coupled with a man before.

She had truly loved Rory, her first love, and had looked forward to becoming his wife. Unfortunately he died on the day they were to wed. An arranged marriage followed six months later, and she had not met Luag until the day of the wedding. She had not been attracted to him; though not a bad-looking man, she simply didn't favor him. She had actually worried over intimacy with him. She needn't have since he died right after speaking his vows.

The memory sent a shiver through her and caused concern, and for a good reason. She was attracted to Reeve. That he was a handsome man was undeniable, but it wasn't entirely his good features that attracted her. What appealed most was that he had called himself her friend. It had been so very long since she had had a friend.

Tears had threatened when he had told her that he was her friend, and she could count on him, but she wouldn't embarrass herself and let them spill. She had fought to keep them at bay. It was at that moment he had stolen a piece of her heart, or she had simply given it to him . . . her friend.

While she would love their friendship to continue, she knew it would be unwise. Her attraction to him and his obvious desire for her could only prove fatal. It was better that he leave her with the clan he felt best suited her situation and she never see him again.

A pang of regret stabbed at her heart, but she ignored it. Disappointment had been her constant companion. And she had grown accustomed to it. It would do no good to dwell when she knew her decision was for the best. She would make a new life for herself, solitary though it might be. At least she would finally be at peace.

It was late morning when they finally stopped and Reeve suggested she have a rest while he hunted for food. She quickly agreed, hoping the respite would help her throbbing ankle. She waited to examine it until he disappeared beyond a thicket of bushes, and she winced while struggling to get her boot off and cringed when she saw how it had swollen considerably.

She didn't remove her wool stocking to have a peek. She immediately slipped her boot back on though with much discomfort; and there it would stay until the swelling went down.

A fire needed to be started to cook whatever game Reeve caught. She didn't hesitate. She got to her feet and ignored the pain that rippled through her ankle. This was not going to be easy, but when had her life ever been easy. Just like so many other times, she had no choice. She would not cause them to linger, placing them in more peril. She hobbled around collecting sticks and fallen branches and went to work on starting a fire.

She was pleased with her efforts, Reeve returning to find a fire and spit ready to use.

"You did well," he said, taking the already skinned and cleaned rabbit and placing it on the pit stick to cook. "You've saved us time. If we can keep a steady pace, we can reach my friend's before nightfall. Then three more days, and we'll reach our destination."

That brought a smile to her face. Pain or no pain, she had to keep pace with Reeve. She could rest when they reached the croft; and hopefully the swelling would be down by morning and the pain diminished.

Excited at the thought of finally starting anew, she asked, "Can you tell me about the clan where I will make my new home?"

"It would be a good idea for us to discuss that now."

"You are sure they will accept me?" Tara asked apprehensively.

"I haven't a doubt," he said.

"You know them well then?"

"Very much so," he said with a nod.

"They are friends of your clan?"

Reeve grinned. "Actually, you'll be making your home with *my* clan."

Shock and a spark of anger had Tara jumping to her feet. A stabbing-hot pain shot through her ankle, and her response was instinctive. She let out a yell and then sunk, like a stone thrown into a river, to the ground.

Reeve was at her side in an instant. "What's wrong?"

"Nothing," she said stubbornly through gritted teeth.

"You're in pain," he said. "You were hurt in the fall, weren't you?"

"It's nothing."

"You're lying."

"How dare you—"

"Show me the injury," he demanded.

"No," Tara said, folding her arms tightly across her chest.

Reeve leaned his face so close to hers that their noses touched. "Tell me, or I will find it myself."

"You wouldn't dare," she challenged.

"Do you truly believe that?"

Tara glared at him.

"Show me, or I will begin to touch you, starting from the top and working my way down."

If he had intended to work from the bottom up, she would not have considered capitulating. And if that didn't annoy her enough, then her traitorous body certainly did, tingling at the mere thought of his exploring touch.

His hands reached out, and she quickly grabbed hold of them. "My ankle."

She released his hands and raised the hem of her dress, knowing he would do so if she didn't. It was easy to see which ankle was injured, and he gently took hold of her leg. He shook his head, saying nothing. He then attempted to ease the boot past the swelling, and she winced.

It had swollen even more, and now the leather refused to release the injured foot.

"Why didn't you tell me?" he asked, annoyed.

"It would have slowed us down."

"Are you in such a hurry to reach your new home?"

"I had been until you told me that it was your clan you were taking me to," she said, knowing it would not do.

"My clan is comprised of good people. You will be welcome there, though . . ."

"You have doubts," she said at his pause, and shook her head at the obvious mess she had gotten herself into.

"I do not, though I think it wise we don't mention that you are a—" He pursed his lips tightly, as if he didn't want to continue.

"Say it," Tara insisted. "I am a death bride. *Death Bride. Death Bride*. I kill husbands. I kill people who love me."

"I don't believe that," Reeve said. "That is one reason I prefer not to tell anyone of your past. It is time for this so-called curse to be broken. With no gossip to follow you, no one will fear you, and the curse will be no more."

"You're willing to take that chance? You know so much about curses?"

"Curses only have the power you give them," he said.

"I've learned otherwise and will not take a chance in causing more harm."

Reeve reached out and took hold of her chin. "Listen and listen well. You requested that I take you somewhere safe. My clan is a safe place. You will be well protected there, and if you wish to keep to yourself, to make no friends, then so be it. But it is where you are going and where you will stay."

It did no good to protest. He was giving her what she asked for. What she hadn't counted on was being attracted to him, though what did that matter. Nothing could come of it. She couldn't allow it to. Or was it that she wondered if anyone could ever love her again? It had been so long, and men were so fearful of her that love simply avoided her. But as Reeve had said, she could keep to herself and not bother with anyone.

It wasn't as if she was in love with him. He was no more than a friend. The problem, no doubt, was that she had been too long without the touch and company of a man, and like a starving person, she now craved it. However, it was an appetite she would have to ignore for his safety and for her sanity. As far as not letting anyone know of her being a death bride? She would bide her time and see if it could truly work to her advantage. She had her doubts, and oddly enough, though she could not say why, for the first time in a long time she had an inkling of hope.

She finally agreed. "All right."

"Believe me, it is a good place for you."

"Since you are an honorable man, I will take your word on that," she said.

"Good, for it is given in friendship."

*Friendship.*

There was the inkling of hope rearing its head. It would be wonderful to have friends again, to be able to talk with other women and perhaps love would stop avoiding her and somehow, some way the curse could be lifted. She truly hoped that such a miracle was possible.

"Now for your ankle," he said.

"I don't think we should remove the boot. Once off, I doubt I will be able to get it back on."

"You cannot walk on it," he said as if he declared an edict.

"I must," she insisted. "At least until we reach your friend's croft. There I can rest."

He rubbed his chin, and once again she noticed his handsome features. She liked the way his dark eyes seemed to match his dark hair and the lines of his slim nose blended so perfectly with his facial features that one would believe his face sculpted by talented hands. But most of all she liked that he cared about her. She could see worry in his eyes, and it was so very nice to have someone truly care.

"We could slow our pace," he said.

"Then we would not reach the croft before nightfall."

"The walk will be too much for you," he insisted.

"Let me be the judge of that."

He grinned. "With how stubborn you are?"

"My stubbornness just might serve a purpose this time."

"The purpose of making your ankle worse and causing you more pain?"

"I can manage this," she said. "And once at the croft, I can rest."

He shook his head, as if in disagreement with himself. "You will tell me if the pain becomes too much?"

"Yes, I promise."

"If we must stay with my friend a few days, you will not protest?"

Since they would not be alone, she had no worry. "I will not protest."

"Then we will try and make it to the croft."

"You don't believe I can," she said, seeing the doubt.

"You can at the cost of pain and more swelling."

"But it will bring us closer to your home, my new home, and that is where I long to be."

"I cannot fault you there," Reeve admitted. "I long to be home myself."

"You miss your family?"

"Aye, I do," he admitted, tucking the hem of her cloak around her feet and stretching his legs out where he sat beside her. "Mercy, Duncan's wife, is expecting their first babe in the summer, and the family can't wait for the wee one to be born."

"How wonderful," she said, trying to keep the sadness out of her voice. She loved children and had hoped to have many. Rory and she had talked about having a large family. He had joked about starting his own clan, and she had been willing to oblige him. They had been so young and so in love. There seemed to be nothing to stand in their way . . . nothing except death.

"Are any of your other brothers married?" Tara asked, not wanting to focus on sorrowful memories.

"None but Duncan," he said.

"And none in love?"

Reeve hesitated a moment. "Trey lost the woman he loved, killed by our enemies."

"How terrible for him," she said, too familiar with the pain of loss.

"It was," Reeve agreed. "The family didn't think he would ever heal. I sometimes wonder if he has, or if he has just found a way to cope with it."

The hiss of the flames drew their attention, and the succulent scent of the roasting rabbit reminded them of how hungry they were. Soon they were enjoying the meal, and soon after that, Reeve was dousing the fire with handfuls of dirt and kicking the last of the charred wood apart.

"Are you sure of this?" he asked.

Tara nodded. Pain or not it had to be done.

They set off, and she didn't know how she kept pace with Reeve, but she managed. Her ankle pained unmercifully until finally it settled into a dull rhythmic throb that, in a strange way, became bearable, or was it that she ignored it as best she could.

Reeve endlessly asked if she was all right, and she endlessly informed him that she was fine. But after a few hours, the throbbing increased, and she began to ask him how long it would be before they reached the croft.

Finally, Reeve stopped abruptly and turned, reaching for her.

She swerved out of his reach. "What are you doing?"

"I intend to carry you."

"You most certainly will not."

"There's no time to argue," he said. "And since you have repeatedly asked how far we have to go, your ankle must be paining you. I hadn't expected you to last this long."

"I can manage," she insisted adamantly, expecting him to argue.

He stretched out his hand to her. "Let me help you."

This time when he stepped forward, she didn't stop him from scooping her up. Even with the weight off it, her ankle continued to throb. But that wasn't what drew her attention. A chorus of chaotic warnings shouted in her head how dangerous it was to be in his arms.

Why then did his embrace feel so utterly wonderful? The brute strength of his arms, the ease with which he carried her, the determination on his handsome face, they all made it seem so right.

Without thinking, she laid her head on his shoulder, tucking the top of her head beneath his chin and snuggling comfortably against him.

"There's another abandoned farm a short distance away. We'll stop there for the night."

Her head shot up.

"Don't bother to argue," he said, cutting off her protest. "You can't walk on this ankle, and the more you try, the worse it will get and the longer it will take us to reach home."

It annoyed her that he made sense, and so she returned her head to his shoulder without making a comment.

He shifted her to sit more comfortably against him. "You know, you're a perfect fit."

He was right. She had felt it herself. She did fit with him perfectly, and that's what worried her the most.

# Chapter 5

"So many farms abandoned," Tara said, as they approached a small croft that had long been deserted. It appeared as if Mother Nature had reclaimed the land and was about to do the same with the cottage.

"The kings demand too much from their people. And King Kenneth, who rules over them all, should be creating laws and enforcing them to protect his people. But he's as busy as the kings taking more than he gives."

"Times are troubling," she said.

"More than anyone cares to admit." Reeve lowered her carefully to the ground. "Stand here and don't move while I remove the debris from around the front door."

Tara followed his instructions, not wanting to prove a hindrance to him. He searched the area before starting, disappearing around the side of the cottage and reappearing only moments later. He held up a half-broken barrel and grinned as if he'd been given a gift.

She smiled herself when he began digging the snow away from the front door and snapping the tree branch that had grown through the lone, small window. He worked with such ease and confidence, like a man comfortable in any task he took on.

What she liked most was that he worked with a smile and no complaints. She had thought he might balk about the delay her ankle caused, but his concern was more for her comfort, and she was grateful.

He used his shoulder to get the door open, it proving a bit stubborn at first. But it was no match for his brawn. He vanished inside, and, with a limp, she approached slowly. She hadn't gotten very far when he appeared in the open doorway.

"What are you doing?" he asked. "You shouldn't be walking on that ankle. It must have time to heal."

She was in his arms before she knew it and carried across the threshold. She was surprised to see a single bed with a limp mattress that needed stuffing, a table with one corner rotted away, and two chairs that had seen better days. And a fair-sized cauldron sat to the side of the cold hearth.

He placed her on the bed. "Those chairs don't look sturdy; besides, I need to get a fire started. Then I'll go hunt us something for supper."

"I should help," she said, feeling a burden on him.

He laughed, shook his head, and bounced down on his haunches to reach out and take hold of her leg.

He held her leg with a tender gentleness while his other hand attempted to work off her boot. It had gone quickly from her not wanting him to touch her to his touching in an intimate fashion. No man had ever caressed the calf of her leg.

"I'm sorry," he said. "This may hurt."

That he offered an apology astounded her. He was proving to be different than she had first imagined him. When he had suddenly appeared out of nowhere, she had grown even more frightened than she had been. She thought he might join the robbers and then, when she had realized he intended to defend her, she had been stunned. And in the few short hours since they had met, she realized he was no common Highlander warrior. Nor was he easy to define.

She had watched him dispose of four men as if they were nothing more than annoying gnats, and he had not a bead of sweat on him when he had finished, nor had his breathing been labored.

He smiled more often than most Highlander warriors that she had known, and he was fearsome when it came to strength and kind when it came to gentleness.

She winced as he eased the boot down over her injured ankle.

"Take your stocking off," he ordered.

"Why?" she demanded.

His grin turned his face wickedly handsome. "If we pack snow around the ankle, it may take the swelling down."

She should have realized that herself. Instead, she appeared the fool, he obviously thinking that she thought he was thinking something entirely different and inappropriate.

"You're right," she said.

"I'm always right." He bounced to his feet. "I'll get the snow while you remove your stocking."

He was even mannerly enough to give her privacy. And she saw to removing her stocking before he returned. He dumped the handful of snow into the broken barrel piece and placed it on the floor by the bed. He lifted her beneath her arms and braced her back against the wall, then stretched out her legs on the bed. He positioned the snow-filled barrel piece beneath her injured ankle and piled the snow over it.

"Now you're all set. I'll get the fire going and then be off to get us supper."

"Thank you," she said.

"No need. You're paying me well to see to your safety."

"Safety yes, kindness is another thing."

"A man protects a woman," he said with a shrug. "It is the way of things."

It might be for him, but it hadn't been for her. Watching him set a fire and seeing that he took the time to gather pine branches and pack them in the window to keep the cold away was a sight she favored. She had seen to taking care of things for herself for so long that it was difficult to believe that someone was now looking after her.

If this was a dream, she didn't want to wake up.

"Lord," she whispered, "please let this work. Let me slip away. Let them think me dead. Let me finally be free."

When she had told the Highlander she would give him all of her bride price, the plan had barely formed in her head. Her first thought had been to buy his protection and see her safely to her intended destination. After all, what else was there for her? When suddenly the thought of freedom gripped her, and her mind was made up before she even attempted to make sense of such an insane idea.

Once it had taken root, it had flourished, and she knew she would pursue it. She felt no guilt in using her bride price; after all, her father was paying to be rid of her, so he would get what he wanted.

The cold had seeped into her ankle and was now traveling up her leg. She wrapped her cloak more tightly around her upper body and rested her head back, closing her eyes. She was tired and would take a few moments to sneak a brief nap. Then when she woke, perhaps she could help Reeve. She snuggled her chilled chin into the fur lining of her cloak and was asleep in no time.

Reeve had the rabbit cleaned and ready for the spit before he reached the cottage. All he had to do was set it to cook in the fireplace. He had even managed to find some onions and turnips in what once had been the cottage garden. Though frozen, he could set them to cook in the cauldron. He bowed his head into the wind, which had picked up, the air having grown colder with the approach of dusk.

He hurried into the cottage, shutting the door against the rush of cold that followed him. He turned to proudly show off his successful hunt and saw that Tara was sound asleep. He rid himself of his plaid and skewered the rabbit on the spit in the fireplace to cook. He made quick work cleaning the dusty cauldron with snow and then adding fresh snow and setting it on the hook in the hearth. He chopped the onions and turnips and added them to the melting snow. When he was finally done, he walked over to Tara.

He reached out and took hold of one of her curls, the ringlet wrapping around his finger. It was soft, silky, and shiny, the color as dark as raven feathers. He took hold of others, and they curled around his finger as eagerly as the first.

Tara stirred with a faint sigh. He wondered over this woman he had just met yesterday. He knew little about her, and yet she intrigued him. She had made certain at first to keep her distance from him, but he knew that wouldn't, actually couldn't, last long. With the snow and the cold, it was inevitable they would be drawn together whether to provide heat to each other or a helping hand as she had needed today.

She had called out to him, and when he had turned with barely enough time to grab hold of her hand, before she went over the edge, he had felt a jolt to his gut. He thought for a moment she'd slip from his grasp, but she stretched out her fingers to him as he did to her, and they grabbed hold of each other and clung tightly, not wanting or willing to let go.

He wondered who waited for her and if her intended would care that she would never arrive. Or would it be her bride price that he missed? Marriages were made more often for the convenience and benefit of the clans. Love was rarely involved, but his parents' marriage had shown him the difference, and he knew that he would settle for nothing less.

Tara hadn't had that choice. He couldn't blame her for wanting to escape a marriage that wasn't of her choosing. But he couldn't help but wonder who would ever agree to wed a woman considered a death bride?

It made no sense.

Her eyes suddenly popped open, and she glared at him standing there, a few of her dark ringlets curled around his fingers. They said nothing, just stared, until Reeve moved, trying to rid his fingers of the possessive curls.

They refused to let go, curling around his fingers again and again each time he tried to tear them away. He was surprised to hear her chuckle.

"They are obstinate like me," she said.

"And soft like you." He turned and walked away, the curls reluctantly releasing him. He smiled, wondering if she would chastise him or graciously accept the compliment.

"Something smells good," she said.

From the hint of joy in her voice, it seemed to have pleased her, and that pleased him.

"A rabbit is roasting and onions and turnips are boiling."

"I wish I could be of more help. I am not accustomed to being idle," she said.

That had him returning and taking a look at her ankle. "The swelling has gone down some. We should pack more ice on it." He glanced at her. "Up to suffering another chill?"

"Just hearing the meat sizzle in the hearth is warming me already."

"One more dose of snow will be enough for the night, and then we'll see how your ankle is in the morning."

"I'll be fine to continue our journey," she insisted.

"I'll be the judge of that."

"It's not your ankle," she said.

"But I make more sensible decisions when it comes to your injury."

Her smile surprised him. He thought for sure she'd argue; most women could be obstinate that way.

"And you're always right."

"You learn fast," he teased.

"That I do."

The bit of sharpness in her response had him realizing it was a warning, and he grinned. "I will remember that."

* * *

The wind howled around the cottage, rattling the thick pine branches that served as shutters. The chilly draft sent the flames in the fireplace dancing wildly and had Tara relieved that no more snow covered her ankle. Her stocking was back on, and she was wrapped snugly in her fur-lined cloak.

Reeve, however, only had his extra wool plaid to cover him, and he shivered beside her in bed. She had almost objected when he had announced that they would share the single bed, and though it wasn't narrow, the size left little room for space between them. But with all he had done for her, she couldn't see him spending the night on the cold earthen floor.

The way he was shivering, though, you would think that was where he was, and it bothered her. He had looked after her, and she lay selfishly beside him, wrapped in a fur-lined cloak while he froze.

While the curse remained a threat, she neither loved him nor was to wed him. They barely knew each other. And with Reeve suffering no dire repercussions thus far, it certainly should be safe enough to share some heat with him for the night, just as they had the night before, though that was by accident.

He'd freeze to death by the time she debated the matter and so before she could change her mind, she said, "You are freezing, share the warmth of my cloak with me." And she opened it for him to slip close.

He didn't hesitate though he shared much more than merely the warmth of her cloak. His arm went around her waist, and he snuggled against her, his leg going to rest between her legs in the crevice of her red velvet dress. He settled his face next to hers, and she startled from the touch of his icy cheek.

"Good Lord, you are ice-cold," she said, and wrapped her arms around him.

They were soon cuddled like lovers who couldn't get close enough to each other. She rubbed his back until she could feel the warmth returning to his flesh. And though she had taken a chance inviting him near, she knew she was safe.

He would honor his word not to touch her intimately.

The long day, the cold, a full stomach, and finally warmth soon had his eyes closing, and soon after he began snoring lightly. While odd to be in a bed with a stranger, Tara found it more pleasing than not. Having not been touched, even a simple friendly touch, in so long made her cherish and want to linger in this moment.

The smell of pine and ash and woods drifted off him, along with a hint of a well-cooked rabbit. She smiled, having missed the scent of a man and not realizing just how much until now. Or had it simply hurt too much to remember and so she had shut the memories away never to visit them again.

But now she had no choice. Reeve was here beside her, and his close presence caused an explosion of memories, including desire. It had been some time since she felt desire for a man. Reeve had sparked it, to her surprise, and now lying here beside him, she worried that he might just ignite it.

# Chapter 6

Reeve woke to a tickling sensation beneath his nose, and he smiled, knowing it came from Tara's springy locks. He opened his eyes and wasn't surprised to find them wrapped in an embrace more common to lovers than friends. And once again he was made aware of how precisely her curves melded with his.

*Two halves once separated coming together as one.*

The thought startled the bejesus out of him, and he suddenly felt the need to place distance between them. Not that he was running, he reminded himself. He never ran from anything. He stood his ground, fought a good fight, fought for what he believed, fought for his clan, fought to protect.

As he gently disengaged her arms and slipped out of bed, he was reminded that he was to protect her, to see her safely home. He tucked her cloak around her and glanced down at her ankle, but only her stocking-covered toes peaked from beneath the red velvet.

He went to the hearth, and though the fire had dimmed, he added no more logs. He would wait to see how her ankle fared. If they could continue, he would need to extinguish the fire; if not, he would add more logs then.

He thought the same about hunting for food. If they could get started soon, they could make it to Old Jacob's place by early afternoon, and that was with a few stops along the way to let her ankle rest.

Taking a quick glance to see that Tara still slept, he turned and headed out the door. He'd see to the weather while seeing to his morning duties. A cloudy gray sky and crisp air greeted him, though it didn't sting his cheeks. Snow didn't seem likely, and he was pleased. He wanted to get home and see his family and see Tara safely settled.

His mission hadn't produced any startling news, though, like an approaching storm, the forces of change were gathering. He had heard it at every croft he had stopped at and in villages, though more in whispers, the villagers mistrustful of prying ears that reported to the king.

One obvious change he had made note of was the presence of the king's soldiers in areas they had not been known to frequent. He wondered if they were scouting for future reference or were there for a particular purpose. It shouldn't have been difficult to find out, and yet he had found no answers. All inquires he had made produced the same results, no one knew why. And not knowing had made the people all the more mistrustful and fearful.

Reeve finished, though before returning to the cottage, he sensed the need to scout the surrounding area. He always listened to his instincts. They never failed him, but then he believed that was the way of all good warriors. At least it was for him and his brothers, the way they had been taught.

After covering some ground and finding no cause for alarm, he took a moment to stand and listen. Silence engulfed him, and that had him listening more closely and his head going up so that his nose could get a good whiff of the air.

The scent hit him, and he rushed to cover his latest tracks and took refuge behind a thicket of snow-covered bushes. He would have to be careful, the snow-covered land making it more difficult to conceal oneself.

He crouched and waited. It took time, but he was patient. The strong scent of a burning campfire always clung to those around it as if the fire had yet to be extinguished. In the cold, crisp air, it was even more easily detectable. And with the scent growing stronger, Reeve knew that more than one person headed his way.

He heard the voices before they appeared, the fools paying no heed to how sound echoed in the forest, especially in the dead of winter. He knew by the raucous talk and unconcerned manner that they were the king's soldiers even before he caught sight of them.

It was unusual for a small troop to be this far north in territory that wasn't friendly to King Kenneth. He had seen small divisions of troops like this one all too often the last couple of weeks, and their sudden presence troubled him.

Reeve remained where he was, watching the four of them pass. The fools were so busy talking amongst themselves that he could have easily attacked them and have kept one alive until he found out what they were doing here, before having him join his comrades in hell. But he had Tara to consider. She had to be awake by now, and he needed to get back to her. And he needed to get them moving, get them to Old Jacob's place and make sure he and his granddaughter-in-law Willow were safe. Not that the soldiers usually bothered anyone on MacAlpin land, but they had been growing bolder, the king making his power known throughout the land, especially those areas that lent him no support.

He waited until he could hear the soldiers' footfalls no longer, and then he quietly made his way back to the cottage.

He entered to find Tara in front of the hearth, cloak and bundle in place and ready to depart.

"Where have you been?" she demanded. "I was about to leave without you."

"You would leave me behind?" he asked with a glint of a smile. He had to admire her courage, but he supposed that had been hard-won. Forced to rely on herself, what other choice had she?

"I thought that was your intention."

"I'm sorry," he said, feeling the need to apologize. Of course she would think he would desert her. From the little he had learned, she was accustomed to people leaving her and some discarding her. He wanted her to know that would not be the way with him. "I meant only a brief absence and expected to return before you woke. You can count on me, Tara."

She seemed to weigh his words, and he could see that she remained unsure.

"What happened?" she asked.

"Soldiers," he said, and explained what he had seen. "I need to get to Old Jacob's farm and make sure he and his granddaughter are all right. How is your ankle?"

"Better," she said, and held out her foot to show that she had gotten her boot on.

A slight bulge protruded out one side of her ankle. It was better but far from healed. He worried that a day of walking and climbing the snow-covered hilly terrain would only make it worse.

She seemed to sense his apprehension and was quick to put his mind at ease. "My ankle does fine. And while I know it will probably swell again after our long trek, at least I can walk on it now without pain. So I suggest we get started."

He admired her resilience and willingness to suffer further pain so that he could see to the safety of another. She was not a selfish woman, and that was a worthy attribute.

"We'll need to be extracautious," he said as he extinguished the fire, dumping a good amount of snow on the last of the dying flames and embers. "I don't know where the soldiers are going. They could backtrack or cut to the west, or do any number of things."

"But you sense they go north toward Old Jacob's place, don't you?"

She was perceptive, keeping good count of what he had told her. And he nodded.

"This area is close to your land?" she asked.

"It is my land," he said, standing and brushing the snow off his hands. He waited for her to ask more, but she simply nodded and turned to the door.

"We better get going." And out the door she went.

He followed with a smile, Tara continuing to surprise him, and he loved women who could surprise.

Tara's thoughts had remained on the soldiers as she walked. When Reeve had told her about them, she worried that they could prove a threat. What were they doing in the area? Did they search for someone? And was her curse the cause of this sudden problem? Was she already bringing danger to Reeve? And what of the farm they go to? Would danger follow them there or arrive before them?

She could not change what she had done. The deed was done, and she so hungered for her freedom. Her only course of action was to remain aware. Be careful of what choices she made from here on and not think that because she was about to embrace freedom, she was free of the curse. She had to remain diligent, not only to protect herself but others as well. She could not, would not, bring danger to others.

"Are you all right?"

Reeve's concerned query startled her out of her musings, and she nodded. "I am fine."

"We will rest in another hour or so unless you need to rest now," he said, as they continued to walk.

"No. An hour or so will be fine," she said; though her ankle tormented her, it wasn't anything she couldn't bear.

They continued on in silence until finally Reeve announced it was time to rest. He found a boulder they could sit behind, and Reeve, in a whisper, suggested they continue their silence.

She nodded, understanding his concern that their voices would carry on the wintry air and through the barren tree branches to be heard even a good distance.

His hand reached for the hem of her dress, and she grabbed his hand. "It's fine."

They remained as they were for a moment, her hand holding firmly to his until she realized what she had done, and then she quickly released him. She should not have touched him. They had been too close of late, and while he might not believe in curses, she certainly knew better. She could not allow herself to feel for this man, or it would be the death of him.

They didn't linger long. After only a short respite, he reached out to help her to her feet. But she ignored his kindness and stood on her own. She had to remember that while he was here now, he wouldn't be for long, and she would once again have only herself to rely on.

Her ankle throbbed, but she would have none of it. Ignoring the pain, she gave Reeve a firm nod and smiled, letting him know she was ready.

Reeve glared at her a moment as if he had seen through her façade, then shook his head, turned, and stepped around the boulder.

Before she could follow, she heard the clash of swords and without thinking she grabbed the dirk from her boot and hurried forward.

Reeve was in battle with two soldiers, and she had no doubt he could dispose of them both. The one soldier turned a shocked expression on her when she appeared at Reeve's side.

"Stay behind me," Reeve shouted.

The soldier's eyes narrowed and turned angry, and he made a move toward her. Reeve was faster and blocked his attempt.

To her dismay, another soldier appeared and stopped dead for a moment, as if surprised at what he saw. Without further hesitation, he advanced to join his comrades, though he circled around them and headed straight for Tara.

Fear gripped her, but didn't stop her from raising

her dirk and with a forceful snap she sent it flying. It landed in the soldier's shoulder, sending him stumbling. Once he found firm footing, he turned and ran.

Reeve finished the two men and firmly grabbed hold of her hand.

"We need to get out of here," he said.

"What of the one that got away?"

"That's why we need to leave. If his wound doesn't kill him, he will alert other soldiers, and they will soon be on our trail. And it seems that the soldiers aren't questioning anyone they stop. They raise their swords and threaten. Something has changed with the king, and I'd like to know what."

Reeve set a brisk pace; he had no choice, and she kept up, ignoring the steady throb in her ankle. She reminded herself that the pain of discovery and losing her chance at freedom would be far worse than what she was presently suffering. However, she feared the curse was rearing its ugly head, and there would be consequences to pay. It had always been that way. Had she truly expected it could be any different? She had wanted to hope, wanted to believe things possible she had once thought impossible. But was she being foolish, or did she continue to believe, continue to take a chance, continue to reach for a new life?

The fear and uncertainty that plagued her decisions and actions gave her the impetus to keep going, through the pain, the doubt, but mostly the fear; the fear of losing all hope.

They kept a vicious pace, and not once did she lag behind until she slipped on a snow-covered rock and went down before Reeve could grab her. He was quick to help her sit up, but he refused to let her stand until he had a look at her ankle.

This time, when her hand tried to prevent him from seeing the damage, he brushed it aside.

"Not this time," he said. "I'll have a look."

They both cringed when they saw the swelling. It stretched the leather of her boot until it looked as if it would split.

"You should have told me," he scolded, though Tara could see in his eyes that the scolding was for him.

"And what would you have done," she asked, not wanting him to blame himself. "We need to get to your friend's farm. We can't let my injury stop us. We do what we must."

"And you suffer for it."

"And if it had been your ankle." She shook her head before he could answer. "Don't tell me that would be different or that you are a warrior and can bear the pain."

He smiled. "If I can't tell you either, then I'm left with no other reasoning."

"Which means I do what must be done." In so many more ways than Reeve would ever know.

"And I do what I must," he said, and scooped her up in his arms before she could protest.

"You can't carry me."

"But I can, and I will." He stomped off, ordering her silent when she tried to protest. And she realized that no matter what she said, he would ignore it. Besides, it felt good, so very good, to be off her feet, and, with a yawn, she rested her head to his shoulder.

# Chapter 7

Reeve heard raised angry voices and stopped to listen. They came from Old Jacob's farm. He feared the king's soldiers had stopped to question them, though it also could be mercenaries hired by the king to torment those who supported the return of the true king.

Such incidents had grown in frequency with fear that the true king would soon claim the throne. The MacAlpin clan had sworn allegiance to the true king, and he and his brothers had been trained since they had been young to protect the rightful man who would become the King of all Scotland. And with their diligence, and God willing, they would soon see success. And then people like Old Jacob and his granddaughter-in-law Willow need fear no more.

But now was a different matter, and until the rightful king took the throne, Reeve and his brothers would do all they could to protect the people.

"Tara," Reeve whispered, giving her a gentle shake. She had fallen asleep not that long ago. He had been glad, sleep relieving her of the pain.

She stirred, and while she was far from petite, she

had been no burden. He had carried much heavier without difficulty. Besides, he favored the feel of her in his arms.

"You must remain silent," he whispered, and her head quickly shot up, her eyes growing wide. "We're at the croft, and so are others."

She motioned for him to put her down, and he did so very gently. He took her hand and guided her to a spot amongst the trees where they had a good view of the farm. She limped, and he worried that the brief respite had not helped her ankle. But there was nothing he could do for her at the moment. He had to help Old Jacob.

He kept hold of her hand, and, surprisingly, she didn't object, as they both peered through the branches. What he saw infuriated him. And if he was not mistaken the four soldiers who tormented Old Jacob were the same ones that had passed by him this morning. His anger had him fisting his hands. A tiny wince drew his attention, and when he turned, he saw that Tara was biting down on her lower lip to stop from yelling. He remembered then that her hand was in his.

He immediately released it and pressed his cheek to hers, whispering in her ear, "I'm sorry."

"I understand," she murmured. "You must hurry and help him."

"Stay here."

She nodded vigorously.

Reeve was relieved that she didn't protest and would heed his order. He left her safely tucked amongst towering pines and thick bushes.

He didn't hide his approach. After all, there were only four of them. He could dispatch them without a problem though he would not do so until he made them pay for the taunting slaps and punches they were inflicting on Old Jacob. He was a feeble man of five-and-seventy years, hunched over from age and hard toil and didn't deserve such harsh treatment or disrespect.

"Leave him be," Reeve shouted, his anger having grown with each step.

The men stopped and turned, and when they saw that he approached alone, they laughed.

"Are you a fool?" one asked.

"Are you a coward?" Reeve shot back. "You taunt an old man who can do you no harm?"

The soldier advanced on Reeve, his face flushed red, his hand on the hilt of his sword. Reeve not only had the advantage of strength on his side, but speed as well. He rushed the man and elbowed him so hard in the jaw that the crack could be heard by all as the man dropped to the ground. With precise swings and substantial punches, Reeve finished off the remaining four men.

He immediately went to Jacob, who was struggling to stand.

"Willow," Reeve asked, concerned for Jacob's granddaughter-in-law.

"Root cellar," Jacob said with a bloody smile. "I'll not let anything happen to her."

"I didn't think you would." Reeve helped the old man up to sit on the well-worn bench by the door. "Stay put until I get rid of them."

Jacob nodded, slowly cupping his elbow in his hand.

Reeve grew more annoyed seeing that the old man had suffered far too much and for no reason. He withdrew his sword and began poking the soldiers as they starting coming to with groans.

"Get up!" Reeve yelled repeatedly, as they struggled to get to their feet. The one whose jaw he had broken had the most difficulty standing. "Go help the idiot," Reeve ordered the first man who finally made it to his feet, and poked him with the tip of his sword to get him moving.

"You'll suffer the consequences for this," another said as he stumbled to his feet.

"The only ones who will suffer any consequences are the four of you if you don't leave MacAlpin land immediately. And if you don't understand consequence, let me enlighten you. I will see you all dead by morning if you do not take your leave of MacAlpin land *now*!"

"The king owns all land," one soldier shouted.

"The king *owns* nothing. He *owes* everything to his people," Reeve said. "Now be gone with you before I regret how lenient I've been."

The four leaned on each other as they hobbled to their horses.

A thought struck Reeve. "Leave one horse."

The soldiers looked angry and argued among themselves over who would lose his horse, until Reeve ordered, "Leave the gray mare."

They did, riding off mumbling.

"Cowards the lot of them," Jacob said, and spat.

Reeve agreed with a nod, then turned to Jacob. "Are you all right?"

"Nothing that won't heal," Jacob assured him. "You'll be staying the night at least, won't you?"

"I had hoped to since I have a woman with me who needs tending, and we could do with some food."

Jacob had trouble getting up off the bench, but he brushed away Reeve's offered hand. "My bones may be protesting, but that's too bad for them. They'll be doing what I want, or I'll not give them a lick of rest. Now go get your friend and bring her here. Willow will see to her, and she already has a tasty stew cooking."

Reeve did as ordered and went and got Tara. He was pleased that she had waited where he had left her. He scooped her up though she protested and had her inside the cottage to find Jacob struggling to lift the door to the root cellar.

Reeve quickly set Tara on a chair and lifted the door before Jacob could object.

"It's all right, Willow, you can come out now," Jacob called down.

A slim woman of medium height, with fiery red curls piled wildly on top of her head and a lovely face, though unfortunately marred by a thin scar that ran across her left cheek, practically leapt out of the cellar.

"Are you all right, grandda?" she asked, going directly to him though acknowledging Reeve as she did. "Glad you came along, Reeve."

"You both truly need to move to the village, for a while at least," Reeve said. "The king's soldiers are suddenly showing a strong presence in this area."

Willow carefully examined the old man's injuries. "Grandda will not leave his land, and I will not leave him."

"No more of this talk," Jacob ordered. "We have a guest who is injured."

Willow looked to Reeve, then to Tara. "What is wrong?'

"A sprained ankle, no more," Tara said. "See to your grandda first."

Willow ignored the old man's protests that their guest be seen to first and went and filled a bucket with snow and sat it on the hearth to melt and heat. She gathered stripes of clean cloth and grabbed a handful of herbs that hung in bunches from the ceiling rafters.

While Willow was busy tending her grandda, Reeve helped Tara out of her cloak. His hand went to her arm, her elbow, her back as he moved her around to slip it off her. When done, he realized the cold had seeped deep into her flesh. He moved a chair near the hearth, scooped her up, though she squeaked in protest, and sat her there to warm.

"There's cider in the pitcher on the table," Willow said. "Put it on the hearthstone and let it heat, then pour a tankard for each of yourselves."

Reeve did as Willow had directed, and in a few minutes, he and Tara were warming their innards with the tasty apple cider.

"Now, are you finally going to introduce us?" Willow asked, almost finished with her grandda.

Reeve shook his head for not having done it sooner. "This is Tara, she'll be joining the MacAlpin clan."

"Welcome," Willow said, her smile growing.

"It's a good clan you join," the old man said. "You'll be safe, especially with Reeve at your side."

"We are not together," Reeve and Tara said in unison.

Willow and the old man laughed.

"We're friends," Tara said, though she blushed.

"That's how my Edward and I started," Willow said with a hint of sadness. "We were friends first and fell in love along the way."

"God bless my grandson's soul," Jacob said with a nod. "He's gone two years now."

"I'm sorry for your loss," Tara said.

"Edward was a good friend and a good man," Reeve added.

"Died saving my life he did," Willow said, turning away as a tear fell from her eye.

Silence followed until finally Reeve spoke. "Jacob, you and Willow need to come to the village until the true king takes the throne."

Jacob waved away Reeve's plea. "Who knows when that will be? I leave my farm, and it will go to rot, and I chance losing my land."

Reeve wished he could share what he knew with the old man, but he couldn't. The plans that were being made had to remain secret, for the safety of many and for the success of the true king. If things continued as they were, it would be less than a year before the true king could possibly sit the throne. And as matters deteriorated for the present king, they would also worsen for the true king's supporters. Meaning life could prove more dangerous for Jacob and Willow.

"Stay, and you could lose your life, you old, stubborn fool," Willow said with more care than malice.

Jacob pounded the table. "I won't leave my land."

Willow shook her head and looked to Reeve. "I cannot leave him here on his own."

"I will talk with my brothers and see what can be done," Reeve said.

Willow drifted over to Tara, and Reeve moved out of her way, going to sit next to the old man and talk.

Getting the boot off proved difficult, and Willow called out for Reeve's help.

"I can do it," Tara said, persistent in her struggle with the boot.

Reeve pushed her hands away and slipped his hand up her calf along the underside of the boot; his other hand took hold of her heel. Then he began to ease the boot back and forth gently, his hand following its descent down along her stocking-covered calf. After a few minutes of tugs and urgings, the boot slipped off with only a modicum of difficulty.

He kept hold of her stocking-covered leg, staring at the area swollen twice its size. "No more walking for you," he ordered, and before she could object, he explained. "One of the soldiers gladly left a horse."

Tara simply grinned, and Reeve gently released her ankle and returned to sit with Jacob.

"Reeve is a good man," Willow said for their ears alone.

"Yes, I find him an honorable one," Tara agreed, rolling her stocking down.

"It's odd," Willow said, "but you seem a good pair, familiar with each other, as though you belong together."

"That's foolish. We've only met."

"Yet you appear more than friends," Willow said, carefully removing the black stocking.

"It's just that we seem to understand each other."

"It was like that between Edward and me. We met when we were young, and we seemed to fit, as if we were two matching pieces who found their way back together. We understood each other and"—she laughed softly—"I fit in his arms perfectly, as if God intended me just for Edward."

Willow tenderly probed the swollen area. "I'll fetch some snow, and we'll pack it around your ankle. I don't feel any broken bones, and I doubt you could have walked a distance if you had broken any."

Willow had Reeve move Tara away from the hearth before she packed the snow around the ankle so that the heat wouldn't melt it.

Reeve grabbed his extra plaid and wrapped it around Tara. "For the chill that surely will follow." He leaned down to tuck it in snugly at her waist, and as he did, his cheek grazed hers. It was warm and flushed from sitting near the fire. His cheek had chilled, and it was like fire and ice coming together, it scorched and melted. He felt the sting all the way to his loins.

He stood rather abruptly. "I better see to the horse."

"I'll help you," Jacob said, easing off the chair.

"No need."

"Nothing for me to do here," Jacob grumbled.

"Then do join me," Reeve said, realizing that the old man didn't want to be left with the two women.

It had been a long time since Tara had sat in conversation with another woman, and she didn't know what to say. She needn't have worried, Willow felt the same, but didn't let it stop her from talking.

"It has been far too long since I have had the opportunity to speak with another woman. Once this area was thriving with farms, and neighbors visited often. But when King Kenneth claimed the throne, he made heavy demands on the farmers, and it forced many to abandon their places."

"You stayed?"

"As you've heard, grandda refuses to leave, and I can understand why. His family has farmed this land since long before he was born. They have survived wars and nature and have flourished in spite of either. Grandda will never leave here. He will die here and be buried here."

As if she preferred to speak of it no more, she asked, "Hungry? I have venison stew that has been cooking for hours."

With that, the two women chatted on about many different things, and for the first time in a long time, Tara felt hopeful. Maybe Reeve had been right when he had suggested they not tell anyone of her past. Maybe, just maybe, this curse could be broken. And she could again live as she once had, having friends and perhaps even falling in love.

While she hoped it could be so, an inkling of doubt taunted her. Was she being foolish and possibly placing this family in harm's way? She had thought herself free once and had allowed herself to fall in love with Rory, and he had paid the price.

Tara rarely allowed herself to go back to the beginning and what had started the curse, and she didn't want to return there now. She didn't want to think that it could happen all over again. She wanted to believe, had to believe, that her past was behind her. She was free, and she could hope.

What were her chances, though, at keeping her freedom? God forbid her father discovered her deception. He would surely come claim her and force her to honor the marriage arrangement he had made. And who could stop him?

She battled her doubts and worries as bravely as possible while keeping a smile on her face and chatting with Willow.

Reeve and Jacob returned, and they were all soon

sitting around the table, though not before Willow insisted that Tara keep her foot raised. Some of the swelling had gone down, and resting it might just chase away what remained. With nothing for her to brace it on, Reeve drew his chair close to hers, lifted her leg gently, and placed it on his thigh.

"Done," he announced with that teasing grin of his. "Now let's eat. I'm starving, and it smells delicious."

Tara couldn't protest his gallantry. She didn't want to. She wanted to enjoy this time, this chance to share a meal with people, to joke, to laugh, to finally live.

# Chapter 8

Tara took one of the two beds in the cottage and Willow the other. Reeve and Jacob slept in front of the hearth. It was with a lighter though cautious heart that Tara woke the next morning. The swelling in her ankle had gone down considerably though Willow warned it would be best for her to stay off it as much as possible.

They had a hearty porridge for breakfast, and Willow wrapped the remainder of the black bread for them to take along. Tara had protested, knowing food wasn't that plentiful for the pair, but Willow would have it no other way.

"Grandda and I will fish later, and I'll make us a nice fish stew, so don't you worry about it," Willow said. "Besides, friends never let friends go without if it can be helped."

Tara appreciated all Willow had done, but most of all she appreciated that Willow thought of her as a friend. In three short days, she had made two friends, and dare she hope it was the beginning of good things with more to come?

Willow and Jacob stood outside to see them off.

It was cloudy, the air not as cold as yesterday, which meant snow was not likely.

"We could possibly reach home by nightfall," Reeve said, resting his hands on her waist, and, with ease, he raised her and sat her sideways on the saddle.

He then hoisted himself up behind her and adjusted her to rest against him, tucking her in the crook of his arm. "Comfortable?" he asked.

She nodded though she was more than comfortable; she was content. Whatever was the matter with her? One moment she was keeping her distance from him and the next she was wrapped in his arms. It wasn't only the curse that concerned her; her attraction to Reeve could also prove fatal. Did she think a man like him could ever truly love a woman like her? A woman burdened with a curse and by life.

"We can't thank you enough," Reeve said to Willow and Jacob. "I will send some men to help."

"Go away with you," Jacob said with a dismissive wave. "We don't need any help."

Willow smiled. "We'll take what help we can get."

Tara smiled as they rode off, leaving the pair arguing.

"They are good people," Reeve said.

"I see that," Tara said, hoping against hope that no harm came to them; that her curse was dormant, or perhaps waning. But could curses simply wear off? Through the years, she had tried to find out more about hexes, but it proved a difficult task. There were none who would discuss such evil doings, and her father had made certain that no seers were permitted on his land. Perhaps now, starting this new life, she could search and hopefully not only find answers, but a solution.

They rode in silence for a distance, each of them lost in their own thoughts.

Tara finally felt the need to speak, to thank him for what he had done for her before they reached home. *Her new home.*

"I am very grateful for your help, Reeve," she said, turning her head to look at him. She felt a twist and squeeze in her stomach and then a sudden thud to her heart. She almost cringed, but forced herself not to.

It couldn't be possible. She had only met this man two days ago. She knew little about him. Why? Why was she feeling for him what she had felt for Rory when they had first met?

*Lonely.*

A simple, direct, reasonable answer that made perfect sense. He was the first man who didn't treat her as if she were a leper. It was only natural for her to feel kindly toward him.

*Kindly?*

Was she a fool? It wasn't kindness she was feeling. It was the stirring of attraction coupled with passion. Something that she hadn't felt in . . . she couldn't remember when.

"Tara?"

She shook her head, realizing she had gotten lost in her thoughts.

"I've been trying to tell you that you're paying me handsomely for services rendered, so no thanks are necessary, but you seemed far away in your musings."

She purposely ignored his remark about her lack of attention. She certainly didn't want to share her thoughts with him.

"Your kindness needn't have been part of our agreement, and yet you treated me thoughtfully, and for that I am grateful."

He turned a grin on her. "How could I have treated you any other way? My mother would skin me alive if I acted improper to a lady."

"Your mother taught you well."

"She taught my brothers and me whether we liked it or not," Reeve said with a laugh. "None of us dared disobey her, or we would feel her mighty retribution."

"She wielded a heavy hand?" Tara asked.

Reeve shook his head. "Mum never raised a hand to any of us."

"Yet you obeyed her?"

"She had other more wicked ways of punishing."

"She doesn't sound very nice," Tara said, not wanting to think of him as a small lad made to suffer harsh punishment.

"Mum may be blunt and makes sure she's heard, but one thing she isn't and that is cruel. She's a good person with a good heart. I think you'll like her."

"You have me curious," Tara said. "In one breath you praise her, and in another you tell me she made you suffer wicked punishments."

Reeve laughed. "There are far worse punishments to make a young lad suffer than to raise your hand to him."

"I must know. Tell me."

"One that had my brothers and me thinking twice was that she would cook for us." Reeve shook his head. "Her food is barely eatable, and we would be made to eat every bit of it." Reeve scrunched his nose in distaste.

Tara laughed. "It truly stopped you and your brothers from doing something you shouldn't?"

"We would argue amongst ourselves, reminding one another how bad the last meal was we were forced to eat, and if that wasn't enough, my father pleaded with us not to make our suffering his."

Tara laughed again.

"Perhaps I could teach her to bake—"

"No!"

His shout made her jump.

"I'm sorry," he apologized. "It's been tried, and we lost a reasonably good cook in the process. We now have a great cook, and my father and brothers will do anything to keep her."

"What other punishments did your mother employ?"

Reeve rolled his eyes. "God help us, she would sing."

"Her singing is not pleasing?"

"Pleasing?" He cringed and shook his head. "The dogs howl, the cats screech, and everyone runs for cover."

Tara couldn't stop laughing.

"It truly isn't funny," Reeve said though he grinned. "She would make us sit while she sang song after song. Then the stupid songs and her grating voice would be stuck in my head for hours, sometimes days, afterwards."

"Does she still find reason to sing now?'

"Not much, but now and again she'll break into song, and we run as far away as we can."

Tara's stomach hurt she was laughing so much. When it finally subsided, she said, "Now I'm going to have to hear her sing to see if you're simply teasing me."

"Please, I beg you, warn me first so that I can hurry off."

Tara laughed again, enjoying hearing about Reeve's family.

"I think we should stop shortly and give the horse and us a chance to rest," Reeve suggested. "Then we can pick up the pace, and if all goes well, we can make it home by nightfall."

"I could use a stretch," she said.

They found a spot, tethered the horse to a pine branch, and Reeve spread his extra plaid on the snow-covered ground. Tara stretched the ache out of her back once off the horse and wished she could rub the soreness out of her backside.

Her ankle was feeling much better, and so, without hesitation, she lowered herself to the blanket. The added pressure produced a sharp twinge in her ankle, and she almost toppled over. Luckily, Reeve caught her around the waist.

"Too stubborn to ask for help?" he asked, bracing her weight against him.

She almost relaxed against him, as if it was the most natural thing to do, but caught her unwise reaction and steeled herself. "Too foolish for my own good."

"A woman who can admit when she's wrong, I like that," he said, giving her waist a gentle squeeze and, with a supportive arm around her, lowered her to the blanket.

"Truth speaks wiser than lies. It's just that no one truly listens to it."

Reeve lowered himself beside her. "Perhaps lies are just easier to hear."

"Not to an honorable man," she said.

They stared at each other for a moment, and Tara had the urge to reach out and touch him as she had done once before, but, as before, she clasped her hands together, preventing herself from taking such liberties.

However, it didn't stop Reeve. His hand reached out, and his fingers faintly brushed along the top of her cheeks just below her eyes. "I've never seen such beautiful-colored eyes."

She yanked her face away. "No intimate touches."

"I didn't mean—"

She swung her head around to face him. "Don't ever touch me like that again. *Ever.*"

Reeve nodded, and they remained silent while sharing the bread Willow had packed for them.

Tara nibbled at her share, no longer hungry. She wished that she could explain to him that it hadn't been his gentle touch that had disturbed her. She had quite enjoyed it. It had sent a pleasant tingle through her, and she would have loved for him to have continued, dangerous though it was.

It had been when he had mentioned the color of her eyes. It had brought back the memories of the curse. Most assumed it had originated with Rory's death on their wedding day, and so she had been deemed a *death bride*, but the curse had come upon her many years before, and she would do well to remember it.

Tara turned her head away from Reeve when his hands went to her waist to lift her to the saddle.

"Don't turn away from me."

Though his remark was stern, there was compassion in it, and so she looked at him.

"I didn't mean to offend, and for that I am sorry. I

am, however, not sorry for letting you know that you have the most beautiful eyes I have ever seen."

His heartfelt confession sent flutters through her stomach, and it was then and there she knew that she was in trouble. She truly liked this man, this Highlander warrior who had saved her and had given her a chance at a new life. And that would not do at all. She could not take the chance of seeing him harmed. She simply could not, and she had to keep reminding herself of that. Once they arrived at his home, she would need to keep her distance. She had no choice. It was the way of it plain and simple. And the truth of it pained her heart.

They rode the remainder of the way in silence. The air turned crisper and colder as the day wore on. And when dusk looked ready to claim the land, Tara feared that they would have to camp for the night. Then, suddenly, beyond a slight rise, she saw a village.

She grew excited to see her new home, and she wished that night wasn't fast approaching. She wanted to see it all though she knew by the time they arrived, night would be upon them, and she would catch just a glimpse.

No matter, though, there was tomorrow and the day after and the day after that and on and on. She would live here, isolated if she must, and have a good life. She would make it so; she had no other choice.

The village appeared deserted when they entered, but then the temperature had dropped in the last hour, leaving the air biting cold. The villagers were surely tucked safe and warm in their cottages. They passed several and a sizeable grain storehouse, but it was too dark to distinguish anything else except the keep. It rose in a cylindrical shape at the far end of the village. Blazing torches flanked the wooden door, and as Reeve dismounted, a young lad stepped out of the shadows and reached for the horse's reins.

"Take good care of her, Robbie," Reeve said, "and I'll see that you get extra sweets tonight."

The young lad, piled thick with extra clothing and a winter cap pulled down tight, grinned, a wide gap being where two front teeth should be. "I'll rub her down and feed her well."

Robbie stood patiently as Reeve reached up and slipped his hands inside her cape and took hold of her waist. He lowered her gently to the ground, and Robbie led the horse away as Reeve asked, "Does your ankle pain you too much to walk?"

She certainly had no intentions of being in his arms when first meeting his family. She intended to portray an independent, viable woman who could look after herself.

"I'm fine," she assured him, and stepped forward.

Her foot connected with a patch of ice, and before she knew what was happening, her feet were flying out from under her, while her hands flayed frantically in the air.

Tara heard his laughter before she felt his arms catch her and scoop her up.

"I'm forever saving you," he teased, and with a slight toss, adjusted her in his arms.

"I can walk," she insisted, keeping her hands to herself though she would have much preferred to wrap her arms around his neck and linger in his embrace. Since, no doubt, it could very well be the last time he ever held her that way.

"That's debatable." He laughed and walked up the steps to the keep.

As much as she preferred to remain in his arms, she said, "I'd rather your family not see me this way."

"In my arms, or injured?" he asked in a teasing whisper.

"Both," she confirmed.

His murmur of laughter tickled her ear. "But it's the way of things."

Before she could argue, he opened the door and strode into a large room, trestle tables and benches scattered about with all but one being empty. The two women and three men gathered round it were busy in chatter sprinkled liberally with laughter and hadn't heard them enter.

"Sure, leave me to handle it all," Reeve shouted, and they turned.

The older, pleasantly plump woman, her curly auburn hair piled high on her head, shouted out, "You've gone and brought me another daughter." She rushed toward them while the others remained where they were, the older man shaking his head, though grinning.

"It's another celebration we'll be having," the woman said when she was almost upon them.

Tara was too stunned by the woman's exuberance to speak, but she did cast an anxious glance to Reeve.

"Don't worry, I'll protect you," he whispered.

"Tell her," Tara whispered. "Tell her now that I am not your wife." A shudder raced through her at the mere thought, or was that a shiver of excitement?

"The thought that upsetting?" he asked, though without a trace of his usual teasing. He actually appeared serious.

"No, that dangerous."

"And why are you carrying her?" the woman demanded once she reached them. "Is she not well?" Her face suddenly beamed with joy. "A babe! She's with babe. Lord have mercy, it's two grandbabies I'll be having soon."

Tara turned, looked at the woman, and shouted though she hadn't meant to. "No, I'm not with child."

"That's all right, dear," the woman consoled. "You will be soon enough."

Tara turned pleading eyes on Reeve.

"Tara, meet my mother, Mara. Mum, meet *my friend* Tara."

Mara patted Tara's arm. "It's good to be friends first. My husband Carmag and me were friends first and we're remained best friends ever since, though he does try my patience at times." She looked to her son. "Why are you carrying her?"

"She's hurt her ankle."

"Why didn't you say so?" Mara scolded, and gave his arm a playful slap. "Come set her down and let me have a look."

Tara almost feared letting go of Reeve once at the table. The men were a large lot, each one of them seeming bigger than the next, though none as tall as Reeve, but certainly wide. How the small petite woman tucked between two of them managed not to get squashed amazed Tara.

The diminutive woman with hair as black as Tara's and eyes as blue as shimmering sapphires moved to stand, and the man to her right instantly stood and, with a gentle grab of her waist, had her up and over the bench in a second.

Seeing her rounded stomach, Tara assumed that

she had to be Mercy, Duncan's wife, and the man who had lovingly lifted her had to be Duncan. He was wide and thick with muscle and had fine features despite the slight crook of his nose and a scar at the right corner of his mouth. And that he loved his petite wife was obvious by his loving touch, tender smile, and reluctance to let her go. The woman eased his hands away and walked around the table to join Mara.

Reeve confirmed it when he made fast introductions of everyone from Bryce, to Duncan and Mercy, and finally his father, Carmag. Trey wasn't present, and when Reeve asked after him, he was informed that he wouldn't be home for about a week.

Tara felt awful that Mara chased her husband off the end of the bench so that she could rest Tara's leg up on it. And she gave a shout for Reeve to take Tara's cloak.

"I hope you didn't let her walk on this," Mara said, glaring at her son.

"I got her a horse."

Mara beamed. "That's my son, doing the right thing."

That started a rash of ribbing among the brothers, and Tara enjoyed listening to the good-natured exchange.

After Mara and Mercy examined her ankle, Mara announced, "Not much you can do but stay off it."

"That's what Willow recommended," Tara said.

"You saw Willow and Old Jacob?" Mara asked of Reeve. Before he could answer, she asked, "How are they doing?"

"They could use some help. The king's men were tormenting him when I arrived, and he had hid Willow in the root cellar."

"The king has stepped up his activities in his pursuit to prevent the true king from claiming the throne," Carmag said.

"But the people continue to rally," Duncan advised.

"Tara being one of them," Reeve said, sending her a nod. "She has offered to give the MacAlpin clan her fortune in return for her making this her home. She only asks for a cottage where she may live peaceably and safely."

Everyone raved about her generosity though truly it was her father's generosity. But she intended to make no mention of it, just as Reeve hadn't mentioned the true reason she was there.

Tara lifted the end of her red velvet dress and tore at the hem. One by one, she withdrew purses heavy with coins and some with gems and placed them on the table, until finally there were no more, at least no more that they could see. She wasn't foolish. If something should go wrong here, she would need money to go elsewhere, and so she kept two purses for herself.

They all sat staring at the substantial amount, except Mara, who said, "Now that looks like a good *bride price* to me."

# Chapter 9

Tara's eyes never failed to captivate him. At the moment, however, they were filled with utter fear, and he knew that she worried about his family discovering the truth. This was her chance to start anew, and he wanted to make certain she got the opportunity. He wanted that dumb curse dispelled once and for all.

However, he could not lie to his family, and so he said, "Tara is a widow."

"Oh you poor thing," Mara said, patting Tara's arm.

"She would like to start fresh." Reeve went with the truth while omitting other facts.

"Well, you're welcome to make your home with the clan MacAlpin," Mara said, and the others sang out their agreement.

Tara smiled. "Thank you all so very much. I know this will be a good place for me."

"There's a cottage not far from the keep, with a sizeable kitchen garden beside it," Mercy said. "I think you would like it."

Reeve knew Tara would prefer to be a distance from others, but for some reason he preferred she remain close to the keep. He supposed his feelings were thus because he had been protecting and saving her ever since crossing her path. Besides, who else was there to look after her?

"There's also old Alan's place," Bryce suggested. "It's close to the keep—"

Mara interrupted shaking her head. "It may sit close to the keep, but it sits alone, removed from the closeness of others, and it has fallen in disrepair."

"I'll take it," Tara said.

Reeve grinned. He knew she would; it was perfect for her and for him. It was what she was hoping for, and it was close enough for him to keep a frequent eye on her.

"Have a look at both first before you make a decision," Mara suggested, handing Tara a tankard of hot cider.

"Thank you, I'll do that," Tara said, wrapping her hands around the offered mug.

She may have agreed with Mara's suggestion, but Reeve knew that her mind was made up. She would choose the secluded cottage.

"I can take care of any repairs that need doing," Reeve offered, knowing that none of them would be going on any lengthy missions until Trey returned from his.

"We all can give a hand," Duncan said, and nods rippled around the table.

"Thank you," Tara said. "I am grateful for your generosity."

"It is you who have been more than generous," Carmag said.

And more than tired, Reeve thought, noticing how her shoulders slumped, and her head rested slightly to the side. She was exhausted and probably in pain though she would not admit it.

"She needs sleep," Reeve said, going around and scooping her up in his arms. "I'll put her in my bedchamber."

He was surprised when she didn't protest. She simply sighed, and, before resting her head to his shoulder, she asked, "I don't wish to deprive you of your bed."

"Reeve can sleep in my sewing room," Mara said.

All heads turned to Mara, her sewing room a sacred sanctum that one could only enter with her permission. Reeve repeated, as if he hadn't heard her correctly, "Your sewing room?"

"Yes," Mara snapped. "And you'll be careful not to mess anything."

Reeve nodded vigorously.

"Now go," Mara said, shooing him off. "There are clean linens on your bed, and I will have hot water and towels fetched for Tara's use, and I will bring a platter of food to her."

"Thank you again, and I am pleased to have met you all," Tara said cordially.

"After you have settled Tara, meet us in the solar," Carmag said.

Reeve knew he needed to advise the others on the status of his mission. He would do as Carmag said though he wished he could linger with Tara for a bit. He had found her company pleasing. And he greatly favored the feel of her in his arms. Missed her when she wasn't there, and the thought startled him.

"You are lucky to have such a loving family," Tara said, as he climbed the spiral stone staircase.

"They are your family now too. Clan is family."

"Unless your clan is not pleased with you."

"My family is pleased with you," Reeve said, the lonely ache in her voice disturbing him.

"For now," she said softly.

"For always," Reeve corrected.

Tara raised her head off his shoulder and looked into his eyes. "I pray you are right."

Her lovely lavender eyes sent a jolt through him, and he felt his body burst alive with desire. Feeling wicked, he turned a sinful grin on her, and whispered, "I'm always right."

Then he did something out of sheer instinct, he kissed her quick, his lips touching hers for a mere instant, though long enough for him to get a taste, and damn if he didn't like the flavor.

The shock of his unexpected actions left her speechless, and he hurried to his room, knowing she would probably explode with anger any moment. And he didn't want his family hearing her.

Surprisingly, her silence continued even when he entered his bedchamber, and he sat her on the end of the bed. He stood looking down at her and noticed that her bosoms heaved, as if she was breathless.

Had his innocent kiss stirred her?

He hoped it had since it certainly had more than stirred him, and he was now thinking how delightful it would be to taste her luscious breasts, sitting high and full in her low-cut dress. The succulent mounds invited, and he was hard-pressed to ignore them.

"You'd best do as your father asked," Tara said.

Reeve scrunched his brow, suddenly unable to recall what it was his father wanted of him.

"Meet him and the others in the solar," Tara reminded.

Reeve nodded, his father's words coming back to him. "You'll be all right?" He didn't want to leave her though he knew full well she was safe. But would she be safe if he lingered?

His thought startled him, and the fact that she had not reprimanded him for kissing her made him realize that they both could be in trouble if he remained even a moment longer. If he did, he most certainly would kiss her plump lips again. And this time, it would not be a brief innocent kiss he gave her. Strangely enough, he didn't think she would stop him.

"Your mother will be here shortly," she said.

She warned that they would soon not be alone, but she did not warn against him kissing her. And he realized that he would kiss her again and soon, very soon.

"I'll come bid you good night when I finish with my father and brothers," he said.

"No!" she said quickly. "I am tired and wish to sleep. I bid you good night now."

"Then I bid you a fond good night and sweet dreams," he said, and bowed gallantly before turning with a grin and leaving the room.

It was obvious she worried that he would kiss her again and that she wanted him to. His grin widened as he descended the steps two at a time to the second floor. She liked his kiss, though it was more of a peck. Wait, just wait until she tasted a full kiss, she'd be wanting more for sure.

He halted before reaching the solar, suddenly struck by an unexpected thought.

*What if he wanted more? Much more than a kiss?*

"Lost?" Bryce asked jokingly, with a slap to Reeve's shoulder.

"You might say that," Reeve said, the haunting thought continuing to nag at him.

"Interested in the widow, are you?"

Reeve swung his head around, a denial ready to spill from his lips, when he suddenly slammed his mouth shut.

Bryce laughed. "Not sure are you?"

"I just met her." Reeve shook his head as they entered the solar, Carmag and Duncan there waiting for them.

"Where did you meet her?" Carmag asked.

"I came upon a band of inept thieves trying to rob her."

"And you saved her?" Duncan asked.

"I did," Reeve said, knowing they expected to hear the details. "And she offered me money to keep her safe and find a new home."

"And her family?" Carmag asked.

"I don't know details," he admitted, which was the truth. "I only know she was not wanted there."

"Do you feel she is telling you the truth?" Bryce asked. "Or could there be more to her story?"

They all stared at him, and he knew they waited for the truth.

"What I share with you stays among us," Reeve said.

"What is said in this room among us always remains in this room," Duncan reminded.

Reeve knew that it did, that they had been sworn to secrecy since they had been young and trained to protect the one who would be king. The reason he was compelled to tell them the truth. There could be no secrets between them. Nothing could stand in the way of the true king taking the throne.

Yet he felt an overpowering urge to protect Tara, and in sharing the facts with his family, could it somehow cause her harm? The brief moment of doubt passed quick enough. If he had actually thought that, he would have never brought her here.

"Tara is considered a *death bride,*" Reeve said, and went on to explain the exact details of when he had first met her and all that he knew.

"I had the feeling she was running from something," Bryce said. "And she confirmed it when she chose old Alan's cottage. She wants to remain separated from people."

"To her way of thinking, to protect them," Reeve said. "I believe there is more to this curse than she tells me, but she refuses to discuss it."

"What do you think of this curse?" Carmag asked.

"I've never been one for the likes of curses and spells and such," Reeve admitted. "It's just nonsense to me."

"Not to others," Duncan said.

"Especially to ones who have experienced it," Carmag said.

"Are you telling me she is not welcomed here?" Reeve asked defensively.

"Not at all," Bryce said, "but we have a duty to our clan. If something does occur, and the people find out that we knew about a curse and had not warned them, they will be angry, and justifiably so."

"Then let their anger fall on me," Reeve said, his chin jutting up. "No one need know that I shared this information with you."

"Would that be fair to the villagers?" Duncan asked.

"Would it be fair to Tara to turn her out alone?" Reeve asked. "And what of the money she has given us? You know as well as I do that our coffers are near empty. Her money will provide us and the villagers with much-needed items. And also help further our mission."

"He is right about that," Bryce agreed. "There are people out there starving and in need of our help and who will fight when the time is right if they know that their families are cared for."

"And a king to the southwest, who for a fat purse, will join our cause," Reeve said.

"So that is how your mission went," Carmag said.

"King Osgar of the Western Isles says that King Kenneth pays him handsomely for his patronage. But more coins could sway his favor." Reeve shook his head. "He will keep no true allegiance to any king who doesn't fatten his coffers, and he doesn't see to the care of his people as he should."

"He will be dealt with when the time is right," Carmag said. "In the meantime, we will seek allegiance from his people by seeing they are given the coins rather than their king."

"We cannot do that without Tara's generous patronage," Reeve said. "Will we accept it or turn her away?"

"You know damn well we would not do that," Bryce said.

Reeve smiled. "I knew I was right. I'm always right."

"Are you right about keeping this from mum?" Duncan asked.

Reeve cringed. "She'll have my hide."

"She'll have all of our hides since she knows we share everything," Bryce reminded.

"It's a chance we must take," Carmag said.

Carmag's serious tone had them all staring at him.

"Your mother has seen the effects of a curse. She believed that her best friend from when she was young had been cursed, the results devastating. She will not take kindly learning that we knew of it and did not share it with her."

"Are you suggesting we confide in mum?" Reeve asked.

"Heavens no," Carmag said, shaking his head. "I fear it would worsen matters since she would feel helpless to help Tara and would warn you against falling in love with her."

"I'm not falling in love with her," Reeve said quickly.

"On the verge then?" Duncan joked.

"Nowhere near it," Reeve protested.

"I don't know," Bryce said, shaking his head. "He was standing in the hall with a mighty lost look on his face.

"I only met her four days ago. You can't fall in love that fast," Reeve said.

"It can start that fast," Carmag said. "I knew I loved your mother the very first time that I saw her, and I still do."

"Had you heard her sing yet?" Bryce asked with a laugh.

Carmag cringed. "No, she saved that surprise for me until our wedding celebration."

The brothers laughed.

"Love knows no time," Carmag said to Reeve. "It simply strikes."

"I'm not in love with Tara," Reeve insisted.

"I wager by the end of the month he will be," Bryce said.

"I say two weeks, and he'll be making a fool of himself over her," Duncan chortled.

"I am not falling in love," Reeve repeated more strenuously.

He wasn't ready to fall in love. Didn't want to fall in love. Wasn't a good time to fall in love. And he'd be damned if he'd let himself fall in love.

# Chapter 10

Tara woke the next morning with Reeve on her mind. Actually, he hadn't left her thoughts since he had kissed her. She hadn't expected it though she couldn't say she didn't welcome it. It had been far too long since she had been kissed and though it had been a mere peck, it had jolted her senses.

"*Fool,*" she whispered to the empty room. "You should have reprimanded him. You did nothing."

She sighed heavily and drew the wool blanket up over her head, trying to escape her musings. It did little good, Reeve refused to vacate her thoughts. He lingered there like a ghost that haunted.

Whatever was the matter with her? She threw off the blanket and sighed again. She knew what was wrong. The last four days had been like a dream. Nothing horrible had happened to her or those around her whom she had come to care for, and it had given her hope. Hope that perhaps she could live a relatively good life. And yet she was afraid. Afraid that the curse would resurface, or her father would discover her whereabouts, and all this joy would disappear in an instant, and she would once again be alone.

The worst part, though, would be if something happened to Reeve. She could not live with the thought of her being the cause of him dying. And that could very well happen if she continued to have feelings for him. She had tried unsuccessfully to chase them away.

Last night, after he had left the bedchamber, she had chanted silently and endlessly that she did not care for Reeve, *she did not, she did not.* And each time she had, she had suffered a sting to her heart.

Mara had made matters worse, though not intentionally, when she had arrived with a platter of food and had informed Tara that she should not feel guilty for loving Reeve. That life goes on whether we want it to or not and that Tara's deceased husband probably would want to see her happy.

Tara tried several times to make the persistent woman understand that Reeve and she were just friends, but to no avail. And that had gotten her thinking. Why would Mara believe that she cared about Reeve? Was it obvious that she cared for him? Whether she loved him or not was too early to tell. After all, they had just met. She couldn't have fallen in love that fast. She was probably grateful for all he had done for her, and so she felt this tug of gratitude.

She groaned pitifully, thinking what a poor excuse that was. She slipped out of bed, taking one of the wool blankets with her, and hurried to the hearth. She curled up in the large wooden chair, the blanket snug around her and her feet tucked beneath her.

She had tossed and turned all night with worry. She wanted very much to remain here, part of the MacAlpin clan. But was it a wise choice? And did she have any other choice?

*Keep your distance.*

She hated that warning voice in her head. She didn't want to keep her distance from Reeve. She liked him. She enjoyed his company. She felt safe with him. And Lord forgive her, she liked the taste of him, even if it had been just a brief taste.

Whatever was she going to do?

*First things first, Tara,* she scolded silently. You are going to look at that cottage, claim it as your own, and establish roots. There is no point of thinking beyond that. A safe home comes first. The rest can wait.

Tara felt a bit relieved confronting the problem and narrowing it down to what she needed to focus on. It was then she realized that her ankle was feeling much better. Riding on the horse yesterday and retiring early to bed, though she hadn't slept much, had given her injury time to heal. She would need to make certain that she didn't think it completely healed and walk on it all day. She would be careful what she did though she would go see old Alan's cottage and begin to establish residency there.

With that thought and a yawn, Tara drifted off to sleep.

Reeve paced in front of the hearth while his family enjoyed the morning meal.

"Sit, Reeve," his mother ordered.

"I'm not hungry," he said. "Are you sure she was still asleep?"

"Last I saw, she was curled up in a blanket on the chair in front of the hearth," Mara said. "I didn't want to disturb her, assuming she had a fitful night."

"I wonder if her ankle pained her," Reeve said. "I should go check on her."

"I already have," Mara said. "Now sit and eat."

Reeve remained pacing. He was concerned that Tara was curled in the chair instead of the bed. What had troubled her that she couldn't sleep and sought refuge in the chair?

Duncan turned to Bryce, and whispered, "I should have wagered one week."

The two men laughed.

Tara woke with a start. It took her a moment to realize where she was, and once she did, she relaxed, though not for long. She wanted to get started on the day. Today she would have her own home. It would be hers and hers alone.

She noticed that on the bed lay a brown wool skirt and a tan linen blouse. A deep green wool shawl also lay there, and freshly washed stockings hung from the mantel. Mara must have been there and had graciously provided her with garments more suitable to her surroundings. After all, her velvet and silk gowns certainly would not do while here, where hard work was part of daily life.

Tara was careful unfolding her legs from beneath her, realizing that it had not been a wise choice to tuck her injured ankle under her. It had swollen though not badly, but it did pain her. She silently chastised her own stupidity and, with a limp, walked over to the bed to dress.

She managed fine until it came to getting her boot over her swollen ankle. She grew frustrated when she couldn't accomplish the simple task.

Reeve would be able to get it on. He had before and had gotten it off with little effort. She needed his help, wanted it, and the thought that she was relying on him frustrated her all the more. She had seen to her own care for years. Why, suddenly, did she need to rely on someone? Perhaps it wasn't that she needed to rely but more that there finally was someone she could rely on.

After several more unsuccessful, frustrating attempts, she grabbed the uncooperative boot and hobbled out of the room to the stairs. A tear touched her eye, and a pang hit her heart. She had someone to go to, someone she knew would help her, and it filled her with precious joy and nagging sorrow. It could not be between them. Why did she continue to torture herself?

Reeve kept glancing toward the stairs while he paced, paying no attention to his family as they enjoyed the meal.

"Oh for God's sake, go and see if she's awake," Mara said, and everyone clapped in agreement.

Reeve ignored them and bolted for the stairs, and as he rounded on the second floor, there was Tara, tears threatening to spill from her lovely lavender eyes and her boot in hand.

His heart tore in two though even more so when she backed up the stairs away from him. Though he wondered if it was the curse she feared or the attraction they shared.

He advanced one step. "What's wrong?"

She raised her chin, kept her tears from falling, and held up the lone boot. "I can't get this stubborn thing on."

"I'll get it on." He took another step up, not wanting to rush at her but intending to have her in his arms soon. "If you let me help you."

"You always seem to be helping me," she admitted.

"And that is a bad thing?"

Her brow creased and she worried at her lower lip and once again his heart hurt for her. That damn curse had simply consumed her and dictated her life. That had to change, and he intended to see that it did.

A tiny single tear spilled from the corner of her eye, and that was it. In an instant, Reeve had her wrapped in the comfort of his arms. He brushed the tear away with the pad of his thumb. "I will always be there to help you. I told you that you could count on me, and I meant it."

She said nothing, simply stared at him, and he knew it would take more time for her to trust him, to believe that she had someone she could rely on.

He scooped her up, something that seemed to have become a constant, and, with a satisfied grin, headed down the stairs. "Mum tells me you were asleep in the chair when she went to see how you fared this morning. Did your ankle pain you?"

"No, my ankle felt better until I fell asleep with it tucked beneath me in the chair."

"Then your sleep was fitful? What bothered you?"

She seemed hesitant to answer.

"It was probably because you are in unfamiliar surroundings," he said, offering her an excuse.

She quickly agreed. "Yes, that was probably why. I am looking forward to seeing old Alan's cottage."

He wondered what it was that made her change the subject so quickly. What had haunted her so badly last night that she hadn't been able to sleep? He wished he could ask her, or that she would simply confide in him. But whatever it was that had disturbed her, he sensed she wasn't ready to share it with him, and so he left it alone.

"I'll take you there after breakfast," he said, eager to get her settled safely and permanently in her own place.

"I'm starving," she admitted with a smile.

"So am I." His appetite had suddenly returned.

Mara was quick to jump up and hurry over to them as soon as they entered the great hall.

"What's wrong?" she demanded.

"A little swelling, that's all," Tara said, wanting to reassure the woman.

Reeve set her on the end of the bench and, with a gentle and careful touch, had her boot on in no time. She gave him a generous smile, and damn if it didn't give his heart a jolt as he sat down beside her.

When Reeve looked up, he saw Bryce and Duncan snickering, and he shot them warning glances that had them snickering even more. A hard poke to each of their sides from Mercy, who sat between the pair, wiped their faces clean.

Reeve acknowledged her help with an appreciative nod, and Mercy smiled.

"Mercy and I will take Tara to Old Alan's cottage and see if it suits her," Mara said.

"With her ankle as it is, it's best if I take her," Reeve said.

Mara scrunched her brow a moment, and then said, "You're right. With the snow on the ground, she'll need a strong hand to help her."

"It's really not necessary, I can walk," Tara said.

"Not with the snow," Mara insisted.

Tara was more persistent. "Snow or not, I prefer it."

Reeve sat silent between the two women, his eyes

on his brothers, who were just as silent though they wore wide grins.

"You are a stubborn one," Mara said, and Reeve cringed. "That's good. You'll need it with the likes of this one"—she gave Reeve a jab—"who thinks he's always right, which doesn't always let him see the truth of a situation."

That had everyone throwing in their opinions about Reeve, and the chatter was soon sprinkled with laughter and stories of Reeve's youth.

Reeve was pleased with the way things were going, his family accepting her into the clan, and with his father and brothers agreeing to keep her secret, he knew the villagers would befriend her as well. With things continuing that way, there was a good chance that Tara could finally be free of that curse, free to care for others without worry, even free to love.

The thought made him feel good, and why shouldn't it? Tara was a good woman and deserved a good life, deserved to find love. That he helped her to achieve it should make him feel good. It had nothing to do with him caring about her. She had become a friend, and that was that. He wasn't falling in love with her. The idea was simply foolish.

Then why was it that the thought of anyone else kissing, touching, bedding her, tore at his gut. And why did he ache to spend the whole day with her?

Reeve was relieved that the cottage wasn't in as much disrepair as he had expected. And from the smile on Tara's face, she seemed pleased with it. That meant that he could settle her here just a short walk from the keep. He could make certain she was safe and visit her often.

*Visit her often?*

Whatever was he thinking? That was it; he wasn't thinking. He'd settle her here and be done with it. Why? Why not pursue the attraction between them? He had all intentions of kissing her again. So why not take it further?

*The curse?*

The thought infuriated him. That had nothing to do with it. And he was damn well going to make sure that was settled once and for all.

Tara drew Reeve out of his musings when she said, "This is perfect."

"This suits you?"

She squeezed the hand that she had held, at his insistence, since they had left the keep. He had worried she might slip, and so he had kept a good grip on her, and she had not let go since. He assumed that she hadn't realized that she had continued to cling to him, and he would make no mention of it, enjoying the feel of her hand in his.

"I love it. I can't thank you and your family enough."

He could remind her that she had paid his clan well and owed no thanks, but he had the feeling that her thanks was for giving her a chance at a new life, and no amount of coins could buy that.

"No thanks are necessary," he said.

"But they are," she said, and stepped closer and kissed his cheek.

Realizing her own actions, her eyes turned wide, and she quickly retreated from him, yanking her hand free of his.

It was his turn to react without thought, and he did. He reached out, cupped his hand at the back of her neck and grabbed her around the waist, pulling her up against him. Then, without the least bit of hesitation, or concern for the curse, he kissed her.

She struggled for a mere second and then melted in his arms and responded with equal enthusiasm. They were soon lost in the kiss, taking their time, exploring, feeling, enjoying the taste of each other. And when it ended, with great reluctance, they rested brow to brow, Reeve's hand still cupping the back of her neck.

"We shouldn't," she whispered.

"But you liked it," he murmured.

"As did you."

"That I did," he admitted eagerly.

"It's not safe."

"True enough, for I want to kiss you again and again and again."

"No," she said, trying to pull away.

Reeve wouldn't let go of her. "Yes, Tara. We will kiss again. I want it, and you want it."

"I want you safe," she pleaded.

"I couldn't be any safer than with you."

She sighed. "That brings joy and sorrow to my heart, for I would forever keep you safe, but the curse—"

"Is gone," Reeve insisted.

"We don't know that."

"I know it," he said, and brushed his lips over hers.

She wiggled from his grasp, and he let her go. "I fear taking the chance."

"Nothing bad has happened—"

"It's been only a few days since we met."

"That's right, and we know not what this is between us," Reeve said. "Let us give it time and see what happens."

Her response died on her lips as Mara and Mercy entered the cottage, arms laden with baskets, brooms, and bundles.

"We're here to get you settled," Mara said.

In no time, Reeve found he was being squeezed out of the cottage as woman after woman arrived to welcome Tara to the clan. He watched as she smiled and greeted each one pleasantly, but he knew that within she struggled and worried that somehow she would hurt these people, who were being so kind to her.

For some strange reason, he had grown to know this woman well in a relatively short time. While he fought against falling in love, he knew he had to pursue this strange connection to her. He had to settle for himself what it was he felt for her.

He gave her a wave and mouthed *later* to her, and she smiled. His heart did a flop, and he left, shaking his head as soon as he was out the door. Her plain features were changed so dramatically when she smiled. It was as if a beautiful woman was trapped inside her and was only released when she smiled. He wondered what else Tara kept trapped inside herself. And damn if he didn't intend to find out.

An empty ache suddenly struck Tara as Reeve disappeared out the door. She smiled and responded to all queries from the women who came and went, leaving small welcoming gifts for her. But her thoughts remained on Reeve and the kiss.

She struggled with how much she had enjoyed it and how much she wished to kiss him again. She tried to convince herself that it had been so long since she had been kissed that she would have reacted as she had to anyone who had kissed her.

But that was a lie, and she knew it.

She was attracted to Reeve MacAlpin, and for the first time in far too long, she felt that she could trust a man; and that in itself was appealing.

A tug at her skirt had her looking down, and she was surprised to see a little lad no more than four or five years staring back up at her.

"You're pretty," he said.

She hunched down in front of him. "Thank you, and what's your name?"

"Rand," he said with a huge grin, leaned forward, and pecked her on the cheek then ran to hide behind a woman who had two good-sized baskets on her arm.

Tara stood, a smile on her face and a hand to her pecked cheek. She silently prayed that the curse had somehow been lifted and was gone. She didn't want this young lad harmed. She didn't want anyone harmed.

Rand remained glued to the woman's side as she approached Tara. "Welcome. These are for you." She handed Tara the two beautifully crafted baskets. "I'm Cora the basket weaver if you have need of more."

"Thank you, Cora," Tara said. "And this is your son?" She gave a peek at Rand.

"Yes, Rand is my youngest, and I have a daughter, eleven years now and—"She patted her flat stomach. "I've just learned I'm with child again."

"How wonderful," Tara said. "I wish you all the best."

"She doesn't need it," Mara said, joining them.

"She has the easiest deliveries I've ever attended. Not a yell or scream, the babe just pops right out."

"I hope mine pops right out," Mercy said, walking over to them.

"You're a wee one, so it might take a bit more than a pop," Mara said frankly. "Now Tara, here, has good birthing hips, wide and firm. She'll probably pop babes out easily."

Babes and birthing chatter went on around her, all the women joining in. She had always wished for many children. She had attended the birthing of a few women until . . .

She almost sighed aloud. She had been banned from attending any birthing once she was proclaimed a *death bride*. No woman wanted to take the chance of the curse somehow affecting her child. Not that any child whose birth she had attended died. It was fear that had caused her to be banned, and she really couldn't blame them. She would not take such a chance if she were having a child.

With the help of so many women, the cottage began to take shape, and Tara was stunned when Bryce, Duncan, and Reeve arrived with a table and two chairs, a chest and a bed, and not a narrow one, one more suitable for two.

The men were chased out as soon as they finished, Tara not even getting a chance to thank them.

Mercy and Cora dressed her bed while still discussing child birthing. The logs that had been started in the fireplace as soon as Mara had arrived had chased the cold from the cottage, and candles flickered on the table and atop the mantel. Fresh rushes had been spread on the dirt floor before the furniture had arrived, and some of the women were now dropping bunches of dried lavender to the floor to mingle with the rushes and add a pleasant sweetness to the air.

By midafternoon, the cottage was in fine shape, the helpful drifting off one by one until Mara and Mercy were the only ones left.

"I can't believe how generous everyone has been," Tara said.

"We are a clan, and that makes us family," Mara said. "And family helps family. We would have it no other way."

Mercy squeezed Tara's arm. "Isn't it wonderful? It took time for me to get used to how friendly and willing everyone was to help. Now it just seems natural."

"You should rest that ankle," Mara instructed. "You haven't kept off it enough today."

"I couldn't let everyone do the work for me," Tara said.

"That was why they came, to help," Mara said. "Like Mercy said, you'll get used to it. Now rest your ankle. I'll have Reeve bring your personal things."

Tara didn't think it a good idea that she and Reeve spend time alone, but she didn't object to Mara's suggestion. The truth of it was that she wanted to see Reeve. In the few short hours they had been apart, she realized that she missed him.

She could scold herself for the thought or try to ignore it, but she did neither. Instead, she allowed herself to feel, dangerous though it may be; she allowed herself to feel. She allowed herself to look forward to seeing him, and she allowed herself to look forward to sharing another kiss with him. The strange stirrings in her might warn, but they also urged that the risk was worth it.

Most of all, those stirrings offered her hope, and a flutter of anticipation ran through her as she thanked the two women again and closed the door behind them to wait for Reeve.

# Chapter 11

Reeve didn't waste a minute when his mother told him to take Tara's personal items to her. She also reminded him to make certain he saw to it that Tara got to the keep safely for the evening meal. She needn't have reminded him. He had planned to escort her, though he had plans to linger at her cottage first and share another kiss with her.

All day he hadn't been able to get her off his mind. No matter what it was he was doing, she had intruded on his concentration. He had taken a ribbing from his brothers while hunting. There hadn't been a time he hadn't had a successful hunt . . . until today. His arrow had missed every target.

The worst ribbing he had gotten had been when their mother had sent them to retrieve some furniture from a cottage long empty. There had been two beds, a wide one and a narrow one. He had insisted they take the larger bed.

Right away, Duncan started chuckling, and Bryce naturally joined in.

Soon they were in a heated debate about the beds, though the heat was more on his side, while the two simply laughed and snickered. Their mother's sudden presence brought an abrupt halt to the encounter, and though Reeve still was annoyed, it was at himself.

His brothers had been right. As soon as he had seen the beds, he knew that the narrow one would never do. It wasn't until his brothers' good-natured ribbing started that he realized why he had wanted the larger bed. He wanted enough room *when* he made love to Tara.

Not even *if,* but *when.*

Only hours before, he had been trying to convince himself that they were simply friends, and now he's thinking of bedding her.

"Take this along with you," his mother ordered as she entered the great hall.

She handed him a basket filled with two tankards, a pitcher, and a crock full of dried leaves.

"Tara will be wanting a nice brew to keep the chill out of her," Mara said. "You could use one too. Now be off with you."

Reeve hugged his mother. "You are the best."

Her pink plump cheeks grew even rosier. "Go on with you," she beamed, and shooed him off.

Reeve knocked though he didn't wait to be invited in but simply entered Tara's cottage as if it were his own. She didn't seem to mind, greeting him with a wide smile. She was quick to stand and offer him help with the items cradled in his arms. Reeve wouldn't have it. He deposited his armful on the table and hurried her back in her seat, noticing she had used an overturned bucket to prop her injured foot on.

"You rest, and I'll fix us a hot brew," he said.

"That would be nice," Tara said eagerly.

Reeve got the distinct impression that she wasn't

only happy to see him, but she was happy that he wasn't hurrying off, that he'd be staying a while to share a drink.

They chatted endlessly, about everything and anything. Reeve had her laughing about tales of him and his brothers growing up. And she seemed ever so curious about the strange way Duncan and Mercy had met. Reeve explained their plight of having been chained together as prisoners of the king and on the run. And how after endless weeks, they had finally arrived home and had been freed of their chains, though by then their hearts had been bound by love, and the strong link could never be broken.

A yawn stole Tara's smile, and Reeve realized she looked tired. With at least three hours left before supper, he thought it a good idea that she take a nap and rest up.

She seemed reluctant.

"A brief nap will refresh you for the evening meal," he said.

She looked ready to debate the matter when a yawn attacked once again. She laughed. "My body appears to agree with you."

A wicked grin surfaced on Reeve's face, which matched his wicked thoughts. He shook his head slowly, silently admonishing himself. "When are you going to realize that I'm always right?"

"That's still to be proven," she said laughing again.

Tara went to stand, and Reeve quickly was at her side. Once again, he didn't ask permission, but then had he ever? He did what came naturally. He scooped her up in his arms and carried her to the bed.

"You needn't carry me," she said. "I can walk."

"Your ankle needs rest."

"It feels fine, and it is but a short walk to the bed."

"That's good." He hadn't meant to whisper, his response simply came out that way. But then maybe now was the time for whispers and murmurs and stolen kisses and exploring touches.

*Rein it in, Reeve,* he silently warned himself.

He sat her on the edge of the bed and knelt down to take her boots off.

"I can do that," she protested.

"It's no trouble."

It was more difficult than he had expected though it wasn't the boot that gave him trouble. It was his own rapidly mounting passion as one hand cradled her calf, and the other worked the boot off. Her calf was toned, though not rock-hard, and his fingers itched to stroke the inviting flesh beneath the wool stocking.

He moved his hand to take firmer hold of her leg, and his fingertips brushed along the crevice at the back of her knee. The itch to explore farther up along her leg overwhelmed him, as did thoughts of how silky smooth the inside of her thigh must feel.

Heat built in his loins, and he knew he needed a slap of cold air, frigid cold air.

With the stubborn boot finally off, he easily rid her of the other one and placed them near the hearth. He planned to leave, let her sleep, not bother with a kiss. A kiss was not a good idea now. And then he looked at her, and he saw his heated desire mirrored in her eyes.

"Damn," he mumbled, and sunk down in front of her, his hands gripping the back of her neck. "I need to kiss you."

He didn't wait for a response, her deep lavender

eyes had told him what he needed to know. She was as eager for his kiss as he was for hers.

Their mouths joined in a dance of passionate hunger. They tasted, melded, and lingered, enjoying the feast that nourished their hearts and souls.

Reeve feared moving his hands from her neck, for if he did, they would surely roam where they should not go . . . at least not yet. In time, though. Definitely in time.

He eased the kiss to an end and rested his cheek on hers, the heat almost scorching his own heated flesh. That they were on the verge of more than a kiss was obvious, and he knew he had to leave.

His hands fell away from her, and he stood quickly. "I must go."

"Yes," she urged. "Go."

"I'll return for you for supper."

"I'll be waiting . . . outside."

He almost argued that she should stay in the warmth of the cottage until he returned and then thought better of it.

"Until later," he said, and turned, hurrying out, not looking back, not wanting to see the passion that had turned her lovely lavender eyes a dark purple and ready to explode with passion.

Tara was still trying to regain her breath. She had never known a kiss like that. Not even with Rory, whom she had loved beyond reason, had she felt the swell of passion so quickly consume her as she had with Reeve. If Reeve had lingered, she feared she would have surrendered not only to him but to her own carnal need.

She was playing with danger here, a danger that could devastate not merely her but many. She had time to see if things continued on in a good fashion. Time to make certain no one got hurt. Time to make certain no one would come retrieve her. But if she recklessly continued on in such a selfish fashion, it could prove disastrous.

Tara dropped back on the pillow and tucked herself beneath the soft green wool blanket. She hadn't realized how tired she was until her head rested on the pillow, and another yawn escaped. She hadn't slept enough last night, and she had had a busy day. Whatever did she expect?

She would close her eyes for a brief nap and be up and waiting outside when Reeve returned. She would not think of the kiss. Her fingers must not have heard her command, for they drifted to her lips, and she thought she felt them pulse.

Reeve had made her pulse all over. It had trickled through her whole body as he had kissed her. The rhythmic pulse had been like a tingling sensation prickling across every inch of her until her skin had turned to gooseflesh. And she had wanted more, so much more.

Her fingers drifted from her lips down to her nipples, and she gasped when she felt how rigid they were. She was in trouble, terrible trouble, for she not only wanted Reeve to feast on her lips, she wanted his mouth on her . . .

She sighed, shaking her head. *Stop! You cannot do this. You cannot!*

She repeated her warning silently over and over and over until she finally drifted off to sleep.

* * *

Reeve approached Tara's cottage with a mix of anticipation and apprehension. Both grew when he saw that she wasn't waiting outside for him. His first thought was that her absence signaled an invitation. She wanted him to come inside, wanted them to continue what they had started.

"Nonsense," he warned himself, though he hesitated to knock and open the door when he reached it.

He shook his head, clearing his wicked thoughts, and gave a tap before slowly opening the door and calling out her name. "Tara?"

Once inside, the door closed, he realized she hadn't woken yet. He went over to the bed and saw that she slept soundly. She wasn't snoring, though a soft continuous sound emanated from her. She was in a deep sleep, and he couldn't bring himself to wake her.

He tucked the blanket around her and, with disappointment, left her alone.

Reeve was quiet at supper, which wasn't his way. Usually, he joined right in the chatter and the good-natured teasing, but not tonight. Tonight he couldn't help but watch Duncan and Mercy. They were a perfect match, though Reeve had warned Duncan against falling in love, the four brothers having been raised and trained to place the mission of the true king reclaiming the throne before all else.

But Mercy had understood, had even placed her own life in danger so that Duncan could do what needed to be done. She had not only trusted him, she had trusted their love. Reeve had often wondered if their being shackled together for a length of time had helped them find that love.

"If you won't admit that you're falling in love, at least admit you're pining for the woman," Duncan teased.

"I'll admit nothing, but I will beat you senseless," Reeve said with a smug grin.

"Now there's my brother," Duncan said with a nod. "I thought we had lost him to—"

"Don't dare say it," Reeve warned.

"Afraid of love?" Bryce asked.

"Are you?" Reeve shot back.

"Deathly afraid." Bryce chuckled.

"Smart man," Carmag said.

"I'm not in love," Reeve said though it sounded hollow to his own ears.

"Time will tell," Mara said with a motherly pat to his arm.

Reeve rolled his eyes, and begged, "I need a mission. Send me on mission."

"That's a good idea," Mara said. "Absence makes the heart grow fonder."

Reeve didn't know why he had suddenly asked to be sent on a mission. He truly preferred to remain here, but then perhaps that was why he had to go. He had to learn for himself if he had simply grown accustomed to Tara. That she had been right there in front of him day and night, so what had he expected? Not to have noticed her? Or grow attached to her?

"A mission," he begged once more, wanting his chaotic thoughts gone and wanting his sane self back.

"There's a message that needs to be delivered," Carmag said. "It should take no more than two or three days."

"I'll do it," Reeve said.

"Are you sure?" Carmag asked. "It isn't of grave importance."

"Doesn't matter. I'll go."

"Let him go," Mara said. "Maybe he'll learn something while he's gone."

"I'll leave at sunrise," Reeve said, feeling a jolt to his stomach. He had to do this, had to go away if only for a few days. Then why did he suddenly feel like he was deserting Tara?

Tara woke, and it wasn't until she peeked outside and saw the sunrise on the horizon that she realized she had slept the night away, her ankle wasn't swollen, and she was starving. She quickly gathered snow in a bucket and dumped it in the cauldron hanging in the fireplace to heat, after adding another log.

While the water heated, she put her belongings that Reeve had brought to her the night before, in the chest, though she kept her bone combs. She worked the tangles from her hair, and, with practiced hands, she pinned her ringlets to rest near the top of her head, letting a few fall down the front and back.

She washed her face with the warm water and then slipped on her boots with ease. She grabbed her fur-lined cloak from the peg by the door and walked to the keep.

Tara felt refreshed and looked forward to the day. She hadn't looked forward to a day in such a long time. She planned on going to the keep kitchen and see if the cook would allow her to bake bread. Reeve had liked her black bread, and she wanted to bake him some.

She spotted Reeve before he did her and she

stopped, seeing that he was getting ready to mount his horse. Her breath caught, not because he was the handsomest man she had ever seen but because for a moment she believed he belonged to her.

*An insane thought and completely improper,* she silently warned herself.

He saw her and stilled, and so she approached.

"You are going somewhere?" she asked apprehensively.

"A mission I must see to."

"How long will you be gone?"

"Three days at the most," he said.

Her hearted thudded in her chest, and words spilled quickly from her lips. "I will miss you."

Her heart pounded more wildly when he did not respond and then he reached out, his arm going around her waist to lift and swing her up against him. His lips came down on hers, and he kissed her with such passion that she wanted to cry with joy.

Her arms slipped around his neck, and she eagerly responded, letting her own desire take flight. And it flew, soared, and reached the heavens. When finally it returned to earth, though with great reluctance on both their parts, their cheeks came to rest against each other.

Not wanting to, but knowing it was necessary, Tara finally moved away. "Come home safe."

"Stay safe," he said.

"How can I not? I am in the bosom of your family."

He smiled. "I will see you soon."

"Promise?" Tara asked, on the verge of tears though fighting them.

Reeve cupped the back of her neck with his hand

and stared into her eyes. "I give you my word. I will always return to you."

*Please. Please let it be so,* she pleaded.

They kissed again, though briefly, and he mounted his horse and rode off.

Tara watched until he was out of sight and then she turned to go into the keep, though she didn't feel like baking bread anymore.

# Chapter 12

Tara woke excited. Reeve should be coming home today. It had been three days since his departure, and she had steadily missed him more each day. And though she ached for his return, she couldn't say the days had been dreadful. They had actually been quite enjoyable, thanks mostly to Mercy. She had gotten Tara quickly involved in stitching clothes for her unborn babe. Each day, they would spend time in the sewing room, stitching and talking, Mara often joining them.

Mercy also took her on walks through the village, introducing her to those she hadn't yet met. And she had introduced her to Etty, the keep cook. Once Tara made her black bread, the MacAlpin men clamored for more. Etty liked it herself and asked Tara to show her how to make it.

In a short time, her life had gone from a lonely, solitary existence to one of family and friends and the possibility of falling in love.

Tara reminded herself to remain vigilant, that the curse for some unfathomable reason could just be lying dormant. And when she least expected, it would pop up and inflict suffering.

For now she simply intended to enjoy her new life and pray that it continued.

She grabbed her cloak from the peg as she reached the door, and when she swung it open, she jumped with a yelp. Reeve was standing there though not for long. In a single heartbeat, he snatched her up with an arm around her waist, walked into the cottage, kicking the door shut behind him, and planted a kiss on her that left them both breathless.

He rubbed his cheek to hers, and whispered, "Damn, I missed you."

His declaration pleased her beyond reason. "I missed you too."

"How much?" he teased with a twinkle in his dark eyes and a quick brush of his lips across hers.

The faint kiss sent her lips pulsing, and she sighed as she answered, "Very much."

"Show me," he murmured, before nibbling along her neck, and his hand slipped to her backside, easing her to fit tight up against him.

She felt him then, hard with desire, and she warned herself to step away, keep her wits about her, wait; wait just a bit longer, or all could be lost.

His lips were at her neck, and, instinctively, she tilted her head back, giving him room to taste. His mouth skimmed the tops of her full breasts, and the shot of desire that raced through her left her momentarily stunned.

His lips once again went to hers, and after feasting like a hungry man, he eased away though he continued to nibble. "You haunted my thoughts the whole time I was gone. I could think of nothing, nothing but you. Damn, woman, you have bewitched me."

His words were what she needed to stop things from going any further. Was the curse bewitching him? Would she love him only to lose him?

Painful memories quickly surfaced to remind her of how much she had not only suffered, but had been the cause of others' suffering as well. And she never wanted to go through it again. She had to keep her senses about her and take her time and make sure that loving this man would not cause his death.

Tara tried to ease herself out of his arms, but he would have none of it. The more she tried, the tighter he held her.

"You're not running from me," he said adamantly. "We're going to see where this takes us."

"Then we'll go slowly."

Reeve laughed. "Do you truly think that is possible?"

Tara sighed. "It will be difficult for sure."

He kissed her quickly and laughed softly. "Then I haunted you in my absence just as much as you did me?"

She chuckled. "You were forever in my thoughts."

"Tell me about them."

Heat rushed to Tara's cheeks, and soon they looked like two shiny apples.

Reeve laughed again, his dark eyes shining bright with joy. "Your thoughts were as wicked as mine."

She slapped his arm playfully. "You're not helping matters."

"Some things are inevitable."

"With time," she warned.

"We'll see."

Tara shook her head. "Promise me that—"

"I will promise nothing," he said bluntly. "I don't

know what this is between us, but I intend to find out."

Tara opened her mouth to further protest, and he took advantage of the moment and kissed her. Not that she minded. While her focus should have been on their discussion, somehow his lips had intrigued her more than his words, and she was aching to kiss him again. So when he did, she welcomed it.

"No worries of the past or future," Reeve said after his lips left hers. "We think only about now and see what happens."

Tara nodded though she should have objected. She wondered if she should tell him about the origin of the curse, perhaps he would then see the wisdom in going slow. Although it could have the opposite reaction, it could possibly cause him to walk away from her forever, and that would plunge her back into a solitary existence.

She shuddered at the thought.

"What's wrong?"

She smiled at his demanding concern. He was a bold, strong man with a heroic and loving heart.

She didn't answer fast enough, and so he encouraged, "I can handle anything, conquer anything, and I'm always right."

This time she laughed and shook her head. "You've never been wrong?"

He grinned proudly. "Never. So, therefore, you should trust me implicitly."

"I believe I've already done that," she said, thinking of when he had appeared out of nowhere and so gallantly saved her.

"You have, and look what has come of it." His grin grew. "You have a home, and you have *me*."

Her heart lurched as if it had been shocked. The mere thought of him belonging to her overwhelmed and frightened her all at once. She wanted to linger over his words and what they meant.

Both their stomachs gurgled simultaneously, and they laughed.

"We should eat," he said. "And once I am finished meeting with my father and brothers, we can spend the day together."

"I would like that."

He nibbled along her lips, stopping only long enough to say, "So would I."

They left the cottage and walked hand in hand to the keep.

The air was biting cold, the sky gray, and the village was just stirring to life.

"Snow," Reeve said with a nod.

"And you are always right," Tara teased.

"You'll see that I am." He gave her hand a squeeze. "You can rely on it."

She smiled, wanting to believe him, needing to believe him, needing to know this risk she took was worth it, worth the possibility of finding love again. "How was your journey?"

For a moment, she thought she saw concern in his eyes, and she worried. She had hoped when she had so spontaneously decided on this daring action that there would be no repercussions. Her father would assume that she had been dragged off and murdered by the thieves who had stolen her bride price. Had her father discovered the truth? Was he on his way here? And if so, then what?

Tara realized that Reeve hadn't answered her, and she asked, "Is something wrong?"

He shook his head. "No. It's just that things didn't go as I expected." He leaned down and stole a quick kiss. "But it is not for you to worry about."

She almost sighed aloud. It had nothing to do with her, nothing at all. If he had discovered the truth, he would have confronted her with it. And then she would have to tell him the whole truth. What would he think of her then?

"I'm starving," she said, feeling ravenous.

"I've been remembering that black bread of yours"—he licked his lips—"and I was wondering if—"

"I baked several loaves yesterday, and as long as your brothers haven't found them . . ." She shook her head and laughed.

"We better hurry," he said, hastening their pace. "They will be up and about soon, and I don't want to have to lay a beating on them before I eat."

Tara chuckled.

"I fight for what is mine." He grinned. "And that bread is mine."

Reeve had half the loaf eaten and the other half sat in front of Tara for safekeeping, as he had adamantly insisted. It turned out to be a wise move on his part, for as soon as his brothers joined them, they berated him for not sharing. Reeve just grinned and kept eating the bread.

Tara still found it hard to believe her good fortune. Sitting here with this loving family was like a dream to her, and each day, she feared she would wake from it and be plunged back into her nightmare.

"Will you stitch with me while the men talk?" Mercy asked, as the meal ended.

"I look forward to it," Tara said eagerly. "I think I will be able to finish the baby shirt I've been working on."

"Perhaps you should rest," Duncan said, looking to his wife with concern.

"Something wrong?" Mara was quick to ask.

"Nothing," Mercy insisted. "I simply had a restless night."

"She barely slept all night," Duncan said, worry etched in the scar at the corner of his mouth.

"An uneasy stomach, that is all," Mercy insisted. "And besides, stitching is like rest to me."

"You'll keep a watch on her?" Duncan asked of Tara.

"Of course, I will keep a good watch on her and tend to her needs."

"That's not necessary—"

"It is," Duncan said with a finality that left no room for debate.

Mercy rolled her eyes and shook her head.

"I'm sure you'll do the same for Tara one day," Mara said. "It is the way with women."

"Listen to mum, she's right," Duncan said.

"I'm always right," Mara said with a sharp nod.

Bryce cocked his head to Tara sitting to his right, and whispered, "See who Reeve takes after."

"I heard that," Mara said, shaking her finger at Bryce.

Reeve laughed. "Forgot about her magical hearing, didn't you?"

"It's a mother's hearing. Your wives will have it soon enough," Mara said, her smile smug.

Carmag sent a conspiratorial glance to each of his

sons before he said, "Husbands have no need to fear magical hearing since they confide all to their wives as their wives do to them."

Mara chortled. "Oh, you don't know the half of it, dear."

That brought the men to full attention.

Mara looked over her rapt audience and smiled. "Someday, I may be gracious enough to explain that." She stood, and her wide smile plumped her already full cheeks. "But I wouldn't count on it." She shooed at the men. "Now be gone on your business and leave us women to ours."

Tara laughed along with Mercy as the men stood grumbling.

Reeve whispered to Tara, "Later."

She smiled up at him and nodded.

As soon as the men had left, Mara turned to Mercy. "Tell me exactly what's wrong."

Mara's direct nature could intimidate, but it was the concern in her voice that let you know how much she cared.

Mercy sighed. "I can't truly say. I only know I don't feel quite right. It's as if something is wrong, but I don't know what it is."

Mara continued questioning. "Pains anywhere?"

"No, none at all," Mercy said with a shrug. "I just don't feel right. I know it doesn't make sense, but that is the only way I know of explaining it."

"Do as Duncan said and rest," Mara said. "And if anything should bother you, let me know right away."

Mercy nodded, and Mara hurried off after explaining that she had a lot to see to today.

Mercy laid her hand across her rounded stomach.

"Even if there is something wrong, I doubt there is anything Mara can do about it."

"I don't know about that," Tara said. "She's a formidable woman."

Mercy smiled. "She is at that, though kind and loving in her own way."

"Let's go to the sewing room," Tara suggested. "You can rest, and we can talk while we stitch."

Mercy nodded eagerly. "And you can tell me about you and Reeve." She shook her hand at Tara when she tried to protest. "There's no point in denying it. Something is going on between you two, and talking with a friend just may help you better understand it."

*A friend.*

Tara was so happy that Mercy considered her a friend that she completely ignored the little niggling thought that kept trying to intrude. Could Mercy be ill and her babe at risk because the curse was once again haunting her? She didn't want to know, didn't want to think about it, and so she ignored it.

Reeve and his two brothers and father gathered in front of the fireplace, each pulling a chair close to the hearth. While a strong fire blazed, a chill still permeated the solar.

"Something is stirring with King Kenneth," Reeve said after they were all settled.

"What goes on?" Carmag asked.

Reeve shook his head. "The person who shared the news had no idea. It seems that there is a well-kept, guarded secret surrounding him, few being trusted with the details."

"Perhaps Neil could find out something," Duncan suggested.

"His spying days are over," Bryce reminded them, and smiled. "Besides, Etty would never let him place himself in danger."

Reeve sat forward. "Etty our cook and Neil our spy together?"

Bryce grinned. "It's a sight that warms the heart. And you don't want to take a chance of annoying Etty." He looked around the room at each of them. "I think we can all agree on that since the result would be mum cooking for us."

They all cringed.

"I wouldn't expect Neil to place himself in danger," Reeve said, "but he may be able to point us in the right direction of who to talk with. It would help having another spy amongst the king's trusted group."

"But with the king suspicious of almost everyone, how would we get anyone to betray him?" Duncan asked.

"Coins and lots of them," Bryce said. "There is always someone who will take a risk for a fat purse."

"Bryce has a point," Carmag said. "I'll speak to Neil about it and see what he suggests."

"Any other news?" Carmag asked.

Reeve shook his head. "Nothing. I delivered the message, heard the gossip about the king, and headed home."

"Missed her, didn't you?" Duncan said with a grin, then looked to Bryce. "I'm going to win the wager."

"Are you looking for a beating, Duncan?" Reeve challenged, a smirk edging its way past his snarling lips.

Duncan laughed. "You're beating yourself up so badly over this that you'll have no strength left to fight me."

"I am not," Reeve insisted. "I'm simply seeing where it takes me."

"Well, watch out," Duncan advised, "you're already falling, and when you finally hit"—he grinned and chuckled—"it's going to be like something you've never felt before."

"That's why I won't be falling in love anytime soon," Bryce said.

Duncan laughed again. "That means you're next since Reeve believed the same." He rubbed his hands together. "Damn, I'm enjoying this."

"Shut up!" Reeve and Bryce yelled out in unison.

Duncan laughed harder.

# Chapter 13

Reeve was eager to see Tara. After finishing with his brothers and father, he had a few other matters to attend to and then he went in search of her. She wasn't in the sewing room and neither was Mercy. He inquired about Mercy since she had mentioned she wasn't feeling well and discovered that she had gone to her bedchamber for a rest.

Next he found his mother, but she hadn't seen Tara since the morning meal. So he grabbed his wool cloak and left the keep, heading to Tara's cottage. Snow must have started falling earlier, a good inch having covered the ground. Children ran around squealing with delight and sticking their tongues out to catch the fat flakes.

The sheer joy on their red-cheeked faces had him smiling and thinking. He had assumed that one day he would have children, not soon, but someday. Now suddenly he found the idea more appealing than ever. He could just imagine playing in the snow with his son or daughter, perhaps both and possibly even more. He had always hoped he'd have a gaggle of children.

Reeve's smile suddenly faded, old memories suddenly tearing at him.

"What stole your happy smile away?" Tara asked, coming up beside him and hooking her arm around his.

"Sad memories," he said, and gave her a quick kiss.

"Share them with me?"

He didn't think twice. "I recall the day in detail, though I was only four years when I lost my whole family. My father, mother, and older sister Netty were killed by King Kenneth's troops, though he was not king yet, in a bid to take the throne."

He paused a moment, seeing the past materialize before his eyes. "I had hid in the woods with Netty. She was ten years, and when she saw what was happening, she ordered me to stay where I was no matter what, and she ran to help our parents."

He took a breath, remembering much too vividly the carnage. "I watched them all die and never moved until hours after the soldiers had gone. I don't know what I would have done if Bryce hadn't happened along. He found me sitting amongst my family's bodies, crying. He gently took my hand and told me we were brothers now, and he would look after me. I went with him, never glancing back, though the scene remains far too vivid in my memory."

"I am so sorry," Tara said softly. "That had to be horrible for a lad of such a young age to witness."

"It was," Reeve admitted. "But if it wasn't for Bryce, I would have never survived. I would have died along with my family, being too young to know what to do."

"I thought you told me Bryce was only a year older than you."

"He is, though he's years wiser, always has been. He kept hold of my hand and spoke to me of how he had lost his family too and how he knew of a good home for us. And he'd get us there, and how, no matter what, we would always have each other. I clung to him and refused to let go. Even when we arrived on Mara and Carmag's doorstep, it took weeks before I would leave his side."

"You truly are brothers," Tara said.

"That we are," Reeve agreed, and took her in his arms. "Where have you been?"

"Looking for you." She held up her arm, a basket hanging from it. "Your mother sent me to bring this to Kate."

"I just saw mum, and she told me that she hadn't seen you since breakfast."

"She hadn't until a few moments ago. And as soon as she told me that you had just been there, she shoved this basket at me and told me to catch up with you, that you would take me to Kate's."

"I best obey mum," Reeve said teasingly. "You can easily miss Kate and Bailey's place. It's tucked behind newly wedded Cowan and Annie's place."

Tara shook her head. "Too many names and places to remember. I'm lucky my cottage is close to the keep."

Reeve grinned. "And glad I am of that, for I can visit often."

"As often as you like," she said.

"Be careful, I may never leave."

He noticed that she hesitated a moment and then, lowering her head, she whispered as if sharing a secret, "I wouldn't mind that."

Reeve didn't respond, though her remark had gladdened his heart.

Kate's pleasant smile, pretty face and lively nature

welcomed them, and soon Tara and she were talking as if they were old friends.

Reeve stood waiting with more patience than he knew he had as the women chattered, Kate's husband Bailey out with the hunting party for the day. He hadn't realized that Kate was due to deliver any day, and he was pleased when Tara offered Kate whatever help she needed. He hoped that she was finally realizing that there was no curse on her and that life could be good if she would only stop worrying about the curse. If truth be known, it was more that words did damage to people than curses. Once someone set something in a person's head, there was no getting it out. It took solid root and grew, being nourished by wagging tongues that had nothing better to do.

"Thank Mara for me," Kate said as she saw them out.

They walked arm in arm, the snow falling heavier than only moments ago. Reeve directed them toward Tara's cottage. He wanted some time alone with her. He'd been aching to kiss her, truly kiss her, since she had come up alongside him. And he wouldn't mind more than kisses, perhaps a touch or two.

*Damn, who was he kidding?*

He wanted to couple with her, and that was all there was to it. He had had his share of women, some more exciting than others, but Tara was different. His attraction to her overwhelmed and consumed him.

He wanted to be with her, kiss her, touch her, talk with her, or simply hold her hand as he did now. And that wasn't something he had ever experienced. He had never wanted to hold on, truly hold on, to a woman's hand, and now with Tara, he never wanted to let go.

She stopped at her door and stepped in front, facing him. "You know if we enter, we will be kissing before the door closes."

"Let's hurry," he teased.

"This is serious," she scolded, though with a smile.

He slipped his hands past her cloak and settled them on her waist. "I take kissing you very seriously." He eased her closer to the door as he took a quick taste of her lips. As soon as he did, he knew that was it. He wanted more.

She rested her hand to his chest. "We should—"

"Make up for the three days I've been gone when I should have been kissing you."

"That is—"

"Lots of kisses," he said, and connected with her lips again as his hand slipped from around her cloak to locate the door latch.

It clicked as her arms went around his neck. He had them inside and the door closed posthaste and they stood just beyond the door lost in a kiss.

Reeve wondered why each time he kissed her, she tasted more delicious. She had suddenly become nectar he couldn't do without. He slipped off her cloak, letting it fall to the floor, and his followed. His hand went to her backside and urged her closer against him, not a wise move, since he swelled thick and hard with passion.

She startled for a moment and then settled nicely against him, a perfect fit.

He ended the kiss with nibbles along her bottom lip, eager to taste the slim column of her neck and once again explore her bosoms. He loved her bosoms, so plump, soft, and delectable, and all his.

He warned himself to slow down, take his time, but he had missed her so much when he was away that he simply wanted to get lost in her.

The thought startled him, and he knew if he didn't slow down now, he wouldn't. He would have her in bed in no time, and they wouldn't be sleeping, not one wink all night.

He eased away from her and took a step back.

Her breathing was labored, her cheeks flushed red, and her eyes overflowing with passion. And damn if he didn't want to grab her and make love to her.

"We should go to the keep," she said, as if trying to convince them both.

"I don't want to," he said truthfully.

"Neither do I," she admitted, "but it is too soon for us to—"

"Make love?"

"Will that be what we're doing?"

He rubbed at his chin and walked around the table to distance himself from her, not trusting that his hands wouldn't reach out and do more than take hold of her. "I don't know."

"How could either of us know? We've only met."

"You have been wed how many times?" he asked.

"Once, though another died on our wedding day before vows were exchanged."

"Did you love either man?"

She nodded. "I loved Rory, the one I never got to wed."

"Did you feel for him when he kissed you what you feel for me when I kiss you?"

She stared at him a moment, and he pondered the

wisdom of his question. Did he truly want to know if she favored another man's kiss over his?

"Rory stirred me with kisses," she said softly, and her lavender-colored eyes deepened to a rich purple. "You consume me with yours."

He smiled, pleased, though he had to know more. "Did your body fit as well with him as it does with me?"

Again, she paused, and again, he worried over the answer.

"We fit well enough."

"That's not what I asked," he said. "Did you fit as well with him as you do with me?"

This time she didn't pause or hesitate. "I thought so at the time."

"And now?"

"Now I see that you and I fit as two parts that make a whole."

"Perfectly put," he said, glad that she felt as he did.

"When did you know you loved Rory?"

"When I first saw him," she said with a sad smile.

"You needed no time to be sure?"

"None. I knew there and then he was the man I wanted as my husband."

He suddenly felt a swell of envy for the dead man. "And what did you think when you first met me."

"I knew you were the man who would save me."

He was pleased with her answer and told himself to stop there. But he couldn't. He had to know.

"Do you miss him making love to you?"

Tara closed her eyes briefly, and when she opened them, tears lingered at the edges. "We never got to consummate our vows. Rory took a tumble before our wedding vows could be exchanged. He hit his head and died instantly."

"How horrible for you," he said. "I can't imagine the pain you must have suffered."

"My father gave me a little time to mourn and made arrangements for me to wed six months later."

"You didn't love this man?"

"I didn't know him," she said. "I met him on our wedding day. I did not find him appealing."

"Then consummating your vows must have been difficult."

"We never got the chance," Tara said. "When our vows were spoken, he turned to me, smiled, and collapsed dead at my feet."

"Good Lord, Tara, how terrible."

"More than you know," she admitted.

He scrunched his brow and rubbed his chin. "You have never been with a man?"

Tara threw her hands up in the air. "I tell you that the curse killed both men, and all you think about is that I've never coupled?"

"You haven't?" He smiled; he couldn't help it.

"What does that matter when I killed a man I loved and a husband. Do you truly want to take a chance and be number three?"

"No, I will be number one, the first and only man who makes love to you."

"I can't say that I don't want to make love with you," she said, reasoning that it was best to be honest with him in hopes that he would understand. "I find myself desiring you most all the time, but I fear if I surrender to my passion, that it may cause you to surrender your life."

"You desire me all the time?"

"Don't you hear what I'm saying?" she demanded.

"I heard everything you have said. Now hear me," he said adamantly. "Your curse will not hurt me and cannot hurt me. Not now, not ever. Besides, Rory suffered an unfortunate accident. Terrible as it was, things like that do happen. Your husband died like many I have seen, talking and laughing one moment, dead the next. It is the way of life. Death claims those it will, not a curse."

Tara shook her head. "You are a stubborn fool.

"No." He grinned. "I'm always right."

He was glad to see her smile, glad he could make her smile, and he wanted to keep making her smile.

"We agreed to take this slow," she reminded, her smile remaining.

"No, we agreed that probably would be difficult."

"But we'll try," she urged.

"I suppose we could," he said, walking around the table and reaching out for her.

She skirted away from him. "We need to."

"There's something I need," he said, inching closer.

She inched away. "What?"

"Another kiss." He stepped closer.

She moved around the table. "That might not be a good idea."

"Why?" he asked, continuing to follow her.

"Because I want more," she admitted in a lusty whisper.

He moved so fast that she yelped and jumped as he grabbed her and wrapped her in his arms. He held her tight and kissed her quick. "I can give you more."

"I know," she whispered. "That's what I'm afraid of."

He whispered close to her mouth before he claimed a kiss. "There's nothing to fear."

Again they feasted like two starved lovers, their hands at each other's garments and their passions ruling.

The loud toll of a bell sounded like a mighty roar of thunder, stunning them and splitting them apart so fast that it was as if a mighty hand had reached down from the heavens and ripped them away from each other.

"What is it?" Tara asked.

"We must go to the keep," he instructed, grabbing her cloak then his off the floor.

"Are we under attack?"

"No, the bell would still be tolling," Reeve explained. "One toll is a warning that an unexpected troop approaches the village."

He hurried her out the door. "You will wait in the keep with the women."

Tara grabbed hold tightly of his arm, forcing him to stop. "Promise me you will not die."

"I have all the reason in the world to make sure I live." He grinned. "I have yet to make love to you."

# Chapter 14

The snowfall had turned into a raging snowstorm, the keep barely visible the short distance away. Tara yanked her hood up and latched on tightly to Reeve's hand. He in turn tucked her against his side as he attempted to keep the bitter cold and swirling snow from pelting her.

Tara kept her head tucked into Reeve's shoulder as he struggled with the keep door, and when he finally got it open, the icy wind blew them inside.

"Are you all right?" he asked, tossing her hood back.

"Yes, I'm fine," she said, though her teeth chattered.

He walked her over to the hearth. "You're cold. You need to warm yourself."

"Don't worry about me," she said, and nodded toward his family, headed their way from various directions in the great hall.

Duncan had his arm around his wife and set her next to Tara.

"Are you feeling better?" Tara asked, though from Mercy's pale face, she could see that she wasn't, and Mercy confirmed it with a shake of her head.

"I don't want her alone," Duncan said. "Could you please stay with her?"

"Certainly," Tara said, and Mercy sent her a grateful glance.

"What's going on?" Reeve asked.

"All we know is that a sizeable troop heads this way," Bryce said. "The snowstorm has made it difficult to ascertain who exactly it is."

"So it could be the king's men?" Reeve asked.

"We've seen no sign of them close to the village," Carmag said.

"Then let's go greet them," Reeve suggested.

"Poor visibility prohibits that," Bryce said.

"The same rings true for them," Reeve reminded. "I say we at least go scout and see if we should prepare to greet or battle."

"You and Bryce are good at that," Carmag said to Reeve. "Go and see what you can find out."

Both men nodded and left the great hall.

Duncan and Carmag wandered away from the trestle table to talk in private, and Mara left after informing them that she better have cook have hot food ready when they returned.

Tara turned to Mercy. "Are you in pain?"

"No," Mercy said, shaking her head. "It's strange. I just suddenly feel very tired, as if something is weighing me down. I don't understand it at all."

Tara grew concerned immediately. Could her curse have returned, or had it never left?

"I do recall my mother complaining to me that when she carried me, I had so exhausted her that she spent most of her time in bed. I'm assuming it could be the same for me."

Hearing that made Tara feel somewhat better, for it did make sense.

Mara suddenly appeared with a pitcher of hot cider and a wooden bowl piled with chunks of bread and cheese.

Tara removed her cloak, the fire having warmed her, and laid it beside her. Mercy filled two tankards for them, and they sat side by side, their hands cupped around the tankards, neither saying a word.

Conversation wasn't necessary. Their thoughts were similar; they prayed that no battle would take place this day.

Mara appeared again, this time with her healing basket. "Just in case anyone should need tending."

Both women acknowledged her preparedness with a nod though, silently, they continued to worry.

It seemed like forever until a message arrived, the courier out of breath and appearing half-frozen. Mara shoved a tankard in his hands, and he cupped it gratefully and took several sips before he was finally able to talk.

"It's the Picts."

"Why are they here?" Duncan voiced everyone's thoughts. "We have no quarrel with them."

The courier shook his head, the tankard still at his lips.

"What is it, Robert?" Carmag asked the young man.

He continued shaking his head after lowering the tankard. "The Picts have Trey with them. He's badly injured."

"No!" Mara screamed, and Carmag had to stop her from running out of the keep in search of her son.

"He'll need you." Carmag needn't say any more.

Mara took a deep breath and started shouting orders. "I need fresh linens spread on a table and water kept hot."

The servants nodded and carried out her every command without question and with tears in their eyes.

Carmag and Duncan immediately left the keep to be ready to help with Trey.

Mara turned to Tara. "I saw the clothes you stitched for the babe. You are good with a needle. With Mercy not feeling well, you will help me."

Mercy tried to protest. "I can help. I want to help."

"I will not have you grow worse and need healing while I need my attention on my son," Mara said. "Tara will help."

Tara realized that Mercy felt useless, so she offered, "We will need someone to prepare bandages and keep the needles threaded if Trey should require stitching."

"She's right," Mara said. "You can start on that now."

The three women worked side by side, each glancing at the door time and time again until finally. . .

The door crashed opened.

Reeve carried Trey in his arms, and from his limp posture, Tara feared he was dead.

"Here, lay him here," Mara instructed, standing by the table dressed in clean linens.

Tara was right at Mara's side when she looked upon her son, and she almost gasped at the sight of so much blood. The woman didn't hesitate; her hands were at her son, peeling away the blood-soaked blanket, trying to get to his wounds.

Tara didn't wait for instructions. She relied on her instincts and recalled what the women in her clan would do when tending the wounded warriors. With a thick towel, she reached for the smaller of the cauldrons in the fireplace. Reeve was quickly at her side to help, and when she looked into his dark eyes, she could see that he pleaded with her to help save his brother.

For a moment, she froze. Could this be her fault?

She felt Reeve's strong grip on her arm. "Please," he whispered.

She could not fail him. She would not, and so she nodded.

Tara had never seen so many wounds on one person. She thought some were arrows, another could have been a sword, and another was too jagged to tell. She did not know how he would survive, for surely fever would set in and claim him. But like Mara, she wouldn't give up. This was Reeve's brother, and she would do all she could to save his life.

Mara had the men turn Trey on his side to examine him further, and Tara said what they both thought. "We need to stitch this wound right away."

Tara worked alongside Mara, stitching and stitching. She allowed herself no thought, only concentration. She worked on Trey as if he were a delicate silk garment that required tender and precise stitches. She hadn't realized that Mara had stopped and moved out of her way as she had made her way along Trey's body. Tara only knew that she had to apply her finest stitches to his wounds, and so she continued working diligently over him, hour after hour.

She didn't know when her back had begun to ache; she only knew when she had suddenly become aware of the dull, steady pain. She gave a stretch and then continued until she finally came to the jagged wound on his chest. She examined it carefully, the flesh torn so badly she wondered if it could be repaired. After considering what stitches would be best to apply, she decided on tight cross-stitch embroidery stitches.

She called to Mercy, "I need the embroidery needle."

It was in her hand before she finished stretching her back, and she never looked to see who had handed it to her, never saw the anxious faces that watched her intently; she was too busy finishing her piece of embroidery.

Thirty minutes later, she was finally done. She cleansed her bloody hands in the cauldron, the water having been refreshed time and time again. She then began dressing the wounds with the bandages stacked on the table next to where Trey lay. When she finished, she cleaned his face thoroughly of all blood, having left it for last since it had been the only place he hadn't suffered a wound.

He was handsome, but in a different way from Reeve. Reeve's features were sculpted whereas Trey's were more natural, as if the heavens had decided to grace him with fine features. He looked to be perhaps a couple of inches shorter than Reeve, and lean, his muscles naturally defined while Reeve's were chiseled.

She poured some warm water over his hair until the blood rinsed out, and his color, dark auburn, shone through. Once done, she straightened with a stretch and a hand to her lower back, her backache beyond bearable.

It was then she realized that complete silence surrounded her, and she turned.

Mara and Carmag stood side by side, his arm

around her. Bryce was next to them, and Duncan stood beside Mercy, where she sat at the table, and Reeve was not far from her side. Had he been the one handing her what she needed? Standing beside her through it all?

Mara stepped forward. "Your stitches proved far superior to mine, and when I saw that, I knew my son would be grateful if I allowed a skillfully elegant hand like yours to tend his wounds. I am forever grateful to you."

Tara was not accustomed to being thanked or her stitching skills being acknowledged, let alone praised. She didn't know how to respond, and so she stepped closer to Reeve.

His arm instantly went around her waist, and he fit her snug against him. "Thank you."

Tara looked from Reeve to all the others. She feared that they believed she saved him, an ironic twist. Usually, it was death she brought to people. "Trey's wounds have a long way to go before they or he heals."

Mara stepped forward. "True, but what you have done has given him a fighting chance."

She could only hope that she had. "He should be moved to his bedchamber before he wakes."

Her sons stepped forward before Mara even summoned them.

"Leave him to me. I'm the strongest," Reeve said.

No one argued, and Reeve carefully slipped his arms beneath his brother's prone body and lifted him. He cradled him like a precious babe, and his mother draped clean linen over Trey.

"Tara," Mara said, "come help me settle him."

Mara led the way, Reeve followed, and Tara trailed behind.

Tara noticed that there was a woman's touch to Trey's bedchamber when she entered. A trinket box lay on a slim table next to a cushioned red velvet chair. And over it was draped a pale blue shawl with braided fringe. White silk ribbons were tied in bows around the pewter candlesticks on top of the mantel, and the hint of roses permeated the air. Remnants, she supposed, of the woman he had loved and lost.

She watched Mara fight back tears as she helped settle Trey comfortably in bed, but she retained her composure. No doubt she knew that it was more important to doggedly help her son rather than succumb to defeat.

"We'll need to take shifts and watch for fever," Mara said, tucking the ends of the soft wool blanket under the mattress.

"I'll sit with him now."

They looked up to see Mercy, followed by Duncan, Bryce, and Carmag entering the room.

"And don't bother arguing with me," Mercy said. "Since I'm feeling tired, it is the best chore for me. I can rest and be useful at the same time."

"I agree," Duncan said, taking the armless, red velvet chair in front of the fire and placing it next to the bed.

"We can all take turns," Bryce offered, and everyone nodded in agreement.

"It is time to talk to the Picts and see if they know what happened to Trey," Carmag said, "and to offer them nourishment and shelter."

That spurred Mara into action. "Tara, we best get the hall cleaned and food set out."

Reeve stepped behind Tara and massaged the tops

of her shoulders. She nearly sunk against him, it felt so good.

"Tara is exhausted, mum," he said.

"When all is done, I can rest," Tara said.

Mara nodded. "Tara's right." And as she walked past the couple, she gave a slap to Reeve's arm. "She's a keeper. See that you don't lose her."

Everyone smiled for the first time since Trey had been brought home.

Reeve turned Tara around and moved his hands to massage around the back of her neck. "I will ease the soreness from your muscles later."

"Promise?" Tara asked with a sigh, his touch exquisite.

"Aye, it is," he said, and kissed her cheek.

Realizing his family was around, her eyes flew open, and her cheeks flushed.

"Only Mercy remains," Reeve said, "and her eyes are intent on Trey."

Tara's shoulders slumped in relief. "I must go help your mum."

He took her face in his hands. "Thank you for what you did tonight. Your hands and concentration never wavered. You remained focused and gave thought to nothing except my brother. Mum saw it too, and she was wise to step aside and leave Trey in your capable and skillful hands."

He stopped her protest with his lips. Though it was a brief kiss, it contented her, and she simply smiled when it was done.

"We must go," Tara reminded, and they did, though not before she checked on Trey one more time. She didn't like what she found. He already felt feverish to her.

# Chapter 15

Reeve listened along with Tara and his family as the Pict Roan explained how on their return home they had found Trey lying in a pool of blood.

"We thought he was dead," Roan said.

The four other Picts at the table ate as Roan spoke, though their eyes often darted around, alert and ready.

"Then I realized there was life left in the fallen warrior and that I knew him. He was the Highlander warrior who had come to our village to see about the injured woman Mercy, and so we brought him home."

"For which we are eternally grateful," Carmag acknowledged. "There were no signs of his attackers?"

"None that we could discern," Roan said.

"Had you seen any signs of another's presence in the area?" Bryce asked.

"The king's men have been seen more often than usual. Thieves have been more prevalent of late, and more clans seem to be uniting. The wind of change is decisively in the air."

"That it is," Carmag agreed. "And again we are grateful that you brought Trey home to us. And you are welcome to seek shelter and food here for as long as you need."

Roan nodded. "Thank you, but as soon as the storm lessens, we will depart. How is Trey doing?"

"Only time will tell," Carmag said.

Reeve knew as did his family that they would not know what happened to Trey until he woke and explained it all. And his father was right, only time would tell if Trey survived.

Mara saw that blankets were provided for the Picts to bed down in the great hall for the night. Afterwards, she had plans to sit through the night beside her son.

"You get some sleep," Mara ordered Tara. "In case you are needed."

"I'll look in on Trey first," Tara said.

"Then I'll see that she's settled in my bedchamber," Reeve said.

Mara sent him a scowl. "Make sure you're quick about it."

Reeve nodded, though his brothers both grinned at him.

Reeve wasn't surprised when Duncan followed him and Tara to Trey's bedchamber and went straight to his wife's side once there.

"I'm fine," Mercy assured him. "The rest has done me good, I'm hungry."

"Mum is coming to sit with Trey for the night," Duncan said. "I'll have food brought to our bedchamber."

Reeve watched relief spread across his brother's face when Mercy had acknowledged her hunger. He hadn't, when first learning of Duncan's love for Mercy, understood how he could have allowed a woman to possibly interfere with their mission. He had even reprimanded Duncan for it, reminding him that they had agreed that nothing, absolutely nothing, would stand in the way of them seeing the true king seated on the throne.

Now, however, he could relate to Duncan's conundrum. When love struck, it could not be ignored.

*Love.*

That word haunted him like a ghost who refused to accept death. Was he refusing to believe that he was falling in love? He glanced over at Tara, her attention fully focused on his brother. Her black ringlets drooped around her face, and her lovely eyes held a mixture of concern and exhaustion. He wanted to scoop her up and rush her to his room, tuck her in bed, and make certain she slept.

He almost laughed aloud. He had to be falling in love. He was more concerned with her well-being than he was with his own needs, with bedding her. But then he didn't simply want to bed her; that he could do with any willing woman. He wanted more with and from Tara, and he wanted to find out just what that *more* was.

Reeve saw that Tara's hand lingered on Trey's face, going from his forehead, to his cheeks, and she even rested her hand on his neck.

"Has he a fever?" Reeve asked worried.

"Does he?" Duncan asked with even more anxiety, Mercy clutching her husband's hand and her eyes filling with concern.

"He's as warm as he was before," Tara said.

"Is that good or bad?" Reeve asked.

"He's warm to the touch," Tara explained, "but he's grown no hotter, which is good. He'll need to be watched closely."

"Do not worry, I'll have my eyes on him all night," Mara said, entering the room, Carmag following her in.

Carmag walked over to Reeve, and whispered, "Bryce is talking with the Picts."

Reeve wasn't surprised that Bryce had remained with the Picts. He had a way of talking with people and finding out things that they hadn't realized they knew, or perhaps had not thought of to share.

"Duncan, feed your wife," Mara ordered. "Reeve, see to it that Tara rests."

Both men assured her they would, both knowing that it was her way of saying I love you both, but your brother needs me now.

Reeve and Duncan exchanged anxious glances when they watched their father go to his wife's side and place his hand on her shoulder. In turn, their mother rested her hand on top of his. They were drawing strength from each other, as they always did in time of crisis; only this time it was obvious that they were frightened. They feared losing their son.

Reeve and Duncan stopped outside the door once it was closed, their hands clutched firmly to their women.

"I wish there was more we could do," Reeve said.

"There is," Mercy said. "Pray."

Though worried about his brother, Reeve also worried about Tara. Once in his bedchamber, she let go of his hand and walked over to the fireplace, stretching, as if easing out the pain as her hand rubbed at her lower back.

He came up behind her, his hand gently moving hers aside, his fingers rubbing where hers had been. He felt the tautness in her muscles, no doubt from the hours she had spent bent over Trey stitching his wounds. He kneaded the stiff muscles, and she sighed.

"That feels so good."

"Lie on the bed, and I'll make you feel even better."

She turned in haste, her tired eyes forced wide.

Normally he would have grinned and teased, but she didn't need that now from him. She needed reassurance that he simply wanted to tend her.

"My only thought is to rid you of this pain," he said.

Her shoulders slumped, along with her sigh of relief, and she eagerly went to the bed.

He knew it would be easier without the interference of her clothes. Besides she would sleep better as well, but he wasn't sure if she would agree. And he wasn't sure if it was wise.

He asked anyway. "You should get out of those clothes. You'll rest better."

She turned. "That is true. And since you are honorable, and I trust you and your word, I shall disrobe."

Reeve groaned silently. He would have no choice but to be respectful and true to his word, no matter how hard. And he was already hard as it was.

"Turn around," she said.

Reeve did with great reluctance, but he had given his word, and he would keep it. He heard her slip her garments off, and his mind couldn't help but take flight. Her full breasts, her slim waist, her wide curvy hips painted irresistible images, and he ached to see her beauty.

He heard the creak of the bed, and he took a deep breath, knowing what he was about to do wouldn't be easy. He warned himself against being selfish and kept that warning strong when she told him that she was ready.

He was ready as well, though not in the same sense, and he turned around with all the courage and strength of a mighty Highlander warrior.

He almost lost it when he saw her lying on her stomach, her arms wrapped around the pillow her head rested on. She was naked down to her lower back, the blanket serving as a boundary he was not to go beyond. Her body was exquisite, just the right curves and mounds that he favored.

*Stop!*

His silent reprimand rang loudly in his head, and he was glad for the warning. He pushed the dangerous thoughts aside and walked over to her. She had left room for him to sit beside her, and he did. He focused on what he needed to do, and his hands went directly to her lower back.

He began kneading from the center out, his hands following the natural, seductive curve of her back. He would have lingered to admire her beauty, but her stubborn muscles captured his attention, and he worked diligently on them. Pressing and kneading, working the obstinate flesh until . . .

She groaned, and he stopped. "Am I hurting you?"

"Don't stop," she whispered. "It feels good."

Damn but he wished she was saying that for a far different reason.

*Stop!*

The warning rang again, and he reminded himself to obey it. He returned his attention to the stubborn muscles and worked even more diligently, attacking them as if they were the enemy. He used his thumb on the most troublesome spots, which always forced a groan from her.

He continued to keep his wits about him, particularly when he hit a sensitive spot that caused her backside to rise and a moan to escape. Finally, to save his own sanity, he shifted his attention to her upper back, which produced a deeper groan but at least no body movement.

"You are truly my hero," she murmured, when he eased the aches from along the tops of her shoulders.

He heard the fatigue in her voice, and he knew that she would soon be asleep. And that was good; she needed rest though he didn't want to stop touching her just yet. He loved the feel of her silky-soft skin. It was like running his fingers over velvet.

He felt when sleep finally claimed her, her body going limp, and with a gentle brush of his hand down along her back, he took hold of the blanket and pulled it up, covering her. He gave her a quick peck on the cheek, not trusting himself to linger, and hurried out of the room.

His hand went to the wall just outside the door for support, and he lowered his head, taking a deep breath.

"I suffered the same once," Duncan said walking toward him.

"And you're not grinning?"

Duncan rested his hand on his brother's back. "Torture is nothing to grin over."

They both laughed, and Reeve shook his head. "I don't know how you remained honorable being shackled to Mercy as long as you were."

"It wasn't easy, but then love never is."

"There you go mentioning love again," Reeve said.

"It's the only thing that makes sense when nothing makes sense."

"Why does that suddenly sound sensible to me?"

"Because you're falling in love?" This time Duncan grinned.

Reeve shook his head again. "How is Mercy?

"Changing the subject won't help."

"Maybe, but I need to."

Duncan kept grinning as he nodded. "My wife wants more food."

"Sounds like she's doing better."

"I believe she is."

"I thought I'd go sit with mum for a while," Reeve said.

"I was going to stop by once Mercy fell asleep."

"Has Bryce found out anything more?" Reeve asked.

"He's still talking with the Picts."

"It's going to be a long night," Reeve said.

Reeve sat beside his mother on a small foot bench. He had thought it might not hold his weight, and so he sat down on it with apprehension, but it held. He reached out to take his mother's hand, draped over the arm of her chair.

She took strong hold of it, as if she needed an anchor to hold her firm.

"You have a good woman. Don't lose her," Mara said.

"It's not long that I've known her," Reeve said.

"That doesn't matter. It's how you feel about her that counts."

"I'm learning how I feel."

"That is the exciting part about love," Mara said. "You learn as you go, and yet love has already grabbed hold. It's keeping that hold that matters."

"You and Da have kept hold of love."

"I sometimes wonder how," Mara said, shaking her head. "I can be difficult at times."

"Truly?" Reeve asked with a grin.

Mara slapped his arm with her free hand while clinging tightly with her other. "Go on with you now, teasing your poor mum like that."

"Da always looks at you with love, even when you're angry," Reeve said earnestly.

"His love is what often stills my anger," Mara admitted.

"You make a good pair."

"We always have. I knew when I was young that he would be mine, and I laid claim to him," Mara said proudly.

"Never let anyone stand in your way, did you?"

"Not a one," Mara said proudly. "You do whatever it takes."

"I'll remember that."

"See that you do, my son," Mara said with a smile.

Reeve suddenly felt guilty about keeping the truth about Tara from his mother. He wondered if it would have been better to tell her. He believed that she would fight to help Tara rather than condemn her. His mum was a good ally and a formidable enemy. She fought for not only what she believed, but for whom she loved. She would fight the devil himself for those she loved, and he had no doubt she would win.

"You should go get some rest," Mara said. "You may be needed later."

"I'll sit with you a while yet," he said, not wanting to leave her alone.

"You must be tired. You returned home early this morning."

"How did you know when I arrived?"

She smiled, and he was glad to see it. "There isn't much that goes on around here that I don't know about."

"I should have remembered that," Reeve said. "There wasn't much that my brothers and I could do that you weren't aware of."

"There still isn't," Mara said with a grin.

Trey groaned, grabbing their attention, and Mara let go of Reeve's hand and sprang out of the chair.

"No! No!" Trey groaned and began thrashing around in the bed.

"We need to hold him down or he may break open his stitching," Mara said, her hands trying to avoid her son's flaying hands as she sought to help him.

Reeve went to his brother's side and as soon as he put his hands on him, he said, "He burns with fever."

# Chapter 16

Tara woke, springing up in bed, a sense of dread causing gooseflesh to rise along her arms and a tightness to settle in her stomach. She glanced around the room and saw that she was alone. She dropped back on the pillow, and memories of Reeve's hands easing away her aches rushed over her.

Lord, his touch had felt so very good, and she hadn't been the least worried that he would take advantage of the situation. He was a man she could trust. It was she, herself, she couldn't trust. The truth of it was that she hadn't wanted him to stop; she wished that it had turned more intimate between them. Even though fatigued, her body had tingled with desire for him and relieved she had been to have exhaustion claim her before she had done something unwise.

She would have liked to have lingered in the luscious memories, but gooseflesh slowly continued to claim every bit of flesh. She grew uneasy and she realized something was wrong, very wrong. And as much as she wished to simply linger in bed with thoughts of Reeve, she jumped up and quickly got dressed. She twisted her hair up and pinned it in haste, several black ringlets falling willfully loose.

She slipped her boots on, never noticing that the swelling had all but disappeared. The anxiousness had now turned to extreme worry, and she hurried to the door and ran, knowing exactly where she was needed.

Tara burst through the door of Trey's bedchamber and was horrified at the scene. Reeve and Mara were fighting to keep his brother in the bed.

"He's wild with fever," Mara said.

To the bewilderment of them both, she ran from the room. She all but flew down the stairs, slipping on a step and twisting her injured ankle. Pain shot through it, but she ignored it, grimacing while she kept moving.

Once in the great hall, she called out to Bryce, sitting with Roan by the hearth, "Trey needs you."

He sprang off the bench. "Where do you go?"

Tara grabbed two buckets near the hearth. "To get snow to bring your brother's fever down."

The wind blew furiously, snow continuing to pelt the ground. Tara shivered but paid no heed to the cold. She hadn't wasted time to grab her cloak. She didn't have time, and with two bucketfuls of snow, she entered the keep and ran up the stairs.

She refused to acknowledge the throbbing pain in her ankle. She was intent on her mission and wouldn't let anything stand in her way.

When she entered Trey's bedchamber, she went directly to the bed, dropped one bucket to the floor, and emptied the other on top of Trey. She picked up the full one after discarding the other and emptied that on him as well.

She hadn't realized that Trey had calmed until she began spreading the snow evenly over him. Mara's hands soon joined hers, and they had him covered in snow in no time. Tara then took a handful and rubbed it over his face.

Trey moaned though it was more a sigh of relief, as if his suffering had been relieved.

Mara grabbed at her arm when she was done. "How did you know?"

Tara shook her head. "I woke feeling something was wrong and came here."

"And the snow?"

"I watched the women in our clan do it. Some they saved; some they didn't."

"Then he has a chance," Mara said firmly.

"We'll need to get him dry when the snow melts and be ready to use more if necessary," Tara explained.

"Whatever it takes," Mara said.

It wasn't until hours later, with them all working together to bring his fever down and settle him comfortably in a dry bed, that Trey finally lay resting, and for Mara to notice Tara limping.

"Your ankle," Mara said, and everyone turned to stare at Tara.

"I gave it a twist on the stairs," Tara admitted.

"You've given enough," Mara said. "It is time for you to rest."

Reeve went to her side, but she limped away from him. "You may need me."

"Trey's fever is down, and he rests comfortably thanks to you," Mara said. "It is now time for you to take care in case you are needed again."

Reeve scooped her up then, and she didn't protest. She was bone-tired, and her ankle was sore though not unbearably so. She rested her head on his shoulder as he carried her out of the room and down to their bedchamber.

*Their bedchamber?*

Is that how she thought of it? As *theirs*?

More and more, she was thinking of them as one; but then, they fit as one. So why not be one?

She would have shaken her head if she wasn't so tired, which made everything all the more confusing. Life had changed so suddenly and drastically that she barely had time to comprehend it all or believe it. She still wondered if she was dreaming, and she would awaken to the horrible life she had lived before.

"I intend to see that you rest," Reeve whispered, and kissed the top of her head.

She wondered how he planned on doing that, and she soon found out.

Reeve sat her on the bed, removed her boots, and ordered her to disrobe, turning his back to give her privacy.

She didn't argue. She was tired, and her garments were damp from the snow. Once done, she crawled under the covers. Every bit of her ached from top to bottom and in between.

"I'm done," she said, and meant it.

Reeve slipped off his boots, loosened the section of his plaid that crossed over his chest, and slipped his black shirt off. He then grabbed another blanket from the chest at the end of the bed and threw it over the blanket that covered Tara and crawled beneath it.

He wrapped her in his arms, kissing her cheek. "Now I know that you will stay put."

"Do not worry," she said with a smile. "I am too comfortable in your arms to go anywhere."

And in no time they were both asleep.

* * *

It seemed that they had just fallen asleep when the door crashed open.

"We need you, Reeve," Bryce shouted, and left.

Reeve was out of bed running in nothing more than his plaid.

Tara rushed to dress and hurried after him, not bothering with her boots.

Trey was once again thrashing about.

Tara felt his head. He was burning up again. "We need more ice." She didn't wait for anyone to respond. She grabbed the buckets and raced down the stairs and outside.

Mara followed. "He was doing well."

"Fever is unpredictable. Up one moment, down the next," Tara said.

Once again, the two women worked over Trey, and this time when they were done, Tara refused to leave his side.

"No!" she said adamantly, and plopped down in the chair beside the bed. "I will remain right here."

No one argued with her.

Mara looked stricken, as if she had failed her son.

"I could use a brew," Tara said, knowing that giving Mara something to do would help. It was the way she had survived many times when upset. She got busy, so no thoughts could intrude, and then be so tired that sleep claimed her before any musings could.

"I'll get you a soothing one," Mara said.

"Bring one for yourself," Tara said, knowing Mara needed to remember that she was not only needed but wanted here. Tara had been starved for both for so long she had almost forgotten how it felt to be needed and wanted. And she almost cried with the joy of knowing it again.

Mara nodded.

"You know how to handle my wife," Carmag said. "I am grateful not only for that, but for all you do for my son."

Gratitude was another thing that had become so very unfamiliar to her, and so she was uncomfortable with it. She reached out to Reeve, standing beside her, for support.

His hand closed around hers. "Tara has a good heart."

"A generous one," Bryce added.

"A loving one," Duncan said.

A smile peeked through Tara's blush. "Sunrise is not far off; you should all get some sleep. If you are needed, Reeve will come for you."

She squeezed his hand tight.

"I'll be right here," Reeve said, easing his brothers' worries.

They left, albeit reluctantly, their father leaving as well, with intentions of helping his wife.

"Are you all right?" Reeve asked, hunching down in front of her.

"I'll get more rest being here than in your bedchamber."

"I have to agree, though I'd rather not." He grinned.

"Neither would I," she whispered, and kissed him lightly.

"Now you're tormenting me."

"You tormented—no, you tortured me," she said with a soft laugh.

"How so?"

Tara decided to be honest. After all, this had to be nothing but a dream, a fantasy for sure. Good things simply did not happen to her. "Your hands—" She paused, not sure how to say it and then simply plunged ahead. "They felt so very good and had me wanting so much more."

"Now you tell me."

"But I can," Tara said softly, "for none of this is real."

Reeve looked at her strangely, and his hand rested on her cheek. "It is all real, my love."

"No." She shook her head. "I will wake, and you will be gone."

Reeve shook his head. "No, I will not. I am here with you, and here I will stay."

"How I wish," Tara said softly.

"Then your wish will come true."

Tara yawned and rested her head back against the chair, and repeated, "How I wish."

Reeve covered Tara with a blanket just as Mara and Carmag entered the room.

"She sleeps," Reeve said.

"She needs it," Mara said, and handed the hot brew to her son.

Reeve took it and sipped it gratefully.

"It's been a long night," Carmag said. "And it has yet to end."

Those words proved true since Trey's fever climbed again, and Mara and Tara were quick to react. Though this time Reeve went and fetched the buckets of snow.

By sunrise, Trey was resting, but Tara didn't like the look of one wound, and she feared that poison had already set in. As the day went on and the fever continued to rise and fall and Trey remained in slumber, she feared the worst.

"We've done all we can," Tara said to Mara, as they watched over Trey.

Mara brushed her son's auburn hair back away from his face. "I won't let him die. There must be something else we can do."

"There might be," Mercy said from the open door.

"Tell me," Mara was quick to demand.

Tara was pleased to see that Mercy looked much better, her cheeks full with color as she approached them.

"Bliss could possibly help," Mercy said. "She is a Pict woman who helped heal me when I was shackled to Duncan after I had been struck with an arrow."

"She is a healer?" Mara asked anxiously.

"As Bliss once explained to me, she is not a healer and yet she heals."

"She is a witch?" Mara asked nervously.

"No," Mercy said, shaking her head. "She is a remarkable woman. You would like her."

"It matters not," Mara said obstinately. "If she can help my son, then she is welcome here."

"I'll go ask Roan if he can bring Bliss here," Mercy suggested.

"I'll go with you," Mara said, and looked to Tara.

"Go," Tara urged.

"I won't be long," Mara assured, and hurried out with Mercy.

Reeve entered shortly after the two women left. He was shaking his head. "I could barely understand mum, something about getting a witch to help Trey?"

"No, a healer of sorts," Tara clarified.

"If she thinks it will help," Reeve said. "Duncan and Mercy will be replacing you soon, so that you can join me in a meal."

Tara smiled and was ready to tell him she was starving when she looked to Trey first and saw his eyes open wide.

"Reeve," she said, standing and waving him to the bed.

Once he saw his brother's eyes open, he rushed to his side. "I'm here, Trey. You're safe."

Trey's eyes darted past Reeve to settle on Tara. They spread wide, and he raised his hand and pointed his finger at her and in a bare whisper before once again closing his eyes, he said, "Death."

Tara collapsed to the chair, her skin rising in gooseflesh.

"He doesn't know what he says," Reeve said.

But Tara wondered if perhaps he had learned something about her, perhaps he had known she was a death bride and in his pain tried to warn his family.

"He doesn't know what he says," Reeve insisted again.

They had no time to argue. Mercy appeared at the door.

"Hurry," she said breathless. "Willow has brought Jacob. He is seriously ill."

Tara froze, being plunged back into her nightmare. Death once again stalked those around her.

Reeve grabbed her arm. "Mercy will stay with Trey. Come with me. Willow may need you."

Tara didn't yank her arm free until they left the room and were near the stairs. "I cannot touch anyone anymore."

"What do you mean?"

"This is my fault."

"That's nonsense," Reeve said.

"No, the curse is real, and it will only get worse. You must believe me," she begged.

Reeve grabbed her arm tightly. "Enough. We don't even know what happened to Jacob and Willow. And Trey is crazy from fever. Keep your wits about you. You are needed."

Tara wanted to believe him, but she felt she would do more harm than good. "You heard your brother, I am death."

Reeve yanked her up against him. "Am I ill? Has anything happened to me?"

Tara shook her head. "Don't—"

"Don't point out the truth?" Reeve argued. "Trey does not know you—" He held up his hand when she tried to interrupt. "He speaks senselessly from fever. And Jacob is an old man. You had nothing to do with either of their misfortunes."

"You don't know that."

"I do," Reeve insisted. "You are a good woman with a good heart. No curse can befall goodness."

"Don't be foolish," Tara warned. "I once was, and it cost me dearly."

"You were vulnerable and believed foolish mumblings."

"No, you don't understand—"

"I do understand," Reeve said. "Let the fear go, or it will keep you forever cursed."

He didn't give Tara a chance. He took hold of her hand and rushed her down the stairs and into the great room.

Everyone was around a table, and Tara heard someone sobbing. Her heart lurched in her chest, and she feared, even though Reeve had warned her against it. She knew what was happening, someone had died, and Trey could very well follow.

Reeve pushed past those around the table, and when Willow saw him, she fell into his arms.

"He's dead. Jacob is dead."

Reeve held her, and Tara looked at Jacob, who lay on the table. The same table where Trey had lain, and she had fought to save his life.

"What happened?" Reeve asked.

Willow moved away from him, wiping the tears from her eyes. "The old fool wanted to hunt even though he wasn't feeling well. I refused to let him go alone. On our return home, we heard raucous laughter, and so approached the farm cautiously."

She stopped and walked over to Jacob, resting her hand on his shoulder. "The soldiers had returned."

Tara saw that Reeve's hands tightened in fists at his sides. No doubt he blamed himself for the soldiers' return.

Willow continued. "Though I often called the old man a fool, he wasn't one. He hurried me away— "She shook her head. "He was forever protecting me." She wiped away the tears that fell. "He told me it was time we came here, and so we began the long walk." She grew quiet.

Mara went to her and slipped her arm around her shoulder.

Willow looked up at her with tearful eyes. "He spoke to me as if he knew death was imminent. He told me I was to stay here at the village, where I would be safe." She glanced down at Jacob again with sorrowful eyes. "He forced himself to live until he knew I was here and safe. He had promised his son that he would take care of me, let no harm befall me, and he did; the old fool kept his promise."

Willow broke down in tears, clinging to Mara. The older woman's arms wrapped around her, offering comfort.

"Jacob was a good man," Carmag said. "He will be missed."

Tara stood stock-still, listening to the chorus of accolades for the old man that circled the room, each more profound than the last. And try as she might, she could not shake the thought that she was responsible for Jacob's death. And then there was Trey.

An icy shudder racked her body and the hand of fear suddenly gripped her hard and strong. She dreaded the overwhelming feeling that something bad was about to happen again.

The door burst open, and Cora, the basket weaver, hurried in. "Please help me. Rand is lost in the storm, and Alida went in search of him."

# Chapter 17

Reeve couldn't reach Tara before she fled the keep. He was grateful that she had the sense to grab her fur-lined cloak off the peg as she went. He knew she blamed herself for everything that was happening, and it would do him little good to say otherwise. The best thing he could do was let her seek the solitude she probably believed necessary while he helped find the children.

As for Jacob, he was an old man, older than most, and he had lived his life as he pleased and died the same way. Reeve was angry that the soldiers had returned to torment the old man, and he wondered if they were the ones who had attacked Trey, a cowardly bunch for sure. If so, he and his brothers would indeed see that they paid for their evil deeds.

None of what happened here was due to any curse. He didn't know how he was going to convince Tara of that, but he was damn well going to make her see reason.

He and his brothers were quick to organize men. Duncan would remain at the keep to help with Trey. Carmag would see to Jacob's body being stored until burial, after the ground thawed, and Reeve and Bryce would lead a group of warriors in search of the children.

Bailey, Kate's husband, was fast to volunteer since he had come upon one of Rand's hiding spots once before. Reeve wished there were time to go comfort Tara, but time was of the essence for the children. They wouldn't be able to last long in the snow. Even though the snowstorm had abated somewhat, snow was still falling, and the air was decidedly crisp.

Mara took charge of Willow, and Mercy went to stay with Trey. Duncan would join her as soon as he helped Carmag take care of Jacob.

Reeve did wonder over Trey's remark about Tara. Why would he point to her and say death? Had it been the fever talking, or had he learned something? Reeve didn't know what to think, and he wondered what Trey would say when he woke and turned clearheaded.

He refused to think anything other than that Trey would grow strong and survive. He had survived the loss of the woman he had loved beyond measure though it was obvious to Reeve and the others that Trey had never fully accepted her death, and it worried them.

It had been a year since Trey had lost Leora, and he continued to mourn her. And he continually blamed himself for her death. No one could convince him otherwise, and the family had stopped trying, knowing that only time would heal his suffering.

Would Trey wish to join his beloved? Would he surrender to death, feeling it was less painful than life? Reeve could only pray that such was not the case.

"Ready?" Bryce asked, handing him a torch as they made ready to leave.

"Ready and hopeful," Reeve said, thinking not only of the children but Tara as well.

Tara refused to feel helpless. She would not let this curse claim innocent children. She hurried to her cottage, relieved that the snowstorm had lost its force though snow continued to fall. At least visibility was better, and she found her way home without difficulty. Before she opened the door, she realized that she had walked the entire way, short as it was, barefooted. Annoyed at herself, she entered her cottage. There was no point in returning for her boots until she was dressed and ready to join the search.

She found her extra pair of wool stockings, which she had no intentions of putting on until she had her boots. She topped her linen blouse with a wool one and wrapped a wool scarf around her head and folded a blanket over her arm. Once done, she returned to the keep and found it nearly deserted.

She made a quick trip to Reeve's bedchamber and slipped her stockings on and then her boots, ignoring the slight swelling that remained but wasn't severe enough to prevent her from getting her boot on.

She hurried out of the room and straight to Trey's to check on him before she left.

Mercy was there alone, and she smiled when Tara entered.

"You go to find the children?" Mercy asked.

"I must," Tara said.

Mercy nodded. "If I could, I would join you."

"You are needed here."

"I know," Mercy said, "but let me tell you some of the places Rand likes to play and, in particular, hide."

Tara listened, nodded, and went to leave. She stopped suddenly, and turned. "What of Bliss?"

"Roan was wise enough to send one of his men to fetch her once they had found Trey," Mercy said, and shook her head. "Roan felt that Trey would not survive and hoped that perhaps Bliss could work a miracle."

"Why would Roan believe that?'

"Bliss has had success in healing where others have not."

Tara nodded and left, wondering if Bliss had any luck with removing curses.

Hours later, the men returned, unsuccessful. They had no plans of stopping their search, they simply needed nourishment and warmth. Reeve had detoured to Tara's cottage, and when he didn't find her there, he went to the keep.

He downed a tankard of hot cider before going to look for her, assuming she was tending Trey, but Mercy was the only one there.

"Have you seen Tara?" he asked, entering and looking to see how his brother was doing. Trey appeared to sleep contentedly, and he was barely warm to the touch, a great relief to Reeve.

He realized that Mercy hadn't answered and he glanced over at her and repeated the question. "Have you seen Tara?'

Duncan entered as he asked, and when Mercy again hesitated, he said, "Did you not hear Reeve?"

"I did," she admitted with a nod. "But I fear he will not like hearing what I know."

Reeve stood tall and alert. "Where is she?"

This time Mercy's answer came quick. "She went to look for the children."

Reeve was out the door so fast that the flames in the fireplace flickered as if a strong wind had brushed past them.

"Didn't you try to stop her?" Duncan asked

Mercy smiled. "Do you truly believe you can stop a woman intent on a mission?"

Duncan hunched down in front of her and rested his large hand lovingly over her rounded stomach. "I couldn't stop you."

"Then you have your answer."

Trey stirred then, and they both turned their attention to him.

They both were shocked when Trey's eyes sprung open.

"It's Duncan, Trey," he said, grabbing hold of his flaying hand. "You're safe."

"De—"Trey choked trying to speak.

Mercy was quick to get him water, and he took it like a man dying of thirst.

Trey tried again, but Duncan warned against it. "Don't speak. There's time for that later. You need to save your strength."

Trey groaned and closed his eyes, sleep once again claiming him.

Tara was lost, but at least she had found the children. They had been huddled against a towering pine in the opposite direction from where everyone had been searching. She didn't know what had made her turn that way, but at the last moment she had the overpowering urge to do just that, and so she had followed the urging and found them.

Unfortunately, the snow had begun falling heavier again, and she had lost her way home. She had wrapped the scarf she wore around Alida's head and then wrapped her shivering body in the blanket she had brought along. She carried Rand in her arms, her fur-lined cloak wrapped around them both. His little body shivered until her body heat and the warmth of the cloak finally penetrated his bone-aching chill, and he remained snuggled comfortably against her.

"There!" Alida shouted, pointing off to the right. "There's the path."

After what seemed like hours, though wasn't, of senseless wandering, Tara tightened her hold on Alida's hand, and said, "Homeward bound."

Reeve was furious when night was near to falling, and they hadn't found Tara or the children. They had no choice but to return to the keep. All he could think about was Tara and those children out in the freezing cold all night. They would be lucky to survive, and that had his heart beating wildly, his stomach clenching, and his anger mounting.

"They're found. The children have been found." Cries of joy rang in the air as Reeve and the men entered the village, and for a moment, he was relieved; that was until he realized no one had mentioned Tara.

He stomped up the steps to the keep and entered with a scowl on his face and an ache in his heart.

He heard her laughter before he saw her, and his heart soared with relief. Tara sat at the table in front of the hearth with the children, their parents and most of his family all smiling. Willow had even joined them, and she wore a smile as well. Everyone was obviously relieved and happy the children had been found.

However, while relieved, he was far from happy. Tara had caused fear to be his constant companion over the last few hours, and his heart to ache unbearably with the thought of losing her.

He marched over to the table, joyous smiles greeting him. He reached out so fast that he caused some to startle with gasps and others to jump out of his way. Their shocking reactions didn't stop him, he grabbed hold of Tara and in one swoop he swung her over his shoulder and stomped out of the hall and up the stairs to his bedchamber.

"Whatever is the matter with you?" she asked when he dropped her to her feet in the middle of his room and walked back to shut the door.

His hand rested on the latch for a moment before he turned and took a deep breath trying to calm his soaring anger. It didn't work. He turned and advanced on her. And when she scurried back away from him, eyes wide, hand out trying to ward him off, he knew his face burnt with a dark fury.

"I know I should not have gone out on my own," she said hurriedly, trying to explain.

He stopped inches from her and ran his hand frantically through his long dark hair. "Can you even imagine the torment you put me through?"

"I didn't think."

"A poor excuse," he said, pinning his nose to hers. "I thought you trusted me."

"I do. It's me I don't trust. I felt responsible." She shook her head. "So many bad things have happened of late and—"

"You assumed they were your fault."

"Didn't you?" she asked.

"Not for one moment," he said bluntly.

"Not a sliver of doubt?"

"No," he said firmly, and took a step away from her. "What is happening is part of life, not due to a curse."

"You may believe that"—she thumped her chest—"but I don't."

He wanted to cringe at his own selfishness. In his fear of losing her, he hadn't given enough thought to what had driven her to run blindly into a snowstorm in search of the children. One terrible thing on top of another had been happening, and each one only added to her fear that it was her fault.

He calmed. His concern now more for her fears than his own. "You should have come and talked with me. I am here for you as I believe you are for me, or haven't you noticed what a vital part we have become of each other?"

"I'm afraid to acknowledge it," she admitted.

"Even now, after you've saved the children, while endangering your life and making me insane with fear of losing you?"

"You truly felt insane with fear?" she asked softly.

"I'm still quaking."

"Now you tease," she said. "You never quake. You are bold, brash, and brave."

"Aye, I am all that, though when it comes to you, I am weak with the need of you and—I think I am in love with you."

Her violet eyes widened. "Think?"

He nodded. "I believe it is love since I don't know how to define what I am feeling for you. I thought I would go mad not being able to find you. I wanted to roar with anger. Punch something, anything. But most of all, I wanted you safe in my arms, where you belong."

He held his hand out to her, waiting for her to come to him and admit the same.

She turned away, and he felt a stab to his heart as if a sword had been thrust through it.

"I fear if we love—"

He rushed over to her, grabbed her around the waist, and swung her around to face him. "Let love rule instead of fear."

"I lost when I allowed myself to love, and I don't want—" She shook her head, her eyes turning sad, the memories hurt. "I couldn't bear losing you."

"You won't," he insisted.

"Not if we remain *only* friends."

He laughed loudly. "That's not going to happen."

"Loving me will only cause you pain," she pleaded.

"Not loving you would be like a living death to me."

Tears pooled in her eyes.

"Tell me you don't feel some undeniable tug between us. Tell me that you aren't eager to see me. Tell me that you don't ache when we're apart. Tell me that you don't love me."

She stared at him, and as a single tear ran down her cheek, she said, "I can't."

Again he offered her his hand, and this time she took it.

He wrapped her in his arms and brought his lips down on hers. It didn't start out as a hungry kiss. It was simply a coming together of the obvious, the undeniable, the truth. But the need to draw closer grew and with it hungry passionate love.

The kiss turned into an erotic mating of tongues until Reeve broke away and rested his brow to hers.

Breathless, he said, "If we keep going like this I will not be able to stop from making love to you. Already I swell with the want of you. So tell me stay or go; the choice is yours."

# Chapter 18

Tara felt frozen with fear yet burned with desire. She wanted so very badly to surrender to passion, but what if she did, and then . . .

"Let love rule, not fear," he reminded with a whisper.

Wasn't she doing just that? Wasn't she thinking how she felt the same as he did, that she believed she loved him? And if she did, did she love him enough to walk away so that he might live?

"Don't do this," Reeve pleaded. "Forget everything but you and me."

"That is the only thing I am thinking about," she said.

With his two hands, he cupped her face. "Good. Then how do you feel at this moment?"

"I worry—"

"No," he argued. "How does your *body* feel?"

She couldn't help but smile. "It tingles all over."

"What else?" he asked.

Her cheeks heated and bloomed bright red in his hands.

He didn't laugh or tease her about her obvious reaction. He simply encouraged her. "Tell me."

"I truthfully don't know how to explain it."

"Close your eyes," he whispered, "*and feel.*"

His hands left her face and drifted faintly down along her body, stopping here and there to stroke more intimately, the crook of her neck, the dip in her blouse, and settled on her hard nipples.

She shuddered and sighed.

"Tell me," he urged again.

"I feel a pleasurable ache that needs tending. It steals the breath, beats at the heart, and tortures the body in the most exquisite way."

His hand roamed down along her waist, gravitating slowly over her hips and nestling firmly between her legs.

"Oh!" She lurched up, only to settle more intimately in his hand.

"Now tell me."

She stumbled for words, for a breath, for sound reasoning. "I can't think."

He rested his cheek against hers and whispered in her ear, "Don't. *Just feel*!"

His hand began to move against her skirt, igniting a small pulse that quickly turned to a throb and made her grow wet.

Her head tipped back as she moaned with sheer pleasure.

His lips settled on her exposed neck, and he was soon nipping and nibbling at the sensitive skin. It fueled her already raging passion. And she thought she would go mad, simply insane, if he did not douse the fire that burned inside her.

"Feel," he urged once more, and took her hand and slipped it beneath his plaid.

She almost yelped when she felt the thick size of

him though it didn't take long for her to realize that she liked the *feel* of him, smooth and soft like fine silk. Enjoying the strength of him in her hand, she explored, stroking him and realizing with delight that the tip of him was wet and ready just like her.

"You must tell me now," he urged. "Go or stay. I can wait no longer."

Reason had fled when desire had fully claimed her, and so without hesitation, she said, "Stay."

He groaned and reluctantly moved her hand off him then in a flash scooped her up in his arms and carried her to the bed, his mouth hungry on hers.

The pounding at the door startled them both, and a steady stream of oaths spewed from Reeve's mouth before he shouted out, "Who's there?"

"Mum. I need Tara."

Mara's anxious voice had them splitting apart in seconds. Tara smoothed her rumpled garments and hurried toward the door. Reeve lingered behind a moment, and once at the door, Tara turned and saw that he hadn't moved.

"I'll go. You stay," she said, seeing that he was trying to regain his composure.

"That's not what I wanted to hear this night."

"There's always later."

His head shot up. "Promise."

"I promise"–she hesitated—"that soon we'll finish what we started."

"But not tonight?"

"I don't know what the night will bring with your brother," she said.

He shook his head and hurried to her side. "I think of myself when I should be thinking of Trey. Let's go."

He opened the door, and they found Mara pacing in front of it.

"His fever has gone up, and it looks as if one of his wounds pulled open from his earlier struggles."

"I'm sure it can be mended," Tara said. "Let's have a look."

Tara changed her mind when she saw the ripped stitches. The area was already red and swollen, and she feared poison had settled in. She much preferred to leave the stitches as they were, hoping the opening, though small, provided an avenue of escape for the poison that could spread all too fast.

An herb mixture had been kept brewing and fed to Trey when possible, and Tara decided to use an herb mixture that the women of her clan had used with some success on his wounds.

She worked a good many hours beside Mara, having decided it would be wise to keep Trey bathed in some snow throughout the night to control his fever.

Sunrise brought success since Trey slept comfortably, not a fit or stir from him and his fever marginal.

Mara chased Tara off to get some sleep, insisting she rest in case she was needed again. Tara didn't argue. She was bone-tired and ached for sleep almost as much as she had ached for Reeve earlier.

The memory had her halting in her tracks in the hall and had her wondering over the wisdom of returning to his room. She could go to her cottage, but what if she was needed again? They would have to go looking for her, and that would waste precious time.

If she did go to Reeve's room, there was a good chance, a very good chance, that she would get no sleep. And while a tiny tingle coaxed her to do just that, she was much too tired to be tempted by it. If so, then why not go to Reeve's bedchamber. He would surely understand and make no demands on her.

But would she be the one making demands on him?

She slumped against the stone wall, pondering her dilemma.

The thought struck fast, and she pushed away from the wall, thinking it would be a good idea to tell Mara that she would be in her sewing room.

Bryce rounded the corner then, and she was quick to ask him to deliver the message for her. He agreed, and she bid him good night though it was early morning. She moved slowly along the hall to the stairs, never noticing his interest in her hobbling gait.

Reeve woke as the new day dawned and wasn't surprised to see that he had slept alone. He had assumed Tara had a long night ahead of her and so he had left her with his mum to look after Trey and sought his bed.

He'd had a fitful sleep, though, surprisingly, he woke refreshed. He was eager to see Tara, and so he hurried and dressed and went in search of her. He assumed she would be with Trey and his mum, so he was surprised when he entered the room to find Bryce signaling him to be quiet and pointing to their mum, sound asleep in the chair.

A quick glance around told him Tara wasn't there.

Bryce signaled him to step outside the room, and once out, he closed the door behind them.

"You look for Tara, I assume."

"I thought she'd be here," Reeve said.

"She's in the sewing room."

"Why? And how do you know that?" Reeve demanded.

"I saw her in the hall a short time ago, and she asked me to tell mum. As for why?" Bryce grinned. "You're better to answer that than me."

"One of these days I'm just going to beat you and get it over with," Reeve said, turning and shaking his head as he walked away.

"Reeve," Bryce called out.

Reeve stopped but didn't turn around. "What?"

"She's limping again."

That had Reeve turning around.

"And I don't believe she even realizes it," Bryce finished.

Reeve shook his head again and grumbled beneath his breath.

Bryce laughed. "Damn, if you don't sound like a man in love . . . utterly confused."

"I'm saving that beating for you and one day . . ." Reeve ignored Bryce's laughter, which chased after him.

Sure enough, Tara was curled up, and looking most uncomfortable, in mum's large wooden chair in front of the dwindling hearth. He was quick to add two good-sized logs to the fire before he went over to her.

That she had obviously been too tired to add the logs herself upset him. He hadn't needed to ask Bryce why she came here, he knew. She avoided him, thereby avoiding the inevitable between them though he could understand she was fatigued. Had she not trusted him to let her rest, or had she not trusted herself?

He liked the latter answer better.

He refused to think of anything but her need for

rest. He would not linger on the softness of her skin, or her luscious curves, or her plump, moist lips.

He grumbled silently, feeling himself already swelling with desire. He'd get her settled in his bed and leave the room.

She didn't even stir when he lifted her into his arms and carried her out. Sleep had laid a heavy hand on her, and he didn't believe she'd be waking up anytime soon.

He laid her gently on the bed once in his bedchamber and went to take off her boots. He stopped when he saw that her ankle had once again swelled. He took off the one and worried that taking off the other would wake her, but if he left it on, and it continued to swell . . .

With a shake of his head and a gentle touch he began to ease the boot off. He grinned, seeing that his endeavors looked to be successful until he reached a point that proved difficult. He struggled, carefully if that was possible, and just when he thought he had it . . .

She gave a yelp as her eyes sprung open wide.

"I'm sorry," he said.

Her eyes fought to remain open. "I twisted it on the stairs."

He almost chastised her for not telling him sooner though he realized that wasn't what she needed from him at the moment. "Is there anything I can do?"

Her eyes had closed, and he knew what she needed . . . sleep.

He tucked the warm wool blankets around her and added another log to the fire. He returned to the bed, leaned over, and kissed her cheek.

"I do believe I love you, Tara—" He eased up to

his full height and stared down at her, wondering what clan she had belonged to. Part of her was still very much a mystery to him.

He grinned as he walked to the door. He'd unravel her one layer at a time, and the thought produced the most delightful image.

With hunger gnawing at his stomach, Reeve hurried downstairs to the great hall. He didn't think his mum would be there, but some of the others would be, and he looked forward to sitting and talking with them.

He saw that Willow was at the table with Carmag and Bryce, and he joined them, taking the spot next to his brother.

"Tara finally sleeps?" Bryce asked.

"She's all tucked in," Reeve said.

"Willow was just telling us of the soldiers," Carmag said.

She continued as Reeve helped himself to food.

"Jacob and I had to huddle in wait while two soldiers stood only inches from our hiding spot. We heard clearly what they had to say. They were worried that the king was in a snit, angrier than they have ever seen him. It seems that he's lost something of great importance, and he wants it returned."

"This confirms what I heard," Reeve said.

"The soldiers must know what they look for," Bryce said.

"If they do, they made no mention of it," Willow said.

"If the soldiers don't dare speak of it, then they must do so under threat of severe punishment," Carmag added.

"Or they don't know what it is they seek," Bryce said.

Willow shook her head. "How can you search when you don't know what you search for?"

"The king could have directed them to look for particular signs or listen for certain gossip," Reeve explained.

"It's done more often than most realize," Bryce said. "Many times it has to be kept secret so that a mission doesn't fail."

Willow scrunched her brow and looked to Reeve. "I recall Jacob mentioning something after you and Tara left. He told me that one of the soldiers asked if any travelers passed this way recently." Tears stung her eyes. "The answer didn't please the soldier, and that's when they began to—" She wiped at her tears.

"The king looks for someone," Bryce said.

"That he does," Willow said. "The true king of Scotland."

Reeve shook his head. "No, he seeks travelers. The true king would not travel obvious roadways."

"You're right," Willow said with a nod.

"Travelers would also lead one to assume he means more than one person," Bryce said.

"Whoever it is," Carmag said, "he's of extreme importance to the king."

Reeve grinned. "That means we should find him first."

"I'll help," Willow offered.

"Mum could use help with Trey," Bryce said.

Willow shook her head adamantly. "I meant in finding this person or persons. I'm not good with just sitting idly by while the men tend to things. My Rory taught me how to handle weapons, the bow and arrow being my favorite. Jacob continued to teach me all he could—"

She paused, tears once again clouding her eyes. "He had been adamant about the lessons, pushing me harder and harder each day, as if he only had so much time left."

"This mission is best left to men," Bryce said gently.

"Why?" Willow snapped.

Bryce rested his hand on her arm. "You're upset—"

"Damn right, I am," Willow said, shoving his hand off her. "I've lost my husband, his child I carried, and his grandda, and if you think I will sit idly by—" She shook her head, her cheeks turning a furious red. "You're wrong. Dead wrong!"

"We'll see if we can somehow use your help," Bryce said.

"Don't placate me," Willow warned, and stood. "Or I'll go off on my own and find out who this person or persons of interest are and damn well make him or them pay for taking the last of my family from me."

The three men watched her march off.

"She'll calm down and come to her senses," Bryce said.

Reeve shook his head. "I wouldn't wager on that."

Duncan all but flew off the stairs into the great hall, two pails swinging from each hand. "Trey's burning up again."

# Chapter 19

The next two days passed in a blur, with Trey needing constant attention. Mercy went through bouts of fatigue and not being able to keep food down, and Rand took ill, running a fever that refused to let go.

Tara, Willow, and Mara ran tirelessly amongst all of them tending them as best as they could, with Duncan remaining by his wife's side doing more for her than anyone. The storm continued to rage outside, leaving the Picts stranded with the MacAlpin clan.

When things seemed settled, though illness continued to plague the clan, Tara took a moment to return to her cottage. She needed time to think, time to refresh not only her thoughts but her body.

She heated a cauldron full of snow so that she could wash and slip into clean garments before returning to the keep. And she worried, worried terribly that she had brought this plague of problems down upon Reeve's clan. How to correct the situation? She wasn't sure. She only knew that she had to do something. She hoped refreshing herself would help clear the muddled confusion in her mind and help her find a way to amend this mess.

Tara sighed and slipped out of her clothes, draping them over the chair, to be washed and dried by the fire when she was done. Getting her boot off had proven a slight chore since her ankle had swelled on and off over the last couple of days. She knew it would have done her good to have remained off it, but that hadn't been possible. There had been too much to do.

Given time, it would heal, and she would not think anymore on it. It was, after all, the least of her worries.

The wind whipped around the cottage, trembling the timber frame and penetrating the wattle-and-daub walls with a chill. She was grateful for the roaring fire that burned brightly in the fireplace and kept the one room warm.

She hurried to wash herself with the heated water in the cauldron. She had wanted to wash her hair, but it would have taken much too long to dry, and so she had twisted it and pinned it to the back of her head with her bone comb to keep it out of her way.

She had placed a fresh change of clothes on the bed, a high-necked, long-sleeved dark blue velvet dress; though not conducive to tending the ill, it certainly would keep her warm.

The fire's light highlighted her freshly scrubbed skin as she finished the last of her scrub. She jumped when suddenly the front door opened, letting in not only a blast of cold air but Reeve along with it.

They both stood staring at each other, a layer of snow quickly melting off Reeve's hair and shoulders.

"I-I-I-" Reeve stumbled over his words.

"Should have knocked," Tara scolded, her arms crossing over the front of her, trying desperately to cover herself.

Reeve flung off his cloak and dropped it on the peg by the door, though he missed and it fell to the ground. Not that he noticed, he was too busy staring at Tara.

"Good Lord, you're beautiful," he said, advancing on her slowly.

The passion that flooded his dark eyes warned that she would be in trouble very soon if she didn't cover herself though it might already be too late.

She searched around her for something to cover herself with, but her fresh clothes lay out of reach. The only thing left was the towel she had used to dry herself, and that was damp. But it was something, at least, and so she reached for it.

"Don't!" he warned sharply. "I love looking at your naked body."

"But it's not a wise idea," she cautioned, her hand creeping closer to the towel on the table.

He grinned. "I don't care."

He was near on top of her when she grabbed for the towel.

He was faster. He reached out and grabbed hold of her wrist and yanked her up against him. "You made a promise. Will you keep it?"

"Now is—"

"A good time," he finished.

"That's not what I was going to say."

"It's what you should be saying," Reeve said.

"I am needed—"

Reeve grinned. "You are definitely needed."

Tara surprised herself when she asked, "Needed or loved?"

"That's a good question," Reeve said. "Shall we find out?"

"I think I would prefer the answer first."

"You want to know *if* I love you before I *make* love to you?"

"I would," she said.

"You're standing here naked in front of me, and you want me to make certain I love you before I ravish you—"

"Out of love or need?"

"Do you know what you ask of me?"

Tara nodded slowly. "The truth."

He sucked in a breath, let her go, and turned away from her, running his hand through his hair before he turned back around. "I think I love you, I believe I do, it makes sense that I do—"

"And yet you cannot say for sure that you do."

"What of the curse?" he suddenly asked.

"Why do you think I ask this of you?"

He wrinkled his brow. "I'm trying to understand why suddenly—" He shook his head, his brow remaining wrinkled with confusion. "Is it that you would prefer that I *didn't* love you?"

"In some ways, it would make things easier," she said, though didn't add that in other ways it would make things much more difficult. What if it was merely lust he felt for her—when she felt much more.

Her naked body was already alive for him, every morsel of her skin sensitive and yearning to be touched. She ached for his hands to cover every inch of her, not to mention his lips, especially those little nibbles and nips she had come to favor. And if that weren't enough, there was the familiar joyous ache of love that consumed her. She had felt it for Rory though not nearly as strong as she felt it for Reeve.

"So should I have my way with you and not concern myself with love?"

"That way may work to your advantage."

She could see that the suggestion bothered him as it did her, but she had to protect him, and she had to protect herself.

"You're not making this easy," he complained.

"You knew it wouldn't be easy from the very beginning when you found me."

Reeve glared at her, pointing his finger. "Cover yourself, or I will see you in that bed and couple with you before you have a chance to protest."

"What makes you think I will protest?"

Reeve shook his head. "So you want me to couple with you, but you don't want me to love you."

"Too much has happened to make me believe other than that the curse is very much alive and active. I don't truly know how to protect anyone from it. I only know that death stalks those who love me, or wed me, and so I refuse to take any more chances."

"So you will couple with me, but not—" Reeve stopped as if unable to speak it aloud.

Tara finished for him. "I will not make love with you."

He took a step back, as if she had punched him hard, and strangely enough, her words had impacted her as much as him, for she felt it deep in her belly.

"You can't stop me from loving you," he said.

"No, I can't, if it truly is love," she said, shaking her head. "But right now, I can refuse to make love with you."

"You made a promise," he said, disappointed.

"I promised that we would finish what we started. Was it love or lust that had brought us to that point?

If lust then"–she stretched her arm out, her finger pointing to the bed—"join me to finally satisfy that lust. If it is love you feel—then please leave."

"I'm not going anywhere," he said sharply. "Get dressed."

"Wh—"

"Don't say another word," he warned. "My anger is too ripe. Now get dressed."

He turned his back, and Tara wisely did as he had ordered, a shiver racing through her, and not from any chill.

She was glad the dark blue velvet dress tied high at her neck, and she rushed into her dark stockings though she had trouble with her one boot and decided to leave them off, not dare asking Reeve for help.

"I'm done," she said.

"Sit," he said, though it sounded more of a command.

She didn't argue. She sat at the table, and he took the other seat across from her.

"Now you will tell me about this curse." He was ready for her protest and raised his hand as her mouth opened and she shook her head. "I've had enough, Tara. You will tell me what happened so that I may judge for myself."

"Will it matter?" she asked.

"It might scare me off and my lust for you as well. The problem would then be settled."

"How can I take you seriously when you wear a grin? "

He leaned his arms on the table. "Then I dare you to wipe it off."

Her heart thudded wildly in her chest. She loved his grin. It made him all the more handsome, and he was handsome enough without it. But there was something about his smile that changed his features and struck her heart, sending it thumping madly every time.

This time, however, was different. This time, her heart beat wildly because she feared that once he heard the truth, he would walk away from her forever. And that very reason, she feared, was the only way of saving him.

Tara began the tale that had started when she was barely ten years. "I was an inquisitive child and therefore adventurous. I would wander off in search of—" She shrugged. "I don't know what it was I searched for; I only knew I wanted to learn things and not only women things.

"One day I followed my father deep into the woods. I had seen him go off there alone many times, and I wanted to know where he went. I watched as he came upon a lone cottage. It had strange symbols carved around the door and a lone window, and a strange scent that bothered the nose surrounded it.

"I thought to sneak up to the window and see what went on within, but a young lad suddenly appeared at my side, frightening me half to death. He looked to be around my age and he beckoned me to follow him. I did, and he took me to a stream, where we sat and he showed me a collection of small stones he kept in a pouch. It took me a moment to realize that he couldn't speak, but it didn't matter to me. I enjoyed his company and what he was showing me.

"His head suddenly went up, and he motioned for me to follow him again. He took me back to where he found me and cautioned me to remain quiet with a finger to his lips. Then he was gone. My father came out of the cottage a short time later, and I followed him home."

She paused to glance at the fire. "I followed my father again and again so that I could visit with the lad I named Stone. He smiled and nodded when I told him that, as if I had guessed his name."

Tara turned to look at Reeve. "Stone was my first love. Soon I remembered the way there myself, and for two years I went to visit him as much as I could. I don't know what it was about him, I just knew that I wanted to be with him. And I knew he felt the same about me."

Tears gathered in her eyes. "My father found me with Stone one day. I think one of my half brothers had followed me and told him. He dragged us both to the cottage and demanded the witch remove the spell she or her son had put on me. I hadn't known that his mother was a witch until then, or that my father believed Stone one as well.

"The woman smiled and tried to tell my father to let us be, that we were in love, and it was a good love. He grew furious and ordered her to do as he said or suffer the consequences. She tried to explain that there was nothing she could do, that love had claimed us and that she could not defy love.

"My father refused to listen, refused to see reason, and so he beat Stone." A tear fell, and she let it. "I tried to stop him. I took a few blows until one of my half brothers dragged me off and held me kicking and screaming. The witch begged my father to stop, but he was furious and kept pounding Stone. Finally, I bit my half brother's arm so hard he let me go; I could taste the blood I had drawn. I ran and flung myself on top of Stone's battered body.

"I suffered a few blows before my father realized and stopped. The witch was quick to fling me off her son and cradle him in her arms. My father warned her to leave his land or he would see her dead along with her son. It was as he dragged me away crying that she screamed out the curse."

Tara turned silent, not wanting to repeat the words that had remained burned in her memory all these years.

"Tell me," Reeve urged. "I want to hear it."

Tara sighed and repeated the words she hadn't muttered since she had first heard them. "Your heart will break just like mine, over and over, time after time. When you claim the love of your heart, the touch of death will see you part. If it is a vow you make, death will visit again and take. And for those men who speak aloud their love for you, death will see them taken too. On this day I curse you well and condemn you to a living hell.

"My father threw me aside and drew his sword with all intentions of striking her dead, but she raised her hand and told him that if he took one more step toward her, he would drop dead at her feet when he finally reached her. My father did not move, and when he did, it was to grab me and once again warn her to leave his land or die. I don't know if Stone lived or died. I never saw him again."

Tara waited for Reeve to say something, anything, but he remained silent. She knew what he must be thinking, the fear that must be racing through him, and so she said, "You can leave now."

He shook his head. "What?"

"You can leave. I understand, and have no worries. I will keep to myself."

"You think me a coward?" he asked.

Her eyes widened in surprise. "Not at all. I think you the bravest of men."

"Then if you believe that, why would you think I would leave?"

"I stunned you silent—"

"You assumed that your tale frightened me?"

"It would most."

He shook his head. "I'm not most. And as for my silence, I was thinking about the witch. If she had such power, she would have used it to protect her son. She lashed out at you to hurt your father, the only way she could, as he had hurt her son."

"But she threatened my father with death—"

"And out of fear, he remained frozen in his tracks. He allowed himself to believe her able to strike him dead. But if she truly had such powers, she would have used them to protect her son."

"I never considered that," Tara said.

"You were too young and full of guilt and fear to think clearly. When either rules, they cloud sound reason and prevent people from taking action."

"But most do not think like you," Tara said.

Reeve smiled. "As I told you, I'm not most, and I have Bryce to thank for that. The day he found me, he began to teach me how to survive, but he never realized that he also taught me to always keep learning, never stop. And as I watched and learned from him, I did the same not only with others, but from the animals in the forest, the birds that take flight, the weather that is unpredictable, and so much more. That is the reason I can hear your tale, question it, and make sense of it."

"I wish I could see it like you, believe it like you, but I am living the hell the witch has inflicted upon me."

"Your fear and guilt give it power. Cast the spell off and let it be no more."

"I haven't the skill to do that," Tara said, while wishing she had.

"Then we'll find someone who can."

Her eyes widened, and she felt a flutter of hope. "Do you think that is possible? Do you truly believe we could find a witch with the power to remove the spell?"

"Why not?"

"I had thought of it," she said. "But I was never able to pursue it. My father forbids witches, seers, anyone with dark powers to cross his land. Are there any witches in your clan?"

"None that I'm aware of, but I'll inquire, discreetly, of course."

"The healer who isn't a healer," Tara said, excited.

"What are you talking about?"

Tara's excitement grew. "Mercy told me of Bliss, the Pict healer who heals but isn't truly a healer. I wondered if perhaps she could help me."

Reeve nodded. "You may be right. I have heard Duncan and Mercy talk of her and her extraordinary skill in healing people with a simple touch."

"You've given me hope," Tara said, smiling brightly.

"Good, now can we make love?"

Tara's smile faded. "I don't want to take the chance of losing you."

He reached out for her hand, but she slipped

away. He shrugged. "All right then, let's make lust."

"So you only lust after me but not love me?" Tara asked.

"You're making this very hard, and while I'd love you to make *me* hard, this is not what I had in mind."

"I love making you hard. And I truly love the feel of you hard in my hand."

"That's it. We need to make lust right now."

Tara stood slowly. "Then tell me it is lust pure and simple. Tell me you have no love for me in your heart and I will gladly, willingly, happily couple with you."

Reeve stood so quickly that he rattled the table. He glared at her, raised a hand and pointed at her, opened his mouth then closed it, shook his head, ran his hand through his hair, and then released a low growl that turned to a grumble that finally burst into a frustrated roar.

Tara took a step back, fearing she had pushed him too far.

Finally, after taking several deep breaths, Reeve calmed enough to speak. He pointed at her. "When I take you to that bed"–he pointed to it and then back at her—"it will be to *make love* to you. I do not lust after you like an animal hungry to mate. There is more here between us, Tara, and I will not demean whatever this strange all-encompassing feeling that nags and torments and batters me every waking and sleeping moment and yet I do not want to do without, simply to share a toss with you."

He paused and shook his finger at her when she went to speak. "Say nothing, absolutely nothing. We will make love in that bed. Our children will be conceived of love in that bed. We will grow old and still make love in that bed. And I will always hold you with love whether in or out of that bed."

He turned, swiped his cloak off the ground, and said, "I will wait outside for you. We go to the keep together."

Tara stood silent, watching the door close behind him. Tears filled her eyes and spilled over.

*Keep him safe. I love him. God help me, I love him. Please keep him safe from me.*

# Chapter 20

Reeve felt like raging, he was so angry. And he knew it showed on his face since the villagers passing by Tara's cottage gave him a wide berth.

*Damn but she could be stubborn.*

"You look like you want to kill someone," Bryce said, approaching him.

"I do," Reeve snapped.

Bryce snickered. "That's what happens when you fall in love."

"How would you know?"

"I learn from watching," Bryce said.

Reeve shook his head. Hadn't he just told Tara the same?

Bryce rested a firm hand on Reeve's shoulder. "Put yourself in her place before you judge too harshly."

Reeve went to argue.

Bryce squeezed his shoulder. "Think as she does, then see how you feel. See you in the keep for the noon meal, though if you take too long, I'll have eaten most of the food."

"I'm going to beat you," Reeve threatened teasingly as he always did, though he never meant it. It was the way between them.

Bryce laughed and waved him off just as the cottage door opened.

Tara stepped out and sent him a skeptical glance.

*Think as she does.*

From the way she stared at him, he knew that he still looked angry, and he didn't want her thinking he was angry with her. It was the situation, not her, and so he grinned and took her hand.

An apprehensive smile lit her face, and she wrapped her fingers slowly around his, and his heart soared. Damn, but this love thing could be unnerving.

They walked in silence, the snow falling softly over them and the air crisp. He did as Bryce suggested and thought how Tara must feel. And suddenly he felt an unbearable weight descend on him.

Was that how she felt, as if she carried a hefty weight? She did feel responsible and a responsibility brought a weight of sorts. He hadn't given enough thought to how this curse had affected her. He had simply brushed it off as unreasonable, but he hadn't suffered from the remnants of it. Tara had.

She had grown excited when he suggested they find a witch to remove the curse, or when she thought that Bliss might be able to help her. He had to approach this differently. He had to stop thinking of how he felt, and his wants and desires, and concentrate on how Tara perceived things. It was the only way to truly help her.

They reached the keep without having exchanged a word. Reeve stopped at the foot of the steps and turned to Tara.

"I will do whatever it takes to rid you of the curse."

Her violet eyes grew wide, and he thought he detected a tear.

"Truly?"

"Truly," he said. "We will find a solution together."

She flung herself at him, her arms wrapping around him. "You truly are a man of honor."

He cringed. "If you knew what I was thinking, you would not say that."

She chuckled. "Then we are thinking the same."

He laughed and hugged her tight. "I am lucky to have found you."

Before Tara could respond, the keep door opened, and Duncan called out, "You best hurry. Between Bryce and Mercy, there won't be any food left for you."

Reeve could see how relieved Tara was when they joined his family at the table and saw that Mercy's appetite had returned, and color now flooded her face. Mara let them know that Trey continued to rest comfortably though he had yet to fully wake, and Rand's fever had broken, and he was eagerly drinking broth.

Willow had offered to sit with Trey so that the family could all have some time together, and they were grateful. It was good to be all together, smiles on faces, appetites robust, and hope strong.

As they ate, Roan and his men entered and sat at a table a few feet away, as if respecting the family's privacy. They were served a hearty fare and were deep in their own conversation when one of their men entered the keep and hurried over to Roan. He quickly stood and followed the man out.

Reeve had watched it all, and said, "Something goes on with the Picts."

"I noticed that myself," Duncan said.

Mercy grasped at her chest, and Duncan turned pure white, fearing the worst.

"Bliss!" Mercy shouted. "Bliss has arrived."

Sure enough, in seconds the door opened, and in entered Roan, three more men, and a woman. She was swathed in a white wool, hooded cloak that unwrapped like a swirl of snow as she walked toward them. Her hood fell back just as she stopped at their table, and Reeve wasn't the only one whose breath caught.

She was an angelic beauty, her long hair shimmering gold, tall in height, slim in body, and exotically stunning.

"I have come to help," she announced, her voice soft and melodic.

Mercy jumped up and pushed at her husband to move so that she could get off the bench. He instead simply lifted her up and swung her off the bench. As soon as her feet hit the ground, she ran around the table to hug Bliss.

"I'm so glad you came," Mercy said.

Bliss smiled. "You knew I would."

Introductions were made by Mercy, and food and rest were offered to Bliss, but she declined.

"I should see to Trey," Bliss said.

Mara hurried to her side. "I'll take you to my son. Any help you can provide will be greatly appreciated."

"I'll do what I can."

The two women walked away and disappeared up the stairs.

"She is a beauty," Tara said.

"In more ways than one," Mercy said, having returned to her seat beside her husband.

"Mercy's right about that," Duncan said.

"There's something different about her." Carmag scratched his head. "I've seen it before in those who have a knowing."

"You mean she knows things before they are told to her?" Bryce asked.

Carmag nodded.

"We need to talk," Bryce said, looking from his father to his brothers."

"Go," Mercy said, shooing them off. "I will tell Tara all about Bliss, and she will soon find her a friend."

Reeve was pleased with the smile of delight that filled Tara's face. He gave her a quick kiss before leaving, happy that she looked hopeful, and he intended on keeping hope alive for her.

The four men entered the solar and made themselves comfortable in the chairs, all except Bryce. He stood, leaning an arm on the mantel.

"If Bliss has a knowing of things that are and yet to come, then our plans could be in jeopardy," Bryce said. "She could know the identity of the true king."

Reeve didn't want to lose Bliss before he even could ask her for help, but he also couldn't see their mission jeopardized. They had worked too hard and long to see it threatened. "Bryce has a point, but her knowing may also help us."

"That's true," Duncan said. "She may provide us with an advantage while she is here, and though I can't say I know her well, I do believe she keeps what she knows to herself."

"But does her visit here put her in danger once she leaves us?" Bryce asked.

"Those I have known with this knowing," Carmag said, "always knew their path. I suggest we bide our time and see what Bliss has to offer us."

"That could prove dangerous," Bryce said.

"Or advantageous," Carmag said. "Time will tell."

"Perhaps she could at least tell us who stole the precious hide so important to the true king," Reeve suggested.

"That's a good point," Duncan said. "It had been kept safe in the chest here in the solar for years with only the four of us and father familiar with its hiding spot."

"We know none of us took it," Bryce said. "So who, then, knew of it and took it."

"Only to give it to Mercy's mother, who burned it before her capture and death," Duncan said. "And why would the person give it to Mercy's mother, mistress of King Kenneth?"

Carmag nodded. "Perhaps Bliss can settle the mystery for us."

Mercy was anxious to have Tara watch Bliss heal, so the two hurried up to Trey's bedchamber to watch. Tara remained to the side with Mercy, her stomach all aflutter, nervous and eager to see if perhaps this woman would have the skill to free her so that she could finally . . . freely love Reeve.

Tara kept her stare fixed on Bliss as she rubbed her hands repeatedly, then brought them to her mouth, holding them against her lips as if in prayer and then lowering them to rest at Trey's brow.

After a few moments she shook her head slowly and moved her hands to rest on his chest.

After a few minutes, Trey's eyes sprung open. "An

angel. I am dead." He closed his eyes again, and Tara saw Mara wipe away the tears at her eyes.

Bliss leaned down, her hands remaining on his chest, and whispered something to him that no one could hear. She then stood, removed her hands, and signaled Mara to follow her. Mercy and Tara went as well, leaving Willow alone in the room with Trey.

Once outside the door, Bliss spoke. "He does not fight to live."

Mara choked back a sob. "I was afraid of that."

Mercy slipped a supportive arm around Mara. "He lost the woman he loved."

Bliss frowned, though she made no comment.

"Can you help him?" Mara asked.

"I'm not sure. His will is weak, but it is imperative he live. I will do the best I can."

"That is all I ask," Mara said.

Bliss placed her hand on Mara's arm. "Go rest, you need it."

"I'll see that she does," Mercy said, though Mara only left after gentle urgings and assurances from Bliss.

Tara waited until the two women were out of sight and then she turned to Bliss.

Bliss spoke before she did. "You have reason to worry. Keep your heart strong, and we will talk."

Tara wished for more, but she knew Trey came first, and so she turned and walked away once Bliss returned inside the room. At least the woman had agreed to talk with her, and that gave her hope.

She was eager to tell Reeve, and so she hurried to the great hall to see if he was there. When she found it empty, she decided that she just couldn't sit and wait for him. She went to the kitchen and found Etty busy as usual.

The woman was as round as she was tall. Her red hair was sprinkled with gray, and while her face wore a constant pinch, it changed miraculously to a brilliant smile whenever Neil, her love and soon-to-be-husband walked in the room.

"I was just going to see if you wanted to bake bread," Etty said, removing her apron and wrapping it around Tara and tying it tight. She then grabbed her cloak off a peg and grabbed a large basket filled to the brim with food. "The kitchen is yours." And with that, she was out the door.

Tara smiled, and then the quiet descended on her. She cast a glance around the large room. Bubbling cauldrons hung on hooks over the roaring flames in the fireplace. Baskets spilled over with rooted plants, and smoked meat hung on hooks from timber rafters. Eggs were plentiful in baskets, and cheeses were wrapped in cloths and piled on one of the three tables.

She had hoped to talk with Etty. Actually, she had hoped to *listen* to Etty talk about Neil and how much she loved him. Tara had been looking for company who would keep her mind and hands busy.

Now she had only silence for company, and silence had been her companion for far too long. With little choice left to her, Tara gathered what she needed to bake the dark bread that Reeve favored and set to work to keep herself busy.

Unfortunately, Bliss's words haunted her.

*You have reason to worry.*

She had been right about the curse. It was real, and she had reason to worry over it. It was good that she had stopped herself from making love with Reeve. She would surely have lost him if she allowed her desire to rule. She had to keep her wits about her and her heart strong as Bliss said.

Tara soon had four loaves set to bake, and once the kitchen helpers arrived, she asked them to remove the bread at a specific time. She dropped the apron on a bench as she left the kitchen, hoping to find Reeve in the great hall. He still hadn't returned, so she went upstairs and peeked in on Trey. Willow was gone, and Bliss sat in the chair beside the bed and looked to be asleep.

Undoubtedly, she was exhausted from her journey through the snow and needed rest, though she had looked rested upon arrival.

She wished they could talk, but she didn't wish to disturb her slumber, so she quietly closed the door. A yawn attacked her after two steps, a few more steps produced several more yawns, and Tara decided that a nap was necessary. If she remembered correctly, she had had only a few hours' sleep in the last couple of days. She'd be wise to catch a nap when she could, and with Reeve still busy, now was a good time.

She hurried to Reeve's bedchamber and slipped off her boots and stockings. She wished she had worn her linen shift beneath her velvet dress, for then she could take off her dress. While it certainly kept her warm, it wasn't suited for sleeping.

She made the choice in haste to take it off and slip naked beneath the covers. It was only a nap. She'd be up and dressed before Reeve found her. Her head no sooner rested on the pillow than she was asleep.

# Chapter 21

Reeve snuck a taste of the dark bread that Tara had made for him cooling on the table. He'd been disappointed that he had missed her in the kitchen though he had been thrilled to discover that she had baked him bread. It meant that she had been thinking about him, and he liked when he remained on her mind. Besides, it was only fair since she remained constantly on his mind.

After sneaking a few more tastes and thinking that perhaps she was trying to avoid him, he went to his mother's sewing room, but it was empty. After that, he made his way to Trey's room, wondering if she had gotten a chance to speak with Bliss.

"I bid you welcome," Bliss called to him when he opened the door.

He entered, and before he dared take the chair beside her, he said, "I don't wish to intrude."

"Your brother rests," Bliss said. "He hasn't truly rested in some time."

"That I agree with."

"But you are not here about your brother," Bliss said. "You look for Tara."

"Was she here?" he asked, excited. "Did she speak with you?"

"We had no chance for a discussion, and time grows short."

"You will leave soon?" he asked. "You've only just arrived."

She reached out and took hold of his hand, and for several moments simply stared at him until finally she said, "An unselfish love will save Tara."

Trey stirred, and Bliss was quick to rest her hand on his chest. Her eyes closed, and her lips moved, as if she was silently praying or reciting or chanting. Reeve wasn't sure what she was doing, but it mattered not to him as long as Bliss healed his brother.

Reeve didn't want to disturb her while she tended his brother, and so he left. He wondered over Bliss's remark and told himself to remember it well. He couldn't be selfish when it came to loving her. If he needed to wait to love her or make love to her or sacrifice for her, he would do it. He would do whatever it took to free her to love him without fear.

He went to his bedchamber, thinking she might be there, but doubting it. And so when he found her naked in his bed, he simply stood there and stared down at her, tangled in his bedding, a leg, an arm, and a breast exposed.

He didn't think, didn't hesitate; he shed his clothes. Only when he was about to climb naked in bed with her did Bliss's words return to haunt him.

*An unselfish love will save Tara.*

If he crawled in bed naked with her and began exploring her exquisite skin, he'd never stop, and that would be selfish.

He yawned, and she turned on her stomach with a sigh, her backside peeking out to torment him.

He should dress and leave. He yawned again. He was tired, his sleep having been brief and disturbed over the last few days. He could use a rest just like her. After another yawn claimed him, he decided to join her. He promised himself he'd be unselfish. He wouldn't touch her; he'd simply sleep cuddled against her.

With an earnest determination in his heart, he crawled into bed with her, cuddling up against her, and, surprisingly, he was asleep in no time.

Tara felt safe, so very safe that she never wanted to leave the lovely warm cocoon that sheltered her. She wasn't sure how she had gotten there, but there was where she intended to stay. There was a lovingness she couldn't describe but could certainly feel. It settled over her, every part of her and deep inside her, so deep it seemed as if it had always been part of her. And she never, ever wanted to be separated from it.

Her body tingled from the protective warmth and she moved closer against it. Her hands explored, seeking what she wasn't sure, only knowing she enjoyed the touch. And she sighed with pleasure when her touches were returned.

Lips soon nibbled at her, and she smiled as the nibbles rushed over her body, sending the most exquisite shivers through her. It was when the nibbles settled between her legs and the sensation grew beyond bearable that her eyes flew open.

"No," she moaned when she realized that it all was real, and suddenly she felt safe no more. "No, Reeve."

Reeve rose up over her. "Don't do this to us."

"Get off me," she said, shoving at his hard chest.

"Don't," he begged. "Let me love you."

Lord how she wanted him to love her, but she wanted him safe and alive more, and so she pushed at him harder. "Get off."

Reeve fell off to her side on his back, and she sprang out of bed, hurrying into her clothes.

He bolted out of bed. "What good does it do to deny our love?"

"It saves your life," she protested, aching terribly for him to finish what he had started. Or had she started it?

"Please, Tara, let me love you," he begged. "Let me end your fear."

She bit at her lip, tempted, so very tempted to say yes. Instead, she shook her head and ran to the door, flinging it open. Bryce stood on the other side and shoved her back in, shutting the door behind him.

"We have a problem." Bryce grabbed Reeve's clothes and threw them at him. "A big problem."

Reeve got dressed. "What's wrong?"

"Neil got word as to what disturbs the king," Bryce said. "It seems that the king had plans to wed, and his intended's caravan was attacked on the way here. At first he had thought her killed and her bride price stolen, but he had come to learn that she along with her bride price simply disappeared. He intends to find both."

The two men glared at Tara, and she knew there was no longer any point in denying it.

"Are you the king's intended?" Bryce asked.

"Yes," she said, her shoulders sagging, as if finally a weight had been lifted. "My father agreed to the marriage arrangement."

"Who is your father?" Bryce asked.

Her chin went up. "That's not important."

"Yes, it is," he insisted.

"No, it isn't," Tara snapped. "I have no intention of returning home, and I have no intention of marrying the king."

"You're damn right you won't," Reeve said.

Bryce shook his head. "Do you both realize the difficultly and potential danger this causes?"

"No one knows that Tara is here," Reeve said, going to her side and slipping a possessive arm around her waist.

She leaned into him, glad for his show of support, but had she expected any different? He had protected her from the very first day they had met, and he had never stopped. He would always protect her. She could count on it.

"Wagging tongues travel over the roads, valleys, and mountains of the Highlands," Bryce said. "Soon someone is bound to put the pieces together. Then it will not be the king who comes to claim his intended. It will be her father, whoever he may be, and"—Bryce pointed at Tara—"she will have to go with him, and her bride price will have to be returned."

"But that has yet to happen," Reeve said. "We have time to find a solution that will benefit all."

"This needs to be discussed between Da and our brothers," Bryce said.

"And me," Tara said curtly. "It is my future, my life that will be discussed, and I will not be left out of it."

Bryce looked to Reeve. "This is your doing. Handle it."

With that, he left the room.

Tara turned around and looked up at Reeve. "You send me to my death if I am sent to wed the king."

"What do you mean?" he asked, his arms wrapping protectively around her.

"I believe the king only agreed to wed a death bride because he had plans to kill me before the curse could take him. He wants nothing more from me but my bride price."

"Have you any proof of this?" Reeve asked, angry and concerned.

"Think about it, Reeve. Why would the king dare take a chance to wed a known death bride?" She shook her head. "King Kenneth is not an ignorant man. I overheard my father say that the king's coffers were near empty, and my substantial bride price would replenish them quite nicely."

"Your father knew this and agreed to the arrangement?" he asked incredulously.

Tara shrugged, though sadness filled her eyes. "I suppose it's a small price to pay to finally be rid of me. After all, there was no man foolish enough who would agree to wed a death bride. And with things not going well in the clan . . ." She shrugged again.

He took tight hold of her shoulders. "You're a member of the MacAlpin clan, and here is where you will stay."

"I want to believe that, but Bryce is right. If my father learns my whereabouts, then I will have no say in the matter; you will be forced to turn me over to the king."

"That's not going to happen," Reeve said forcefully.

"How will you stop it?"

"I'll find a way," he said adamantly, "but you're not going anywhere."

"Believe me; I'm right where I want to be."

His arms went around her. "And here is where you shall stay and where you belong."

"Perhaps Bliss could help," Tara said. "If the curse could be removed—"She didn't finish, though she blushed. It was presumptuous of her to think that Reeve would wed her to save her from wedding the king.

"What then?" Reeve asked.

"I'd be free—"

"To still wed the king," Reeve reminded.

"Or someone else," she said cautiously.

"Anyone in mind?"

She smiled at his grin, which seemed to keep spreading, and the merriment that danced in his dark eyes.

"You tease me," she said.

"If I protest your wedding the king, what makes you think I would agree to have you wed any other than me?"

Her heart thudded, and her stomach fluttered. But the question was . . .

"Why would you wed me?" she asked.

If he claimed that he would wed her for love, then surely the curse would take him and he would die. But whether he claimed it or not, didn't she already know that he did love her? Was she so fearful of ever being loved again that she didn't recognize love when it was right in front of her?

He leaned down and whispered in her ear, "That's a secret I have yet to share with you."

"Why not share it?" she asked, disappointed, and yet she knew the answer or at least hoped she did.

"Because the time is not right. When the time is right, I will share the secret with you," he said. "Now you go see if Bliss has time to talk with you, and I will go talk with my family."

"I should be there."

"I understand why you want to be, but you cannot," Reeve said, and continued before she could protest. "There are matters that will come up in the course of the debate that you cannot know about, matters vital to the true king's return. Know that I will share with you all I can and trust that what I can't will not affect you in any way."

"I do trust you," she said, "though I still wish I could be there."

He leaned down and kissed her quick then returned to linger before releasing her lips. "I will fight for *us*."

"Of that I have no doubt."

They kissed again.

And when it ended, Reeve said, "I had no intentions for what almost happened when I joined you in bed. I simply wanted to nap wrapped around you."

"Naked?" She chuckled.

"Well, my first thought may have been—"

She placed her finger to his lips to still his words. "It's all right. Your embrace was so loving, warm, and welcoming that I never wanted to leave it. I truly wished that we could have finished what was started."

"I'll make sure of that."

"When the curse is gone," she reminded.

"When the time is right."

Tara tried to argue, but he shook his head and hurried her to the door. "We must get busy. Time is short." And out the door he pushed her, following behind.

*Time is short.*

Reeve wondered, as he took the steps two at a time. Was that what Bliss had been trying to warn him . . . time was short because the king was searching for Tara?

Suddenly there was an urgency he hadn't felt before. He needed to make certain that Tara was protected and that the king, or her father, could not lay claim to her, and there was only one way of doing that.

He burst into the solar to find Duncan, Bryce, and their father waiting there.

"I suppose you have a plan," Bryce said.

"What makes you think that?" Reeve asked.

"You're grinning from ear to ear," Duncan said, smiling along with Reeve.

"This is not a situation that calls for smiles," Carmag scolded.

"Unless the smile is because of a perfect solution," Reeve said.

Bryce shook his head. "You cannot tell me that between the time I left you and now, you have come up with a solution."

"Honestly, I cannot say that," Reeve said. "Your news simply forced me to evaluate and better understand my own misgivings and procrastination in the situation."

Carmag shook his head along with Bryce, who said, "You're confusing me."

Duncan clarified it for them. “Reeve has finally accepted and is admitting that he loves Tara.”

Bryce scrunched his brow, even more confused.

Duncan laughed. “It takes a man who has been there to understand.”

“Love cannot rule a situation,” Bryce said staunchly.

Reeve and Duncan laughed.

“You’ll understand better when love finds you,” Carmag said.

“I have no time for such foolish folly,” Bryce barked. “We have a mission, and this situation with Tara could easily damage our plans. Need I remind you all that we have already used some of the money we accepted from her?”

“And we will continue to use it for our benefit,” Reeve said.

Bryce crossed his arms over his broad chest. “It’s her bride price. It belongs to the man she will wed.”

Reeve smiled and nodded. “That’s me.”

Duncan clapped. “I knew it.”

“You don’t win the wager,” Bryce reminded. “It’s been over a month.”

“Why do you do this?” Carmag asked, looking to Reeve.

“He loves her,” Duncan answered.

“I didn’t ask you,” Carmag snapped. “I want to know why. Do you love her, or is it for the good of the true king of Scotland?”

“I’m lucky that it can be for both,” Reeve admitted. “I do love Tara—”He stopped, hearing his declaration roll off his tongue so easily gave him a punch to the gut. “I have debated my love for her far too long instead of simply accepting it. I made it more difficult for myself than it needed to be."

"True," Duncan said, "though I think that time of doubt and questioning is needed to get a firm grasp on love."

"You may be right," Reeve agreed.

Bryce snorted. "Listen to you two. You make something that supposedly you admit is so simple so very difficult. If you love someone, tell them, wed them, and get on with it."

Reeve and Duncan laughed again.

Bryce grew annoyed. "Wait until I find love. I will show you how it is done."

Duncan and Reeve burst into a fit of laughter, and this time, Carmag joined in.

Carmag finally cleared his throat, more of laughter than anything else, and asked, "What of this curse on her? Do you not fear it?"

"Not truly," Reeve said confidently, "but Tara is going to speak with Bliss and see if she can help with it. Regardless, though, I will wed Tara."

"And you believe this will solve the problem?" Bryce asked.

"How would it not?" Reeve said. "Tara weds me, which makes me entitled to her bride price. Who can argue with it? The deed is done, and I'll make certain our vows are consummated. No authority would dare rescind the vows."

"That leaves one problem left before all this can be done," Bryce said.

"What's that?" Reeve asked.

"You have to get Tara to accept your proposal."

# Chapter 22

Tara was relieved when she found that Bliss had time to speak with her. She was also remarkably surprised to see that the redness around Trey's wounds had diminished considerably. And that his fever hadn't returned since she had gotten there. If Bliss had such notable healing powers, then was it possible that she could help Tara?

"Is there a private place where we can talk and share a hot brew?" Bliss asked, as they left Mara to watch over Trey.

Not that Mara had wanted Bliss to leave, and Tara couldn't blame her. It had been only a short time since her arrival, and already there had been marked improvements in Trey. Tara had no doubt that Mara would find a way to keep Bliss with the clan until Trey was healed to her satisfaction and relief.

"My cottage is not far if you don't mind a brief walk in the snow," Tara said.

Bliss smiled. "I love the way the snow paints the land in swatches of winter white. It's such a beautiful sight to behold."

"I never thought of it like that," Tara admitted.

"Because you have never taken the time to look."

Bliss was right. She hadn't. She had been too absorbed in her lonely world to see beauty anywhere. Now, however, it was different. It was as if colors suddenly appeared brighter to her, scents richer, and touch simply divine.

She blushed, turning her head away, thoughts of touch producing naked images of Reeve that she was quite enjoying.

"You're afraid to love Reeve," Bliss said, startling Tara.

Tara sighed and nodded, too taut with anguish to speak.

Bliss rested her hand on Tara's shoulder. "Get your cloak as you intended, and let's go to your cottage and talk."

Tara was only too eager to obey, and it wasn't until they had left the keep with a sprinkle of snow falling upon them that Tara stopped abruptly.

Had it been a logical deduction that Tara intended to get her cloak? After all, they were going out in the snow.

Tara shook her head. "How did you know—"

"Sometimes I simply know what people intend to do, and other times I don't," Bliss said. "It is a strange skill I have and one that I have still to make sense of."

The two women were soon sitting at the small table in front of the hearth in Tara's cottage. Hot cider filled their tankards while a pitcher was kept heated on the hearth.

Tara didn't waste any time. "Can you remove curses?"

"Curses are a difficult lot."

Tara's shoulders sagged, and she felt hope drain away.

"It depends on the curse and who cast it, but it's intention that matters the most."

Hope returned, though cautiously, as Tara said, "I don't understand."

"When curses or spells are cast, they are done so with intention. Whether it is to hurt, to harm, for joy, for love, for help, it is the intention of the caster that gives it power. If someone is angry and wishes harm or hurt to another, then the cast is made with the power of hate. If it is with annoyance or as a nuisance, then its sting is not as strong."

"So the stronger the intention, the more difficult it is to be rid of the curse?"

Bliss nodded. "That is what I have discovered through the years."

"Have you ever removed a curse from someone?"

"A curse or spell can only be removed by the person who cast it or one more powerful than she or he," Bliss said.

"You are powerful," Tara said, her violet eyes turning wide. "I saw how you have healed Trey and in such a short time."

"Trey has yet to fully heal," Bliss said. "I but help him along."

Tara refused her explanation. "No, I have seen your remarkable power to heal. Trey's wounds were near to filling with poison. You stopped that and reduced the redness to almost nothing. That is power."

"To heal," Bliss reminded.

"You're my only hope," Tara pleaded.

"Unselfish love is your only hope."

"What do you mean?" Tara asked.

"An unselfish love in your life counters the curse, but only when you realize it."

"How can that be when you just told me that a curse can only be removed by the one who cast it, or one more powerful?"

"I'm not sure what I mean," Bliss said. "That is the problem with this knowing of mine. I don't always understand what it is I know."

Once more Tara felt the heavy weight descend on her shoulders, which sagged from the burden.

"You should smile," Bliss advised. "There is a way for the curse to be lifted; you must just realize it."

"If I haven't realized it by now, how will I ever?"

"Love has a way of bringing to us what we need," Bliss said, "especially when it is given as a gift from the heart."

*Gift from the heart.*

The words resonated in her head like a bell tolling in the distance, a familiar bell.

"Think on it," Bliss advised. "It will come to you."

Peaceful warmth settled around Tara like the arm of an old friend wrapping around her, and she suddenly felt confident that Bliss was right. It would come to her. The problem was what would she do until then?

"You must trust in love," Bliss said, as if hearing Tara's silent question.

"So far that has been dangerous for me."

Bliss tilted her head and scrunched her brow. "I believe what it has done is brought you where you were meant to be."

"You often speak in riddles."

"That eventually make sense," Bliss assured her. "But that doesn't help when you worry over what you can do now."

"Time grows short."

"Yes, I know," Bliss confirmed. "But a solution will soon present itself."

"It will settle the matter?"

"Only if you trust in love," Bliss warned.

Reeve was sitting at the family table in the great hall when Tara entered with Bliss. He had hoped to catch her alone so that he could ask her to marry him. His brothers and father had shared their thoughts on how he should go about asking her.

"Be honest with her," Bryce had said.

Duncan had shaken his head. "Don't listen to him. He doesn't know what he's talking about. Tell her you love her before you do anything."

"Isn't that being honest?" Bryce had argued.

But his father had given him the best advice. "Let your heart speak for you. It never lies."

While Tara and Bliss approached, he wondered how he could politely get rid of Bliss.

She smiled at him as if she knew his secret, and said, "I'm going to visit with Mercy." And turned and hurried off.

Tara eyed him strangely as she slipped off her cloak. "I've spent only a short time with Bliss, but I have come to know her way. She sensed something from you, and so she left us. Is something wrong?"

Reeve reached out for her hand. "Sit with me. I have something to ask you."

Tara discarded her cloak to a nearby table and joined Reeve.

Different scenarios had run through his head, but he rejected most of them. They simply did not fit the situation, and theirs was a situation. There was so much more involved with a union between them than just love. But the biggest obstacle he knew he would face with her was that she believed herself a *death bride*. How, then, did he approach this?

"We agree that you cannot be sent to the king," he said.

She nodded anxiously.

"But the problem remains that eventually your whereabouts will be found, and demands will be made by the king and your father, and you will have no choice but to obey—unless . . ."

Her eyes brightened, and Reeve was captivated by their color once again, deeper violet, almost purple, and her lips were a plump, soft pink, while her chilled cheeks shone a berry red. Damn, if she didn't tempt him.

"Tell me," Tara urged, squeezing his hand.

He gave an inward shake, clearing his head and focusing his attention on the matter at hand. There would be time soon enough for intimacy with her.

"I want you to marry me, Tara," he said bluntly.

Her hand shot out of his, and she scrambled to her feet and walked around the table away from him.

"Think on it," he warned curtly. "I am not proposing a love match. I am proposing a union out of necessity." He knew if he told her that he loved her, which he did more than he thought possible, she would adamantly refuse him. Approaching it this way, he felt he might have a chance of convincing her.

"You cannot wed me, you will die," she reminded with a heavy sadness.

"No," he said, shaking his head. "I've been thinking about the curse." And he had been, trying to find a way around it.

"If it is a vow you make, death will visit again and take," she said, repeating the relevant section of the curse.

"Right," Reeve said, aching to go over to her and wrap her in his arms, but knowing it was best to keep his distance and not display any signs of affection while trying to convince her. "And it isn't vows we will exchange. It is a decision that will benefit all."

He saw by the way her brow wrinkled, and her eyes narrowed that she was giving it serious thought. And he said no more, allowing his suggestion to take root.

"What of love?"

He had anticipated that question, and, wanting no untruths between them, he was careful how he answered. "What of it? We have touched on it, yet we have yet to fully express it? So it isn't relevant at the moment."

His heart ached when he watched her quickly contain the cringe that surfaced, and he knew his words had hurt her.

She recovered with a brave smile. "That is true. We have declared no love for each other."

"And with no vows, simply a decision to wed, the curse cannot touch us."

"What if—"She paused, hesitant to ask.

Reeve knew the question, had anticipated it since he would have asked himself. "What if we find ourselves in love?"

"We have discussed the possibility."

"And we have agreed that we weren't sure. We were still finding our way with it."

Her eyes returned to their lovely lavender color

though it was filled with sadness. "Then I suppose we should stop finding our way—with love."

Reeve had to keep himself from doubling over, that was how hard her words had hit him in the gut. He knew she didn't mean them, but it didn't help. Hearing it aloud troubled him, and yet in order to get her to wed him, he had to make her believe that love had no part in the decision.

When his father had told him to speak from the heart, he hadn't realized it would cause him and her so much pain.

Bryce and Duncan entered the hall, preventing Reeve from responding, and he was glad for the interruption. It would have been too difficult to agree with her.

They were both grinning like fools, and since they knew that Reeve loved her, they could damage the progress he had made. He jumped up and went to Tara's side, slipping his arm around her waist.

"I convinced them that we were in love, or else they would have protested my decision," he whispered.

Tara never had a chance to reply.

Duncan called out, "So we will have a new sister?"

Reeve grinned and hugged her close. "We wed as soon as arrangements can be made."

Burly hugs and tender kisses were followed by a wrenching screech of delight as Mara came barreling into the hall, Carmag quick on her heels.

"Another daughter, how blessed are we?" Mara cried out, and flung herself at Tara, wrapping her arms around her. "I knew as soon as I saw you that you were just right for Reeve. He's not an easy one to deal with, but I could see you had the strength to handle him."

"Mum, you wound me" Reeve said, feigning hurt though knowing his mother was right. Tara had handled him well from the start and continued to do so.

Mara brushed his protest off with a dismissive wave and continued fawning over Tara. "We'll have a grand feast. I'll cook—"

"No!" All the men yelled in unison.

Mara, her back to them, winked at Tara. "Come, we must tell Mercy and Bliss, and where has Willow gone?"

"I sent her to claim one of the empty cottages for herself," Bryce said.

That had Mara swerving around. "By herself?"

Reeve and Duncan backed away from Bryce as Mara marched over to him.

Bryce's hands went up like a shield. "I had important matters—"

"Nothing is as important as seeing that one of our own is taken care of," Mara said. "Now go find her, and then let me know which one she has chosen so that the women may help her settle in."

Bryce opened his mouth, and Reeve and Duncan grinned at him.

He sent them evil looks, which made the men grin all the more.

"Go now!" Mara ordered, her arm outstretched and her finger pointing to the door.

Bryce mumbled beneath his breath and turned to do as his mother bid, though not before sending death stares at his two brothers.

"What are you two grinning at?" Mara said, turning on her other two sons.

"Happy. I'm happy, Mum," Reeve said.

"And I'm happy for Reeve," Duncan confirmed, draping his arm around his brother.

"Good, then you two happy men go hunt us something special for supper tonight," she ordered.

"With pleasure," Reeve said, Duncan nodding beside him.

"Can I speak with you for a moment, Reeve, before you go?" Tara asked.

He hurried to her side while Duncan made his way to the door, and Mara joined her husband by the hearth, affording the couple privacy.

Reeve stepped close to Tara, and she whispered, "Tell me that you don't love me."

# Chapter 23

Tara could see that Reeve was relieved when Bliss entered the room with shouts of joyous congratulations and for hurrying over to Tara and hugging her. It gave him time to make a sneaky and hasty exit.

Carmag soon followed the men, leaving Mara to join the two women to chatter away about plans for the wedding. She soon had Bliss and Tara hurrying upstairs to tell Mercy the good news and include her in the planning.

The women chatted quietly, Trey still caught in a deep slumber though he no longer suffered with fever. While offering opinions on the wedding plans, Bliss laid gentle hands on Tara's ankle, after Mercy had mentioned it was slow in healing.

Tara enjoyed the camaraderie with the women. They truly were pleased about the coming nuptials and excited about making it a memorable day for Tara. And while she should be thrilled or at least hopeful, it troubled her that Reeve had hurried off rather than give her a quick answer.

Her concern grew as Reeve continued to avoid her throughout the day, and the more he did, the more she dreaded hearing his answer.

If he loved her, she couldn't marry him.

Tara waited anxiously in the great hall. Supper wasn't far off, and while the whole family would appear soon enough, including Reeve, she would request a moment alone with him.

Bryce was the first to arrive though it appeared as if he was trailing after Willow.

"You are the most *willful* woman," he shouted at her back as he kept pace behind her.

She halted so abruptly that he almost collided with her, and Tara watched the exchange with amusement.

"I'm a capable woman," Willow shouted, jabbing at Bryce's chest. "Who doesn't need a *brute* telling her what to do."

Bryce's flared nostrils looked as if they were ready to snort smoke.

Duncan and Mercy drifted in during the heated exchange and joined Tara at the table.

"Someone has to make you see reason," Bryce said.

"Make *me* see reason?" Willow finished with a sharp jab to his chest.

"Jab me again and so help me—"

"What?" she challenged, her chin jutting up.

Bryce let out a roar and stomped off, shaking his head and heading in their direction.

Duncan was grinning from ear to ear.

"Open your mouth, and I'll beat you," Bryce warned, reaching for the pitcher of ale and filling a tankard until the liquid sloshed over the sides. He picked it up and downed almost half then slammed it on the table.

Willow disappeared up the steps, and Duncan said, "Not good."

"Better she retreat than stay here, or I might just wring her neck," Bryce said.

"Think again," Duncan said. "She's going to relieve mum from watching Trey, so that she can have supper with the family."

"Oh shit," Bryce said, and cringed.

Tara couldn't help but laugh, as did Mercy, and for a moment, Tara was free of worries, though only a moment.

Mara skipped the last two steps, looking as if she flew off the staircase and into the great hall, her face aflame with annoyance. At the same moment, Carmag and Reeve burst through the front doors, a chilled wind following them in.

"We have a problem," Carmag said.

"Yes," Mara agreed. "Your son is being rude to our guest."

Tara grew anxious when Reeve hurried to her side and wrapped a strong arm around her.

"That will have to wait, Mara," Carmag said firmly.

"What is it?" Mara asked, her arm going to rest on his.

Carmag turned to Tara. "King Carnoth of Carlig along with a troop of his warriors is but an hour away from arriving here. Is King Carnoth of the west Highlands your father?"

The truth had finally caught up with her. And the thought that her father was but a short distance away terrified her, and so she grabbed tight hold of Reeve's hand before she answered. "Yes, he is my father."

"What's going on?" Mara demanded. "Since obviously there's something you haven't told me."

"Tara has been promised to the king of Scotland," Reeve said.

"Reeve wasn't aware of that until recently," Tara said, not wanting his mother to think that he had intentionally kept it from her.

"It doesn't matter when I learned of it," Reeve said. "You're not going anywhere."

"Then I suppose the plan was to wed Tara before the king or her father learned where she was," Mara said.

"That was the plan," Carmag admitted.

"But there's more to it," Tara said, wanting the whole truth revealed. Mara had been good to her, and she was tired of deceiving her and others.

"Tara—"

"No, Reeve," she said, clinging even more tightly to his hand. "It's time your mum knew the truth."

Tara noticed Duncan wrap his arm around Mercy, as if ready to protect or comfort her. Carmag even took a step closer to his wife.

Tara took a breath, and said, "I'm a *death bride.*"

There was an audible gasp from both women, and for a moment, there was complete silence.

"You've lost one husband?" Mara finally asked.

"One, but also a man I loved," Tara said, and wasn't surprised to see Mara cringe.

"It makes no difference," Reeve said.

"It makes all the difference," Mara argued. "I'll not lose a son if it can be helped."

"I agree," Tara said. "I will not see another suffer because of me."

"I'll not see you dead because a curse was feared," Reeve said vehemently.

Mara shook her head. "It's as though you talk in riddles. Explain it all to me, *now*!"

Reeve did so, keeping it brief and finishing with.

"King Kenneth will kill Tara after vows are exchanged."

"And he keeps her bride price, the only thing he ever wanted from her," Bryce finished.

"This is a problem," Mara confirmed. "We certainly cannot surrender Tara to her father."

"I knew you wouldn't, Mum," Reeve said with a grin.

Mara shook her finger at Reeve and proceeded to do the same to each of her sons and Carmag. "I'll deal with all of you later, keeping this from me. For now we need to protect Tara."

They each had the good sense to look contrite.

"We need time to wed," Reeve said.

"That decision needs more consideration," Mara said.

"I agree," Tara said, relieved that she finally had someone who saw things as sensibly as she did.

"In the meantime, let's make certain we greet King Carnoth with a substantial feast," Mara said.

"My father would expect it," Tara said.

Mara nodded. "Then we will not disappoint him."

"Mum is right," Bryce said and received a generous smile from Mara. "We'll stuff them with food and drink, giving us time to revise our plans."

Mara turned to Tara. "Go make yourself ready for your father. It will be good for him to see how you have prospered here in spite of the curse."

Tara nodded and eased herself out of Reeve's arms.

He, however, refused to let her go. "I'll go with you."

"No," Mara snapped. "You will stay here and

talk with your brothers and father and see what can be done to correct this mess."

"No," Reeve said. "I'm going with Tara."

Before Mara could argue with him, Tara stepped in. "Do as your mum says. I need time alone."

She walked away before Reeve could argue, and, after grabbing her cloak off the peg, she hurried out the door and to her cottage. Tears were running down her cheeks by the time she closed the door behind her.

Try as they might, the MacAlpin warriors would find no way to save her. Her father was near, and he would demand her return. Her fate was sealed. She would wed the king of Scotland and die on her wedding day.

She couldn't stop the tears from falling as she prepared to meet her fate. She would say nothing to Reeve. She would wait until her father's arrival and confess her sins to him, making him understand that Reeve never knew who she was and that she had given her bride price to them in good faith and that he could not ask for its return.

Tara knew her father had hoards of money and could well afford to let the MacAlpins keep her bride price and still pay the king it as well.

It was the only sensible thing to do, and it was the right thing to do, the unselfish thing to do.

She freshened her appearance, letting her dark hair fall freely and thinking how only a short time ago Reeve had proposed marriage under conditions that just might have proved successful against the curse, and now . . .

She sighed and shook her head slowly, not believing how it had all changed in such a short time. With her cloak wrapped around her and her head bent against the cold wind, Tara returned to the keep.

Reeve hurried right over to her, taking her hand. "It will be all right. I promise."

At that moment, Tara felt the urge to tell him how she truly felt about him. After all, she might never get another chance, and she also knew she would regret it if she never told him . . .

"I love you," she whispered after leaning close against him.

She felt him grow rigid next to her, and she knew she had shocked him. She had even shocked herself, but it was something she had to do. Her father would no doubt want to leave early in the morning, and she wouldn't be surprised if the king's men waited in the woods to take her directly to the king to be wed.

Her time with Reeve was short, and she didn't want to waste it. She wanted him to know she loved him and always would.

"Always," she murmured. "I'll love you always."

His arm curved around her waist and he drew her up against him. His dark eyes danced with passion and joy, and he grinned. She just loved his grin, and she smiled in return.

He pressed his lips to her temple, looking to all as if he kissed her, but instead he whispered, "You're mine, and your father will not take you from me."

Her smile grew. She hadn't expected words of love, he would save them for when he was sure it was safe and could not be used against him, could not be used to prevent them from marrying.

Besides, in an odd way, his response was better than his admitting he loved her. It settled deep in her heart and gave her a smidgen of hope.

Bryce rushed into the great hall, a flurry of snow covering his shoulders. "Carnoth has arrived."

Reeve was quick to hurry her over to the table by his family. Tara noticed that Bliss and Willow were not present, and she wondered if Trey was all right. She didn't have a chance to ask; her father stormed into the hall, shouting her name.

Tara wanted to cringe, but she didn't. She held her head high and squared her shoulders, prepared to do whatever it took to keep Reeve and his family safe.

Reeve watched King Carnoth march toward them. It didn't surprise him that Tara took a heroic stance beside him. He was aware that she planned to sacrifice herself for him, she had been sacrificing herself for years, and when she had admitted she loved him, he knew she was saying good-bye.

He had no intentions of letting her go anywhere even if he had to battle her father's entire troop to keep her here.

Carmag stepped forward. "Welcome to the MacAlpin clan."

Reeve was proud at the way his father stood tall and reminded his guest that he was on MacAlpin land, which meant he should tread light or suffer the consequences.

Unfortunately, Reeve could tell that King Carnoth was too angry to listen to reason, and he approached like a man ready to battle, a mistake he'd be certain to regret.

"You better welcome me, Carmag of the clan MacAlpin, and explain why my daughter resides with you."

With the man only a few feet away, Reeve assessed him quickly. He was not a tall man though he was broad and thick, though more round, his long hair was all gray, and his face wore a multitude of wrinkles.

Tara moved out of Reeve's arms before he could stop her, and his heart lurched in his chest, fearing at that moment he had lost her.

"I requested shelter from the MacAlpin clan, and they were kind enough to give it to me," she said. "In return, I offered them my bride price."

"You what?" her father shouted. "Your bride price belongs to your future husband."

That was all Reeve needed to hear. He stepped forward, moving to Tara's side. "That would be me."

"The hell it is," King Carnoth spat. "Tara has been promised to King Kenneth, and it is King Kenneth she will wed."

"Not anymore," Reeve said vehemently.

"Get over here, daughter," King Carnoth ordered, his hand snapping at his side.

Reeve tried to grab hold of her arm, but she avoided his effort to stop her and went to her father's side.

"How dare you think that you can do as you please. The king's men wait to take you to him and be wed. You leave in the morning."

Tara tried to accept her fate, she truly did, though what troubled her more was the thought that her father held so little regard for her that he would send her to possible death without thought or care. That hurt terribly, especially after spending time with Reeve's loving family and seeing how they all cared and looked after each other.

"And if I don't," she bravely asked.

Her father's face exploded red, spittle flying from his mouth. He was too angry for a coherent reply. His hand was as quick as ever, and he raised it, Tara only having time to brace for the blow.

It never reached her. Reeve stepped forward and grabbed her father by the wrist before his heavy hand could do any damage.

While her father struggled against Reeve's strength, he said, "Tara belongs to me, touch her, harm her in any way, and I'll kill you."

A group of six who had entered with King Carnoth quickly stepped forward, hands on the hilts of their swords. Reeve's brothers and the MacAlpin warriors who occupied the hall had their swords drawn as they stepped forward.

"Enough," Carmag declared. "There'll be no bloodshed here."

"Then tell your son that it is not his decision as to who my daughter weds," King Carnoth said loudly.

"Perhaps an agreement can be reached," Carmag suggested.

King Carnoth yanked his wrist free and stepped away from his daughter, while his eyes remained intent on Reeve. "My daughter weds the king. There is nothing else to discuss." He snapped his fingers at his men. "Take her and see that she stays put."

Reeve stepped in front of the men who came for her. And when they hesitated, Tara glanced at Reeve. His look was feral, like an animal ready to attack his prey and enjoy every minute of tearing them limb from limb.

"What do you wait for?" King Carnoth yelled.

Tara thought she had imagined the growl, but

then she heard it again. It came from Reeve, a snarl of sorts that developed soon enough into a low, predatory growl, the rumble coming deep from his chest.

Her father's men quickly retreated several steps.

"Carmag," her father shouted. "I expect you to honor my rule when it comes to my daughter. The choice is mine, not hers or yours."

"I certainly have no intentions of usurping your rule," Carmag assured him. "Though I do suggest that we all sit and partake of the bountiful feast my wife has seen prepared for you and your men."

"First, I will have a private word with my daughter," King Carnoth said.

"As you wish," Carmag said, and waved Reeve away.

Reeve went reluctantly though not before whispering to Tara as he passed her, "I will not fail you."

Tara wanted to cry. That he should still believe that he could save her against all odds proved to her just how much he loved her. It also proved that she could not marry him, for he would surely die. And she would rather see him live and lose him than love him and see him dead.

Her father stepped so close that his hot breath felt like it singed her skin when he spoke. "I can see you wed this fool here and now, if you wish. And when he dies at your feet or before the night ends, then I will take you to the king and see that you honor the agreement I have made with him. I give you that choice."

Fear tickled down Tara's spine. She could not wed Reeve. She could not take the chance. She would never be able to live with the thought that she had been the cause of his senseless death. She also didn't wish to wed the king. But how she would escape that, she had no idea.

"I'll have your answer," her father snarled.

She had no choice and her father knew it and that was why he had enlisted her aid in seeing this matter settled before it escalated into a battle.

"I'll wed the king."

"Tell all here that you have agreed," he ordered sharply.

Tara stepped away from him, and her glance fell on Reeve. He would live and that was all that mattered to her and she was glad, so very glad that she had had the courage to confess her love to him. Her strong voice carried throughout the hall. "I will wed the king."

Reeve shook his head slowly, a snarl spreading across his face.

# Chapter 24

Reeve kept the appearance of a man in control, but inside he felt like a caged animal waiting to be released. He knew Tara was once again sacrificing herself for the sake of others. She had done it so often that it had become a natural thing for her to do.

He had until morning, though he had the feeling that Carnoth would probably sneak her out in the middle of the night, and therefore he needed to hurry and devise a feasible plan. He knew his family was thinking the same.

It was a difficult situation for sure. The MacAlpin clan had no business denying King Carnoth his daughter. The king had the right to do with her as he pleased, his clan, his laws. But as a Highlander and a defender of the true king of Scotland, Reeve had been raised with a strong moral code. He was there to protect the people, fight against injustices, and see that the man who could bring all of that to Scotland be seated on the throne.

Until that could happen, he presently needed to protect one particular person—the woman he loved.

*Love.*

How had it ever happened to him? He certainly

hadn't been looking to fall in love, but somehow love had found him. It had laid claim to him whether he was ready, willing or not. And while he had never given love much thought, being too busy in seeing that the true king took the throne, love had crept up on him and settled firmly in his heart.

He was in love, and there was no denying it. He just hadn't expected for it to be this difficult, to face so many obstacles, and each more insurmountable than the next. He refused to give up. He told Tara he would not fail her, and he wouldn't. A plan was already bubbling in his mind. He would stir it around, let it simmer, and when it was finished, he would serve it up hot and ready and most likely not to everyone's taste.

He had tried to capture Tara's attention, but she had avoided looking his way. His heart ached for how much she must be suffering, but he'd soon remedy that.

Bryce came over to stand beside him, his hand on his shoulder. "Let me know when you're ready."

Reeve loved the unspoken understanding amongst his brothers. Bryce had no idea what Reeve had planned, but he was letting him know he stood beside him regardless. Reeve never doubted he would, and it was good to know that he could always count on that.

"He will take her before sunrise," Bryce whispered.

"Agreed."

Duncan joined them, smiling and retaining his grin as he said, "Don't leave me out."

The brothers smiled and nodded, all the while planning.

* * *

Tara was relieved when Willow entered the room and explained that Tara was needed in Trey's room. Mara grew upset and was quick to jump up, ready to go to her son.

"Stay. You have guests," Willow urged with a strong grasp of her arm. "Tara can see to this without any help."

Mara returned to her seat, and Tara looked to her father, knowing if she didn't seek permission, he would make a scene.

"May I?"

"Be quick about it," her father snapped. "It grows late, and we leave at first light."

Tara left with Willow and was surprised when the woman stopped abruptly on the staircase as they neared the second floor.

"Bliss, Mercy, and I have talked and decided that you must leave here, not only if you wish to live but if bloodshed is to be avoided."

"When have you had the time—"

"That doesn't matter. What does matter is that you are much like us—"

Tara shook her head. "You are all so strong."

"As are you, which is why we know you can do this."

"Do what?" Tara asked, a bit fearful yet eager.

"Escape to the protection of the Picts."

Tara felt a smidgen of hope. Her father often spoke about avoiding the pagan Picts. He wanted nothing to do with them. They lived by their own rules, guarded their land vigilantly, and were fierce fighters.

Willow continued explaining. "Bliss has offered

you sanctuary with her people and insists that you stay at her cottage. She will not be returning until she makes certain that Trey is healed. You should be safe there."

"And with Reeve and his family not knowing where I've gone . . ."

"Your father cannot hold them responsible."

"When do I leave?" Tara asked. Thanks to the help and caring of her new friends, she didn't feel as isolated as she had felt for so many years. Their courage gave her courage, and she finally felt that she just might be able to survive this ordeal and hopefully find a way to conquer the curse and, please God, be free to love Reeve.

"Now," Willow said. "Follow me."

Willow took her through passages in the keep that she hadn't known existed, and she surmised that Mercy must have shared their secrets. That these women trusted her without question and believed in her made her all the more determined to succeed.

In the night shadows of the towering keep, Willow stopped and searched behind several barrels. She pulled out a wrapped bundle, untied it, pulled out a thick wool cloak, and handed it to Tara.

Willow retied the bundle. "There is a change of clothes and food that should last until you reach Pict land. Bliss thought of having Roan and his men take you home, but if she did, that—"

"It could start a war, since my father would never believe that I would willingly go with the Picts."

Willow gave Tara a hug. "You can do this. You're a strong woman."

"Thank you. You don't know how much your encouragement helps me."

"We'll see you again," Willow said with teary eyes. "Bliss says so."

That knowledge brought a smile to Tara's face though it didn't prevent a tear or two from falling. "I look forward to it."

"Go," Willow urged. "Don't stop and don't look back."

Tara did just that. She disappeared into the woods, following the trail Bliss had outlined to Willow though it was more a trail of trees that she had been advised to follow. Willow had assured her that she would not get lost, even with its being the dark of night.

Willow had also explained that if she should accidentally deviate from the prescribed path, she could possibly come upon the king's men since they waited in the woods to take custody of her. And so Tara kept a keen eye on the towering trees, with particular notches that guided her along the way.

Reeve watched Carnoth grow more and more agitated as an hour passed, and Tara hadn't returned. He had grown concerned himself. What was keeping her?

Anxiousness grew as chatter slowed, and whispers began circulating the hall as another hour passed and still no Tara.

Carnoth stood angry. "Bring me my daughter now."

"I'll go see what's keeping her," Mercy offered.

When Mara said she'd go, Mercy hurried off, ignoring the woman and even avoiding her husband's hand that reached out to stop her.

Reeve sensed something wasn't right, but there wasn't much he could do right now but wait and see.

Carnoth started pacing between the tables while his men sat rigid, eyeing the MacAlpin warriors. Tension was brewing, and if Tara didn't make an appearance soon, a fight just might erupt.

Mercy returned just as Carnoth looked ready to explode.

"Tara is busy tending Trey's stitches. She will be a bit longer and bids you to retire if you wish."

Carnoth glanced around at the MacAlpin clan, and Reeve knew what he was thinking, for he would have thought the same. With the MacAlpin family present, Carnoth felt safe that no one was attempting to help his daughter escape. None of the MacAlpins, not even the warriors, had left the hall, so he obviously felt confident in his assumption.

Not so Reeve. He could feel something was going on. Willow had come for Tara and had brushed off Mara's help. Then Mercy hadn't even acknowledged Mara's offer. Something definitely was brewing. He wanted to go find out for himself, but if he left now, it would look suspicious. And if the women were up to something, would his actions interfere?

Reeve waited, feeling ever more the caged animal hungry for release. When Willow finally entered the hall and explained that Tara was still not finished, Carnoth exploded.

"I will have my daughter here now!" he screamed, shaking his fist in the air.

Carmag had no choice; he stepped forward. "Tell Tara that her father demands her presence. She must come now."

Willow sighed and shook her head. "Tara is not with Trey."

Carnoth kicked at benches, sending one or two

sprawling as he approached Carmag. "What have you done with her?"

"I know nothing—"

"He doesn't," Willow said, before Carnoth could accuse him otherwise.

Carnoth took an abrupt step closer to her, his round chest near bumping her. Reeve and Bryce were at her side in an instant.

"Where is my daughter?" Carnoth demanded.

"I don't know," Willow said with a shrug.

Reeve was impressed that the blustering man hadn't upset Willow in the least.

"After Mercy let us know you inquired about her, Tara simply said she was leaving and to please give her time to make her escape."

Carnoth turned to his men. "Go find her."

"We will help," Carmag said. "It is cold and dark out there. She certainly couldn't have gotten far."

Reeve admired the way his father didn't give Carnoth a choice while making his concern for Tara known. Carnoth couldn't turn him down, or he'd look the fool.

Carnoth accepted the help, though reluctantly.

There was a scramble for the door, and, in the chaos, Reeve took Willow by the arm and guided her to a dark corner of the hall.

"Tell me what is going on," he demanded.

Tara kept on the path, careful not to wander away from the trees that marked her course. Having spent so much time alone, the solitude of the forest didn't disturb her though the darkness was a bit frightening, as was the crunch of snow beneath her feet, which sounded much too loud to her ears.

She kept walking, knowing she needed to place as much distance and time between her and her father as she could. She would need to keep her hurried pace, tired or not. She could not take time to rest. She needed to keep going and not stop until she reached Pict land.

The crunches of her footfalls remained constant in her head until she suddenly stopped, it dawning on her that she was leaving a trail that anyone could follow. Her father would find it in no time.

She remained frozen, not sure what to do when suddenly the dead silence of the night was broken by . . . footfalls. She cocked her head and listened, not sure where they were coming from, or if they were moving toward her or away, their volume remaining steady.

Had her father finally found out that she had left? Had he informed the king's men? Was danger closer than she thought? She was grateful that the moon was just a sliver tonight, her dark, hooded cloak making it easier for her to blend with the night shadows.

The question that most disturbed her was that if she had heard their footfalls, had they heard hers?

Tara wasn't sure of her next move. Stay or go?

Suddenly the footfalls grew louder, and she feared someone had picked up her trail and was heading toward her. She took off, her pace even faster than before.

Hours later, when dawn broke, and her body was racked with fatigue, she thought herself safe, and she stopped for a moment to rest. Leaning against a large boulder for support, though she dare not let herself sit for fear of not getting to her feet again, she closed her eyes and took a deep breath.

The air was cold, though, gratefully, no snow was falling. Enough already covered the ground to prove challenging at times. Snowdrifts had also tested her endurance, and no doubt those who followed her as well. In the last hour or so, when she had stopped to listen, she hadn't heard the footfalls. Before that they had remained in the distance, which allowed her to linger if only briefly.

With aching arms, she shoved away from the boulder, ready to return to her arduous, but necessary, journey.

"You'll be going with us now."

Tara let out a shout she was so startled by the unexpected voice. And when she saw that she was surrounded by five of the king's men, she grew angry. She had not come all this way to be caught.

Her eyes narrowed, and her lip curled in a snarl as she said, "I'm not going anywhere with you."

The soldiers laughed, and the biggest one, in height as well as width, who seemed to lead them, stepped forward. "You'll be going with us like it or not. And we might just be having a little fun along the way."

Tara knew what he implied, but the king would never allow it. She was his future bride, and so she reminded them. "You dare touch me, and you will answer to the king."

The big one thought that funny and laughed again. When his amusement subsided, he informed her, "It was the king who suggested we have fun with you."

Now she knew for certain that the king had no intentions of seeing her live past their vows. The only thing left to threaten them with was the curse.

"If you touch me, you will be doomed," she warned calmly.

Two of the soldiers' brows furrowed though her words had no effect on the other three.

"We don't plan to make you our bride," the big one snickered. "Though you will surrender to each of us if you know what's good for you."

He stepped forward as did the two behind him, though the two that raised their brows in doubt remained where they were.

Tara dropped the bundle and made a fist.

"A feisty one," another soldier said. "I like that."

"I'm first," claimed the big one.

"Good, then if you drop dead, we'll know not to touch her," one of the reluctant ones said with a laugh.

"He'll drop dead, I promise you that, though it will be before he gets anywhere near her." Reeve stepped out of the woods, his sword drawn, and walked over to Tara, his hand going out to gently stroke her cheek.

"Are you all right?" he asked.

"Now that you are here, I am."

Reeve smiled. "You must have known I'd come for you."

"You weren't supposed to," she scolded with a smile.

"And miss a chance to save you once again?" He shook his head and grinned, though it faded as he positioned himself like a warrior's shield in front of her.

# Chapter 25

Reeve was furious. He didn't want to think what would have happened to Tara if he hadn't shown up when he did. And he intended to make each of the soldiers pay for what they had planned to do, and it had to be done quickly.

The big one made the mistake of laughing. "There's five of us and one of you."

Tara peeked past Reeve's shoulder. "You need more men?"

Reeve grinned, pleased with the confidence she had in him and pleased that she knew he would not fail her, as he had promised.

The big one courageously or rather foolishly stepped forward. "I'll let you watch while we have our way with the woman before we kill you."

Reeve's fist came up fast and furious and struck him before he had a chance to react. The one solid blow to the soldier's jaw sent him reeling back, and he bounced as he hit the ground, unconscious.

Though startled, the other soldiers reacted as taught, and, with swords drawn, they advanced on Reeve. He pushed Tara back and out of the way and rushed at them with an angry roar that shook the tree branches and had two of the soldiers halting in fear. Their hesitation gave him all the time he needed to deal with the first two and then finish off the next two in quick succession. They were no match for his extraordinary skills and strength, and it took little effort to see the job done. He left the big one for the cold to finish off or the animals and grabbed hold of Tara.

"We have to go."

She reached for her bundle. "My father follows?"

He nodded. "I did what I could to cover your tracks, but if your father has a good tracker, he'll find the trail in no time."

"How did you—"

"Willow told me everything."

Tara was so relieved to see him that she wrapped her arms around him and pressed her face to his chest, comforted by his familiar woodsy scent.

"There'll be time to thank me later."

She chuckled, happy to hear his teasing. She so feared the possibility of never seeing him again, and for the moment she didn't care about anything except that he was there with her.

"Let's go," he urged, "for if I take you in my arms right now, nothing will prevent me from making love to you."

She felt the same, her passion burning so deeply that she actually felt hot enough to want to rip her clothes off. Not a good idea, and there was still the curse to be dealt with.

They hurried off, knowing it would take almost two days before they reached their destination and safety, all the while knowing they could be captured at any moment. Whether it was by another group of soldiers or her father, her fate with either would be wretched.

They walked a good distance before Reeve spoke again. “We must find a way to wed. It is the only way to stop your father from giving you to the king.”

Tara needed him to understand her fear of that happening, and so she confessed. “My father offered me the chance to wed you.”

That stopped him dead, and he turned to glare at her as she stepped up beside him. “And you didn’t take it?”

“You would have died,” she argued.

“We had worked that out.”

“No, you lied to me. You do love me, and I love you.”

He grabbed her and brought his lips down so hard on hers that she thought he would crush the breath from her. But he didn’t. Instead, he fed the frenzied passion that had remained vibrantly alive in them.

He finally tore his lips away. “I will have you this night and put an end to this nonsense.”

“No, you mustn’t. We love each other. You will surely die,” she pleaded.

“Then it will be a good death.”

With that, he released her and started walking. “There is a vacant croft. It will take until after dark for us to reach, but reach it we will. And there is where I will make you mine.”

Tara followed. She was already beyond exhausted, as he must be, neither of them having slept since the previous night, leaving her too tired to argue with him. There would be time to debate whether they would make love or not. Truthfully, she was willing.

She wanted him to make love to her, but she feared the cost was too high a price to pay.

They discovered tracks around the croft that disappeared into the woods to the east, away from them. There were also remnants of recent occupation of the cottage, the hearth ashes still warm. A traveler no doubt had made use of the vacant place and had left without extinguishing the flames, leaving the fire to burn out on its own. Unless soldiers canvassed the area, a thought they would need to keep in mind.

Tara was glad that Reeve had made her wait along the way while he had set about misdirecting anyone who followed. She felt safe enough that whoever had been there wouldn't return, though that didn't mean they could take a chance and light a fire. And they would need to be vigilant, meaning they would need to take turns sleeping.

There would be no making love tonight.

The cottage retained a small amount of warmth, which was sure to dwindle as the night wore on.

"We'll huddle by the hearth where the heat remains." Reeve held his hand out to her.

She hesitated, wondering if he still planned to do as he had claimed.

He seemed to know what she was thinking. "As much as I want to make love to you, this is not the time or place. Once we are safe, I promise you that nothing will stop me from making love to you."

She walked over to him slowly, her hand outstretched. "I will attempt to make you see reason before then."

He smiled and reached out to grab hold of her hand. "And I will convince you otherwise."

"We'll see about that," she said, as his arms wrapped around her, and she melted into him.

"You surrender already," he whispered, and pressed his lips to her temple.

"I am cold and hungry."

"I can keep you warm and full," he murmured, much too invitingly.

Her stomach answered with loud, grumbling protests.

Reeve laughed. "I guess I got my answer."

They feasted on what foods Willow had packed, and they made sure to save some for tomorrow. Soon they found themselves huddled against the corner of the hearth. Tara sat curled in his lap, her head resting against his chest. Her cloak as well as Reeve's wrapped snugly around them, keeping them warm along with their body heat.

His hand slipped from her waist to cup her breast. "I love the feel of you."

"You said you won't—"

"Make love to you, though I didn't say I would not touch you."

"Is that wise?"

"Tell me to stop," he whispered.

"I should—"

"But you can't, can you?"

He was right, and her nipple responded, hardening to his unmercifully teasing thumb.

"If we were in a safe place, I would strip you of your clothes and take my time exploring every inch of your exquisite body."

The image his words evoked sent a shiver through her.

"You would do more than shiver at my touch. I promise you that."

Tara hadn't realized that she had grabbed his shirt as he continued to torment her breasts and inflame her passion. A small moan escaped her lips when his hand drifted away from her breasts and settled between her legs.

She knew the danger of letting him linger there, and though her velvet dress and linen shift provided a barrier between their bodies, it didn't stop her from feeling him grow hard beneath her.

Why, then, didn't she warn him to stop?

Because it simply felt too deliciously wonderful, and the more he teased and tormented, the more delicious it felt.

"Your skin is much like this velvet dress, so soft and alluring that I can't stop touching you."

Somewhere in her mind, where reason and sanity still reigned, though she much preferred that it didn't, she found the courage to say, "You should . . . stop touching—"

His hand stilled. "Is that what you want?"

The absence of his touch devastated her, and her body protested by writhing in an effort to force his hand's return.

"It isn't, is it?" he whispered.

Tara tilted her head back, not having had the courage to look into his eyes, knowing what she saw would only make her want him more. And it did. Passion burnt as deep in his eyes as she knew it did in hers.

"Even so, we shouldn't." Sensibility struck again, and she silently cursed it.

He brushed his lips over hers, and it heightened the tingling sensation that already ran through her body. He did it again and again, until her lips finally grabbed hold of his, and they kissed.

Reasoning completely vanished as she quenched, or was it fired, her passion with a never-ending kiss?

She didn't know when his hand started moving against her again or when her body responded to a new yet familiar rhythm. She only knew that she didn't want him to stop. She wanted to embrace the rising passion, lose herself in it, and finally surrender to it.

And she did.

She buried her face against Reeve's chest, drawing in the scent of him as her breathing turned rapid and her body responded to his intimate strokes, but it was when his hand found its way beneath her dress and connected with her flesh that she gasped and began to moan.

Nothing made sense. Nothing seemed real except for his touch.

She thought she moaned his name, but she wasn't sure. And as his fingers caressed, stroked, and tormented, she writhed against him as if begging for more. She couldn't control herself, didn't want to.

When he whispered softly, "Let go," she did, and the world exploded around her, her head falling back, her body arching against his touch, and he capturing her moan with his lips and sharing in her climax the least dangerous way he could.

When her senses finally returned, and she saw that he was staring at her, she blushed.

He grinned, and said, "Now you belong to me."

While she had no objections to that, there remained many obstacles, but even so that was no reason to deny the truth. "I would have it no other way."

"I'm warning you now that I will never be able to keep my hands off you."

"I cherish the thought, and if all goes well, I fear it will be me whose hands are always on you."

Reeve was quick to say, "I'll make sure all goes well, and your hands are welcome on any part of me anytime."

"You may be sorry you said that."

"Never," he said with an adamant shake of his head.

Her eyes suddenly turned sad, and he was quick to notice. "What's wrong?"

"Being intimate with you has made me realize how very lonely I have been. No one to talk with, no one to be close with, no arms to comfort me or simply hold me. I had let myself believe that my forced solitude was not a bad life, but now"–she shook her head and placed her hand on his warm, flushed cheek. "I don't believe I could live without you."

His arms tightened protectively around her. "You're not going to."

"But—"

"No buts," he said firmly. "We are going to wed, raise a family, and grow old together, and since I cannot live without you as well, we shall die together, or at least within days of each other."

"That's a lovely thought; if only it could be so."

"Have no doubt, it will be."

"You talk as if you know it is so," she said, wishing she could be as confident.

"I do know, for I will see to it."

"See that you do," she said teasingly, and yawned, exhaustion finally catching up with her.

"Orders already, and we're not even wed yet."

"You are not a man to order about," she said, her eyes closing. "You are a man to love, and I love you with all my heart."

Reeve felt sleep claim Tara, her body going limp against him, and he held her close, never wanting to let her go. He hadn't planned on bringing her to climax, but once he started, and he realized how much she desired it herself, he couldn't stop, wouldn't stop. He wanted her to taste the love he had to offer her.

What he hadn't counted on was how it had made him feel. It had made him realize how real his love was for her. He hadn't thought about satisfying his own needs, only hers. And he had never known such a feeling before.

He knew now more than ever that they were meant to be. And he would let nothing, absolutely nothing, stand in his way. It struck him then how that would not be possible. His first pledge was to the true king of Scotland, and he could let nothing stand in his way, not even love. His mission affected too many for him to simply disregard it. And his pledge was his word and his honor.

It troubled his heart to think that he could lose her so that the true king could take the throne, but he also knew that love defied even the most powerful of men and nations. He would honor his pledge, but he would also honor his love for Tara.

She had nearly broken his heart when she had confessed how lonely she had been. He could not imagine not having his family around, or their refusing to speak with him, completely ignoring him as if he didn't exist. How could her father, her clan, have done that to her? And how had she survived it and retained her sanity?

His heart went out to her, and he wanted to keep her close and protect her not only from her father but from loneliness. He wanted her to know that she need only reach out, and he would be there.

*Always. He always would be there.*

He wished he could declare, shout, sing out his love for her, but he held his tongue. He knew that was the last barrier they would need to breach before she agreed to marry him. And he would not take the chance of her using it against him. She might believe he loved her, but it was to his advantage not to voice it just yet.

He was glad that they would have some time alone together. He didn't know how long he could stay with her. Bryce was aware of the situation and had told him that he would send word when the time was right for him or them both to return.

He hoped for more than just a few days. He hoped they would have weeks to love and to let their love take firm root and grow. Then nothing could stop them, not even a curse.

He still wasn't sure how he would work his way around the curse. How he could convince her that it could not affect them and even how he knew it held no power against their love.

He would take one step at a time, and the first step was getting Tara to see the power of their love. And the more he made love to her, the more time they spent together, the more she would realize that and the better chance he'd have of convincing her that their love was more powerful than the curse.

He made sure their cloaks were tucked around

them, the last of the warm ashes having died off and the cold already seeping in through the walls. Their bodies, however, had retained the heat of their passion and were warm and snug beneath the cloaks. He would keep watch over her and listen for any unusual sounds.

He would let nothing happen to her. *Nothing*.

He pressed a kiss to the top of her head and whispered what he wished he could shout. "I love you. I will always love you."

# Chapter 26

Reeve had slept for only a few hours. Tara had woken suddenly a couple of hours before dawn and insisted that he sleep even though he could see she was still fatigued. He didn't argue, knowing a couple of hours would refresh him enough for the day.

He had been trained as a warrior since a very early age and had learned to exist on little sleep. Tara, however, had not, and he knew the fast pace he set would wear her down though they had little choice.

The king's soldiers and Carnoth's men would not rest. They would keep a pace more grueling than the one he and Tara set. And he explained this to her.

She yawned and slipped her bundle on her arm. "Then we will need to set a more strenuous pace. And if I'm correct, that would mean we will reach Pict land by nightfall."

"It is possible if we can keep a good pace."

"Then I suggest we get started," she said, and opened the door.

Reeve grinned and followed her out. Clouds greeted them and a brisk chill, though no snow fell. Reeve took the lead, and Tara remained close behind. He glanced back often to make certain she kept up, and she did, though he wondered how long she could last. They didn't converse much, a word or two here and there. Instead, they conserved their strength for their laborious journey.

They stopped briefly to grab the food left from last night and ate as they walked. Reeve knew Tara was feeling the pace, but she bravely matched his strides. He was glad for the silence between them, his warrior instincts always more alert in the silence.

The day dragged on, but not their feet, and soon dusk would be falling. An hour or more, and they would reach Pict territory. Though the day had gone well for them, Reeve wouldn't let his guard down until they were safe, and even then he would be watchful.

He heard it too late, though he was able to draw his sword and shove Tara behind him as he braced for attack. They came charging from the woods, only three, and he knew he could easily do away with them. Then three more charged from another direction, and he felt he'd be able to dispose of them as well, though he worried that in the melee Tara could be taken from him.

"Stay close," he ordered. "Don't let them separate us."

Her back slammed against his.

"Keep alert and let no one near you."

There was no more time for talk, only time to fight. They attacked from all sides and Reeve took two down right away. The others did as he expected; they tried to separate them. He was impressed and grateful that Tara hadn't let fear intrude. She bravely kept to his back and he heard a soldier yelp now and again.

"Get her, you fool," one soldier yelled.

"She's throwing stones at me," he answered.

"She's only a woman."

"A cursed woman," Tara yelled. "Look what I've brought down on this fool."

Her threatening words gave the soldiers a brief pause, and Reeve took advantage. In no time, he disposed of two more. He wasn't happy to see two others emerge from the woods, and he wondered how many more waited in the shadow of the trees.

He fought with the fury of ten men, intent on keeping the soldiers from separating them, and Tara did the same, staying at his back and fending off their attackers with stones.

Reeve took another one down, but they were getting smart, and he feared they would somehow drive a wedge between him and Tara.

"Stay close," he yelled, as his sword clashed with three, the others circling behind him.

Another soldier fell, and Reeve felt confident that he'd have them all down in no time. When suddenly one circled in a run and charged him from the side, Reeve turned to fend him off, but too late. He went sprawling to the ground, leaving Tara vulnerable.

He scrambled to his feet, and what he saw stabbed at his heart and made him roar with anger. A soldier had hold of her by the hair and was dragging her off into the woods. She was screaming and kicking and clawing at his hand, but he held firm.

Reeve turned on the remaining soldiers with a vengeance. They were no match for his fury, and he disposed of them quickly and made a dash after Tara. He stopped for a moment once in the woods and listened.

God bless her, she was still screaming, and he followed the sound.

He almost panicked when he heard the sound of

horses snorting. If they got her on a horse and rode off, he'd never catch them. He broke into a dead run that nothing could stop. He mowed down small bushes, shoved branches out of his way, vaulted over large rocks, and never once slowed down.

He focused on her scream all the while mumbling, "I'm coming for you, Tara. I'm coming for you."

He barged through a clumping of bushes onto a large boulder and as he did he saw one of the two soldiers land a punch to Tara's jaw, snapping her head back and knocking her unconscious.

A feral snarl started deep in his chest, and as he launched himself off the boulder, sword in hand, it burst into a spine-chilling roar.

The soldier paled as the mighty Highlander came hurtling through the air toward him. Shock and fear froze the soldier, and, with one forceful swing of Reeve's sword, he was dead. He turned to dispose of the other soldier, but he was gone.

Reeve kept his sword in hand as he hurried to Tara, draped over the horse on her stomach. She was still unconscious and a bruise was darkening her chin. If he could kill the fool soldier all over again, he would, he was so furious that he had hurt her.

It would be a while before she regained consciousness, and he intended to take advantage of that. After sheathing his sword, he mounted the horse and hurried them away from the carnage and possible further attack.

In no time they would be on Pict land, and the soldiers would dare not follow since the Picts blended with the land and one never saw them coming until it was too late. He and Tara, however, were expected, Bliss having sent one of Roan's men with a message days ago, having sensed that someone would need sanctuary though not knowing who.

They crossed the border though no line of demarcation could be seen; it was simply known. This was the land of the Picts. The land of the old ways and old beliefs, and one trod with respect or not at all.

Reeve brought the horse to a stop as soon as he heard Tara groan. He was off the horse and had her in his arms just as her eyes struggled to open.

"You're safe," he said, and his heart ached as she struggled to fight through the haze that engulfed her. He continued to encourage. "You were so very brave, and I am so very proud of you."

Her eyes finally opened, and a full smile bloomed though it turned to a quick wince, her bruise having worsened considerably. "We survived?"

"We did." He grinned. "But then I would have it no other way."

"You are an obstinate one."

"I will take that as a compliment since it comes from someone with the same quality."

She laughed, but a painful grimace soon stole it.

"No laughing," he ordered, her pain bringing him pain.

She lifted her hand and tentatively touched his face.

He knew what disturbed her. "I told you the curse can't affect me."

Her look asked, are you sure?

"No curse will touch me," he said, and gave her a gentle kiss.

She, in turn, gave him a weak smile, and he laughed, saying, "You don't believe me, but just wait, you'll see I'm right. I'm always right."

She almost laughed but stopped herself, the slight

crease of her mouth causing her to wince. The lack of a smile didn't prevent her merriment from showing, for it danced boldly in her lavender eyes.

Reeve felt a catch to his heart. Never had he seen someone as beautiful as her. He had gazed upon her many times, but not until this very moment did he see her true beauty, and it astounded him. And he felt it, actually felt her beauty. It seeped slowly and steadily into him, and as it took firm root, he knew it was life-sustaining and that never, ever would he be able to live without it. Never before had he experienced such an overwhelming sensation, and he knew then and there that he loved Tara with a deep abiding love that he had never known existed until now.

He kissed her gently. "We need to find shelter for the night."

"What of Bliss's cottage?'

"It is too far. If we get an early start tomorrow, we'll reach it before nightfall. Bliss made mention of a run-down croft just over the border."

"Then let's find it," Tara said, struggling to sit up.

Reeve got her to her feet with ease and held her firm until he was sure she had steady footing. And even though she insisted that she was fine, he scooped her up, carried her to the horse a few feet away, and lifted her to the saddle. He swung himself up, coming to rest behind her.

His arms went around her, and she snuggled against him as he took the reins in his hands.

By the time Reeve found the dilapidated croft, Tara was asleep in his arms. Exhaustion had finally claimed her, and he wished he didn't have to disturb her. His worry was for naught since when he dismounted, she barely stirred in his arms.

The cottage had a partial roof left, and one wall had crumbled in half. It would be more like sleeping under the stars, though the remaining walls would keep the wind from whipping at them. And the fireplace appeared intact, so they would have a modicum of warmth for the night.

Reeve shook his cloak off his shoulders and, with his booted foot, spread it out on the floor. He carefully lowered Tara down on it, tucking her cloak more tightly around her. He then set to work, his first chore getting a fire going. Afterwards, he saw to the care of the horse, finding shelter for the animal in an old lean-to. With no food left, he ignored his grumbling stomach and figured it would be best to sleep and get an early start in the morning. He stretched out beside Tara and eased her cloak from around her, intending to wrap both of them in it. He yanked a little too hard, and she rolled into him, her chest slamming against his.

Her eyes fluttered open, and the tip of her tongue peeked out and licked her dry lips until they were plump with moisture. Being that her mouth wasn't far from his and her lips glistened invitingly, Reeve didn't think twice. He kissed her.

She returned the kiss with more passion than he had expected, igniting his own passion, which sat far too close to the surface and had been for some time. He wasn't sure if she was fully awake, or perhaps thought herself in a dream, for her eyes remained closed. Either way, it didn't matter; they had hungered for each other far too long, and it was time to quench that hunger.

He slipped his hand inside the bodice of her dress and took hold of her plump breast. He gave a slight squeeze and she moaned into his mouth and he deepened their kiss.

To his utter surprise, she rolled on top of him and wiggled her body against his. His body instantly responded, and she settled herself comfortably against his bulge as if nesting on it, in hopes that her heated warmth would bring it further to life. It was his turn to groan, and she took advantage, taking charge of the kiss.

Her teasing tongue had him wondering how it would feel if she should taste the size of him with as much enthusiasm and made him grow all the more hard. Which sent her moving against him in a steady rhythm and had her mewling like only a woman in need could.

He tore his mouth away from hers and tore at the ribbons of her bodice to plant his face in the crevice of her bosoms. Lord, but she smelled good, the perfect blend of sweetness and woman. His mouth soon found a nipple, and he suckled it, not like a thirsty babe but like a man needing to satisfy, not only himself, but her as well.

She moaned and rubbed herself against him harder, and he joined in her frantic rhythm; the scent of her moisture drifted up to sting his nostrils and sent him over the edge of passion and into madness.

He grabbed at her waist, flipped her on her back, and came to rest over her, his hands rushing her dress up her legs. Her eyes spread wide open. They were the deepest purple he had ever seen and sensual, almost as if her passion had heated her usual lavender to this raging purple.

"I—I–"

He kissed her quick. "Don't ask me to stop."

His fingers found the opening between her legs he was searching for before she could respond, and the sleek moisture that welcomed him had him groaning. "You're wet and ready for me."

She nodded, her body arching against his playful fingers.

He knew she wanted this just as much as he did, but he wanted to hear her say it. He moved his fingers, positioning himself to enter her, and then he rubbed enticingly against her, entering just far enough to tease. "Tell me you want me, Tara. Tell me."

Her passionate groan almost had him plunging into her, but he held firm. He would hear it from her. He would hear her say that she wanted him. She had to. She had to surrender willingly, for to him it was the only way to break that wretched curse she believed in.

With her eyes wide and her lips trembling, she said "I—"

Reeve slammed his hand over her mouth and shook his head. In the split second before she spoke he had heard the crunch of footfalls.

"Quiet, I hear something," he murmured in her ear, and she nodded.

He moved off her, and Tara quickly fixed her garments.

The sound came again, and Reeve looked to her. Her eyes were wide with fright, and damn if passion didn't remain strong in them. He placed a finger to his lips, warning her to remain silent, and she nodded.

His sword was already in his hand, since he had grabbed it from where it lay beside him. He couldn't believe that the soldiers would be foolish enough to cross over into Pict territory. They had to know that they would never survive against the indigenous Picts.

Still, Reeve had to remain cautious. The king could very well have ordered his men to bring her back at all costs. And only in the condition that she be able to speak her vows. The thought still infuriated him, and he hoped he would be the one lucky enough to see to King Kenneth's demise.

"Greetings clan MacAlpin."

Reeve didn't take any chances, he called back. "Who goes there?"

"A Pict. Who else would dare tread on our land without invite?"

Still cautious, Reeve signaled Tara to remain there while he went to make certain it was a Pict who greeted them. He returned in no time to find that Tara had secured all their belongings and was ready to run if necessary.

He smiled. "You did well, and thankfully we are safe. Odran has come to take us to Bliss's cottage."

"Now?" Tara asked.

"He says a severe snowstorm approaches and will be here by morning."

Tara nodded, staring at Reeve.

He stared back. They both understood the urgency of their departure, but they both also understood that passion still ran like fire through their bodies. Though Reeve was no longer as hard as he had been, there still remained a thickness to him. And from the color of Tara's eyes, purple, he knew that she was still wet and ready for him. It was not going to be easy sitting behind her on the horse, and damn if the thought didn't harden him all the more.

"We best go," he said abruptly.

She nodded, grabbed the sack, and hurried out the door.

He followed after, first taking a deep breath and giving the wall a punch.

Odran explained that the snowstorm would probably last a few days and that they would be snowbound, though not to worry. Bliss's cottage was stocked with all they needed.

Reeve rolled his eyes to the heavens in gratitude. He'd have Tara all to himself for days on end, and he intended to make love to her as often as possible, in every which way possible. And he'd start as soon as they got there. He'd have to; he'd have no other choice since riding like this, with her bottom tightly against him, had him on the verge of exploding.

She shifted against him for the third time, and he tightened his arm around her waist. "Sit still," he whispered harshly in her ear. "That tight bottom of yours bumping against me is tormenting the hell out of me."

"And what do you think that bulge of yours is doing to me?"

He knew as soon as the words spilled from his lips and his hand moved beneath her cloak that he was causing them both a world of agonizing ache, but it didn't stop him.

"Let's see," he said, and his hand found its way beneath her dress and shift, slipping up her leg, tickling across her thigh, and settling between her legs, where his fingers slipped their way inside her.

Tara let out a soft, "Oh my!"

"I can feel what it's doing to you," he whispered, and then teased along her ear with a nibble. "You're wetter than you were before."

"You shouldn't—"

"Ah, but I want to."

"You can't—"

"I can."

"I'll come," she whispered.

"Not this time," he murmured against her ear. "This time you wait for me."

"I can't wait—"

"You will. I'll make you."

"That's not fair."

"Oh, but it is," he murmured. "This time we climax together."

She shuddered against him, and he chuckled.

"I promise you a most memorable ride now and when we arrive."

# Chapter 27

Tara had tried to wiggle free of Reeve's teasing touches, but she had only managed to make it worse. It seemed the more she moved, the deeper inside her he went. She had finally resorted to pleading, but he had just grinned.

Finally, she had threatened. "I will return this torture one day."

Reeve had laughed. "Is that a promise?"

She had remained quiet after that, biting at her bottom lip to prevent the heated moans from bubbling over. Reeve had continued to fuel the fire he had started, detailing things he intended to do to her in soft, hungry whispers that stained her cheeks molten red.

So by the time they arrived at Bliss's cottage, she was ready to ravage him. And damn if after all the begging for him to stop, when he finally did, she was disappointed. Her only thought was that he had to finish what he had started, or she would kill him.

The thought struck her like a splash of ice-cold water to the face. Good Lord, what had she been thinking? If she made love with him, the curse would kill him. She had allowed her need, her never-ending ache for him, to blind her to what she must do.

Snow had started falling shortly before they arrived at the cottage, big fat snowflakes that quickly stuck to everything they settled upon. Reeve dismounted first and then, with a quick grab at her waist, he had her standing next to him.

Odran and Reeve talked for a few moments, though Tara had no idea what they discussed. She was much too worried about spending time alone with Reeve and trying desperately to ignore, chase, and be rid of the passion that so thoroughly consumed her.

Reeve took hold of her hand, and it was then she noticed that they were alone. Not only Odran was gone, but so was the horse. Snow was falling fast and hard. And she was surprised that the flakes that fell on her weren't melting, her burning desire for Reeve having flamed even more instead of dying to tiny embers.

He hurried her into the cottage, shutting the door. And before he turned, she scurried around so that the table stood between them.

When he turned, his grin faded though he said nothing. He removed his cloak, hanging it on the peg near the door. Then he pulled his black shirt from his plaid, stretching his arms up to shed it with a careless toss.

Tara felt her legs buckle, and she leaned on the back of the chair for support. He was simply delicious. His lean form was defined by taut muscles, and each stretch and turn defined those muscles even more. He was a gorgeously crafted male and he loved her and she loved him and this should be so easy, but it wasn't.

He yanked his boots off and tossed them to land

near the hearth. He then grabbed his plaid at the waist, where it sat tightly tucked, and once he pulled the strip loose and let it fall, he would be completely naked.

"Don't," she said sharply.

"You don't want to make love with me?"

Damn him for asking her that. "You know I want to make love with you."

He grinned and let his plaid fall.

Tara almost shut her eyes, almost, but then thought better of it. She would not appear a coward. She had to make him see reason though how she would do that with him naked in front of her was the real question.

She tried not to focus on his obvious desire for her, but damn if she couldn't keep her eyes off it. *Large, long, thick*. She startled at the fast throb that struck between her legs.

"You can't deny we want each other," Reeve said.

Tara felt like raging at the injustice of all she had endured and still continued to endure, and tears were quick to fill her eyes.

Reeve stepped forward, but she swung her hand up. "Don't."

"I am going to make love to you," he said adamantly.

"Then you will die," she said, shaking her head and letting the tears fall. She was exhausted from fighting, exhausted by the loneliness, exhausted from the passion that just would not dissipate.

Reeve moved so fast that Tara had no time to react. He had her in his arms before she could protest, and once there, she didn't want to leave. She rested her head on his bare chest and let the tears fall.

He held her close. "Cry all you want. I am here

with you, where I want to be, and with you is where I intend to stay forever."

She let the tears fall, not sure why she was crying and not caring, knowing only that she needed to shed them. Perhaps they fell because she would not make love with him, or perhaps she would and then regret it, for she would be the death of him. She didn't know, didn't want to know. She simply wanted to remain safe in his arms forever.

"We need to do this," he said.

"Why? Why can't we remain like this? Me forever in your arms."

"You know why as well as I do."

"Love," she said. "You won't say it, won't admit it, but it is love that drives our passion, our need, our never-ending ache for each other."

"That need, ache, whatever you wish to call it needs to be satisfied."

"And the consequences? What of them?"

"We leave them to fate," he said.

"Don't ask that of me. I can't."

"I can, and you will." He took gentle hold of her chin and raised her face to look upon him. "Trust me. Let me make love to you."

He didn't wait for her answer. He scooped her up and carried her to the bed.

She covered his hand when it went to grab and lift her dress. "Do you know what you do?"

He grinned and laughed. "I've never had a woman ask me that."

She shook her head though she smiled. "You know what I mean."

His hand snaked around to take hold of the back of her head and brought her mouth to his so fast she had no time to take a breath. He kissed her like a man starved for love, and she responded with equal hunger, her arms going around his neck and her body pressing invitingly against his.

At that moment, she surrendered to her passion, she had no choice. Her need was too great, as was his.

He kept his mouth glued to hers while he struggled to lift her dress and shift. Impatient herself, she tore her mouth away and yanked her garments over her head, tossing them carelessly aside. Her boots followed.

He took hold of her waist and held her a short distance from him, glancing slowly over her body and smiling. "You are so very beautiful."

Joy flooded Tara's heart, and tears tickled at her eyes.

His thumb wiped them away. "I'll see you shed only tears of happiness from this moment on."

"I am happy," she said, "though I will be much happier when you rest between my legs." And she pulled him down with her onto the bed.

"You are a wicked woman," he teased, coming down on top of her and bracing his hands on either side of her head.

"You prefer me not to be wicked?" she asked innocently.

He grinned and stole multiple kisses before responding. "I encourage you to be as wicked as you want to be with me."

She nibbled at his lips. "Be careful what you ask for."

"I don't want to be careful. I want us to explore, experiment, examine all there is to making love."

Tara shivered at the erotic images that assaulted her.

"I'm going to make love to you all night, Tara. I'm going to taste and touch and tease and torment—"

"And I shall do the same to you."

"Promises. Promises—" Reeve gasped.

Tara grinned, her hand having slipped quickly down to take a firm hold on his manhood. Actually, she quite liked the feel of him, velvety soft, thick, and hard.

"Keep stroking me like that, and I'll be the one pleasured."

Tara didn't have a chance to react. Reeve moved her hand off him and snuggled his way between her legs while settling his lips to play across her mouth, down her silky neck, and over her full bosoms, finally resting, in turn, at each nipple, which hardened instantly to his teasing taunts.

Her body squirmed beneath his in an effort to help him gain entrance.

He raised his head to look at her, her nipples budding tightly from the cold air that hit them, and she yearned for the return of his warm lips.

"Not yet," he said. "We play first."

"We've played enough," she insisted, rising her hips to push against him and meeting his thick bulge. She moaned with the want of him.

But he made her wait, his hand moving down to please and torment all at the same time, while his lips pleasured her budding nipples. After a moment or two, he moved down along her body, planting kisses and stealing nibbles as he went. It was when he settled between her legs that she almost bolted, if it hadn't been for his firm hold on her hips.

His tongue darted into her over and over until she thought she would go mad with desire.

"Please, Reeve, please," she finally begged, after his torment turned unbearable. "I need you inside me."

He rose over her and eased his way between her spread legs, slow and easy. "Know once I enter you, you belong to me."

She nodded and grabbed at his face. "And you belong to me."

He slipped into her then as if sealing their bargain, and she gasped and stiffened for a moment.

"All of you. I want all of you," she demanded.

He plunged into her then in one swift motion, and she cried out, grabbing his arms tightly.

He stilled instantly, and asked, "Are you all right?"

The concern in his voice had her smiling; that he should put her comfort before his pleasure pleased her beyond reason.

"More than all right," she whispered. "I think I will want you inside me often, it feels so very good."

He grinned and kissed her. "I want you to always feel good."

They set a rhythm then, not taking their eyes off each other. Tara could see his passion grow and peak in his dark eyes and knew his mirrored her own. Then there were the moans she couldn't help. He felt so good sliding in and out of her, teasing her senseless, that she responded with the deepest groans and sighs and moans, which seemed to please him just as much.

His rhythm suddenly changed, turning more rapid and insistent, and she followed suit, rising to match his hardened thrusts and relishing the tremendous pleasure it brought her. She closed her eyes, feeling the strength of her wildly beating heart, savoring the erotic beat that pulsed through her body and holding firm to the pleasurable ache swirling like a whirlwind through her.

Her fingers dug further into Reeve's arms, and she anxiously pleaded for release.

"Soon," he whispered, and kissed her with a hunger she returned.

"Now," she begged again. "Please now."

And with a sudden plunge, he sent her over the edge, tumbling into an abyss of pleasure she never thought possible and she never wanted to see end. And he didn't let it. He moved inside her, causing her to burst with pleasure twice, consuming her, captivating her, and completing her. The second time, she felt his release, his groan of pleasure filling the air until, finally, he collapsed on top of her, and she wrapped her arms around him.

She didn't know if it was that she was trying to keep death away, or if she was afraid he would simply disappear, and this would all turn out to be nothing more than a dream. Either way, she didn't want to take a chance. She held him tight and wouldn't let go.

He tried to move off her, but she held firm.

He looked up at her, and she knew her eyes were wide with fright, knew her fear was palpable.

"I'm not going anywhere. I—"

She rushed her hand to cover his mouth. "Don't say it. I long to hear it, but please don't say it. I fear if you do . . ." She didn't finish, she couldn't. As much as she wanted to hear Reeve declare his love for her, she still feared the curse.

He brushed her hand away and rolled off her, taking her with him to tuck and hold in his arms. "I intend to keep you right here beside me."

She sighed with relief and snuggled against him. He understood her fear, and she knew his actions declared his love for her, but she wasn't ready to hear him say it yet. She wasn't ready to believe that the curse could not hurt him. She still feared it could. After all, she loved him, and that was enough to bring the wrath of the curse down upon him if she claimed it aloud. But if he should admit his love, he would certainly suffer for it.

"Here is where I want to be," she said.

"Here is where you shall stay."

She wanted to ask how. How would he manage to keep her with him? But she didn't want to disturb the peace and beauty of the moment. She preferred to believe that he held the power to make it happen. That he was a mighty Highlander warrior impervious to curses, to death itself.

"Trust me, Tara, I'll see that it all turns out well for us."

"I want to believe," she said, glancing into his dark eyes, eyes that retained a hint of passion. "I truly do, but we face so many obstacles."

"You can believe that, or believe that fate intervened and placed us where we are meant to be," Reeve said, wrapping his legs around hers. He reached down and pulled a soft wool blanket over them.

"Then that would mean that fate sent you to rescue me."

"More than once," he chuckled.

She jabbed his chest playfully.

He grabbed hold of her hand and brought it to

his lips to kiss, a tender, loving kiss. "You and I were meant to be. Fate decreed it, and we can't fight fate."

She smiled. "I keep forgetting. You're always right." Her smile faded. "But what if—"

"No what-ifs."

"But if fate decrees otherwise?"

"Then I defy fate," he said, with a shake of a fist to the heavens and a grin. "And fate learns I'm always right."

Her chuckle was broken by a yawn.

"Sleep," he urged, stroking along the length of her back.

"I love when you touch me." She sighed.

"Then I'll touch you to sleep." And his hand began to work magic over her, caressing and kneading along her back, her shoulder, her arm.

She sighed aloud. "Don't stop. Please don't stop."

He nipped at her ear. "Never, Tara. Never will I stop touching you."

# Chapter 28

Exhaustion crept over Reeve, but he couldn't sleep. He closed his eyes, but they soon drifted open. He tried to calm his mind, but it soon filled with thoughts. Try as he might, sleep eluded him. All through his restlessness, he had kept Tara snug against him. She hadn't moved since falling asleep over an hour ago, which meant she was content, and he intended to see she remained that way.

He hadn't considered how they would avoid the obstacles already in their path or those to come. He only knew that he would protect her with his life, even against fate if necessary.

He yawned, had been for the last hour, though it hadn't helped him sleep. It more tormented him, letting him know just how tired he was but that nothing would come of it. He'd lain there awake, his musings haunting him.

Then there was his mission to consider. It would soon make more demands of him, and there would be times he would have to leave Tara and see to his duty. He and his brothers knew that, and it was the very reason why they had planned not to fall in love . . .

just yet. They had concluded that there was no time for it, but as he had learned, love doesn't consider time. It arrives when and where it pleases.

The next yawn had him squeezing his eyes tight and spreading his mouth wide. Lord, he was tired and wanted to sleep. Here he could finally sleep, feeling safe, not worrying about someone bursting in and stealing Tara away from him. He was glad for the snowstorm that raged outside. It meant they would have time alone together. They would have time to talk, to plan

And—to make love as often as they liked.

Tara stirred, stretching as she turned away from him. He almost didn't let her go, turning to take hold of her, but she snuggled her back against him. And he, in turn, draped his arm and leg over her, cuddling her tight.

Warmth and the scent of their lovemaking drifted around them, not to mention the sweet aroma of her hair. He took a deep breath, breathing in her rich scent. And he smiled as his eyes drifted closed, and this time they didn't open.

Reeve opened his eyes slowly. He lay on his side, hugging the edge of the bed, and he smiled when he thought of who lay behind him. His eyes opened fully, and he was about to turn and take hold of Tara when his eyes nearly popped out of his head.

She stood completely naked in front of the fireplace, her backside to him. She was washing herself from a bucket by the hearth. Her pale skin glistened from the fire's light dancing across it.

Good Lord, she was a beauty. He loved the fullness of her hips, the roundness of her backside, and the slender strength of her legs, which he was thinking would fit quite nicely around his waist as he slipped comfortably inside her.

The image had him slipping out of bed as quietly as he could to sneak up undetected behind her though he wasn't as subtle as he had thought. She went eagerly into his arms as they wrapped around her, and her damp, shimmering skin was like quick fire to his loins.

"I thought you would never wake," she said, resting her head back so that their cheeks met.

"And imagine my surprise and delight when I caught a beautiful water nymph washing in front of the fireplace." He nibbled hungrily along her ear, and she tilted her head, offering her neck to him. He kissed along the silky column, enjoying the fresh taste of her.

She rubbed her backside against him, and he ran his hand down between her legs to tease, but she turned quickly in his arms.

"No time," she whispered, nipping at his lips. "I want you inside me now."

Reeve didn't waste a minute. He threw his arms around her and hoisted her up, her legs swinging to wrap around his waist. Once she settled, he eased his way into her, not wanting to jab into her like a rutting animal. But she wanted none of his gentleness; she plunged down on him, taking the full length of him inside her. She threw back her head with a sensual moan, and all thought of tender lovemaking vanished.

He grabbed her backside and forced her to match his urgent rhythm, and she did. She rested her brow against his as they both concentrated on the passion that built like a raging storm inside them.

"Don't stop; good Lord, Reeve, please don't stop," she begged.

His labored breathing didn't allow a response. He rushed with her to the door to brace her back against it so that he would have more leverage to quicken their movements even more, and he did.

He drove into her again and again.

"Reeve," she cried with bated breath.

"Let go," he urged, and increased the tempo.

She let out a scream, and her legs tightened around him, her fingers digging into his arms. Her explosive climax forced his own, and a groan that he couldn't stop erupted from deep in his chest and burst forth in a mighty roar.

They clung to each other, their bodies trembling from lingering ripples of pleasure. Reeve braced one hand to the door for support while his other hand held firm to her backside. Her head rested on his, and her arms lay draped over his shoulders.

He took a few deep breaths, then held her tight and carried her to the bed, following her down to lie beside her. When the heat of passion began to fade, and their bodies cooled, he pulled the blanket over them.

"That was the greatest morning greeting I have ever had," he said with a chuckle.

"I wholeheartedly agree." She sighed.

Reeve reached out and took hold of her hand, bringing it to his lips to kiss. "Your beauty is beyond words."

She remained silent, and he turned his head to her. She was staring at him, her cheeks still flushed, her lips still plump, and her eyes soft lavender, the color speaking volumes to him though the hint of tears disturbed him.

"My words upset you?"

She shook her head and sniffled in an attempt to hold back the tears. "No. It is just that it has been so very long since anyone has told me that. And I didn't realize how very much I have missed such loving words until hearing you say them with such sincerity again and again."

"Who spoke of your beauty as I have?"

"Rory. He was a good man."

"You still miss him?" He was glad that she didn't hesitate to answer him.

"Not as I once did. I will keep the good memories he left me with, but it is you who now constantly fill my thoughts and dreams."

He kissed her hand again. "And I always will."

"You are so sure?" she teased.

He turned on his side, releasing her hand and running a finger along her cheek and over her lips. "You and I will live a long life together."

"You are so sure of this?"

"Need I remind you again that I'm—"

"Always right," she finished.

He took hold of her chin. "Believe in *us,* and you will know it too."

Both their stomachs rumbled at that moment, and they laughed.

"See how alike we are?" he said. "We're both in want of nourishment."

"I have bread baking."

He grabbed his chest, feigning shock. "I didn't think this morning could get any better, and it just did."

She gave him a playful shove. "Wait, you'll get tired of being stuck here with me soon enough."

He gave her a gentle kiss. "I will never grow tired of you. I dare say we will have our battles at times, though never ever will I feel stuck with you. Besides, I can't live without that delicious bread you bake."

She gave him another playful shove, and, laughing, they got out of bed and dressed, and Tara got busy fixing them breakfast.

Reeve grabbed his cloak off the peg. "I'll be right back." He stopped before opening the door and glanced at the two buckets of water by the hearth. "You went out in the snow this morning?"

"Briefly," she said. "You must remember that I am used to doing things on my own. There were none who extended a helping hand to me."

"That is no more. You have me now, and you have a family to help you."

Her smile was hesitant, as if she wanted to believe him, but uncertain if she should. He knew he couldn't force her to believe that he spoke the truth. She would need to learn it on her own.

"Do you need more snow?" he asked.

"Not at the moment," she said. "Be careful, the wind and snow blind."

He threw his hood over his head. "Fear not. The weather knows better than to torment me."

His dramatic exit left her laughing.

Later in the day, with the wind and snow picking up in intensity, they stripped and climbed beneath the bedcovers and made love. They took their time exploring each other, and Tara allowed her inquisitiveness to take control. Soon she was kissing and tasting places on Reeve she had only dreamed of doing.

It was a lazy play of teases and taunts until they

finally joined as one to finish in exploding bursts of pleasure. Afterwards, she lay in his arms, and when reason finally returned, they began to talk.

"Do you think we will need to remain here long?" she asked.

"God, I hope so."

She smiled, for she felt the same, but there was his duty to consider. "What of your missions?"

"Presently, all parties are settled in for the winter, making plans, seeking direction, and continuing to choose sides."

"And waiting for the true king to make himself known," she said.

"He'll show himself when the time is right."

"You have met the true king?" she asked surprised. "I had begun to wonder if he was a myth the people created to give them hope."

"He's no myth. He is a man born and bred of strong conviction, honor, and distinction."

"You sound as if you know the true king well?"

"Well enough to know he is a good man who will serve his country and people fairly."

"You sound honored to serve him."

"I am," he admitted, "but enough about the king. There will be time for me to deal with that soon enough. I presently only have thoughts of you."

"And I will see that it stays that way."

"How?"

She slipped her hand along his leg and began to stroke him.

Later that night, Tara sat by the hearth in the lone wool nightdress that the women had packed for her. Reeve slept soundly in bed, snoring lightly. It was a scene she would have never imagined possible only a few months ago. She had thought death was just a matter of time after her father had explained that he had made arrangements for her to wed King Kenneth. She had never expected to be rescued, let alone fall in love. But how did she protect the man she loved from the curse. She wondered why the curse had yet to claim Reeve but had come to the conclusion that it was because he had yet to claim aloud his love. Rory had claimed his love for her and had died before they had exchanged vows. And no love was involved when it came to her second husband. It was when they exchanged vows that he also died. The curse brought suffering and death to anyone who loved or wed her.

So, as much as she wanted to wed Reeve, she couldn't, for exchanging vows would surely kill him. Bliss had told her to *remember* when it came to the curse, but what was it that she was supposed to remember?

Tara wished that she could find the witch who had cast the curse and have her remove it, but she had disappeared that day so many years ago never to be seen again. She often wondered what had happened to her. She remembered screaming when her father had her torn away, and though Stone had never spoken a word, she had thought she heard him say, "Go, all will be well."

At the time, the curse meant nothing to her; her only thought had been for Stone's safety. It hadn't been until much later that she had learned the power of the witch's words. Tara wondered if it was possible to find a more powerful witch than her. Bliss had said that a more powerful witch could remove the curse. But where would she find one?

She felt as if she ran in circles, round and round, again and again getting nowhere. She felt completely helpless, and she had felt that way far too long. There had to be something she could do to stop the madness.

A yawn warned that sleep was approaching, but she paid it no heed. She had thinking to do, solutions to reach before they were reached for her. Never again did she want decisions made for her. Choices from now on belonged to her; she would have it no other way. How she would see to that, she didn't know. But she was determined, and that was half the battle.

She yawned again, and her eyes drifted closed. She would rest for a moment and then think again on finding feasible solutions to her dilemma. One more yawn, and sleep laid claim to her.

Reeve woke and rolled over in search of Tara. When his hands found empty space, his eyes shot open, and he cast an anxious glance around the cottage. Relief poured over him when he saw her in the chair by the fireplace.

He leapt out of bed and padded over to her, ignoring the cold air that rushed to nip at his bare feet. He was about to playfully scold her for deserting him when he saw that she was sound asleep.

She wore her worry even in sleep, and he surmised that it was her concerns that had brought her to sit in front of the hearth. He wished she understood that he had no intentions of ever letting her go. They belonged to each other and always would. He had no doubt that his family would find a feasible solution to the matter. He worried the bigger problem might be getting Tara to wed him.

He leaned over and lifted her gently into his arms. He smiled, for she was toasty warm, and, at the moment, his body felt chilled. He held her close, sharing her body's heat, and once he placed her on the bed, he hurried under the covers and cuddled her close.

He tenderly tried to stroke away the worry lines from her brow, and, surprisingly, in only moments, his gentle persuasion worked. Her brow relaxed, and he thought he detected a slight smile. If only he could chase away their problems so easily.

He watched her sleep with one thought constant in his head. He loved her; beyond all reason, he loved her. And he wanted desperately to tell her so. Speak the words loud and clear so that she would hear the conviction in his voice.

He continued watching her, and, when finally he heard a slight snore, he smiled. He leaned over and kissed her softly on the cheek and whispered as he had done before while she slept, "I love you. I will always love you."

# Chapter 29

Tara struggled with the two buckets of snow. How she would love a good soak in tempered water. She'd been washing with the melted snow for the last few days, and while it served the purpose well enough, she longed for a soak.

She plunked the buckets down in front of the door, the snow gobbling them up to the bottom rim reminding her that several inches had fallen since their arrival. And though the snow had stopped yesterday, she couldn't say she was pleased. It meant that departure was imminent, at least for one of them.

The door suddenly swung open, and Reeve greeted her completely naked.

"You left me to wake alone," he said with feigned sadness.

Tara looked him up and down and smiled. "And you woke in your usual state, the cold not shriveling you a bit."

"It's you who keeps him at attention," he teased, and swiped the two buckets up before retreating completely inside.

Tara followed, admiring his taut backside and

rock-solid legs. She smiled, closing the door behind her. Before she could turn, Reeve cozied up behind her, his arms wrapping her snugly against him.

"We should go back to bed," he said, nibbling at her ear.

"You're tired?"

"And you're funny," he said, turning her around in his arms.

He went to kiss her, and she stopped him. "I need to wash though I would much prefer a good soak."

"If I provide a good soak for you, will you spend the rest of the day in bed with me?"

She knew he teased by his grin though she also knew that a good portion of the day would be spent in bed enjoying each other in so many ways. Whether it was touching, kissing, coupling, laughing, talking, they enjoyed every minute of each other.

"I most certainly will," she said, though wondering how he would ever accomplish such an unlikely feat.

He gave her a quick kiss. "Give me a minute to get dressed."

"What are you up to?" she asked skeptically.

"You'll see." And as soon as he was done, he took hold of her hand and out the door they went.

Reeve stood a moment, as if getting his bearings, and then turned, tugging her behind him. He stopped here and there along the way and gave a quick look around before proceeding with what appeared confidence. In one sense, he appeared to know where he was going, and in another, he wasn't quite sure.

Then suddenly he said, "There it is."

Tara looked though didn't see anything until they got closer, and then she saw it, an opening to a cave.

A bit excited about their mysterious destination, she followed along eagerly. At first, upon entering, it seemed like any cave until they proceeded deeper inside, the yawning-wide cave producing enough light to follow the twist and turn that lay ahead. Then a turn that led into a narrow passageway lit with dusk-like light, followed by another turn that had her stopping suddenly and staring in shock.

It opened on a cavern, light from beneath the water illuminating the place and steam rising from the water.

Tara clapped her hands, and her face lit with pure joy. She grabbed Reeve's face, and said, "You wonderful, wonderful man. I adore you." She kissed him quick and then almost ripped off her clothes, so eager was she to soak in the water.

"Be careful," he cautioned. "Bliss warned that the water can get hot."

Tara tested it with her foot and sighed with pleasure. "It's perfect." Anxious to be fully submerged, she hurried in, the water greedily devouring her up past her breasts.

Reeve was beside her in no time, groaning with pleasure as he dunked himself to his neck. "This is—"

"Heaven," Tara finished. "Bliss told you of this place?"

He nodded. "I had forgotten about it until you told me you wanted a soak. Bliss had told me you might want to bathe and that there was a perfect place for it near her home."

"Bless her," Tara said, and dove beneath the water. She came up with a cheerful jump, her hair soaked through.

"Soap," Reeve said.

Tara laughed. "I wish."

Reeve wrapped his arm around her waist and pulled her close. "I can make wishes come true."

Tara chuckled. "Bliss told you where she keeps the soap."

"I prefer to think of it as me making your wishes come true."

Her smile faded, and she touched his cheek ever so gently, almost as if she wasn't sure he was real. "You've made so many of my wishes and dreams come true."

"And I'll make many more come true."

Her smile returned. "I'll settle for the soap wish right now."

He laughed, let her go, and left the water to retrieve the soap from behind a small outcropping of rocks, tossing it to her before he joined her once again.

Tara caught it and proceeded to scrub her hair with sheer delight. When she had lathered it good, she passed the soap to Reeve.

"I can help scrub you if you'd like?"

She chuckled again. "I'd never get washed."

"You know me well."

As Tara scrubbed, she realized that she had gotten to know Reeve well, except for his involvement with the true king. She knew only bits and pieces of that part of him. And she wondered why. Why hadn't he discussed it with her?

And so she asked, "Tell me of your missions for the true king."

He stopped scrubbing. "I cannot. And before you think it is because I don't trust you, it isn't. My missions must remain secret for the good of the king and for your own protection. You must trust me on this."

"I do," she said without hesitation.

"You believe me so easily?"

"You are an honorable man. I see no reason to believe otherwise."

"That tells me much about you," he said with a satisfied smile.

"Which is why I inquired about your missions. I want to know everything about you."

"Someday I will tell you all."

She hoped that day would come; she hoped that this time spent together was not the only time they would have. That they would, as Reeve promised, grow old together.

"What do you think of the true king?" he asked.

"I had believed the prophecy no more than a myth at first, or perhaps it was because I didn't believe there was someone strong enough to overthrow the present king. Then I began to hear people grumbling, my father among them. King Kenneth was demanding too much from his people and giving nothing in return, not even to those who had helped him gain the throne."

"Then you began to believe?"

"I began to hope that perhaps there was a man wiser and more powerful who could give the people what they needed, what they yearned for—a fair and honest leader."

"Not an easy task with the different kings who demand more than their share," Reeve said.

"My father being one of them, though presently he has more money than the king, not that he would want that known."

"King Kenneth must have suspected as much if he arranged to wed you."

"A fear that had my father worried," she admitted.

"And so he gives his only daughter to the king in fear of losing his fortune and in fear of the curse he had brought down on her," Reeve grumbled. "I should have beaten him when I had the chance."

He reached out and took hold of her. "You belong to me now, and no one—*no one*—will ever take you from me."

He said it with such fervor that, at that very moment, Tara believed him. Or was it that she wished to believe him? Regardless, she wanted more than anything for his words to be true.

She reached out and touched his lips ever so gently. "I wish–" She smiled. "I've already been granted my wish."

He didn't smile. Instead, passion soared in his eyes, and he kissed her.

They came together in a frenzied heat though Reeve took command, and Tara surrendered. His hands glided over her wet body, touching every part of her, as if laying claim to her, branding her his.

He took her fast and furiously, and she didn't object. She wanted him as much as he did her, and she had no patience to wait. Her climax was so explosive that she cried out, her shout bouncing off the cavern walls and echoing back at her.

Spent, her head dropped to his shoulder, and there she rested until she calmed, regaining control. He began to walk out of the water with her in his arms.

"No," she protested. "I don't want to leave yet."

"Neither do I," he said, and settled down in the water, letting the heat cover them like a warm blanket.

He liked that she wanted to linger in the serenity

of this moment, this place, and forget that anything outside of it existed. There were just the two of them, and this time to love freely and safely. And they did. They lingered in the cavern, talking, making love, and enjoying the silent moments that crept over them from time to time.

Neither one of them wanted to leave, but Reeve pointed out, "We have yet to eat."

Tara laughed. "I was thinking the same."

They hurried out of the water, Tara using her shift to dry herself and then giving it to Reeve. They dressed and, hand in hand, left the cave. Their steps were brisk though slowed as they grew nearer the cottage.

Tara knew what he thought, for no doubt her thoughts mirrored his. They both worried that someone would be waiting for them. And their time together would be done. He would have to leave, or they both would be forced to depart and once again meet their fate.

They rounded the bend slowly, and when the cottage came into sight, they both breathed a sigh of relief and hurried forward with smiles.

They were still alone.

After eating a hearty porridge and the last of the dark bread, Reeve was pleased to see that Tara intended to bake more bread. He was content being here with her and was relieved, upon their return to the cottage, to see that no one had come for them. He was hoping for more time with her. He intended for this time to be a fostering of their love. And that the strength of their love would win out against all odds, against that damned curse.

He watched her long, slender fingers work with the grain, adding ingredients, a pinch of this, a smattering of that, and then her fingers worked joining them all together, soft and gentle then hard and forceful.

He jumped up from the chair, moving to stand behind her, his hands slipping down along her arms until they rested at her hands.

"Teach me to work the bread."

She shuddered against him, and he knew it was from the soft whisper of his breath against her ear. It was so easy to spark her passion; just a simple touch, and he could sense she wanted him. It was the same for him; though a single glance from her could set his loins on fire.

"You truly want this?" she asked.

The soft wispiness of her voice was all he needed to hear to confirm what he had sensed. She wanted him, and she was asking the same of him.

"Truly, I do," he said with a nibble along her ear.

"Good," she said firmly. "Go stand on the side of the table."

"What?" His hands dropped away.

She turned around with a grin. "Go to the other side of the table." She gave him a push.

"This isn't what—"

"You truly wanted?" Her grin had grown with each word. "Is the warrior too mighty, not humble enough to bake a simple bread, or perhaps he hasn't the wit for it?"

Reeve nodded slowly as his grin grew. "Challenging me, are you?"

"Are you up to it?"

"I'm always up to it."

"Then the gauntlet is dropped," she said. "Go to your side of the table."

He did as she said, rolling up his sleeves as he went.

"I will finish mixing this dough and then separate it into two portions and show you how to knead one of them. Once it's baked, we'll see which one tastes better."

He watched her add ale to the mixture. "Aha, now I know how you get your bread so tasty."

"It helps the bread to rise and adds a bit of flavor," she admitted. "But a good working with the hands also helps produce tasty bread, so let's see who does the best."

Reeve rubbed his hands together. "I've got good, strong hands."

"Bread needs caressing," she said, and ran her hands softly over the mound of dough.

Reeve watched enchanted as her fingers caressed, squeezed, pinched, and rolled, and made the dough respond to her every touch. Damn if he didn't get images of her hands working on him, and damned if his body didn't respond.

When she finally handed him his portion of the dough, he slammed it down on the table. "This is war and I'm going to win and to the victor go the spoils. That means my bread will be the tastier, and, later tonight, your hands will have to caress me as skillfully as they do that dough."

"And if I win?" she asked, her smile confident. "Then your hands will skillfully caress me?"

"I always skillfully caress you."

"Only caress, nothing more," she said.

"Are you trying to rob me of my sanity?"

"You said it yourself, to the victor go the spoils, and to me, the spoils are my whole body being caressed by your strong hands."

Reeve laughed, shaking his head. "Why argue with you? I'm going to win."

"Then I have your word that you will simply caress all of me?"

"You do," he said, and plunged his hands into the dough.

Reeve spat out the piece of bread, and Tara laughed.

"I don't understand what I did wrong," he said, reaching for a hunk of Tara's bread. He sighed with pleasure as he chewed it. "Yours is delicious."

"Because I caressed the dough, not beat it senseless." She continued to chuckle.

"Laugh," he warned with a nod. "I'll honor our bargain and do no more than caress you, but remember the bread responded with each and every touch."

Tara stopped laughing. "Well, I could change my mind along the way."

Reeve shook his head. "A bargain is a bargain. You won the spoils fairly, and I will see that you receive them."

"But—"

"No buts, it is done, or it just begins," he said, and scooped her up and carried her to bed.

Tara was soon in the throes of passionate torment, and no amount of pleading with Reeve would change his mind. He kept reminding her that a bargain was a bargain. He would do no more than caress her.

"Not fair," she begged.

"Your choice," he reminded her with a grin.

Then Tara realized that two could play the game, and her hand slipped down to firmly grasp his hard manhood.

It was Reeve's turn to gasp and warn and have it do little good, and it wasn't long after that they both enjoyed the spoils of battle.

# Chapter 30

The days passed all too rapidly for Tara and Reeve, and by week's end, and with no more snow falling, Reeve knew he'd be hearing from his family all too soon. Carnoth would have made extreme demands by now, and to avoid unnecessary bloodshed, something would have to be done.

He had enjoyed every moment he spent with Tara, especially making love until they were exhausted. He had also cherished their talks. They had shared stories of their early years and secrets they had told no one else. They had discussed their hopes and dreams and weren't surprised at how similar they were. It had taken time, but eventually she began to discuss the future with him as a couple. They talked about having children and argued over names until he had her believing that it was all possible.

It was during those discussions that an idea took root in his mind, and it had begun with something Tara had told him. He had wondered why he hadn't thought of it sooner, but then he supposed this time away with her was needed. Perhaps now she would have more confidence in their future and not balk at his plan, though he wondered if he should even mention it to her.

He wanted trust and honesty between them. He felt both were the makings of a good marriage; without them, respect would be lost, and once that was gone, love would soon follow.

They sat at the table, finishing the morning meal, and he decided to broach the subject and gauge her reaction before revealing his plan.

"It has been days since the snow has stopped," he said, knowing that would speak for itself.

Tara nodded. "I expect we'll hear from your family soon."

"Your father probably wonders if I have found you, and if so, what has gone on between us."

Her chin went up, and her large eyes turned wide. "I care not for what my father thinks."

Her response warned him to proceed with caution. "Whether you care or not, your father is a powerful man. He will not allow you to reside here with the Picts. And I do not believe you would be obstinate enough to place a generous people in harm's way."

Her chin remained firm. "There are other places I can go."

"Where?" He hated to back her into a corner, but he wanted her to see for herself the futility of remaining stubborn.

Her shoulders slumped ever so slightly. "I have to think on it."

"There is little time for that."

She reached her hand across the small table and took hold of his, hugging it tightly. "You are my best friend. I will never forget the day you told me that you were my friend. I believe that day is when you stole my heart, and I gave you my trust. You brought me to a safe haven once before. Have you any suggestions where I would be safe now."

He could play this safe and not tell her his idea, or he could—he stood abruptly, his chair tumbling backward. He walked over to her and swept her out of the chair and into his arms.

"Here is where you are safe. Here in my arms. Here with me, always." His mouth grabbed hold of hers, and they kissed like starving lovers, though just an hour ago they had lingered in bed making love.

Reeve wasn't surprised by the intensity of the kiss. It only proved that their love and need for each other was as powerful as her father's desire to find them.

He nibbled along her lower lip, reluctantly bringing their kiss to an end, and holding firm to her arms, he took a step away from her. "Together we can conquer anything."

"What are you suggesting?" she asked.

He heard the apprehension in her voice, but also the courage.

A pounding at the door interrupted any response, and they both eyed each other skeptically.

Was that fate knocking?

He wrapped his arm around her waist, tucking her against him. "Whatever awaits us beyond that door, we face together."

She nodded, her arm slipping around his waist.

"Enter," he called out.

Odran walked in and wasted no time in delivering the news. "One of our men has returned with a message." He looked to Reeve. "Your father requests that you both return home. He says it is imperative that you do so."

"Trouble brews?" Reeve asked.

"King Kenneth has sent a cleric to have Tara wed to him by proxy. Following the vows, his soldiers will escort her home. Carnoth agrees with the king's plan, and there is little your father can do about it unless he wishes to go to war now with the king."

"I will never reach the king's home," Tara said. "He will see me dead first."

"That will not happen," he assured her.

"How can you stop the king?"

He rested his brow on hers. "We'll do it together."

She shook her head, and Reeve, with a kiss, stopped any protests that would spill from her lips.

"We'll escort you home," Odran said.

"Your help is appreciated," Reeve said.

"Bliss warned us it would be necessary. We leave soon, so that we can reach shelter before nightfall." With that, Odran was gone.

"What will we do?" Tara asked anxiously.

"You will marry me," he said bluntly.

Her eyes rounded in fright and turned deep purple. "I cannot do that."

"You have no choice," he said adamantly.

"But I do. I must."

"Do you love me?'

"Of course I do," she said, as if angry that he needed to ask.

"Do you wish to wed me?"

"More than anything, but—"

"Is there a chance you carry my babe?" he asked.

She gasped and smiled, her hand going to her stomach. "Oh my, I had not thought of the possibility. But of course." She nodded vigorously. "Yes, there is."

"Would you not protect my child?"

"That's not fair," she said, understanding dawning. "You ask me to trade the father for the child."

"The father isn't going anywhere," Reeve said firmly. "We will return home, and you will tell your father that you may carry my babe and therefore wish to wed me. If he protests, you can remind him that he had asked you that very question once before and that you have decided it is exactly what you want to do."

"You will die," she said, fighting tears.

Reeve laughed. "I will not die. Besides, it is your only chance."

She walked away after giving him a shove. "What you are saying is that you are willing to give your life so that I, and possibly your child, may live."

"You believe in that wretched curse more than you believe in me," he said angrily. "I need you to believe in me, in us. When do you finally do that? When do you finally allow love the strength it needs to fight that damn curse."

"What if love isn't strong enough?" she argued.

"Do you believe that?" he snapped. "Can you honestly stand there and tell me that what you feel for me isn't strong enough to slay whatever stands in our way?"

"You wish to protect me and keep me safe, don't you?" she recounted.

"Of course I do," he said.

"Then don't you see that I wish to do the same for you. And sacrifice is what will slay anything that stands in my way of protecting you."

"No!" he shouted with a roar. "You have sacrificed enough for others. You will sacrifice no more, and certainly not for me."

"Yet you take the chance of sacrificing *your life* for me."

He rushed around the table before she could avoid him and grabbed her around the waist. "You have lived with fear long enough. It is time to live with courage. Trust me. Trust our love. Do that for *us*."

"I don't want to lose you, Reeve," she said softly. "I think I would die from the pain if I lost you."

He held her close. "We have no choice in this matter, Tara. There is no place for you to hide. No place for you to be safe, except in my arms. You need to be courageous and take the chance in choosing what you want, choosing to love."

Tara rode her own horse, the Picts leading the way. They had been traveling several hours, and though Reeve rode alongside her, they had spoken little since their departure. She had been deep in thought, musing over how only a few days ago, she had decided to make her own choices. And here she was faced with a choice.

According to Reeve, the choice was simple, trust in him, trust in love.

Did she have the strength to do it? Not only to trust but to truly love without fear or apprehension. Not only to defy her father's dictates and follow her heart, but to defy the curse as well. Reeve had been right about one thing; she had lived with fear far too long.

But again, did she have the courage to not only embrace love, but to accept love?

* * *

Reeve took Tara's hand as they entered the keep. They had exchanged few words since last night, and he knew that she had been agonizing over her decision. He wanted to believe that her love for him would overcome her fear, but he couldn't say for sure. Fear was a powerful deterrent. And he had no doubt love had lost out to it at times. He only hoped this wasn't one of those times.

Voices hushed as soon as they walked in, and Tara's father stomped toward her.

Reeve was quick to step in front of her. "Recall what I told you I'd do if you raised your hand to her again?" He didn't let Carnoth answer, but he knew from the fuming look in his eyes that he recalled every word. "I meant it."

"And I mean it when I tell you that my daughter will wed King Kenneth here and now." Carnoth waved at a wiry, short man who hurried to his side. "The king has sent his cleric. He will wed them now, for all of the MacAlpin clan to see."

Reeve looked to his family, his brothers' hands already on the hilt of their swords. He knew he couldn't allow this to turn into a battle. It would upset all plans made for the true king's return. But how did he stop it? How did he protect the woman he loved if she wouldn't help protect their love?

His answer came just in time, and he smiled with pride.

Tara stepped around him, her shoulders thrown back, her chin up, and her eyes glowing deep purple. "I will wed Reeve of the MacAlpin clan."

"You wed the king," Carnoth shouted at her.

She threw her chin up higher. "I will not. Once

before you gave me a choice to wed Reeve. I foolishly refused. I correct my foolishness right now. I will wed Reeve."

"That was before, this is now," Carnoth argued. "You will wed the king."

"I will not wed another man when I could possibly be carrying Reeve's child."

That had Mara running over to her, and, like a battling ram, she pushed Carnoth out of the way and hooked her arm with Tara's. "She's right. If she carries a MacAlpin babe, she has the right to wed the father."

Carnoth glared at both women. "Fine, wed the fool, right now. He will be dead shortly afterwards and then you will honor my agreement with the king."

# Chapter 31

Mara had everyone in place in no time, whispering to Reeve and Tara that they would have a proper exchange of vows and celebration another time. For now this would do.

Reeve couldn't have agreed more. He wanted vows exchanged right now, before anything else interfered. Unfortunately, the next interference came from his family.

Willow flew off the steps and into the great hall yelling, "Trey is awake."

"Let him wait," Carnoth yelled angrily. "I want this done."

Tara turned on her father. "If as you claim, Reeve will be dead shortly after our vows are exchanged, then I insist that he be given the chance to speak with his brother one last time."

Reeve grinned. "Your daughter has a point, Carnoth."

The man mumbled beneath his breath before waving them away. "Be quick about it."

MacAlpin warriors roamed the great hall, their presence a warning to Carnoth and a relief to the parents and brothers as they hurried up the stairs.

Mara was the first one in the room, but then everyone moved out of her way, including her husband, who followed on her heels. Tears filled her eyes, seeing her son lying back against a mound of pillows instead of lying prone as if in death.

"Welcome back," she said with glee and tearful eyes. "You are feeling all right?" She reached out and checked his brow for herself.

"I hurt, but that is good, for it means I am alive," Trey said with a stronger voice than any of them had expected.

"You gave us quite a scare," Mercy said, standing beside her husband, his arm around her.

"That you did," Duncan said. "It is good to have you back."

"Damn good," Bryce added.

"Pleased that you're finally among the living," Reeve teased.

Carmag simply placed a firm hand on his son's shoulder.

Mara started her fussing. "You'll need some food, and I'll get you a shirt and—"

Trey grabbed hold of his mother's hand and Mara stilled, her tears of relief ready to fall. "Your stitching saved my life."

"I wish my hands had been skilled enough to have saved you. But it was Tara who stitched you up and gave you a chance to live."

Reeve tugged Tara from behind Duncan, where she was attempting to hide, and he knew why. When Trey had woken briefly and his eyes had caught hers, he had pointed at her, and said, "death." Since she had just faced her father, who had reminded her that she was a death bride, she hadn't needed another reminder. Not that he believed it would cause her to renege on her decision though he believed it would play on her fear.

"My about-to-be-wife," Reeve said and, with a firm arm around her waist, approached his brother.

Trey's eyes widened, and he shook his head. "You can't wed her. She will bring death."

Reeve was quick to defend her. "Tara is a good woman. What nonsense do you speak?"

"Before the soldiers attacked me—"

"The king's soldiers did this to you?" Bryce asked angrily, as if repeating it would confirm it.

"I thought I had been cautious, farmers at the crofts where I stopped warned me that soldiers were in the area and in the foulest of moods. They believed it had to do with a mission for the king that was not going well."

"How many?" Reeve asked.

"Not nearly enough to be a threat to you, but enough of a serious threat to me. With little choice left to me, I defended myself the best I could. I landed solid blows to a couple, but one large fellow struck me a blow that took me down fast and hard, and that was the end. I heard one say, "Let the animals feast on him." I thought I was doomed, the pain too great to move."

He scrunched his brow. "I believe I lost consciousness for a while and then I thought someone approached, knelt beside me, and whispered for me to hold on, help was on the way." He shook his head. "I must have imagined it. The next thing I knew I was here; other times I thought it a dream; and still other times I felt as if I was burning in the depths of hell."

"You'll be revenged," Bryce said.

"The day the true king takes the throne will be revenge enough," Trey said.

"With that settled, tell me why you believe Tara brings death," Reeve said wanting this done with here and now.

"In my travels, an old woman approached me in one of the villages. She told me to beware of a woman with hair the color of raven feathers and eyes the color of heather, that she would bring death to my family."

"Why would you believe a stranger who babbled nonsense in search of coins?" Reeve asked.

"I didn't," Trey said, closing his eyes briefly. "And she asked for no coins. She had also told me that I would suffer great wounds, and when I finally woke, a beautiful woman would be sitting beside me and that she would be my future wife." Trey searched the room. "I thought I had seen a fair-haired woman here when I opened my eyes, but I don't see her now."

"Bliss," Mara said.

Trey looked to Mercy. "The Pict woman who helped heal you?"

"She helped heal you as well," Mercy said.

"Where is she?" Trey asked.

"That doesn't matter now," Reeve said, growing impatient. "At the moment, it is important that Tara and I wed, or she will face death herself."

Trey looked at him confused.

"There's no time to explain it to you now," Reeve said. "I'm about to wed."

"Wait," Tara said, slipping from Reeve's grasp. "This old woman who warned you about me, what did she look like?"

"What difference does it matter?" Trey asked.

"Many years ago a woman my father believed a witch cast a curse on me. There are only two ways for me to be rid of it. One is to find the person who placed the curse on me and have her remove it."

"It could be her," Reeve said, realizing what Tara was implying.

She turned to him. "She described me as if she knew me. It has to be her."

A servant lass appeared at the open door. "Sorry to disturb, but King Carnoth grows restless."

Reeve grabbed her hand. "We go wed."

"We should find her first," Tara said.

"There isn't time to search for her. We wed first and then we search for her," Reeve insisted, wrapping his arm around her waist. "There is no other way. We wed, or your father has his way."

Mara tucked the blanket around Trey. "You rest. We have a wedding to attend."

They all marched out of the room before Reeve and Tara.

Trey called out to Reeve just as the couple reached the door. Reeve nodded to Tara to wait in the hall, then he turned and walked over to his brother.

"I know nothing about what is going on with you and Tara. I just want to know that you're sure about this," Trey said.

"As sure as I am that the true king will claim the throne of Scotland."

Trey stuck his hand out. "Then let me be the first to congratulate you."

Reeve took his hand with a firm grip. "That means a lot to me."

"We'll talk later. Go get married."

Reeve was out the door and hurrying Tara down the stairs. Her father was pacing around the tables and looked ready to explode when he caught sight of them.

"Let's be done with this now," Carnoth said.

Mara once again hurried everyone into place, and Reeve reached out and took hold of Tara's hand and smiled. She bravely forced a smile, though fear dulled her lavender-colored eyes.

There was no point trying to reassure her. She would see for herself soon enough that nothing would happen to him. The cleric started with a rush of words and finished with a hasty blessing, then stepped aside as if he feared something would happen if he remained too close to Reeve.

It seemed that everyone waited, staring at him with apprehension. He ignored them all and took Tara in his arms and kissed her. It took a moment for her to return the kiss, but she did. When it finished, she glared at him, her hand patting his cheeks.

"I'm still alive," Reeve said, grinning.

"You'll be dead by morning," Carnoth spat. "And then I'll be taking my daughter with me."

"You acknowledge that Tara is my wife?" Reeve asked.

"I stood here and watched you exchange vows, you fool."

"You may have watched, but you're the fool if you didn't realize that once she wed me, she became part of the MacAlpin clan. If anything should happen to me before morning, Tara remains with the clan; she no longer belongs to you. She is and shall remain a MacAlpin. So take your men and leave. You are no longer welcome here."

Carnoth's face flushed bright red, and he sputtered when he spoke. "Tara is my daughter."

Reeve stepped right up to within inches of his glowing red face. "Tara may be your daughter, but she is now *my wife*, part of *my clan*. You no longer have a say in her life."

"I thought your clan fought for the true king to take the throne," Carnoth said. "If you had but let her wed the fool king, he would be dead by now."

"Are you telling me that you arranged for Tara to wed the king in hopes that he would die?" Reeve asked, his anger rising.

"The selfish bastard is bleeding me dry," Carnoth yelled.

"Watch your mouth in my home," Mara scolded harshly.

Carnoth was so livid, he looked as if he would snort smoke from his nostrils. "King Kenneth demands more and more of my money. I thought my daughter could be the solution to many problems."

"He planned to kill her," Reeve said, disgusted.

"The consequence of battle," Carnoth said without an ounce of regret.

His callous remark infuriated Reeve, but what drove him over the edge was turning to see tears in his wife's eyes. She had suspected as much, but hearing her father announce that he knowingly and without regret had planned to send her to her death must have torn at her heart.

Reeve threw his arms out from his sides, fisted his hands, leaned his head back, and let loose with such a spine-chilling roar that everyone in the room took a step back. He reached out and grabbed Carnoth by the throat, dragging him across a table, sending tankards and food flying. He slammed him down atop another table, the wood groaning and Carnoth's head cracking a pitcher of ale. Reeve roared again and, with two hands, grabbed the man and sent him flying over the last table in the long row. He then hurried over to grab him off the floor and start the process all over again.

No one interfered, not even Carnoth's men, but that was because MacAlpin warriors prevented any of them from moving. Finally, Reeve slapped the man down on a table, his body bouncing from the force, and pressed his nose to Carnoth's.

"Bother my wife, come near her, make her cry, make her sad, speak to her as if you own her, and I will see you gutted and strung from the highest tree." He tossed the man to the floor like a piece of garbage and walked over to Tara. As he stepped behind her, he wrapped his arm possessively across her chest and pulled her back against him, so there could be no mistake that she belonged to him.

Carmag stepped forward. "I suggest you leave. All has been settled."

Carnoth stood, his hand going to his throat, Reeve having left a sizeable imprint on it, and choked as he spoke. "This is not over."

"Yes, it is," Carmag said. "As Reeve said, Tara is now a MacAlpin. Our warriors will escort you off our land."

Carnoth glared at his daughter. "You have brought disgrace to our clan. And have caused nothing but problems for me, so it is glad I am to be rid of you. As far as I'm concerned, I have no daughter." He turned his back on her, snapped his fingers, and his warriors followed him out of the hall, MacAlpin warriors right on their heels.

Reeve could feel the tremor that rumbled through Tara. While Carnoth was never a good father, he was still Tara's father, and to hear him admit, before all, that he purposely sent his daughter to her death had to have caused her immeasurable pain.

"It's over," he whispered in her ear. "You belong to me now, and as you can see, I'm still here." He wanted her to understand that she had a home and was safe, and that he wasn't going anywhere.

Her tremors continued, and she didn't respond. He knew something was amiss when he saw his mother's eyes turn wide when she glanced upon Tara.

Reeve coaxed Tara around in his arms as Mara approached. Her face was as white as freshly fallen snow. And tears trickled one by one down her cheeks.

Mara reached them before he could do anything and yanked her out of Reeve's hands, though she nodded for him to follow. Mercy hurried ahead of Mara, rushing to grab one of the wool cloaks that hung on a peg by the keep's double doors.

"It's the fire's warmth and a hot strong drink you need," Mara said.

Reeve then realized that Tara's father had actually chilled her to the bone in shock. He took the cloak from Mercy and wrapped it around his wife then sat her at the table closest to the fire's heat and joined her on the bench, his arm going to her back to rub warmth into her.

Mara filled a tankard with hot cider and added more than a splash of acqua vitae. She then filled enough tankards with ale for them all and raised hers high.

"Blessings to Reeve and Tara."

They each in turn offered their own congratulations and, with acknowledging nods, drifted off, leaving the couple alone.

He was relieved when she turned and finally spoke to him. "I thought my father might have planned it this way, but I didn't want to believe it, and even now hearing it—" She shook her head, and a few more tears fell. "How could he? I'm his daughter." She shook her head again. "He never loved me. My father never loved me."

Reeve tried to ease her into his arms, but she pushed him away and stood.

"I've been nothing but a burden to him, an annoyance he wanted out of his life, and he thought to be rid of me along with another annoyance, the king."

Reeve remained silent, letting her spew out her anger and hurt.

Her shoulders slumped, and, again, she shook her head. "My second wedding ceremony, and again it is filled with heartache."

"And in a sense, death, which takes care of the curse," Reeve said.

Tara turned wide eyes on him. "With my father's shocking rant, I forgot all about the curse."

Reeve silently cursed himself for having reminded her. "You must admit that your father's departure is very much a death."

She sighed, another tear dropping. "It is, isn't it?"

"So the curse has been fed, and we have no need to worry," he said, hoping she would see it his way.

"I wish it was that simple."

"I'm still here," Reeve said, throwing out his arms to her. She didn't run into them, and he didn't like that.

"We need to talk with your brother about the witch."

"There's time for that." Since she wouldn't come to him, he walked toward her.

She raised her hand to ward off his advance, and he stopped, his eyes narrowing and his brow knitting in a frown.

"We must find this witch and have the curse removed before we take our vows any further," she said.

He didn't like what he was hearing. "Define take our vows any further?"

With some hesitancy, Tara said, "It's best if we not consummate our vows—"

"We've already consummated," he said.

She shook her head adamantly. "We weren't wed at the time."

"What difference does it make? We coupled, and I lived." He thumped his chest. "And we wed, and death has not claimed me. You can't believe that by consummating our vows as a married couple that death will take me."

"I don't know, and I don't want to take a chance that death still stalks you. With finding the witch who placed the curse on me now a strong possibility, I feel that is what we should do before anything else."

"Like making love or me telling you that I—"

Tara raised her hands to her ears. "Stop! Don't dare say it. If there is the slimmest chance that the witch might help then we must find her."

"And not consummate our vows until we do?"

Her hands dropped to her sides, and she gave a firm nod. "Yes."

Reeve grinned and shook his head. "That's not going to happen."

# Chapter 32

"I'm trying to protect you," Tara said, stepping back as Reeve advanced on her much too fast.

"I don't need protection," he said, reaching out and wrapping a strong arm around her waist. "What I need is me on top of you, or beneath you, or whichever way you want."

"Be sensible," she scolded.

"I am," he said, yanking her against him and teasing her lips with a rough nibble and a forceful kiss.

It took her a moment to get her breath and calm her senses when the kiss ended. Damn him for igniting her desire, though who was she fooling? As soon as he mentioned being on top of her, she had grown wet. She wondered if perhaps there was something wrong with her that it took so little for her to desire him. He had only to touch her, a simple touch, or suggest with wicked words, and she found her body tingling.

"You need—"

"That's right, I need you. Do you want to feel how badly I need you?" he asked

The itch to touch him was unbearable, and she squirmed to get out of his arms and place some distance between them, or else this encounter would end in his favor. He, however, would not let go; he held her firm.

"We'll speak with my brother tomorrow. Right now, you and I have a matter to attend to."

A distinct cough startled Tara, but had Reeve only turning his head.

Willow stood there with a smile. "Sorry to disturb, but Trey has been asking for you both. If you have a moment?"

Tara silently thanked Trey. Reeve would not turn down his brother's summons, not after all he had been through. This would at least give them time to calm their passion and approach things more pragmatically.

Reeve took hold of Tara's hand as if letting her know that she was not getting away from him that easily.

Willow didn't join them when they entered Trey's room, and Tara was surprised that no one else was there. Trey was alone.

"Where is everyone?" Reeve asked, obviously surprised himself.

"I asked for some time alone with you both," Trey said. His voice wasn't as strong as before, and he looked fatigued.

Reeve must have noticed the same, for he said, "You are tired. This can wait until morning."

"I don't think it can," Trey said firmly. "I remember something the witch said, and I thought Tara would want to hear it." He didn't wait for a response from either of them. "I'm not sure if the old hag wanted me to hear it or not, but I did. Though it made no sense to me at the time, after hearing Tara's tale, it just might fit."

"Do tell," Tara said, eagerly slipping away from Reeve to sit in the chair close to the bed.

Trey kept his attention on Tara. "After the old woman finished *advising* me as she had claimed, she turned to leave and that is when I heard her say, 'Deserves it she does, stole my son from me.' "

Tara gasped, and even Reeve's eyes turned wide.

"Did you take her son from her?" Trey asked.

Tara retold the tale to Trey from beginning to end.

"Then it seems she is the one you look for," Trey said.

"Where is she?" Reeve asked.

"Last I saw her, she was traveling north toward Grunnhil."

"The Norse settlements," Reeve said. "That's a distance."

"Time would be needed for such a journey," Trey said.

Tara knew by the look in both their eyes that it was time that could not presently be spared.

"This is for you both to discuss," Trey suggested.

"What discussion?" Tara asked with resignation. "I know that your mission to seat the true king takes priority over everything. And I cannot fault that. I just worry the curse she placed on me could adversely affect your family, your clan, your mission. What then?"

"You said there was another way of ridding yourself of the curse," Trey reminded.

Tara nodded. "To find someone more powerful than the one who cast the curse and have her or him remove it."

"Then that is what must be done," Trey said.

"Reeve has tried that with no success."

"So far no success," Reeve said, and gave her shoulder a comforting squeeze. "But we're not giving up. We'll find who we need."

Tara was relieved when she felt Reeve's reassuring touch. She knew he thought their love could solve everything. And she wanted to believe it herself, but she worried. She couldn't help it. Too many years spent facing too much heartache to simply think that she could dismiss the curse so easily. And though nothing had happened to Reeve since exchanging vows, there were many hours left before morning.

Trey groaned when he moved, and Reeve went to his side. "Need help?"

"I need to sleep," Trey reluctantly admitted.

Tara stood. "Lift his head and back some, so I may fix his pillows."

Reeve did as directed, Trey grabbing hold of his arm to help. When all finished, Trey sighed with comfort as he lay flat, his head resting on one pillow.

Tara was fussing with the soft wool blanket when Willow entered.

"Your father requests your presence in the solar," she said to Reeve.

Trey reached out and took a firm hold of his brother's arm. "You'll tell me what was discussed?"

"All of it," Reeve assured him, and gave Tara a quick kiss before leaving.

Willow joined Tara at the bed and helped her arrange the blankets over Trey.

"You look familiar," Trey said, staring at her.

"You've stopped at my family's croft on occasion. I am Willow, Edward's widow."

"Old Jacob's place," Trey said with a smile. "How is he?"

"He died," Willow said with audible sadness.

"I'm so sorry. He was ill?" Trey asked.

"Sadly, no. He was as stubborn about dying as he was about living. I believe if we hadn't been forced to leave our farm and walk here in a raging snowstorm, the old fool would have outlived me."

"What happened?" Trey asked curious.

Tara excused herself before Willow recounted the heartbreaking story. She was eager for some time to herself. Not so much to think, she had done enough of that for today, just simply to be. And the best way to accomplish that was to keep her hands busy. With busy hands, her thoughts would fade, her worries would calm, and, for a while, just a while, she'd be somewhat at peace. She could sew, or she could bake bread. She chose the more strenuous of the two and hurried off to the kitchen.

Reeve's father and brothers were waiting for him, and he dropped into the only unoccupied chair in the room.

"Sorry to take you away from your wife on your wedding night," Carmag said. "But I felt this meeting could not wait."

"After all that has happened tonight, I expected it," Reeve admitted, and his brothers nodded in agreement.

"The king grows bolder, as do his soldiers," Carmag said. "They prowl our land whereas before they kept a respectful distance. Something has changed."

"We know that the king has suffered money woes of late," Bryce said. "Could be his coffers are bone-dry, leaving his troops to suffer."

"He found a way to appease the soldiers he sent to collect Tara," Reeve said. "He told them to enjoy her and return her in good enough condition for him to wed her."

"Her father deserves to die," Duncan said, "along with the soldiers who almost beat Trey to death."

"That beating makes no sense," Bryce said, shaking his head.

"I have to agree," Reeve said, having given it some thought. "Why not just kill him and be done with it? Why beat him and leave him to die? I think Da is right, something is going on."

"We have plotted the return of the true king for years, and I daresay King Kenneth has plotted just as strongly to see that his throne is not taken from him. Two plots at work, with many people involved. If we have spies, the king certainly has spies—"

"Here among us?" Bryce asked.

"Who else would have stolen that piece of hide relevant to the future king?" Carmag asked and answered. "None in this room. I believe we should be more cautious in our discussions and more aware of those around us. I have asked Neil to keep alert. He spied for us; he could certainly spot another who spies."

"The time draws near," Duncan said. "Many wonder if blood will cover the land before all is done."

A gentle knock sounded at the door, and cautious glances were exchanged. No one ever disturbed them when they retreated to the solar, not even Mara.

"Who goes there?" Carmag called out.

"Bliss," came the soft reply.

The brothers immediately stood, fearful something was wrong with Trey, and Bryce hurried to the door and opened it.

Bliss entered and, slipping the door from Bryce's, grasp closed it. "I need to talk with all of you." She walked to the center of the room.

Carmag offered her a chair, but she shook her head. "I don't wish to disturb you. You have much planning to do. I'll say what I have come to say and take my leave."

"As you wish," Carmag said, and the men gathered closer to her.

"More goes on around you than you know, and there is one who has spied before and will spy again. But there is another who you think betrays you but does not. This one knows more than any of you know. This one knows the true story of the true king."

"Who?" Bryce demanded sharply.

"I cannot say," she said.

"You cannot or refuse to?" Reeve asked.

Bliss shook her head. "I do not refuse."

"She doesn't know," Duncan said.

Bryce looked on her with angry eyes. "What of this spy?"

"Keep your eyes open and your heart clear, and you will find the person."

"You talk too much in riddles," Reeve said.

"I can only say what I know, and it is not always clear until it comes to pass."

"What good is it then?" Bryce said.

"I ask the same myself," Bliss said, "but no answer is ever provided."

"What of the one who you say we think betrays us?" Carmag asked.

"This person holds the answers to many questions, and when the time is right, this person will provide the answers."

"This person is friend not foe?" Reeve asked.

"I'm sorry, I don't know." Bliss turned to Bryce before he could comment. "I understand that does you no good, but I can only tell you what I know. The rest is up to you."

Bryce summed it up. "So there is a spy among us and a person who knows much more about the king than we do."

Bliss nodded, and before Bryce could say another word, she said, "I know the true king is one of the four brothers."

They all stood tall, their eyes wide, their mouths stern, and stared at her.

"You all wonder how someone can know more about the king than he does himself. And I tell you that if you open your eyes and clear your heart, you will have your answer."

"Do you know the true king's identity?" Carmag asked.

"I would never reveal such information," Bliss said, and walked to the door. "Open your eyes, or you will miss what is in front of you." With that, Bliss left the room.

The men were too stunned to speak until, finally, Duncan said, "She knows who the king is."

Reeve shook his head. "She never admitted that she did."

"And if she does know?" Bryce asked. "Do we trust her?"

"Bliss has proven a good friend. Besides, do we have a choice?" Carmag said. "The first thing we must do is find this spy. Until then, we must be extravigilant in what plans we let be known. I will map out a plan, and we will discuss it. For now, go to your wives. It has been a long day."

"Bryce has no wife," Reeve said with a grin, and his teasing manner lifted the weight of their heavy burdens and the long arduous day, if only for a while.

"Thank the heavens for that," Bryce said smiling.

Reeve laughed, and Duncan snorted.

Duncan elaborated. "You just may be the last of us to find a wife, you poor soul."

"True enough," Reeve agreed. "According to the witch, it looks like Bliss is Trey's future wife."

"Good for him," Bryce said, shaking his head. "I certainly wouldn't want a wife that had the kind of knowing that Bliss does. Lord, there wouldn't be anything you could do that she didn't know about. I'll stick to tending to the missions while you fools get wrapped up in love"

Both brothers laughed.

"He's jealous," Duncan said, heading to the door.

"Definitely jealous," Reeve agreed, following.

"I am not," Bryce called out, as the door shut behind them.

Carmag placed a hand on his son's shoulder. "Your time will come."

"With so much to be done, I prefer to wait," Bryce said.

Carmag shook his head. "Love waits for no one."

# Chapter 33

Tara was enjoying herself. Etty had been just finishing up in the kitchen and was eager to get home to Neil when she had entered. When Tara had informed her that she was going to make her black bread, Etty begged that she make extra loaves.

The last two loaves of the four Tara had made were cooking. She rolled her shoulders back, easing the stiffness from them, and though she was tired, she also felt refreshed. Baking the bread had cleared her mind, and she was certain she'd have a good night's sleep tonight.

*After making love.*

She shook her head, the silent words resonating like a clanging bell in her mind. How could she prevent her vows from being consummated when she was eager to make love with her husband?

The thought hit her then. Both Rory and Luag had died before consummation of the vows. Would it be any different with the vows consummated?

It was doubtful, but it was worth a try, and besides, she was aching to make love with Reeve. A huge smile filled her face at the thought, and when she heard rushed footfalls approach, she turned, eager to greet her husband.

She froze when she saw that it was Allen, one of her father's most trusted warriors.

"What do you want?" she demanded, though she feared she knew.

"Your husband dead," he said bluntly.

"That's *not* going to happen."

She and Allen turned to see Reeve sending just inside the arched doorway, his arms folded over his chest as if what he had heard did not disturb him at all, confident that he was right. But then he was always right, and that brought a smile to Tara's face.

Allen glared and pointed a finger at Reeve. "You die, and Tara comes with me to fulfill her duty to her clan."

Reeve shook his head and walked slowly into the room. "No. You die, and I send your body back to Carnoth to show him that he has failed again. And to remind him of my warning to leave my wife alone."

Tara knew Allen was skilled with a dirk. He'd been known to kill a man with a single blow, and that, she feared, was his plan. He was fast and accurate even from a distance. Fear raced through her. Would the curse prove true after all? Was there nothing she could do to save her husband? The horrible thought squeezed tight at her heart, and she inched closer to Reeve, wanting to save him, but not sure how.

"Of course, I could let you leave now and thus spare your life," Reeve said.

Allen laughed, and Tara knew it was a diversion. She had seen him use it before. The dirk was in his hand and sailing through the air before she realized he had reached for it. And with no regard for her own life, she launched her body in front of Reeve's.

In one fluid motion she felt Reeve's arm circle her waist, yank her against him and shield her body with his as he dipped them both to the floor. He released her with a jolt and stood so fast that it took her a moment to realize what had happened. From her prone position, she watched as Reeve retrieved the dirk from where it had embedded in the wall and walked toward Allen.

"Let me show you how to properly use this," Reeve said, and, with a fierce roar, launched the dirk and himself at Allen.

Tara sprang to her feet, her eyes wide. With the look of fury she had caught in Reeve's eyes before he released her, she knew that he had intentionally missed hitting Allen with the weapon. He was itching for a fight, and Allen had given him the opportunity.

"Damn, this one might be a match for our brother," Duncan said, entering the room, Bryce following him in.

"Do something," Tara ordered sharply.

"We are," Bryce said. "We're here to cheer him on."

"What's taking you so long, Reeve?" Duncan shouted.

Reeve delivered a vicious blow to Allen's jaw that had him stumbling backward. As Reeve advanced on the man and without a backward glance to his brother, he yelled, "I'm going to beat *you* when I'm done with *him*."

Duncan and Bryce laughed, and Bryce grabbed one of the freshly baked loaves of bread and tore it in half to share with Duncan. They ate the bread while shouting encouragements to Reeve.

"You better hurry up and finish him off before we eat all this delicious bread your wife made," Bryce called out.

Reeve's head snapped around, his face in a feral snarl. Allen took advantage of the moment and landed a punch that sent Reeve stumbling back though he remained on his feet. The snarl returned as he said to his brothers, "Eat all my bread, and I'll kill you both."

"Then stop playing with the fool and finish it," Bryce challenged, and took another bite of the bread.

Tara stood frozen with anger. How could they make light of the situation? Didn't they realize their brother could die? Didn't they know that the curse could rear its ugly head any moment, and Reeve would be dead? It didn't matter that he had battled many men and had won. He hadn't been cursed. It was different now. He was more vulnerable, and the two fool brothers simply stood there and did nothing to help him. Even Reeve didn't take it seriously. He continued to think himself impervious. She wanted to pound on all of them for their stupidity.

It was only moments later that Tara was finally able to breathe a sigh of relief. Reeve pounded the man so badly that Allen raised his hand in surrender. Reeve picked him up by the scruff of his shirt and dragged him to the door.

"If Carnoth dares send another, I'll kill him," Reeve said, and tossed the beaten man out the door, slamming it behind him.

He turned with a grin then winced, his lip split, bloody, and bruised. His right eye was darkening as well, and while Tara wanted to run and tend his wounds, she was so angry with him that she remained frozen where she stood, her hands fisted at her sides.

Reeve grabbed a loaf of bread and tore off a chunk.

"For a minute, I thought we were going to have to help you," Bryce said with a smirk.

Another wince cut off Reeve's laughter. "That will be the day, that I need help in defeating one lone fool."

"It was two fools in that fight," Tara shouted, and all three men turned wide eyes on her. "Go on with all of you and glare at me like the fools you are."

"We better go," Duncan said, and Bryce nodded.

"Don't you dare move," Tara ordered with a shake of her finger. "You'll stay put until I have my say."

The two men remained where they were.

Reeve unwisely opened his mouth. "There's no reason to be upset. I saved you as I always do."

Duncan cringed, and Bryce shook his head.

"Saved me and then fought with not an ounce of wit," she snapped.

Reeve made another grave error by taking a step toward her.

"Stay right where you are," she yelled, her hand going up to ward him off.

Duncan and Bryce tried to ease toward the door.

"If you two move again, *I'll* beat you," Tara threatened.

They stayed put.

She threw her hands up in the air when she looked at Reeve. "I can't believe you took such a chance. Does your life mean so little to you? Do I mean so little to you?"

He looked stricken and tried advancing on her once more.

She wouldn't have it. "Don't you dare come near me until you take this curse seriously. Why do you think I threw myself in front of you? I would rather die than see the curse take you from me. I love you, damn it, I love you more than life itself."

Tara stormed out of the room, tears falling as she went.

Reeve stood, staring after her, then turned to his brothers. "What do I do?"

"Give her what she wants," Duncan said.

"I don't know how," Reeve said, frustrated. "I do understand how she feels about the curse, but witches don't exactly shout out their presence in the area. I have Neil making inquires, and he's found a prophet, but no witch."

"Perhaps the prophet can help," Bryce suggested.

"He can't remove the curse," Reeve said, frustrated.

Duncan smiled. "But he can advise if it will affect you."

Reeve's face brightened. "True enough, and it could put Tara at ease."

"Unless he tells you that you're going to die," Bryce said with a grin.

"Seriously, I'm going to have to beat you one day," Reeve said.

Bryce laughed. "You can try."

"My wager is on Reeve," Duncan said.

Reeve scrunched his brow. "There is one thing we are not considering."

"Which is?" Duncan asked.

"The prophet could very well know who among us is king," Reeve said. "Do we take that chance?"

"We take a chance every day of his identity being discovered," Duncan said. "Besides, he may be able to add to or explain what Bliss has told us about the spy and about the theft of the hide."

"He does make a good point," Bryce said.

"We should discuss this with Da first," Reeve said.

Bryce placed a firm hand on Reeve's back. "Then let's go find him, so that you can put your wife's mind at ease and enjoy your wedding night."

Duncan laughed. "Or else you'll be sleeping alone."

Reeve approached his bedchamber with apprehension, not something he had ever thought he'd be doing on his wedding night. He had never meant to hurt Tara, was shocked that his actions had, and was even more surprised when she had claimed she would give her life for him. That's something a man would do for his woman, give his life to protect her. Tara was so much more courageous than she realized. And if anyone could defeat this nonsensical curse, she could.

However, she didn't see it that way, and in a way she had been right. Though it wasn't the curse he hadn't taken seriously, it was how the curse had affected her that he had failed to consider. He had expected her to simply believe that their love would be enough to battle the curse. But he had not lived through the ordeal that the hex had cost her. Year after year, losing those she loved, living alone without so much as a comforting touch. The curse had been a costly ordeal for her, and he had expected her to dismiss it as if it had never affected her. He had been a fool.

Carmag had agreed about the prophet, and word was sent to Neil to have the prophet brought there. He wasn't sure it would appease Tara, but it was worth a try. And he intended to let her know just how seriously he was taking the matter.

He entered his bedchamber with trepidation, though determined. He stopped dead once inside and grew angry. She wasn't there. He hurried to his mother's sewing room, and when he found it empty, he grew angrier. He hurried to Trey's room and quietly opened the door to peek in, but it was Willow who sat watch over his sleeping brother.

Now he was furious. There was only one other place she could have gone—her cottage. And by returning to her cottage, it all but told him that she didn't consider them wed. He stormed downstairs, through the great hall, and out into the night.

A light snow fell, and though the air was bitter, his anger had him much too hot to notice. He didn't bother to knock at the door; he grabbed the latch and shoved it open. His eyes narrowed, and his mouth tightened as her head shot up from where she stood in front of the fireplace. She had already changed into her soft white wool nightdress, the fire's light silhouetting her naked body beneath.

He slammed the door shut behind him.

"If you have not come to your senses, then take your leave now."

"And what of you, wife?" he argued. "Deserting her newlywed husband on their wedding night?"

"You'll not lay the blame on me for this," she spat.

"And I should lay it on me for saving you?"

"You took a chance of—"

"Keeping us both alive," he snapped, "and successfully."

Tears clouded her eyes, but she kept her head high. "For the moment."

He grumbled beneath his breath. He couldn't bear to see her cry again. She had shed enough tears and had suffered enough hurt. He didn't have to cause her more, and it hadn't been his intention. Again he was thinking of himself, being annoyed that she had left the keep, in a sense leaving him. But if he truly understood his wife, he would have realized that her absence spoke loudly of her love for him. By returning to her cottage, she felt that she somehow was protecting him.

With his anger abating, he took a cautious step forward, and when she didn't order him to stop, he took another and another until he stood beside her. He didn't reach out and touch her; he didn't trust himself. Once he did touch her, he'd have her in that bed making love to her, and things needed to be discussed between them first.

He started with words that he truly meant. "I'm sorry."

Her eyes popped wide, and a tear broke loose and slipped down her cheek.

"You are right. I have not taken this curse seriously enough."

She sighed and wrapped her arms around his waist, laying her head on his chest.

His arms went around her as her warmth spread over him, chasing the chill that had crept into his bones and the ache that had settled in his heart.

"I will do whatever it takes to get this curse off you," he said.

She looked up at him and smiled. "Thank you for understanding."

"It's about time that I actually did," he admitted. "To me, it seemed an easy thing to be rid of, but I haven't lived with the curse and the heartache it brought. And I want no more heartache for you. I want you free to love and live."

"You have no idea how much I have wished for that."

"You shall have it; I'll make sure of it."

"I believe you," she said as if just realizing it. "I truly believe you."

He grinned. "Finally, we both understand each other."

"Now what?" she asked eagerly.

"I'd like to scoop you up and carry you to bed and make love to you, but—" He paused and gave her a quick kiss. "I have something I wish to discuss with you first."

"I'm listening though I am just as eager to make love."

"Damn I lo—"

She pressed her fingers to his lips. "Not yet, I know what you want to say, I can feel it, but not yet."

"When the time is right, I'm going to shout it."

"A soft whisper in my ear would serve just as well." She kissed him soft and sweetly.

He eased her away from him as he took a step back. "I need a bit of a distance, or the discussion will be forced to wait."

"Tell me," she urged anxiously as she moved farther away from him.

"You know that I have been trying to locate a powerful witch—"

"You have found one?" she asked, excited.

"No," he said, and was sorry to see her joy plummet. "I have found a powerful prophet."

"What good does that do?"

"He could tell us the future, warn if there is danger ahead for me, and perhaps let us know where to find the witch we need."

"I never thought of that," she said, nodding. "You're right."

"I'm always right."

"Will I never learn?" She laughed.

"I'll keep reminding you even when we're old and gray."

"The prophet could tell us if that will be so."

"From what Neil tells me, this man is a powerful prophet and knows much," Reeve said. "He may be able to help us more than we realize."

"Have you sent for him?"

He was pleased to tell her, "He's been sent for and should be here in a day or two."

Tara walked over to him, laying her hand on his chest. "I am grateful."

"So am I."

"Grateful for the prophet?"

He shook his head and stole a kiss. "No. That our discussion is done, and I can now get you into bed."

# Chapter 34

Tara cuddled closer to Reeve, a chill creeping up and over the bed. Had they forgotten to add logs to the fire before going to bed? She smiled, recalling what she remembered of last night. Reeve had made wickedly delicious love to her, his exact words of what he had intended to do to her. And oh how he meant it.

She didn't think there was a part of her that he hadn't tasted, teased, or tormented with his lips, tongue, and she giggled, thinking about her favorite appendage of his that had delighted her.

Worried that she was becoming too sinful when it came to her own desires, she had confessed her concern to him. Bless him, he hadn't laughed, he patiently explained how there was nothing wrong with her zeal to make love, and he fervently hoped that it would remain that way.

Feeling more at ease with her unquenchable desires, she had climbed on top of him and eagerly confessed that she loved riding him. He had offered to let her practice riding as much as she wanted to.

It had been a glorious wedding night though she had woke on and off checking to see that Reeve was all right, that death hadn't claimed him. She had never had a husband survive past the wedding day, and she was hopeful that perhaps the curse wouldn't rear its ugly head.

She suddenly recalled a dream she had during the night. She sat by a river talking with someone. She didn't know who, she couldn't see him clearly, though she felt she knew him. He urged her to remember, and then he told her that love had freed her, and she was so very happy. She woke after that and wondered about it and had soon returned to sleep and forgotten all about it until now.

Reeve stirred beside her, and his arms soon found their way around her and pulled her tighter against him. He nibbled along her ear. "It's damn cold in here."

She laughed softly. "I thought the same myself. We must have forgotten to add logs."

"Your fault," he said, wrapping his leg around hers. "You attacked me almost all night."

She laughed again. "I beg your pardon, sir. It was you who scooped me up, stripped me bare, and had your way with me."

"And what of the many times you rode me."

Tara sighed. "I've had no better rides."

Before he could respond, a sharp pounding rattled the cottage door.

"Go away," Reeve yelled.

The door burst open, and Bryce walked in. "Damn it's cold in here." He rubbed his arms and went straight to the fireplace, where nothing but embers remained. "Are you trying to freeze yourselves?"

"It was stifling hot in here all night," Reeve said.

Tara snuggled farther under the covers, which her husband pulled up to her neck.

"There's a problem," Bryce said, standing after the fire began roaring.

"What's wrong?" Reeve asked.

Bryce shook his head. "Carnoth is here with a few of the king's men. It seems that the king isn't recognizing your marriage and insists that Tara honor the agreement her father signed."

"The king's cleric wed us," Tara said.

"That's the problem," Bryce said. "The king claims he never gave the cleric permission, and that your vows are invalid.

"We gather our warriors just in case," Bryce said, worry lingering in the corners of his eyes. He walked to the door. "Hurry, we need to see this done."

Tara rushed into her garments with as much speed as Reeve. She didn't waste time on her hair; she let the black ringlets fall where they might. And after grabbing their cloaks, they joined hands and hurried to the keep.

Neither spoke, neither had to. They both knew that nothing, absolutely nothing would separate them.

"What nonsense is this?" Reeve demanded, as they approached her father as soon as they entered the great hall.

Tara remained by his side, her eyes wide and alert. She would protect her husband however she could.

King Carnoth stepped forward. "It is King Kenneth's doing."

"How did he learn of this so fast?" Reeve demanded.

"He is not far," the soldier beside Carnoth said. "He had planned to surprise his new bride and was met with the troubling news. But it matters not; Carnoth promised her to the king, and to the king she goes."

"Not going to happen," Reeve said vehemently.

"You have no choice," the soldier protested. "She is the property of King Kenneth."

"Tara is my wife," Reeve argued.

"Not according to King Kenneth, and the king's word is law," the soldier said.

Before the argument escalated, Tara stepped forward. "Father, can I speak with you?"

Carnoth nodded, and Tara stepped away from her husband, her father following her to a discreet corner in the hall to talk privately.

"King Kenneth cares naught for me. He wishes nothing more than my bride price. Pay the king and free me."

"Get it from your husband," Carnoth snarled low.

"That is his to keep," Tara said. "Besides, your coffers spill over, you have more than enough money to give the king and still have a sizeable amount left."

"And it stays that way," Carnoth said in a threatening tone.

"Not if I inform the guard of your hefty coffers. I'm sure he would be rewarded with bringing the king such good news."

"If King Kenneth found out, he would take until I was bone-dry," Carnoth complained.

"Unless you simply pay him the bride price and be done with it. He's not interested in me. He wants only the money. You will free yourself, and you will free me with this charitable expression, or–" She shrugged. "I speak up. Something you have not let me do for a very long time."

"You are no daughter to me," Carnoth spat.

"You're right, Father," Tara said sadly. "I am no longer your daughter."

She stepped away from him and returned to Reeve, his arm going possessively around her waist.

"Take me to the king," Carnoth balked. "I have an offer I know he will not refuse."

When her father and the soldier left, Reeve asked, "What did you say to him?"

"I spoke in terms my father would understand," she said, and smiled.

"It is good that you are now part of our clan; the true king can make use of your negotiating skills when needed," Duncan said.

"I would be honored to serve him," Tara said.

Mercy and Mara entered the great hall.

"What goes on here?" Mara demanded, walking up to her sons. "The king's soldiers here, and I am not made aware of it?"

"How is Trey?" Tara asked.

"He does well, improves with each day. Willow is with him now." Mara wagged a finger at her. "But don't think to divert me from the question. "What goes on here?"

"Nothing that Tara couldn't handle." Reeve beamed with pride.

"That's my daughter," Mara said with equal pride.

Both beaming faces almost brought tears to Tara's eyes. No one had ever shown or expressed pride in her, and it filled Tara's heart with joy and with a sense of family.

"We'll celebrate with a hearty breakfast and then I will begin plans for a wedding feast," Mara said.

"I'll help," Mercy offered.

"You should rest," Duncan said, going to her side and scooping her up with ease before plopping down on a bench and settling her in his lap.

The family gathered round the table, while pitchers and bowls and heaping portions of food were brought out.

"Where is your father?" Mara asked just before everyone began to eat. "We don't start without him."

The brothers looked from one to another, and they all suddenly stood.

"He had gone to ready the warriors," Duncan said.

"Yet no warriors have joined us here," Reeve said. "Something is wrong."

"Good Lord!" Mara said, wringing her hands. "Go find your Da," she shouted at her sons.

They never reached the door. It opened, and in walked Carmag, accompanied by a tall man who appeared a hardened warrior. Old scars covered a good portion of one side of his face, and under the bulk of his fur-lined cloak, which swung open, was more bulk, though it was one of muscle and form. He looked to be a man seasoned in many battles and not always victorious ones.

"Where have you been?" Mara snapped. "You scared me half to death."

"I went to greet our guest. He arrived sooner than expected," Carmag said.

The man looked around the table and his eyes settled on Tara.

Her eyes had been drawn to his face as soon as he had walked in. She couldn't tear them away; his face captured her attention, though he was not near as handsome as her husband. But there was something—something—there that drew her to him.

She hadn't noticed that the room had turned silent, the only sound the pop and crackle of the fire in the fireplace.

Tara suddenly turned completely pale. "Oh my God!" She scurried off the bench and ran around the table. The stranger smiled and spread his arms wide, capturing her as she flung herself into them.

"I don't believe it," she said, hugging him tight.

"Nor I," he said, his voice deep and strong. "But as soon as I heard, I knew it could be no other."

"I feared you were—"

"As you can see, I'm fine," he said.

Her hand went to his face and gently caressed his scars. "But left with reminders."

"That have long since faded, except for you."

"I'm so very glad to see you," she said.

"And who is it you are glad to see?" Reeve said, walking over to her with a scowl.

Her smile refused to fade. She reached out her hand to her husband, and said, "I want you to meet a good, dear friend. Stone." Her smile grew wider. "Or so that is what I called him."

"You called me correctly," Stone said.

"I could think of no other name that fits you more," she said.

"You are the son of the witch who cursed Tara?" Reeve asked.

"He is the prophet Neil told us about," Carmag said.

Tara dropped Reeve's hand and grabbed hold of Stone's hands. "You can help rid me of the curse your mother placed on me."

"We need to talk," he said seriously. "Alone."

Tara turned to Reeve, and he looked none too pleased.

"I know you have waited for this, so go and do what you must, but first—" He pulled her close and whispered in her ear. "You are mine."

"And I am yours."

They kissed, not caring who watched, and when Reeve bought it to an end, he took her hand and walked with her over to Stone. "She belongs to me."

"I know, and I knew that Tara would find you, and you would save my friend." Stone held his hand out to Reeve.

Reeve took it, and they shook.

"I'll take Stone to my cottage," she said.

Reeve frowned.

Mara stepped forward. "Why not use my sewing room?"

Reeve smiled and slipped his arm around his mum's shoulders.

"You'll be telling me more about this as soon as your wife leaves the hall," Mara whispered.

"Anything for you, Mum," Reeve said, and kissed her cheek.

Tara hurried Stone up the stairs to Mara's private room. The roaring fire kept the small room toasty. Stone removed his cloak and draped it over the back of the chair then sat, stretching his hands out to the fire's warmth.

Tara sat in the seat beside him and waited, though she itched to ask him if he could remove the curse. Could he help free her?

"I've already told you that you were free."

Tara glared at him. She hadn't spoken her thoughts aloud, had she?

"Don't you remember how we would talk without talking?"

"I thought it was simply the way between us because you could not speak."

"I didn't speak for the longest time," he said. "I was too busy listening. With you, however, it had been different. I found it easy to hear your thoughts and was surprised that you could hear mine. But you don't want to talk about that."

Her hand reached out to rest on his arm. "I believe you were my first love."

He smiled. "And you mine though I knew I would not be your last."

"Or I yours."

"You are patient when you rather wish to know if I can remove the curse," he said.

"Can you?" she asked, squeezing his arm.

"It has already been removed."

Her eyes widened. "What do you mean?"

"You had a dream."

"Last night," she gasped. "Someone told me that love had freed me." She gasped again. "It was you?"

"Let me explain," he said, and Tara fell silent. "The woman you know as my mother is my aunt. My mother died when I was young. She was a powerful seer, and I inherited her skills. My aunt was good to me and treated me as her son. But she was a woman who found it hard to forgive. As I lay beaten and thought I would die, I sensed that my aunt would curse you. I wanted so badly to help you and then my mother's voice came to me and I repeated the words I heard in my head.

"My gift to you comes from the heart. It will allow you a fresh new start. No matter what words follow mine. There will come a time. When love refuses to let go. In a dream you will know that you are forever free. And that this special love is meant to be."

"You protected me," she said tearfully.

"The only way I could."

Tara stared at the fire for a moment. "Rory and Luag, the curse killed them."

"No one can say for sure, Tara, if it was the curse or simply time for that person to die. Some will believe it was the curse that struck, and others will insist it was death who laid claim. I have learned and seen for myself that fear and love are potent powers. It depends on how they are used. My aunt chose fear for revenge; I chose to combat it with love."

"Reeve was right. He told me to trust our love, and the curse would have no power."

"He's a wise man."

Tara smiled. "He's always right."

# Chapter 35

The day finished with a joyful feast, the brothers having started it in Trey's bedchamber, letting him know all that had happened. They taunted and laughed with each other and regaled the women with stories of their younger days, Mara often correcting their memories.

When Trey had grown tired, his eyes closing, Willow chased them out and offered to sit with him so the family could continue feasting.

It wasn't until late that everyone retired, happy and content. Reeve and Tara, while eager as always to make love, found themselves talking first.

In bed, wrapped in each other's arms, Reeve said, "So now you finally realize that I'm always right."

Tara laughed. "I'll concede to that."

Tara had hurried to tell Reeve everything Stone had told her. His family had heard as well, and Mara had declared it was time to rejoice. Tara was free of the curse and Trey was healing nicely and Mercy was feeling good and even Willow was finding peace here. All was well, and a celebration was called for.

"Please tell me there is no impending mission,"

Tara said, "that we will have time together before you must go off to serve the true king."

"There are no missions presently planned," Reeve assured her. "I'm all yours. You may grow tired of me."

She shook her head. "Never will I grow tired of you."

He kissed her, a soft, lingering kiss.

She ended it, easing away, her brow scrunched. "I've been thinking about something."

"Tell me."

"For some reason the prophecy about the true king kept ringing in my head this evening. I don't know why, but it wouldn't leave my thoughts."

"It is a myth many people find comfort in repeating," Reeve said. "It gives them hope of a better day, a better future."

"It does more than that," Tara said. "It gives a hint as to the identity of the true king."

That had Reeve sitting up. "What do you mean?"

Tara sat up beside him, the soft wool blanket dropping away to reveal her lovely breasts, but she noticed that Reeve didn't pay any heed to her breasts as he usually did. Anytime they were in front of him, he couldn't keep his hands or mouth off them, and here he was ignoring her bosoms. His wide eyes were focused on her face, and that was an indicator that what she had been thinking might just prove true, and so she proceeded to find out.

"It's very visible. Anyone could see it," she insisted.

"What?" he snapped. "What could they see?"

"Listen. Hear it yourself," she said softly, and began to recite. "When summer touches winter and the snow descends. The reign of the false king begins to end. Four warriors ride together and then divide. Among them the true king hides. When he meets death on his own. That is when he reclaims the throne."

Reeve shook his head. "I see nothing that hints at the true king's identity."

"Nothing?" she asked, shaking her own head.

"Nothing at all," he confirmed, falling back against the pillow and taking her with him to cover him.

Tara frowned, resting her elbow on his chest and her chin in her hand. "It seems so obvious to me."

"Forget it. There's nothing there," he said, his hands beginning to explore her.

"But there is," she said, her soft tone suddenly changing to a forceful one as she repeated. "*Four warriors* ride together."

His hands abruptly stopped exploring, and he stared at her.

"Want to tell me something?"

"There's nothing to tell," Reeve insisted.

"Then let me tell you what I think." She didn't wait for him to agree. "Four men were raised as brothers to protect the true king and to help him claim the throne. What better way to make certain that the true king was protected than to raise him in the bosom of loving and protective brothers? They would not only fight for the king, their brother, they would also die for him. And so four young lads were raised together, the true king among them. The four warriors are the four lads raised as brothers. The four brothers are you, Duncan, Bryce, and Trey, which means . . ."

She waited to see if he would finish it, and when he didn't, she did. "One of you is the true king."

He groaned and shook his head.

"Don't try to deny it. I know I'm right." Her smile grew.

"You know nothing," he said.

"I know, but I will *say* nothing, or don't you trust me?" she asked with a tinge of disappointment.

Reeve's arms went around her. "I trust. It's just that it's a difficult burden to carry."

Tara laughed. "I carried a far heavier burden."

"Precisely, I don't want you to carry another."

"We carry it together as you did with mine," she said.

He nodded. "I see the wisdom of that, and it would be nice to finally share it with someone I can trust as Duncan did with Mercy."

"She knows who the true king is?"

"No, and neither will you," he said. "What you do know that others don't is what you have already surmised. One of us—me, Duncan, Bryce, or Trey—is the true king of Scotland."

She grinned. "You mean I actually could be married to a king after all?"

"It's possible," he said. "Would you mind?"

"Mighty warrior or powerful king, I love you no matter."

"That is good to know," he said, and brushed his lips over hers. "You can say nothing of what you have learned to anyone."

"I understand. The king must be protected at all cost," she said. "Did you know since you were young?"

"I can discuss no more with you," he said firmly, "for your safety as well as his."

She nodded and then grinned. "So I could be sleeping with a king tonight after all."

"You're going to be doing far more than just sleeping," Reeve said, and with his arm around her waist, he swung her off him and under him.

She gasped, startled, when she came to rest beneath him.

"But first I have something to say, I've been aching to say to you. You refused to let me say to you. And now I am free to say it to you." Reeve brushed his lips across hers and whispered, "I love you, Tara. I will always love you."

A smile burst across her face. "Tell me again."

And in between kisses, he did.

*Please turn the page for an excerpt*

*from the next book in*

*the Warrior King series.*

*Coming 2012*

*from Donna Fletcher*

The little urchin ran like the devil was after him. His worn boots pounded the dirt, leaving a wake of dust in his trail. He couldn't let the soldiers get him. He couldn't. They would give him a thrashing for sure and then? He shivered as he ran, not wanting to think of what would happen if they discovered his secret.

He hadn't been able to help himself. Hunger had gnawed at his gut until it had pained him. It had been two full days since he had eaten, and he had to have food, even if it was a stale piece of bread cast carelessly to the ground by a noblewoman.

No sooner had he scooped it up than the woman had started screaming, "Thief! Thief!"

It had been little more than a crumb and had done nothing to appease his pain. While the woman looked like she had not suffered from missing a meal in some time. It mattered not. Once the trio of the king's men heard, they jumped into action and ran straight at him.

He barely had time to put distance between them, and fright gave his bone-tired body the strength to flee. He dodged and darted in and around the marketgoers and ware-barterers, slipped under makeshift tables, jumped over barrels and yanked free of the hand that grabbed at the back of his wool vest. His skinny legs pumped as fast as they could to avoid the soldiers gaining on him, perhaps even toying with him, making him believe he'd escape them when he truly didn't have a chance.

His dark eyes darted in panic, desperate to find

an avenue of escape. At the last minute, he spotted it: big, broad, and solid. Surely, he could take shelter beneath it. With all the strength he had left, he hurled himself at the solid mass, sliding on his stomach between the two limbs that stood rooted to the ground. Then he hurriedly wrapped his arms around one thick leg and held on for dear life.

A quick tilt of his head had his eyes settling beneath the Highlander's plaid, and he gulped. Good lord, he was a big one, which meant he was strong and could protect, and the lad needed protecting.

"*Please*. Please, help me," he begged, peering past the plaid to the giant Highlander, who stared down at him with a look of bewilderment.

"Hand him over," one of the three soldiers ordered, while almost colliding as they came to an abrupt halt.

The urchin hid a smile, relieved at their reluctance to approach the large man.

"And what will you do with him?"

The urchin liked the sound of the Highlander's voice; it confronted and dared all in one breath. He was not a man to argue with, but one to fear and respect.

"That doesn't concern you," the soldier said with trembling bravado.

"Why wouldn't it?" the Highlander demanded sharply.

"He stole from a woman and must pay the price," another soldier spoke up, not daring to step from behind the soldier in front.

"What is the price?" the Highlander asked.

"A good whipping and service to the woman to pay off his debt," the soldier in the front said, a bit more daringly.

"It was nothing more than a crumb off the ground," the urchin snapped. His dark eyes glared menacingly, while his arms clung tenaciously to the Highlander's thick-muscled leg.

"It wasn't your crumb to take," the soldier snapped.

"The lad looks in need of more than a crumb," the Highlander said, much too calmly.

From the way the three soldiers took several steps back, each tripping and trying to get out of the other's way, the urchin knew that the Highlander must have sent them a menacing look.

"He broke the king's law," one soldier said from behind the other two.

"The king wants his subjects to go hungry?" the Highlander asked, his voice rising in anger.

Before the soldiers could respond, the woman whose crumb the urchin supposedly had thieved came upon them with laborious breath. Her large bosoms heaved, and she fanned her flushed face with her hand.

"That dirty little lad"—she stopped for a breath—"stole from me." She took another needed breath and stopped fanning. "Now he owes me, he does."

"What will you take for him?" the Highlander asked.

The woman stared down at the urchin. "He's worth a good amount."

The Highlander lurched forward, causing the soldiers and woman to retreat in haste and huddle closer together. While the urchin, having no intention of letting go of the intimidating Highlander's leg, was dragged along with every step he took.

"Don't think me a fool, madam," the Highlander

snarled. "He's a skinny lad not fit for most chores. He isn't worth a pittance." And with that said, he tossed a meager trinket at her feet. "Take it and be satisfied."

The one soldier was quick to pick it up and hand it to the woman. She took it and, with a snort and toss of her head, stomped away.

"We're done here," the Highlander said.

The urchin heard the tight anger in his tone, and as the soldiers turned and walked away, he grinned. That is until the Highlander's large hand reached down, grabbed him by the back of his shirt, and lifted him clear off the ground to dangle in front of his face.

"Have you no sense, lad?"

A shiver ran through him. It wasn't only the breadth and width of the Highlander that intimidated, but his features as well. His long, dark hair the color of the deep rich earth was swept back away from a face with defined features. Wrinkles ran across a wide brow and at the corners of his light blue eyes. He had a solid chin that no doubt could easily deflect a hefty fist, and a nose so finely shaped that it proved he had been the victor of many a fight, for it looked to have never been broken.

"Answer me," the Highlander demanded, giving the lad a quick shake.

"I'm starvin', I am," the lad snapped.

The Highlander put him down, and fear crept over the lad. It was one thing to look the mighty warrior in the face, but standing beside him, the top of the lad's head was level with the top of his chest.

This Highlander warrior was the tale of legends that his father had told him about. Suddenly, his hunger didn't seem important, and he choked back tears.

He had to find his father and set him free. His father had told him not to worry about him, to run and stay safe, but he was his da, and he loved him with all his heart. He had raised him alone since he was barely five years, his mother having passed in childbirth along with the babe. He was a good, loving father. He would never leave him to suffer the king's torment. He would find him and set him free and then together they would go as they had planned to join those who supported the true king's return.

"I'll feed you," the Highlander said, casting an anxious glance over the marketplace grounds. "We'll get what we need and be gone. I don't trust the soldiers. They'll find more of their kind and be after us soon enough."

The Highlander was right about that, and the lad had no problem with filling his belly and then taking off on his own. He had a mission to accomplish, and he intended to see it done.

"Don't wander off," the Highlander warned. "Stay close to me."

The lad stuck to his side as the warrior made a hasty round of the market, slipping the lad a hunk of cheese he traded for. He ravished the piece in seconds and hungered for more, but didn't ask. They would be done soon enough, and soon he'd be feasting, the Highlander having gathered more than enough food.

The lad had a feeling that the warrior was acquiring more than simply food. Whispers and mumbles were exchanged at most every place he stopped. Something was afoot, and the lad wondered if perhaps the Highlander was in some way connected with those warriors who fought to see the true king take the throne. A prophecy has been circulating for some time now about the true king, the king who possessed the inalienable right to the throne of Scotland. It was a prophecy his father had recounted many times to him until he could recite it by heart.

*When summer touches winter, and the snow descends, the reign of the false king begins to end, four warriors ride together and then divide, among them the true king hides, when he meets death on his own, that is when he reclaims the throne.*

His father had believed strongly in the prophecy and had claimed that the true king would one day appear, and his reign would bring peace and prosperity. Perhaps if the warrior was connected with those who fought for the true king, he could help the lad rescue his father and see them settled in a safe place.

Suddenly, the lad was glad for his near brush with danger, for it had provided him with an introduction to the Highlander and a better chance to free his father.

The Highlander dropped a sack to the lad with a warning. "Eat, but do not show your hunger. It demonstrates vulnerability."

The lad understood, and, though anxious to devour what food staples were in the sack, he reached in and tore off a hunk of bread. With hunger that crawled up and out of his mouth, the lad managed to eat slowly as he walked beside the Highlander, taking two, sometimes three steps, to the Highlander's one.

"Your name, lad?" the Highlander asked, as they approached the end of the marketplace.

"Charles, sir."

"Call me Bryce."

"Thank you, Bryce, for helping me," Charles said.

"Help you? I bought you, lad."

Charles stumbled, and Bryce grabbed hold of his arm. "Watch your step."

The Highlander kept a firm grip on his arm until the market was far behind them, and they entered the woods lush with fresh spring growth.

What a fool he was, forgetting that the Highlander had purchased him. He was now the warrior's property. And the strength of his grip had only served to remind him of the invisible shackle that duty-bound him to Bryce.

Questions assaulted the lad's mind and spilled rapidly from his lips. "What do you want with me? How long am I beholding to you? Where will you be taking me? Will we be going far from here—"

"Stop!" Bryce snapped. "You're a bit of a thing that not only needs feeding but help in growing into manhood."

"And what?" Charles halted in his tracks. "You expect to make a man out of me?"

Bryce peered down at him. "That's exactly what I intend to do."

He kept walking, and Charles had no choice but to follow, with only one thought in mind.

There was no way this mighty Highlander would ever accomplish making a man out of Charles. And for a very good reason.

Charles was actually Charlotte, a woman!